THE SURGEON
SHE COULD
NEVER FORGET

TINA BECKETT

ONE SUMMER
IN SYDNEY

ANNIE CLAYDON

MILLS & BOON

First published in Great Britain 2023
by Mills & Boon, an imprint of HarperCollins*Publishers* Ltd,
1 London Bridge Street, London, SE1 9GF

www.harpercollins.co.uk

HarperCollins*Publishers* Macken House, 39/40 Mayor Street Upper, Dublin 1, D01 C9W8, Ireland

The Surgeon She Could Never Forget © 2023 Tina Beckett

One Summer in Sydney © 2023 Annie Claydon

ISBN: 978-0-263-30612-5

07/23

This book is produced from independently certified FSC™ paper to ensure responsible forest management.
For more information visit: www.harpercollins.co.uk/green.

Printed and Bound in the UK using 100% Renewable Electricity at CPI Group (UK) Ltd, Croydon, CR0 4YY

THE SURGEON
SHE COULD
NEVER FORGET

TINA BECKETT

MILLS & BOON

For moms everywhere

PROLOGUE

"Why do you have to go?" If Lyndsey Marshall asked the question enough times, surely that resolute finality she saw written on Misha's face would change, and he'd go back to the warm, funny guy she loved so very much. He had to realize how much he stood to lose—how much *they* stood to lose—by his moving back to Belarus with his family. They'd just graduated from high school a week ago, had made plans for the future. One in which she'd envisioned the two of them being together forever. Having children. A home. "Surely you could get a student visa for college. Can't you stay on your own? I'm sure your parents would understand. And my mom could let you stay with—"

"I must. My parents must get their visa situation straightened out or they could be deported and denied reentry later on. And my dad…" His throat moved as if some powerful emotion swept through him. "Maybe someday…"

His words drifted away, but all she heard was her own father's voice five years ago telling her that he had to leave, but that they would have all kinds of fun together. But they never had. Instead, he'd started another family with another woman he'd met on one of his business trips. His calls to his daughter had been few and far between and filled with, "Hey, someday we need to…" Only those "somedays" had never materialized. His new daughter deserved his love and attention, but Lyndsey evidently didn't.

She was never going to accept that answer again. Not from Misha. She couldn't. Not if she was to survive his leaving.

"No. Not someday. If you leave now, it's over between us."

If anything, the withdrawal she'd sensed in him grew. She knew she should stop talking, but it was as if all the impotent rage she'd felt when her dad left came boiling out, pushing words she'd never be able to retract past the ball in her throat. She knew she wasn't being fair, but the hurt in her was so big. So overwhelming.

God, if he left her too…

But he's going to. You know he is.

He reached out to touch her, but she batted his hand away trying not to break down like she'd done five years ago when her father broke the news to her. If he touched her, she'd be lost. She'd fall apart, just like she had back then.

This time she wasn't going to be staring at her cell phone for days and months on end willing it to ring. Willing him to come back. If he was going to leave, she wanted it to be a clean cut that might at least have a chance to heal.

"Please, Misha…" She drew a deep breath. "Leave if it's what you have to do. But don't prolong it. Don't call me. Don't contact me. Just…" her arms waved in the air like an injured sparrow. "…don't." The word ended on a sob before she could press her hand to her mouth to contain the sound.

She leaped out of the car and ran up her front driveway, never looking back. Pushed through the front door, slamming it behind her as she bolted up the stairs to her room, vaguely hearing her mother calling to her. But she didn't stop. She kept running, mentally, long after she'd thrown herself onto the bed, sobbing in earnest until no more tears came, only dry racking cries that hurt her chest and stole the breath from her lungs. Then she lay there, ignoring her mom's soft knock, her mind and emotions completely numb.

After what seemed like an hour, she finally pried herself from the mattress and went to the window, hoping beyond hope that his car would still be there. That he would have changed his mind. After all, his dad was a doctor here in Lafayette. Surely he wouldn't leave his practice behind and drag his family halfway across the world?

According to Misha, that's exactly what he was prepared to do.

When she peered through the sheer curtains, the spot where he'd been parked was empty. As empty as her heart now was.

She didn't know how she'd get through it, but she'd

show him that she was a survivor. She'd survived her father leaving. She'd survive this too.

Only it didn't matter. Because Misha wouldn't actually be there to see her rise and conquer. Somehow that just made it worse.

When the light tapping on her door returned, it made her flinch, and she ground her palms into her swollen eyes to hopefully erase any sign of her tears. Except when she opened the door, her mother was there, seeing right past her smile and pulling her into the safe haven of her arms. Lyndsey promptly fell apart all over again.

But this was the last time. The last time she would shed tears for Mikhail Lukyanov. Because tomorrow she was going to get up and start gluing her shattered world back together again. One tiny fragment at a time.

CHAPTER ONE

CHERT VOZMI!

MIKHAIL LUKYANOV DROPPED into his office chair, muttering about how far off the rails his day had already gone. And he'd only just arrived for his very first day after opening his own practice. It was funny how Louisiana had always been home, despite the fact that after high school he'd spent five years in Belarus. In the midst of finding out his dad had leukemia, it turned out that his dad's work visa to the States— unbeknownst to any of them—had been forged by a family friend who claimed he had an "in" with the US consulate.

No one had caught the problem until Misha's dad went to renew their visas and a quick check came back saying there was no record of a work visa for Dmitry Lukyanov. They had no choice but to return to Belarus. Fortunately, Dmitry was eventually able to prove that he'd immigrated to the States in good faith and had been offered a chance to return. Except that by then, five years had gone by, and after a long, hard fight, his dad's leukemia had become a monster that could no longer be controlled with chemo, and he'd been too ill to travel. When his dad passed away a few months later, Misha decided to make his own trek to the States, with his mom's blessing, and finish medical school there. Which he'd finally finished three years ago. Then he'd opted to spend another two years studying surgical options for hearing loss under one of the top surgeons in the United States.

And here he was back in southern Louisiana. Lafayette was about fifty miles from where he'd graduated high school, but he hadn't been able to bear moving back there with all the memories. He'd toyed several times with the idea of visiting and trying to find Lyndsey, but as the years went by, he finally decided it was better to leave things alone. Why barge in and disrupt her life again after all this time? Plus, the idea of seeing her happily married with a passel of children made his gut churn.

He shook off the thoughts as one of his office staff poked her head in. "We were able to juggle your schedule, Doctor. Most of the patients you missed this morning are able to come back this afternoon. All except one, who said she'd wait for as long as it took for you to get here. And we canceled your surgery for this morning at the hospital."

A swear word flashed through his mind. He hated that someone had been waiting on him for over three hours, especially on his first day. But it had taken almost two-and-a-half hours to get the loaner car when his own vehicle had refused to start that morning.

Maybe this was some deity's idea of a joke, forcing a now rigidly inflexible Misha to loosen his grip on his sense of order. But it was what had gotten him through those first horrible months back in Belarus, when his grief over his dad's diagnosis and how he and Lyndsey had left things had almost overwhelmed him. Somehow he'd gotten through it. And now whatever he and Lyndsey had once had was firmly in the past.

"Is she in a waiting room?"

"Yes. The son will be the patient, though."

"Name?"

"Brody McKinna."

He stood. "Okay, which room?"

"Exam room three."

He mentally went through the layout of the set of rooms that comprised his practice. "When you get a chance, could you print a list of my patients, so I have an idea of who's coming when?"

Nelly smiled and handed him a sheet of paper on a clipboard. "Already done." She gave him a smile. "And don't worry about it. Things tend to work out the way they're supposed to."

Misha used to believe that, but he didn't any longer. But he also didn't have time to stand here and argue with someone who was just trying to make him feel better. So he smiled and thanked her before heading down the hallway toward his first patient of the day.

She was nervous. So terribly nervous.

She'd never expected to see Misha again, much less

find out he was the hospital's new ENT and had specialized training in hearing loss cases. But it wasn't for her. When her son's doctor had heard about a new doctor who was coming to Lafayette with great credentials, he'd written down the man's name. She'd stared at the slip of paper in shock, unable to breathe for a second or two. Then her fingertip had slowly traced over the letters on the paper. Surely not. It had to be a fluke. But what were the chances of another Misha Lukyanov coming to Louisiana.

And now he was here. At the very hospital where she'd worked for the last year. An hour from where she'd grown up. Where they'd graduated from high school.

It would be pretty hard to avoid each other when they were going to be working on the same floor.

If he declined to take on her son as his patient today, would seeing her day in and day out make him change his mind? She could go to another doctor if she had to, but the waits were long. And with Misha being new to the hospital, surely he would be more likely to have openings in his schedule, right? And Brody's condition had progressed far faster than expected. Thankfully his doctor had been able to wrangle an appointment with Misha today.

But she'd come alone, while Brody was in school. She didn't want him to be witness to whatever reaction her high school sweetheart might have to seeing her again. She'd been pretty harsh the last time she'd seen him. And pretty broken up inside after he'd left.

She'd paid the price for the rabbit hole she'd gone down after he left the country.

She squirmed in her chair as she waited for someone to update her on how much longer they thought it would be until he arrived. She'd been the only one who'd opted to wait. And she would wait here a week, if she had to.

You can do this. You have *to do this.*

She couldn't let Brody suffer because of her pride. Her son was an innocent party to all that had transpired since his birth. And if Misha hadn't left, Brody would never have been born. So no. She wouldn't go back and undo the past. Even with all that had happened leading up to his birth.

The door to the exam room opened so suddenly that she flinched, something she didn't do as often as she used to, and she gritted her teeth over the muscle memory that still provoked the response.

And then he was there in the doorway, as large as life. He'd put on a bit of weight since the last time she saw him. But it looked good on him. The tall, lanky boy she'd known in high school had morphed into a man. One that was devastatingly attractive and whose unwavering eyes found hers with the precision of a scalpel. She forced herself to hold still, afraid to even breathe, even as a boatload of emotions resurfaced with a vengeance. She bit her lip as her eyes skimmed his shoulders, unable to stop them from venturing lower...

"Lyndsey?"

His deep voice made her gaze jerk back to his as the low tones rolled over her name in that strange but wonderful accent that used to turn her inside out. He would murmur it as his lips slowly trailed across her cheek. As he chuckled at something she said. As he said goodbye that last day. Another wave of emotion—stronger this time—rose, and she fought against it. Even as she noted the empty ring finger on his left hand, she knew there was no going back. For either of them. She needed to remember that. She was not here for herself. She was here for Brody.

It had become a litany she'd repeated for the last week and a half as she'd waited for the new doctor's arrival in Lafayette.

She forced herself to nod. "Yes."

His jaw tightened, glancing down at a piece of paper in his hand. "I'm not sure what this is, but I have a lot of patients to see, and I don't have time for…"

She filled in the word he hadn't said: *You. I don't have time for* you.

Neither had her father. Another pang hit her. Her half sister and brother were virtual strangers to her. She'd only seen them a handful of times in all these years. And with her father's passing last year, she didn't see that changing anytime soon.

"It's not for me. It's for my son.*"*

"And where is he?" He glanced again at the paper. "Brody… McKinna?"

She licked her lips, hoping he didn't recognize the last name. "I—I didn't bring him. If you threw me out of your office, I didn't want him to be here. I know you're busy, but please just hear me out. I brought his chart." She offered him the manila envelope in her hand.

Misha stared at her for a long moment before he took it and lowered himself onto the rolling stool that put him at eye level with her.

Eye level was good, right? Except when those eyes were electric blue and evidently still capable of sending shivers of heat through her.

At least he hadn't thrown her out. Hadn't told her to take Brody's chart and find some other specialist. Not yet, anyway.

He spread the paperwork on the exam table next to him before putting on some reading glasses. If anything, those dark frames made him look even more devastatingly handsome. Her insides shifted at the effect he still had on her. She felt shaky and out of sorts with him being so close, his knee almost touching hers. But she needed to get control of herself. This Misha was not the carefree kid he'd been in school. The one with a smile that just wouldn't quit and a sense of humor that used to keep her in stitches.

No, this man had a deep furrow between his brows that was there as he studied Brody's chart. And he'd not smiled. Not even one time. In fact, it was as if he was totally unaffected by her presence.

Would she rather him try to worm his way back into her affections?

No. Not after all this time. After all that had happened since he'd left.

His finger tapped one of the sheets. "Otosclerosis?"

"Yes. Progressing much faster than anticipated. We thought we'd have at least a year to get things in place to save his hearing, but it looks like he may not have that much time. He's only fifteen and I can't imagine—"

His head came up. "Your son is fifteen?"

She swallowed. Oh, God, she'd hoped to avoid this particular discussion.

"Y-yes. His birthday is in March."

His face was still as he mentally did the math. When his eyes speared hers again, the blue irises had chilled and there was ring of anger in them. "Despite the timeline, I take it he's not mine. Where's his father?"

The question wasn't exactly something a doctor should ask, but she understood.

Before she could answer, though, he spoke again as if he'd just realized something. "McKinna.... Is it *Wade* McKinna? The guy who asked you to prom right before we started dating?"

Leave it to Misha to put two and two together so quickly. Wade had been high school quarterback and she'd been flattered when he'd asked her to the dance. But even then, she'd only had eyes for Misha. But once he left for Belarus, Wade had stepped in with a show of empathy and offered the comfort she'd so desperately needed. She'd been sobbing, clinging to his shoulders. When he kissed her, she didn't resist, but she needed something that no one could give her. One thing led to another as she tried to bury her grief and she wound up pregnant. Wade immediately offered marriage, said he loved her and would love their child.

And Misha, in her eyes, was gone forever. So she'd said yes, praying she'd somehow learn to feel something for Wade.

Only it wasn't love she came to feel. Because her idea of love and his were poles apart.

When she realized Misha was still looking at her, she forced herself to answer. "Yes. But he's no longer in the picture. He won't be making any decisions about Brody's care."

"I see."

His face was hard as he turned his attention back to the pages in front of him. "What exactly is it you're expecting me to do for Brody?"

Was he serious? There was no way he didn't know. "I'm hoping you'll take him on as a patient. Perform his surgery."

His eyes closed for a second before reopening. "There are other surgeons who could do it. Why me?"

She understood why he was asking, but she needed him to know that it had nothing to do with their past. "Because his other ENT says you have a good reputation and trained under the best of the best in this particular surgery. And I don't want to uproot Brody from his friends and school. He's dealt with enough in his life with his..." Realizing she was saying more than she'd meant to, she ended with, "...getting his diagnosis, I mean." The less she talked about Wade the better. She didn't want to dredge up that painful past any more than she wanted to revisit the last time she set eyes on Misha.

They were both over and done, and she couldn't change either outcome.

Except her body's crazy reaction to him was putting her on shaky ground when it came to being around him. Surely, it was just the shock of seeing him again. Those emotions would slink back to whatever dark corner they'd emerged from, right? Especially since there was no sign of any renewed attraction from his end.

"I need time to look over his chart, and I'd like to consult further with his other ENT." A muscle worked in his cheek. "And I'll need to meet Brody."

The way he said it made her think it was the last thing he wanted to do. But she didn't care.

Hope and desperation made her reach out and grab his hand before realizing what she was doing. She let go of it just as quickly, before saying in a low voice. "Misha, please don't hold our past and what happened afterward against my son. He played no part in my decisions."

A muscle ticked in his jaw as he leveled his gaze at her. "I would never blame a child for things over which he had no control. Over who his mother chose to be with."

She knew how it had to look to him. That she had fallen into bed with someone almost on the heels of his departure. But things weren't always like they seemed.

And he could be mad at her as much as he wanted, as long as it didn't affect Brody.

He sighed and stood up. "As it is, I'm already late for many appointments today, so if there's nothing else…"

And just like that, he'd dismissed her. As if it was the easiest thing to do.

If only she could be more like that. But this time she needed to push for what she needed. Because her son's hearing was at stake.

"So you'll at least consider taking him on?"

"Like I said, I'll need to take my schedule into consideration, since I'm still getting the feel of things at the hospital. But stop at the front desk and make another appointment. This time, bring your son with you."

She stood as well. "I will."

"I'll see you soon."

As he went through the door, she almost gave a sharp laugh. Yes, he would. And he didn't know how soon. She hadn't mentioned that she worked at the hospital as well. She'd meant to throw out some humorous quip about them now being colleagues, but his attitude had not invited humor, or anything else. So he was just going to have to learn about it on Monday morning.

And she had no idea if working in his department would help Brody's cause or blow her chances completely out of the water.

Misha's Monday morning was already going much better than his Friday had. He glanced at the nurse's desk on his way through Louisiana Southern's busy ENT department. He'd definitely been thrown into the deep end. He already had two surgeries scheduled for today. A tympanomastoidectomy to treat a stubborn ear infection and a cochlear implant. The implant surgery would take a couple of hours in and of itself.

And he was still trying to learn names and faces of the people he was working with.

As his gaze skipped over the two nurses he recognized, they landed on the third one, who sat a little to the right of the other two. Her head was down as she looked at something on her computer, and a long wavy strand of hair rested against the side of her face, having escaped its confinement. He recognized that hair. And the graceful way her neck curved as she tilted her head to read something on the screen in front of her.

Lyndsey?

He blinked, his steps slowing. Lyndsey was working *here*? Why had she not said something when he'd seen her on Friday?

A thread of anger went through him, and he stalked over to the desk. Faith smiled at him and then reached to tap Lyndsey on the shoulder. "Hey, Lynds, have you met our newest team member?"

Team? As in they would be working in the same department? He wasn't sure what she was playing at, but there was no way her working here could be a coincidence. Or she would have mentioned it on Friday. So why hadn't she?

"Actually, Ms. McKinna and I went to high school together. And I had no idea she was working here."

She was now looking at him, the guilt in her eyes telling him all he needed to know. He addressed her, unable to force a smile to his lips. "Actually, can I talk to you for a minute?"

Faith looked surprised, while Meredith, the other nurse, lifted her brows. He'd been short and he knew it, probably not making the best impression on the pair, but he didn't have time to dance around and try to figure out what was going on. He wanted to hear it. From Lyndsey.

"Of course." She sent the two nurses an apologetic glance and came out from behind the desk, her hands tugging the hem of her scrubs over her backside. If anything, it just emphasized curves that still had the power to make his mouth go dry. *Dammit!*

He strode ahead of her to avoid staring at it, shoving his hands into the pockets of his jeans, before rounding the corner and stopping out of view of the desk.

"What is going on here? You said nothing about working at Louisiana Southern during your appointment on Friday."

She moistened her lips, and he did his damnedest not to fixate on the move. Instead, he propped his shoulder against the wall to his right and waited.

"You didn't ask me."

He stared at her. "Try again."

"Okay, look, I know. I should have mentioned it.

But you weren't actually very approachable during our appointment."

"Finding out you slept with the high school quarterback almost immediately after I left the country was…well, not what I would have expected from you."

Her chin jerked up. "Not that my actions were of any concern of yours once you broke things off between us—"

"I seem to remember it being you who asked me never to contact you again."

Although he could understand why she had. He'd been in shock over the spiraling events that had sent his world on a collision course.

She paused for a minute as if pulling herself together. "What's done is done, Misha. Neither one of us can change the past. Can't we just go on from here?"

"As in…?"

Her face turned pink. "As in working together as colleagues?"

That brought him back to why he'd wanted to talk to her. "So you're going to tell me this is all one big coincidence?"

"Actually it is. I've been working here for a year. So unless you were angling for this job as a way of getting back in contact with me…"

Which is what he'd just basically accused her of doing. "No. But I did want to come back to Louisiana. New York was too big of a city for me."

And the fact that he'd broken off a brief relationship with a nurse at that hospital had made the offer at Louisiana Southern look even more attractive. But he didn't want to go into any of that. Especially not with Lyndsey.

"I get it. And I'll be honest. Brody needs this surgery, and I'm willing to do almost anything it takes to make sure it happens."

One of his brows lifted before he could stop it. She hadn't meant that the way it had sounded, despite all kinds of X-rated images that were now dancing around in his skull.

Her face suddenly suffused with color as if she'd been privy to his thoughts. "That didn't come out quite right. I—I mean finding him the help he needs. My pride means nothing compared to what awaits him without this surgery. And if that means asking someone who hates me to take him on—"

"I don't hate you, Lyndsey." His heart contracted even as he said the words. Because it was true. No matter how that shard of jealousy over her and Wade McKinna had dug deep into his flesh, he wasn't going to punish her son for it. "I told you I would never turn down a patient, especially a child, out of spite." He studied her. "You didn't know me as well as I thought you did, evidently."

"I thought I did. But…" She shrugged. "People aren't always who you think they are. And Wade, well…"

Something about the way she talked about the man gave him pause. Even after all his years in the States, there were still nuances of the language he didn't always grasp. And he didn't have time to work through it right now. She'd said Brody's dad was no longer in the picture, so she and Wade must have split up. But how long ago?

Did it matter?

Hell, he didn't know how he felt about having to see her every time he was at the hospital. She'd hurt him badly fifteen years ago. Had written him off without even hearing him out. But then he knew he'd hurt her too. But it couldn't have been helped at the time. He could have told her about his dad, but somehow even voicing the word *leukemia* had been beyond him at that moment.

He sighed. "I don't have time to hash all of this out with you right now, but we do need to talk if we're going to work together on a daily basis. Do you have plans tonight?"

"Tonight?"

Damn, he hadn't phrased that well. "I'm not talking about a date. I just don't want there to be any misunderstandings about what is happening here." He tightened his jaw. "If I do the surgery, it will change nothing between us on a personal level."

She licked her lips. "I wouldn't expect it to. Nor would I want it to any more than you would."

He hoped to hell that was true. Because her scent was wrapping around him in a way that spelled danger. The sooner he left the vicinity, the better. "Good. So tonight? You have plans?"

"No. Brody has a club meeting after school, so

maybe we can meet at the coffee shop next door. Say at five? It's when I get off work."

"Five it is. I'll see you then."

"Yes. See you."

They stood there for a few seconds as if unsure who was going to walk away from whom. Then Lyndsey spun around and headed back the way she'd come, leaving him to continue down the corridor on his way to his first patient's room. All he could think was that the day that had started out with such promise had just imploded in spectacular fashion.

His cochlear surgery had taken longer than expected, and when he glanced at his watch, he saw he was already five minutes late for his meeting with Lyndsey and he didn't have her cell phone number. He discarded his surgical scrubs and made his way through the hospital exit, before turning right toward the coffee shop. He was now ten minutes late. As someone who was particular about appointment times, spacing his further apart than most doctors so that he wouldn't fall behind, he hated being tardy. Of course, Friday hadn't worked out well in that regard either.

When he arrived, the scent of strong coffee hit his nose with a welcome sense of familiarity, and he spotted Lyndsey already hunched over a cup of brew. He gave her a nod of acknowledgment before putting his order in and then heading over to her table. "Sorry I'm late. Surgery ran longer than I expected."

"I know." She gave a quick smile. "I work there too, remember?"

Of course. She would have known that it ran over. He wasn't sure how he felt about her knowing things about his life and routine. But there was no changing it now. She was still in her scrubs, but any hope that they might dull the attraction that hummed just below the surface was quickly crushed. Because he'd once known every inch of that body. Becoming a mother had only enhanced those dips and curves. He steeled his voice to respond in as normal a tone as he could muster.

"Yes, I remember." The barista came over with his coffee and set it in front of him. He gave her a quick thank-you before turning his attention back to the woman in front of him. Studying her for a moment, he noticed fine lines next to her eyes that spoke of either worry or concentration. Her hair was still long and wavy, like it had been in school, the strands catching the light and turning them honey gold. She'd freed them from the confines of the clip she'd had on earlier. And hell if he didn't remember all too well threading those locks between his fingers when he kissed her. His fingers curled into his palms as he tried to banish the sharp sense of need that flooded him over the memory.

She took a drink of her coffee before saying, "I'm sorry. I'm sure seeing me at the nurses' desk today was a shock. But I promise I'm not stalking you, despite how much I want Brody to have this surgery."

That thought had never even crossed his mind. He leaned forward. "Lyndsey, even if he isn't a candidate for surgery, there are other options."

"If you're talking about an implant, I know that. But he's experienced natural hearing, and I think it would be harder for him to adjust to the change in perception. Plus, from what I read, there's a chance for ossification of the cochlea, after implant surgery, right? And the electrical current can affect facial nerves?"

He was impressed. "You've done quite a bit of research."

"I've read everything I can get my hands on. If he can have surgery before his hearing loss is profound, it provides the best option to preserve what hearing he has left."

"You are correct." This was not someone who just took a medical professional's words as coming from God. This was someone who was willing to stretch her knowledge and make the best decisions based on research rather than emotion.

"So…?"

"I still have to look through everything. I need to make an informed decision too. The last thing I want to do is go in there and do something that does more harm to your son than good.

"His name is Brody."

Yes, Brody McKinna. He knew the boy's name. It was already burned into his subconscious with a fire that scorched its way from his chest to his gut. She'd had a child that should have been theirs, had the fates been kinder to them. But they hadn't. And the fact that she'd jumped from his arms right into someone like Wade's just about killed him. He hadn't liked the star football player from the moment she'd mentioned that he had asked her to the prom. Yes, she'd said no, but on some level she must have been attracted to the guy, right?

Even when she'd been involved with him?

He would never know the answer to that, because he was never going to ask the question. Best to just put it behind him.

"Okay... Brody...would benefit more from a measured approach rather than a rush to surgery. Which is why I need some time."

She blinked at him, her blue eyes filling with a moisture that punched buttons he thought he'd deleted not moments earlier.

"So you were serious about taking him on?"

"There was never any question. Like I said on Friday, I would never penalize someone for things over which they had no control."

He hadn't meant the words as a jab at their past, but if it came across that way, so be it. He'd had no control over whether he stayed or went. He'd had to help his family during a time of crisis. In his mind, there'd been no other option. And as his dad fought his illness and his mom leaned on him more and more for comfort and decision making, he knew that decision had been the right one.

So, what to do about Lyndsey and Brody? He sure

as hell wasn't going to tell her to leave and never contact him again, that was for sure.

He was going to "do unto others as he wished she'd done unto him." Wasn't that basically what that old sage piece of advice meant? Yes, it was. And he was going to do his best to follow it, even if it was the second hardest thing he'd done in his life.

CHAPTER TWO

LYNDSEY PARKED IN the lot outside of the emergency department of the hospital. It provided the most direct route to where she worked. As she entered the space, she caught sight of a team rushing a young girl toward the double doors she'd just come through. The bulge of her abdomen as they went by said she was expecting a child. Just then, she caught the unmistakable gurgled wheeze of someone who was struggling to breathe and failing. Again and again it came, and a clench of fear gripped her, as she stared at the passing gurney.

She recognized that sound. Had *lived* that sound while pregnant with Brody.

A touch to her arm made her recoil until she caught herself. Misha was looking down at her with a strange look in his eyes. "Come. I need you."

A second later he was striding after the gurney. She swallowed when she realized he meant he needed her help with the patient. She hurried to catch up with him just as he reached the nearest curtained-off area. The closer she got, the more pronounced the stridor became.

Restricted airway. A true medical emergency.

"We couldn't intubate," one of the EMTs said. "The swelling is too much."

"What happened?" Misha's voice was calm and measured, no sign of panic or hurry. Unlike Lyndsey's own chaotic thoughts.

"Car accident. No seatbelt, and it looks like she hit the dashboard."

She moved closer, waiting for him to tell her what to do, even as her fear grew in time with the girl's struggle to draw every breath. With every second the baby in her belly went without precious oxygen.

Misha was already examining the girl. She was about the age Lyndsey was when she'd been pregnant with Brody. God. It was a wonder he'd survived. It was a wonder he hadn't been left with some kind of deficit afterward.

She put her hand to her throat as if the young woman's struggle was her own all over again.

"We need to help the baby." Her voice came out thin and thready.

He shot her a glance. "And we will. I need a trach kit." He frowned. "Now!"

Lyndsey quickly forced her hand away from her neck and donned gloves. Regathering her composure, she found the kit.

She ripped it open and sloshed the antiseptic solution over the girl's neck, the purple bruising and swelling telling a story that made her swallow. They needed to get this done before the swelling closed off the area completely.

She handed Misha a scalpel and watched as he felt for the correct spot and then with unerring accuracy made the cut through skin and cartilage, as she waited with the tubing components.

He held his hand out, and she gave them to him.

It took him two tries, and he muttered something she recognized as Russian before the tubing slid home.

She hadn't realized how tense she still was until the girl drew her first unencumbered breath. Then Lyndsey released her own in a rush, her limbs feeling suddenly trembly and weak.

A nurse stuck her head in. "Obstetrics is on their way."

"Good." Misha gave her another glance, his frown deepening.

God. She didn't want him to see her fall apart. She hadn't felt this way in a long time. Had thought that the years of therapy after her disastrous marriage had banished most of her reactions to unexpected situations.

It had to be this girl's pregnancy bringing back the trauma of what had happened during her own pregnancy?

She wasn't sure. She just knew that for a second she hadn't been able to breathe, and the old panic had risen up, swamping her. Or maybe Misha's presence back in her life had somehow unearthed the memories. But why? He'd never treated her badly. And he'd definitely never hurt her physically.

"Are you okay?" he asked.

"Yes. I'm just late for my shift, and I…" What else

could she say? She didn't want to tell him what had happened to her. Couldn't bear the look of pity that would surely come her way. She'd encountered plenty of those looks as she'd recounted her story from the witness stand of a courtroom.

His eyes narrowed, and she did her best to hold herself still and force a smile that was as fake as her words. But he simply nodded. "Go. I've got this. I'll need to get her to surgery to finish up anyway once obstetrics checks the baby's vitals."

"Thank you."

Through a mist of nausea, she somehow made her legs carry her from the room and made it to the nearest bathroom. She raced into a stall and vomited into the toilet, the feeling of relief immediate as if the act worked to release her emotions.

Afterward, she washed her face and rinsed out her mouth, and found a breath mint in her purse. Looking at herself, she realized she was as pale as death. Hopefully, it wasn't visible to anyone but her.

She waited a moment or two longer, then, still shaky, but at least rid of the crippling fear and sense of foreboding, she exited the bathroom. Somehow, she made her way to her department and got through the first part of her shift until her lunch break. There was no sign of Misha, and she was glad. He'd almost witnessed something that would have mortified her.

She got a light lunch from the cafeteria and took it out into the courtyard, finding a spot to sit away from others. She lowered herself onto the concrete bench and thought about the events of the morning. She hadn't reacted like that in a long, long time. Maybe Misha's presence really had triggered something, but why?

As if she'd summoned him, he was suddenly there. "Care if I join you for a minute?"

Rather than try to speak, she shrugged, horrified that the shaky feeling from the ER was returning. But at least she wasn't nauseous this time around.

He studied her. "What happened?"

Her heart clenched for a second before she realized he wasn't talking about her past with Wade. Rather, he was referring to the emergency trach procedure.

She sidestepped the question. "Is she okay? The baby?"

"Yes, they both are. But are you?"

Lyndsey swallowed. "Of course. Why do you ask?"

"You know why."

Damn. He'd always been able to read her. The fact that he still could irked her in a way she couldn't quite understand.

"It's always distressing to see someone on the knife's edge of life and death."

"Yes. But surely you've seen that many times before."

She had. She wouldn't be able to work as a nurse if she couldn't handle terrible outcomes—those times when nothing they did succeeded in saving a patient's life.

"Yes. But that doesn't mean I'm hardened to it."

For some reason, she didn't want him to know what a colossal mistake she'd made by becoming involved with Wade. Part of it was she didn't want to relive it again by telling him. But there was also part of her that didn't want him to know how long she'd waited before leaving the relationship.

He didn't say anything for a long minute. "I think maybe it's more than that. But I won't press you for something you don't want to give."

He never had. It was one of the biggest differences between Misha and Wade. And she wondered all over again how she could have fallen for her ex-husband's words. Maybe she'd been trying to get back at Misha for leaving her. If so, she'd only ended up hurting herself. And Brody.

She decided to at least answer this question truthfully. "Thank you. I appreciate that."

He drew a deep breath and then looked at her. "So. Tell me more about Brody."

Glad to talk about something other than herself, she talked about his condition, filling him in on how he'd been diagnosed. Otosclerosis was rare. Very rare. And it tended to be inherited. If one parent had the gene, there was a chance of passing it down to their offspring. Lyndsey had gone through genetic testing, in case she decided to have more children, but her test had come back clear. And there was no way she was going to ask Wade to take a test. She did not want him in Brody's life in any way, shape or form.

"It started in his right ear. Originally, they thought it

was the remnants of an ear infection. But then his left ear started to show signs of slight hearing loss as well. That's where we are now. He's had a tympanogram to measure hearing conduction to his eardrum and a CT scan, both of which seem to confirm otosclerosis."

"Yes, that follows the pattern. He's on the younger end of the spectrum." Misha said, as if thinking out loud. He glanced at her again. "You already know surgery involves putting in a prosthesis to bypass the stapes, then."

The stapes was one of the three bones of the middle ear. And in otosclerosis, that bone gradually becomes cemented or "stuck" in place and unable to transmit sound vibrations.

"Yes." Before he had a chance to say anything, she continued. "I also know there's a chance that surgery could make his hearing worse. Which is why I'd rather have it done in his right ear first, before attempting the other ear."

"I would totally agree with that plan." He sat back. "Now. Tell me about Brody."

Her head tilted. "But I just—"

"No. Not about his condition. I want to know about him as a person."

"But why?"

He smiled. "You chided me for referring to him as your son and made sure I knew his name. So I want to know more about him." He touched her hand. "Believe it or not, I do view my patients as people."

His fingers were warm on her skin, and it was hard

not to turn her hand palm-side up and link her fingers through his. But the days of doing that had long passed. And Lyndsey couldn't afford to try to rewind the clock. She'd been hurt by him. Not physically, but a deep emotional wound that had taken a long time to heal. She knew part of that had been because of what she'd been dealing with at the time with her dad. But it didn't make the hurt any less real.

But Wade… Well, he had hurt her in ways that had taken years of therapy to get past.

More importantly, she had Brody to think about. He had to come first, no matter what. She couldn't risk dragging him into something that could turn into as much of a disaster as the last time around.

Not that Misha would even be open to that. Nor should he. Especially as Brody's doctor.

With a sense of regret, she pulled her hand free under the guise of picking up her glass of water and downing a big sip, welcoming the icy splash as the liquid hit her stomach. It also helped clear her head. "Rather than me telling you about Brody—as a person—I'll let him tell you about himself. He's really a great kid. Despite my mistakes and missteps."

She didn't voice what those were, but Misha was a big boy. He'd understand what she'd left unsaid.

He nodded. "Okay, I'll let Brody tell me what he wants me to know. And I'm sure you need to get back to work soon."

She realized her pulling away hadn't gone unnoticed. There was an aloofness to him in the way he now sat. In the impersonal words he'd just said.

"I do." She hesitated before trying to at least say what she should have said earlier. "And Misha…thank you for agreeing to see him. For considering doing the surgery."

"Of course. I'll let you eat in peace now."

With that, he stood up and walked away, leaving her with an uneasy feeling that she had somehow thrown what was a nice gesture—an attempt to build some kind of bridge between them—back in his face. But she wasn't sure how to undo it, or if she even should. Maybe aloof was good. Maybe it would save her some heartache in the end. She couldn't want something that wasn't offered to her, right?

So she just had to make sure he didn't offer.

As if he would. From all appearances, he was as over her as she was over him.

Ha! Except right at this moment, she wasn't quite sure that she was. Wasn't so sure that her heart wasn't rebuilding the bridge between them that she'd burned down fifteen years ago. And if it succeeded in spanning the gulf between them, then she was in trouble. Big, big trouble. And she might even jeopardize having Misha as Brody's doctor. So she needed to concentrate on that right now. Not on herself. Or her feelings. But on the reality staring her in the face: If Misha wouldn't do this surgery and if she couldn't find someone else in time, then her son might very well pay the price for her own stupidity.

* * *

Brody looked just like her.

Taller than his mother, he had sandy blond hair that was a little on the longish side and a smile that tilted up on the right side, just like Lyndsey's.

"So you're Brody. I'm Dr. Lukyanov, but you can call me Misha."

The boy hopped up on the exam table without him asking and smiled. "My mom says you used to go to the same high school."

Misha had wondered if she'd tell her son anything about their past. It looked like she had, but she'd left out the fact that they'd once been crazy about each other. Although it seemed like she'd been able to leave those memories behind easier than he had. Besides the woman in New York that he'd been involved with, he'd also dated a woman in Belarus once he realized Lyndsey had been serious about never having contact with him again. But the relationship had been more physical than anything, and when she'd pressed for more, he ended things. A year later, he'd found himself going through the process of emigrating once again from his home country. He'd thought about reconnecting with Lyndsey. But he'd been certain she'd be married with children. And he'd been right. Although she wasn't married any longer, since her last name was no longer Marshall, she and Wade had been husband and wife for a time.

Misha was in no hurry to form an attachment like that. In truth, after Lindsey, he'd never quite met anyone special enough to consider marriage. And he was happy to keep things that way.

"So, Brody, what kinds of things do you like to do?"

He expected him to say he played sports. He may have looked like Lyndsey, but his physique was like his father's.

"I'm actually in band in school. And some friends and I formed our own band. We meet in one of their garages. I play keyboard and sing backup."

Music. Okay, that was something he hadn't expected. But it explained why Lyndsey didn't want to go the cochlear implant route. Her earlier words about his natural hearing made perfect sense now.

He sat on his stool and tapped his otoscope on his knee. "I'll have to come hear you at one of your gigs."

He immediately regretted saying that. But only because it was Brody. What he'd told Lyndsey was true. He did try to see his patients as people. And it was something he might have said to any of his patients. But somehow it was different this time. And he wanted to tread carefully.

Brody grinned, that lopsided smile making something tighten in Misha's chest. "We're not quite there yet, but we do have friends over that listen to our jam sessions. You're welcome to come out."

Lyndsey quickly intervened. "I'm sure Misha—er Dr. Lukyanov—is pretty busy with his patients."

If he treated Brody differently than he would his other patients just because of his and Lyndsey's past relationship, then maybe he should rethink taking him on. No. He was going to do exactly what he would have, had Lyndsey been a complete stranger.

"I'm sure I could find a half hour or so to come out and hear you. It'll give me a better idea of your goals for your hearing."

Brody's smile faded. "The thought of not being able to play anymore…of not being able to hear tones and notes…" A muscle worked in the boy's cheek. "It kills me."

The tightness squeezed harder.

"I'm going to do my best to make sure that doesn't happen. I'm going to examine you, but I've gone over all your tests, and it looks like your other ENT has been very thorough." He paused. "Did your mom explain what the surgery we've been discussing entails?"

"Yes. It's kind of like a heart bypass. Only instead of the heart, you'll be bypassing one of the bones in my ear." Brody's eyes met his, and for the first time, Misha saw a hint of fear in the boy's expression.

"Yes, that's a good analogy."

"Will it work?"

Misha's free hand gripped the other end of the otoscope. "I can't make any hard and fast promises. But I'm hopeful that it will."

"Me too."

A few minutes later, Misha completed his exam and rang a tuning fork, pressing it to the bony region just behind Brody's right ear.

"Can you hear that?"

"Kind of."

He repeated the process on the left side of his head. "How about now."

"Yes. That one is a lot better."

"How much better would you say?"

"About fifty percent. On the other side, I'm not sure if I'm just imagining the sound or if I'm actually hearing it."

Misha felt rather than saw Lyndsey's fingers curl into her palms, and she inched her chair closer to her child, a sign of protection that he had seen in many of his patients' parents. But there was something different about the way she did it.

His father is no longer in the picture.

He mentally heard her voice when he'd asked about Brody's dad. Was his absence due to apathy on Wade's part? Or was it something else? Was there some reason Lyndsey didn't want Brody to have any contact with his dad?

Her hand going to her neck during the treatment of the car accident victim came back to him. It had seemed like such an odd reaction for a medical professional to have.

Speculating would get him nowhere, though, and really the reason for Brody's dad not being around was none of his business.

The teen's voice shook him from his thoughts.

"So what's the next step?"

He was mature. More mature than Misha would have expected. He didn't wait for his mom to ask the hard questions, he was asking them for himself. A testament to Lyndsey's parenting skills.

"The next step is we talk about your goals, which is why I'd like to hear your band. But I also want to show you a short video of how the bypass surgery is done, if you're up for it?"

"Definitely. Can we do it now?"

Misha smiled. "I was hoping you'd say that. I just so happen to have already cued the video on the monitor behind me."

"Great."

Picking up the remote, he pressed play and watched the video he'd seen many times. Except Misha wanted to view it through the eyes of his patients. They were the ones who would ultimately decide if the risk was worth it. Brody had already answered that question. For him, it was definitely worth it.

And for a musician, Misha could definitely appreciate why.

The video showed how the stapes would be separated from the other two bones of the middle ear and carefully removed, leaving its footplate in place. Then a prosthesis would be measured and fitted onto the footplate and attached to the bone next to it. The ultimate goal was for the graft to take over what the stapes—in its undamaged form—would have done.

When the two-minute video finished, Brody released a breath. "Cool. So I'll be able to hear as good as I used to?"

"Maybe not quite as good, because there's been

some damage. But it should be measurably better than it is right now. I daresay you'll notice a difference afterward."

"How soon can I have it done?"

"I'm going to look at my schedule and see where the best slot is. I don't want to try to squeeze you in just to get it done quickly. I need to give myself enough time to be meticulous." He squeezed the boy's hand. "You can understand why. I'm going to say it'll be three weeks at least."

"Three weeks. I thought maybe it would take months." The kid smiled. "Thank you. My mom and I appreciate this so much."

Lyndsey spoke up for the first time since they had arrived. "Yes, we do. So much."

He wondered if Brody even knew his mom was working in his department. Well, if he didn't, Misha was sure not going to say anything about it. And it was a relief that she'd only told the boy that they'd simply known each other in high school. That way there'd be no expectations either positive or negative on Brody's side. He didn't want the kid picturing some Hallmark movie moment and trying to play matchmaker.

They wrapped up the appointment, and he told them to have the front desk schedule another appointment for next week, when they would start talking dates and specifics. He also asked if they would give him some idea of when Brody's band would be playing and he would let them know if or when he'd come by to hear them. In the meantime, he would have his office contact their insurance company to start the ball rolling on getting the surgery preapproved.

Misha could only hope he could keep things on his end going just as smoothly. Like not letting his past relationship with Lyndsey influence his decisions with Brody. He'd told him the truth. That he needed to be meticulous in performing the surgery, and if there were any reasons why he couldn't, he would have to hand him off to another surgeon.

But Misha didn't want to do that. And he had no idea why. To make up for hurting her when he'd told her the news that he was returning to Belarus? Lyndsey had obviously gotten over it, so why was he still thinking about it?

He had no idea. But it was time—way past time, actually—to put what had happened between them behind him. Once and for all.

CHAPTER THREE

LYNDSEY HANDED MISHA the list three days later. It was the first time she'd seen him since their appointment and Brody had asked her every night if she'd given it to him yet. If she had her way, the ENT would have as little contact with her son as possible. But she did understand why he wanted this small peek into Brody's life. The nurse in Misha's office had told her how lucky she was to have Misha taking her son's case. She already knew how lucky she was. What might not turn out to be so lucky was working in the same department as the surgeon. But there was no way she was going to make any kind of change before the surgery. She didn't want to do anything that might jeopardize that. If she requested a transfer right now, she was pretty sure he would question it. Might even question if he was the right person to be performing the surgery.

"Thanks, Lynds. I'll let you know which of these I can make."

His shortened use of her name was a remnant of their past, and it made her tummy shiver in a way that was all too familiar.

Could she stay?

She had to. At least for now. She took her commitments seriously and she'd heard the hospital was short on nursing staff, so to move to a different medical center now seemed totally selfish. And despite Misha saying he would never hold someone accountable for something they couldn't control, she couldn't be sure he wouldn't drop the case if she did leave. Or pass it to someone else.

She was almost positive he wouldn't. But almost wasn't good enough. She would stay here for as long as necessary. And after Brody's surgery?

She still believed in doing the best job she could no matter what the circumstances.

Realizing Misha was standing there waiting for some kind of response, she shook the thoughts away. "Okay, thanks." She swallowed before asking the next question. "I know you told Brody he probably wouldn't get all of his hearing back, but can you give me any idea about how much of an improvement we can expect?"

"I won't really know until I see how much ossification there is, and how much cleanup I have to do after getting the stapes out. But if everything goes according to plan, he could get up to eighty percent."

She closed her eyes and breathed a prayer of thanks. "That's good. Better than I'd hoped."

"There's always the chance of complications, so let's adopt a wait-and-see approach once the surgery has been done.

"That makes sense."

Misha folded the slip of paper and slid it into the pocket of his jeans. Black jeans. Jeans that fit his form far too well. She bit her lip and looked away.

Trying to redirect her thoughts, she said, "I looked in on our trach patient a little while ago. It looks like the swelling is starting to recede and they'll be able to reverse the procedure. And the baby is still doing great."

His head tilted. "Is she on our floor? I understood she'd been moved to obstetrics."

Oops. "She was. I...um...went to see her."

Unexpectedly, the corners of his mouth turned up. One of the few times she'd seen him smile since she'd come to work, and this time it was aimed squarely at her. The change in his face was stunning. Her tummy shiver turned into a shudder that was probably visible.

Oh, God. Not good, Lyndsey.

"I'll let you in on a little secret. I went to see her too."

"You did?"

His smile faded. "Is that so surprising? That I would care for my patients?"

"No. Of course not." She found she mourned the loss of his smile more than she should have. "I just thought with how busy you are, you might not have time to follow up on cases that were transferred to another department."

"Sometimes it's not a matter of having time, it's a matter of making time. I do my best not to overschedule myself."

"But I'm sure like other hospitals, Louisiana Southern has quotas you'll have to meet."

He gave a half shrug. "Yes, they have them. But they agreed to give me the time I feel I need. It was one of the conditions I made when I agreed to come here."

Or he wouldn't work for them. He didn't say it, but he didn't have to. And the hospital probably couldn't afford to lose a prestigious surgeon, and Misha knew it. Wow. She already had respect for him as a skilled surgeon. But she found she now respected him as a person. Just like she used to. And Lyndsey probably couldn't afford to think of him in terms of anything other than a surgeon. But it was hard. So hard.

And those damned black jeans kept catching her eye and making her gaze venture to places it shouldn't. Places she'd been before. Places where love and ecstasy could walk hand in hand.

No. Do not think about that. Especially not right now.

She pulled the conversation back to the patient. "Any idea when she'll be able to get the trach reversed?"

"As soon as the swelling goes down enough. Maybe another four or five days. She's still got four weeks until her due date, so they're going to try to keep that baby in place as long as possible."

"So they won't do reconstructive surgery on her trachea right now?"

"They don't think it'll be needed. Surprisingly, it's intact, when by all accounts it should have been crushed."

Something in his phrasing rolled around in her head,

trying to find a place to land. Like a pesky insect, she swatted it away before it could. Because she was afraid she might somehow apply it to her and Misha's breakup.

Because it was a completely different thing. Their relationship had been crushed. Destroyed, actually. No part of it remained intact. And if by some weird accident there was something left, she would have to make sure it didn't have a chance to do anything except linger in her subconscious.

"Well, I'd better go look in on my patients," she said.

"Okay, I'll get back to you on the dates. Is the address on here, or do they meet somewhere different each practice?"

"No, it's on there. Brody made sure of it."

For some reason it was important for her to stress that this was Brody's doing and not hers. She did not want him to think that she was eager to see him outside of work.

She could opt not to be at whatever practice Misha chose. Except she drove Brody to practice and normally waited there for him. Sometimes in the garage, where friends normally gathered to hear the group, or in her car. But if she opted for sitting in the car, Misha would think it was because of him.

And it would be. Lyndsey did not want him to know that he still affected her on a physical level, even if it no longer reached her emotions.

At least she hoped it didn't.

Surprisingly, it's intact, when by all accounts it should have been crushed.

No. It was definitely crushed. She remembered that day as clearly as if it were yesterday.

And she was not planning on letting anything "uncrush" it.

Misha sat next to Lyndsey on a folding chair in the humid night air. The band was tuning up in preparation for practice, and there were seven other young people who were either up by the band talking with its members or sitting in a cluster talking among themselves. He felt slightly out of place, but Lyndsey said she regularly sat in on their sessions. When Brody spotted him, he came out from behind the keyboard and walked over to shake his hand. "Thanks for coming. We cover a lot of groups, so hopefully you'll recognize some of the songs."

"I'm sure I will."

It didn't really matter. He'd come to see what Brody's passion was. He'd done it with some of his patients in New York, too. Not as a guide to whether or not they were worthy of surgery, but as a guide to what surgical candidates hoped to get out of whatever procedure was being considered.

Five minutes later, the band started playing in earnest, and true to what he'd said, the first number was something from the nineties and Misha did recognize it. "The Stillness of Love" was something he remembered hearing on the radio as he and Lyndsey sat in his car and talked about their dreams for the future. They'd joked about the number of children they each wanted, and Lyndsey had laughed when he'd claimed he wanted fifteen. Instead, he had none.

He glanced to his side to see that Lynds had her hands clasped tightly in her lap and was holding herself stiffly erect. She wasn't moving in time with the music or tapping her foot.

Because she too remembered that night? It was the first time they'd made love, parked next to the river in the dark with no one around. But it hadn't been the last. Not by a long shot. If she'd gotten pregnant by him, would he have opted to stay in the States rather than leave with his parents?

But she hadn't. And it would have placed him in the untenable position of choosing his dad's cancer battle over a possible child. He could only thank God that he hadn't had to make that choice. But the choice he had made was just as terrible. His dad, or a love that might or might not last? In the end, he couldn't help but think he'd made the only decision he could have under the circumstances.

Damn. He wasn't even sure why he remembered the song, or why it stirred up all those old memories. Maybe coming here was a mistake. But surely Lyndsey had heard them play this song before, so it wouldn't have taken her by surprise like it had him.

Or maybe she'd even forgotten this was one of the songs on the radio that night.

Then the notes faded away, and he found himself

sagging in relief. The band started its next number, and thank God it wasn't anything he recognized. Lyndsey too seemed to have relaxed, her hands no longer clenched together. And this time, her foot was tapping to the beat of an upbeat rock number. So maybe she did remember.

He forced himself to concentrate on Brody.

The band was actually good. Better than Misha had expected them to be. He understood why Lyndsey had pushed so hard for him to have the surgery. If Brody were his, he would have done exactly the same thing.

But he wasn't his. And he needed to keep some semblance of objectivity, or he would be in trouble. And so would Brody.

Worse, he found he liked having Lyndsey sitting next to him as the group moved from one song to the next. If things hadn't turned out the way they had, they might have still been together. Married. With at least one or two children.

But they weren't. And if he had it to do all over again, he still would have gone with his parents. He'd made his decision. And Lyndsey had made hers.

They were the people they were today because of those decisions. Misha had to believe he'd done the right thing.

And not contacting Lyndsey? Respecting her wish for him to leave her alone, had that been the right decision?

But if he had, would she have still chosen Wade over him?

He would never know the answer to that. And in truth, maybe Lyndsey didn't even know the answer to that question.

And dissecting the past wasn't going to change it. So he decided to just take this moment for what it was and enjoy the band's music. And allow himself to enjoy Lyndsey's presence.

Why the hell not? It wouldn't change anything between them. But he could still like sitting here with her, just like he would with any other friend or acquaintance.

It didn't matter that she was neither friend nor acquaintance. She was something else. Something he didn't have to define or categorize.

So he let the music wash over him, watching Brody put his heart into each note he played.

And he knew that whether he wanted to or not, he was going to be the one to perform that surgery. And he was going to do his damnedest to make sure he gave that boy every ounce of hearing that he possibly could.

When the group finished playing, Brody hurried over to them, his face alight with energy and exhilaration. "So what did you think?"

Misha could honestly answer that question. "I think you guys are phenomenal. And you might not have any paid gigs right now, but if you keep playing the way you do, you will. It won't be long."

"You really think so?"

"I do."

"Our goal is to be a part of the big music festival in Gerard Park."

Misha's head tilted. "I think I remember someone mentioning that festival. You said it's big. How big is it?"

"You mean you've never heard of it?"

Had he? Maybe. But if so, he hadn't paid attention to announcements about it. He'd been so caught up in his work in the short time he'd been at the hospital that he hadn't gotten out very much. By the time he got home, he was pretty much wiped. In fact, this was the first "outing" he could remember going to in ages. Even in New York, he'd been driven and focused, finding very little time to do much outside of work.

"I guess I must have, but I've never been."

"You have to go, doesn't he, Mom? It's like *the* thing in Lafayette. I've been a bunch of times, and we live an hour away from there."

Since it had taken him almost an hour to get from the hospital to where Brody's band was playing in Centerville, he could see how the festival would have to be good to be worth traveling that far to see it. He glanced at Lyndsey. "Do you commute from here to Lafayette every day to get to work?"

She nodded. "I don't want to move if I don't have to. Brody loves his school, and he might have to give up his band if we moved closer."

And yet she'd been working at the hospital for a year. That was a long time to wait. So why hadn't she looked for something closer to home. Maybe because

Lafayette was so much larger, she felt she would have a better chance of finding help for Brody through whatever contacts she made there. And after his surgeries, would she take a job closer to home?

It might be easier for him if she did, but there was a part of him that gave a funny lurch at the thought of it. And yet he'd moved an ocean away from her. It had hurt to do, but he'd been so focused on his dad that he hadn't really thought as much about Lyndsey's hurt as maybe he should have. Then again, he hadn't been able to think much beyond the crisis his family was going through at the time. To expect her to wait would have been living in a fantasy world.

She'd done the right thing in moving on. It just stung that she'd done so as quickly as she had.

Honestly, he had no right to ask her what her plans were. But to drive over an hour every day to get to work and another hour to get home? It was taking time that she could have spent with her son. And yet it was Brody who drove all her decisions. If he were a father, he imagined he would move heaven and earth to get his child the help they needed.

"I can understand that. It's a big leap. Especially when you have someone else to think about."

"Yes. It is."

He thought he heard a hint of irony in her words, although he could have imagined it. Looking at it from her perspective, he could see that being the one left behind was harder than being the one who left, although at the time, he'd placed them on even footing.

Brody chose that moment to break in. "Why don't you come with us to the festival. It starts next week, and we always just buy tickets at the gate. That way you can see what it's like."

Lyndsey's eyes went wide. "Brody. You can't just try to force people to join us."

There'd been no forcing involved. It had been a simple question from a teen who was eager to share something he was passionate about. And somehow, Misha didn't want to disappoint him by turning him down.

"I think I might be able to manage it, depending on what day it's on." He would just have to make sure it didn't interfere with any of his surgical cases, which were on Mondays and Fridays. The rest were appointment days at his office, which was connected to the hospital.

"Brody, why don't you go say goodbye to your friends while I talk to Misha for a minute."

The boy looked from one to the other, before shrugging and moving away from them.

Then Lyndsey turned to him. "You don't have to go just because he asked you to, you know."

"I do know. But I've never been to the festival. Hell, I'm not sure I've even heard of it before he mentioned it. Was it here back when we were dating?"

"Of course. And there's no way you can live in Lafayette and not know about the festival. Most of the literature is written in French Creole. It's a celebration of Cajun culture."

He shook his head. "I haven't been living here all that long."

"So you've seriously never been? Not even with your folks when they lived here?"

"Not even then."

Lyndsey actually laughed before she swallowed the sound. "Seriously, though. You don't have to go."

"Do you want to use the word seriously a few more times?"

"Jerk."

The word made him blink. Their back and forth reminded him of old times. Times that he found he missed more than he realized. Suddenly he wanted to go. Not because he expected to ever get back together with Lyndsey, but he wanted to see it through her eyes. Through Brody's eyes. And since he'd never been, who better to enjoy it with than people who went to it every year.

"Will it bother you if I join you for the festival?" If she minded, he would back off. But if she didn't...

Then he would go with no expectations other than to enjoy something different.

"No, it's okay. Although I'll warn you that Brody will probably provide a running commentary the entire time. He's passionate about music. And the festival. Just like I'm passionate about his ability to hear."

He wasn't sure it was a good idea. But right now with her beside him, he found he wanted to be with her away from the hospital. Where conversations didn't just revolve around patients and conditions. Where they could just...talk.

And not about their past. Just about life. And what she'd done over the past fifteen years. What had made her choose nursing as a profession. And what had ended her marriage to Wade.

Hmmm...that was really none of his business. If he went, he wasn't going to bring the man up. Not even once. Besides, he didn't know what Brody knew or didn't know about his dad.

"Since I know nothing about the festival, a running commentary will be welcomed."

Lyndsey laughed again, and the sound filled him with a warmth the surprised him. A warmth from the past that threatened to leak into the present.

"Well, don't say I didn't warn you."

"I would never say that." He paused. "Do I need to pack a lunch, or will they have food there?" Some of the festivals in Belarus had concession stands and some were just open air where you brought a blanket and a picnic lunch and enjoyed the company of family and friends.

"Lots of typical foods, and regular things like hot dogs for those who prefer simpler fare."

"I'm not sure how anyone can prefer hot dogs."

She smiled. "That's right. You were never a fan of them at the ball games in high school."

"Not American hot dogs, no. Ours are more of a kielbasa, and it's what I grew up eating. They just taste completely different to me."

"I'll have to try one sometime."

"Maybe I'll make you one, sometime." When she smiled again, he realized this conversation was taking a turn he didn't want it to take. It was better to keep things on more impersonal footing. Especially since he would be taking on Brody's surgery.

So while he didn't retract his offer, he did steer the conversation back toward more professional footing, and when Brody came back after a few minutes, he'd already said his goodbyes to Lyndsey. He did the same with Brody, then he got the hell out of there.

Before he could change his mind and set a date to cook up one of the most famous Russian comfort foods: sliced kielbasa fried up with potatoes.

CHAPTER FOUR

"I DON'T KNOW if you heard. Joanna went home today."

Misha had stopped by the desk to check on a patient's chart, and Lyndsey blurted out the first thing she could think of.

"Joanna?"

"Our trach patient."

His brows went up. "That's great news. I meant to check on her yesterday, but one of my surgeries ended up more complicated than I expected."

She tensed, hoping she would never hear those words in reference to Brody. "Did it come out okay?"

"I'm hoping. We did a graft over a perforation, and the skin we harvested from the patient ended up being too delicate and came apart. The second attempt held. We're hopeful it'll take." He paused. "Anyway, I'm glad she was able to go home."

"Me too. They extubated her yesterday afternoon and she was able to breathe on her own, despite some residual edema. But that should go down on its own over the next several days and she and the baby were deemed stable enough to be released."

"That is good news." Misha's light brown hair

looked mussed, like he'd run his fingers through it one too many times. She could remember many a time where she'd been the one who'd dug her fingertips into that thick hair during a make-out session and had to smooth it back down before she got out of the car, hoping no one would guess what they'd been up to.

Only she was no longer allowed to run her palms over that sexy head or kiss the tip of his nose when she was done.

Had he had another difficult case today?

"I thought so too." She glanced at where he was struggling to locate something on the computer. "Who are you looking for?"

"Max Sheffield. He has a suspicious lesion on his vocal cord, and I wanted to go in and get a biopsy of it today. But I wanted to look at his scans again, first."

Lyndsey sat down in the chair next to where he stood, only realizing afterward that it put her dangerously close to him. So close that she could smell the clean scent of his soap and a hint of whatever shaving cream he'd used that morning.

Forcing her attention to the screen in front of her, she typed in the name. Nothing came up, so she edited the spelling to Maxwell Sheffield. The entry popped up immediately. "Here it is."

Misha leaned down to look as she scrolled through the screens until she arrived at the scans of the patient's vocal cords. His hair brushed her cheek, making her shiver. The last time she was this close to him, she was kissing him, and he was...

Her whole body tightened in remembered anticipation.

What was wrong with her?

He grabbed a Post-it pad and pen as if he felt no different than he did with any other nurse and jotted down a few notes. "Got it, thanks."

He'd moved on a long time ago. She thought she had too, until he'd brought the past roaring back to taunt her. So not fair.

Trying to nurse the sting, she nodded. "No problem."

When he looked at her, though, his blue irises were darker than they normally were, and as he stood quickly his shoulder accidentally brushed across her breast, causing the nipple to tighten and gooseflesh to ripple across her skin.

Desperate to find something to say that would distract her senses, she blurted out, "I'll check with Brody when I get home about the music festival dates."

Ugh! Reminding him about that wasn't a good ploy. In fact, she was wondering how good of an idea it was for him to go with them. But she couldn't retract the words, and right now she just wanted him to move away from her before her system went into critical meltdown and he noticed how hot and bothered she'd become.

"Feel free to text me once you know."

Text him. Good idea or not? Probably not.

But it was way better than calling him and having to listen to that low, smooth voice pour its magic over her.

Oh, jeez, working with him was going to be a disaster if she couldn't get herself under control. And it wasn't like he was trying to do anything. He wasn't. And he definitely wasn't Wade, who she'd found out had tried to hit on her best friend Brittany a few months after they'd gotten married. By then, she was six months pregnant and Wade's college football scholarships hadn't materialized like he'd hoped and he wasn't working. They were living in a camper and things between them were spiraling downhill fast. And to hear that he'd propositioned a friend... She'd confronted him, realizing too late that there were crushed beer cans littering the floor and a college game on TV. Not a good combination. Wade had stood and grabbed her before she could get away. He let her know in no uncertain terms that she was never to question anything he did. And never ever to interrupt him during a game.

Somehow she'd clawed her way free of him before he was able to make her lose consciousness and had fled the camper with the clothes on her back and a fresh set of bruises around her neck.

But at least she'd been alive. And she hadn't lost Brody.

The memory made her throat tighten for a split second and she took a wheezing breath. She quickly righted it. But it was too late. Misha was now looking at her with concern on his face.

"Are you okay?"

"Fine. I was just suppressing a cough."

"I don't think so. Tell me what's going on."

She hesitated, fighting the tiny voice inside of her

that told her to tell him everything. But how could she? Despite the fact that she knew none of it had been her fault, there was still a part of her that was embarrassed she'd gotten into the relationship at all. And damn it, it was no one's business. She would choose who she told. And when. She gritted her teeth and stood. "I'm fine. And if that's all you wanted, I have a few patients to check in on."

Good going, Lynds. Use the same excuse you did last time when you wanted to escape his eagle eyes.

"Is one of them Max?"

What could she say? No? It was pretty obvious he would have been on her list of patients to check.

"As a matter of fact, it is."

"Mind if I head over there with you? I'd like to get a fresh set of vitals, and since I don't see Jacelyn anywhere around, maybe you could assist. I'm just going to give him a local and go in with the endoscope and swab the area. Pathology should pick up any suspicious cells when they go over it."

Did she have a choice? Obviously not, since she couldn't think of an excuse under the sun that would keep her out of that patient's room. Other than *you still affect me more than you should.* And there was no way she was going to admit that to him. Not today. Not ever.

"I don't mind." What was one little white lie among ex-lovers?

Too bad she didn't affect him the same way.

Or did she? He'd gotten up from his chair pretty

quickly back at the desk. She'd been so stuck on her own physical reaction to him that she hadn't had time to analyze that until right now.

Somehow that made it better. Or at least it made her feel better to pretend that was the case.

And when she went to move past him, he took a step back.

Okay. Maybe she wasn't crazy after all. With a jolt of fresh confidence, she walked ahead of him, allowing her hips to tip maybe a little more than usual as she went, although she'd never been very good at trying to have a sexy walk. She normally ended up feeling more like a penguin, making Misha laugh back in the day.

Of course that had been back when she'd been able to laugh at herself too. She tempered her pace and ordered her hip movements to settle down to a normal rhythm. They made it down the short corridor with no incidents, and when they went into the room, they found the thirty-eight-year-old patient reading a book, looking completely at ease. When he saw them, he closed it and set it on the nightstand beside him.

It was rare to find a patient quite so blasé about a possible cancer diagnosis, although Lyndsey knew people could bury their feelings so deep that others had no idea what they were going through. Hadn't she done that with Wade? Pretended life was fine when it was really a train wreck she'd felt she couldn't escape from?

Misha stepped forward. "I'd like to get a little swab

from that area we talked about. Are you okay with doing it now?"

"Yep." Max folded his hands in his lap, looking totally at ease, even sending them both a smile that was wider than it should have been.

Misha sent her a look. He'd noticed it too.

He leaned closer and looked in the man's face. "Mr. Sheffield, have you taken something?"

The man scratched his neck and shrugged. It was then that she saw where Misha was headed with his question.

"I took a valium to help me relax, just in case."

"Is it your prescription or someone else's?"

"Mine." He pulled a bottle from his pants pocket and handed it to Misha, who studied it carefully before handing it back. "You should have checked with me first. Some medications can react with the spray I'll use to numb your throat. Fortunately, valium isn't one of them. Did you just take one?"

"I did. Sorry, Doc."

Misha sighed, obviously not happy with his patient, but he went about his preparations, directing Lyndsey where to find some of the equipment he would use. She wasn't trained as a surgical nurse, but she had helped with routine endoscopies before.

She sprayed the back of the patient's tongue with the anesthetic and waited for it to take effect.

"I normally do this in my office, but since you were already in the hospital for another procedure, I thought

we could just do it here rather than have you make another appointment at my practice."

He began to feed the endoscope down as they
watched its progress on a nearby monitor. "Entering
the vocal folds now."

Lyndsey saw the area immediately. It was red and
irritated, but not very large at all. Misha saw it too,
and readjusted his equipment so that he could rub a
special swab across it to collect a specimen.

It took less than five minutes and when he pulled
the scope out, the man seemed even more relaxed than
he'd been when they arrived. She could see why Misha
was irritated with him. But he'd kept his cool better
than she might have, simply placing the swab in a collection tube for the pathologist to process.

"Okay, Max, that should do it. Do you have someone to pick you up?"

He nodded. "My brother is down in the waiting
room. He'll take me home." There was a slight hoarse-
ness to his voice that she'd noticed earlier. Probably
why he'd been referred to Misha.

Misha motioned her to the side and in a low voice
said, "Could you call down there and make sure he's
telling the truth. I don't want him on the road like
this."

She agreed and went over to Max. "Can you tell
me your brother's name and I'll have him come up?"

"Gary. Gary Sheffield."

"Okay, I'll be back in a minute."

She went out to the nurses' desk and called down

to the main waiting room. Gary Sheffield was indeed there and was on his way up to their floor to collect his brother. She gave a sigh of relief and went back to the room, giving Misha a quick nod. "He'll be here in a minute."

"Good." Placing his hand on the man's shoulder, he said, "I've printed off instructions for aftercare. Try to rest your voice as much as possible tonight. If you start coughing up any blood, call my office immediately and they'll get in touch with me. For anything more serious, dial 911. Understand?"

Max smiled again. "Perfectly, Doc."

Misha muttered something in Russian before nodding at him. "I'll wait for your brother outside. Lynds, could you help him gather his things?"

"I sure can." She grabbed a plastic bag emblazoned with the name of the hospital and put his book and a few other things he'd laid on the table into it, then handed it to the man.

A minute or two later, Misha entered with another man who resembled Max. Only this person was fully in control of his faculties. "I'm sorry. I told him not to take anything before getting the procedure. Obviously, he didn't listen."

She smiled at his obvious frustration.

Then Gary shot his brother a look that could kill.

"They're sending up a wheelchair for him," she said, then added, "It's hospital policy."

"Okay. Thank you for everything." He glanced at Misha. "You'll let us know what the results are?"

"Yes. I should have them in a couple of days. I'll call as soon as I do."

With that, Misha exited the room with Lyndsey close behind.

She eyed him as they walked back the way they came. "Does that happen often?"

"Fortunately, no. But when it does, it infuriates me."

"Really? I couldn't tell." She batted her eyes at him before laughing. "And did I just hear you cuss in front of a patient?"

He smiled as if it had been drawn from somewhere deep inside of him. "Let's let that be our little secret, okay?"

She'd heard him speak Russian many times when they'd been together. Most of the time, it was when he was in the throes of some passionate emotion, whether anger or something a little sexier. And it never failed to pluck just the right notes in her.

He was one of the sexiest men she'd ever known, and when he dragged his fingers through his hair in an effort to shove a few errant locks off his forehead, they fell right back to where they had been and made her smile. She loved his hair. His chin. Almost everything about him.

Except his decision to leave. And that had just about killed her.

But that was a long time ago, and she needed to push it back in the past where it belonged and leave it there. Along with her anger.

He couldn't change his decisions any more than she

could change hers. And in the end, they'd both come through the years a little older and, in Lyndsey's case, hopefully a whole lot wiser.

And that's what she needed to be where he was concerned for as long as he—or she—worked at Louisiana Southern: A whole lot wiser.

Brody's surgical date was set for two weeks from now. But today he was to go to the Cajun Music Festival. The former he was sure about. But the latter? Well, he wasn't positive that pushing to go with Lyndsey and her son was one of his better decisions. And he had a feeling Lynds felt the same way. But what was done was done. And to back out at the last second would look suspicious to Lyndsey and it might upset Brody, who'd really wanted him to come. He wasn't sure why. He'd been nothing but professional with the kid and it needed to stay that way. But then again, Misha held the boy's hearing in his hands, and Brody probably wanted him to see firsthand how important this surgery was to him.

He knew. It was important to Misha too, for a variety of reasons. Some of which were not as smart as others. He wanted to do this for Lyndsey. Maybe to make up for causing her pain all those years ago?

Possibly. But he'd also sensed a hint of sadness in her that he hadn't understood. He had the sense it wasn't directly tied to what had happened fifteen years ago between them. Maybe if he could take this one weight off her shoulders, it would take away that heaviness. At least that was his hope.

They'd agreed to meet at the hospital and go in his car. He figured if they stayed a couple of hours, he would have done his duty, and he could drop them back off at the hospital. It would be easy and painless. At least that was his hope.

When he got to the parking garage, he saw they were already there waiting for him. Great. Late again. This time it wasn't due to a patient, but due to his own reticence about going. He did not need to get attached to the boy.

Or to his mom, for that matter. Standing next to her as she'd looked for Max Sheffield's name had done a number on him, and from what he'd read in her body language, he wasn't the only one who'd felt it. If they'd been alone, he couldn't guarantee that he wouldn't have turned her to face him and looked deeply in her eyes before drawing her closer.

Proklyatiye! Not something he should even be imagining, much less admitting to himself.

"Sorry to keep you waiting." His voice was gruffer than he'd meant it to be and Lyndsey shot him a look.

Brody shrugged. "We just got here, actually. Our car wouldn't start, and Mom had to ask a friend to bring us."

He frowned. "I could have picked you up."

"It's an hour out of your way. I'll just call her when we're done, and she'll come and get us again."

"No need. I'll take you home."

"That's okay, you don't have to—"

"I know I don't have to. But I want to. It will be nice to see Centerville again. I assume it hasn't changed much."

Lyndsey glanced at him, but she didn't smile. "No, it hasn't. But then people seem to like it that way."

"Do they?"

"I think so. They get stuck in the memories of the past and don't want to move beyond them." She bit her lip. "I'm talking about the people who live there. Not me."

"I didn't think you were talking about you." He clicked the button on his fob to unlock the car, and Brody opened the door to the backseat, climbing inside. Misha opened the front passenger door and nodded at Lyndsey. "Go ahead. It's fine."

He then walked around to the driver's side and got in, pressing the button to start the vehicle.

Fifteen minutes later, they were on the grounds of the festival, and Brody had their path all mapped out on a sheet of paper.

"I want you to see it all."

Misha glanced around the venue. It was huge. "I'm not sure that's even possible." But he was impressed by Brody's diligence. Lyndsey had done a wonderful job raising him.

"It's not. But you can at least see a little of everything, starting with some of the Cajun jam sessions. They're this way."

Brody whisked them from space to space. It seemed

everything had its own tent or stage. Traditional music, modern, dance, it was all there, along with something for the kids. And food. Hell, the food. He tried a little of everything. The heat levels went from mild to atomic. He was pretty sure he'd just blown a hole in his gut with the last bite of spicy shrimp.

He glanced at Lyndsey. "You do this every year?"

"Every. Year. It's a tradition in our little family of two." She smiled, glancing at Brody with obvious affection and ruffling his hair.

No mention of Wade once again. But then, she'd said he wasn't in the picture. So where was he? Had he moved on to someone else? He did seem the type. The type to up and leave.

Like Misha had done?

That was different. Or so he'd thought back then.

But evidently she'd never remarried, since she still carried the McKinna name. And her ring finger was undeniably empty.

"It's a tradition to stuff yourself full enough to…?"

"Don't say it. I'm struggling to keep a lid on my stomach as it is. I'm glad we're walking."

"You and me both. I should be done digesting things about ten years from now." He sent her a smile. "But I have to admit this was nice. A great tradition you have here, Lynds. You're very lucky, you know."

The words were out before he realized it. But he meant them. She was happy with her "little family of two." It was evident in the shine in her eyes every time she looked at her son. Every time she talked about him.

"Lucky?" She shrugged, looking out over the venue. "I don't know that I'd go that far. It's taken me a long time to get where I am. A very long time. And Brody… he's everything to me. He's why my heart is still beating in my chest."

He turned and looked down at her. "He's a good kid. You should be proud of him."

"I am. More than you can ever know."

Their gazes met. Held. His hand lifted to cup her cheek, then Brody came rushing toward them like a whirlwind. "They've started the last set that I want to see."

Lyndsey, evidently unaware of what he'd been about to do, sent him a shrug. "Brody is being Brody." She might not realize what had almost happened, but he did. And he needed to check himself before he did something he couldn't take back. Something that might change what could—and would—happen in regard to Brody's surgery.

He and Lyndsey followed the boy back to the stage where the jam sessions were being held. Brody was obviously enthralled by everything that was happening on stage.

He glanced at his watch. Wow, they'd been here for almost four hours. That had to be a record for Misha. And he'd had fun. Something he couldn't remember having in a long, long time. Maybe since high school.

That seemed like a lifetime ago, and yet he remembered so much about those days. He'd been so young back then. Impulsive and sometimes stupid. He glanced at Lyndsey before pulling his attention back to the stage. Right now he couldn't afford to be either impulsive or stupid.

The band ended with a long, loud riff that went on for probably ten minutes. And when it ended, people all around them were standing on their feet and clapping and yelling. He couldn't blame them. It had been a workout for both the musicians and the audience, which seemed to throw as much energy into the mix as the band members had.

Brody turned to him. "Did you like it?"

"I really did. Thanks so much for inviting me."

Surprisingly, Brody glanced at his phone. "What time were you thinking of getting back?"

"Whatever time you think." In all honesty, he was ready to go now.

Lyndsey must have read something into her son's words. "Do you have something going on tonight?"

"Me and the boys were going to have a jam session of our own if I got back in time. If it's all right with you, that is."

"It depends on what Misha's plans are." She glanced at him. "I can certainly get Brittany to come out and get us. I know this has lasted longer than you probably thought it would."

There was no way he was going to let her and Brody sit around for an hour waiting on a ride when they could already be home.

"I'll take you home. It's not a big deal."

"Are you sure?"

"Absolutely."

With that decided, they piled back into Misha's car and headed toward Centerville and the end of what had been a very pleasant evening.

CHAPTER FIVE

MISHA PARKED OUTSIDE of Lyndsey's house, a move that felt both familiar and foreign. It had been years since they'd sat in a car together. And of course Brody was there, so it wasn't the same at all.

Before she could exit the vehicle though, Brody leaped out of the car. "I'll be back by nine, okay, Mom?"

"Yes. Nine o'clock for sure, though. Tomorrow's a school day."

A second later, the boy wheeled a bike from the garage, hopped on and was gone, pedaling out of sight.

"He makes my head spin sometimes, I swear." She looked at Misha. "But it's been good to see him smile like that. With the fear about his hearing, it's been a while since I've seen him so carefree. But now that a date for surgery has been set, he's got hope."

They exited the vehicle, and he walked her to the door. "Thanks for tonight," he said. "It was good to get a peek into Brody's passions. I had a good time."

"So did I."

They stood in front of her door. And she couldn't quite bring herself to turn toward it and let herself in.

Instead, she leaned back against it and looked at him. He was so damned gorgeous.

Neither of them moved for a long moment. Then her hand slowly lifted and pushed a strand of hair off his forehead, allowing her fingers to trail across his skin as she did. He was so warm, just like he'd been on so many nights in their past. The times when his gentle touch carried her to places she'd only dreamed about. And now they were alone. There was nothing to stop them if they might want to…

"Lynds…" As if he heard her thoughts, he took a step forward, crowding her against the door. Once upon a time that might have startled her. Frightened her, even. But this was Misha. And he would never physically hurt her.

He stared at her for a long moment, then leaned his face toward hers. And suddenly he was doing what she'd longed for him to do. He was kissing her.

The first touch of his mouth to hers was ecstasy. How long had it been since he'd done this?

A lifetime.

How could this be happening?

He moved closer, his body connecting with hers, bringing to life old and familiar nerve pathways that hurried their preparations.

His tongue touched her lips, pushed past them. And she welcomed him inside. Welcomed his touch, his taste. Her fingers found the warm hair at the base of his skull and tunneled deep, relishing the feel of his skull and the warm skin that covered every inch of his body.

It could be hers again. Tonight. Brody wouldn't be home for almost two hours. All she had to do was reach behind her for the doorknob and open the door.

Her hand reached back and found what she was looking for. But instead of turning it, she felt the cold reality of what that would mean.

She'd be opening herself up to be hurt all over again. Misha didn't want promises of forever. She wasn't sure what she was looking for here, but…

No!

Before she could say the word out loud, though, Misha's head came up and he took a step back.

Withdrawing.

And the loss… She didn't want to feel it again. But it was already creeping through her. How much worse would it be to get involved with him? This time it wouldn't just hurt her. It could potentially hurt her son as well.

"Lyndsey. This can't happen. For so many reasons."

She bit her lip hard enough to hurt. Hard enough to force her to separate fantasy from reality. And that kiss…was make believe. Even Misha recognized it.

"I know. I've managed to give Brody a stable life after Wade…left."

No. She didn't need to bring her ex-husband into this. "I'm just not willing to risk that again. Not for anyone."

And especially not you.

She didn't say those words out loud. But then again, she didn't have to. His face had already morphed from sexy to closed the moment he stepped back from her.

"I understand. Believe me. I'm not looking to start anything anymore than you are. And if we did, you'd have to find a new surgeon."

"No!" The word exploded from her mouth, and she forced herself to repeat it in a lower tone. "He trusts you. I'm not sure he'll let another surgeon move forward with the surgery. He...he trusts you."

She was repeating herself, but she was desperate not to let what almost happened ruin things for her son. He deserved this chance. "Please don't make us start from scratch."

"I wasn't saying I wouldn't do the surgery. I only meant we have to keep things professional."

"Of course. If anyone has a chance to make Brody's dream a reality, it's you."

He nodded, face unsmiling. "We'll just consider tonight a blip of something from the past that never should have raised its head."

Was it that easy for him to just pull back and forget tonight had ever happened? Evidently. After all, he'd left for Belarus and seemingly forgotten all about her. He'd been in the States for how long now? And never once had he tried to get in touch with her.

Working with him was going to be torture if she couldn't get past this. But she would...somehow.

And once Brody's surgery was over and done, she could make the decision about whether to keep working in his department or request a transfer. Or, once she no longer needed to be at a big hospital, she could go back to a hospital closer to her hometown. Where she never had to see Misha again.

The next couple of days were hard. Misha found himself avoiding the ENT department of the hospital, except today when he actually had a surgery he couldn't get out of. But what he'd said at her doorstep was true. They could not have a relationship for any number of reasons, but the first and foremost was because of Brody's surgery. Conflict of interest was never a good thing. There was a reason they didn't let doctors treat family members or those closest to them.

As he rounded the corner, hoping to avoid the nurses' station, he spotted a familiar face. He just couldn't place who she was.

But when she saw him, she stopped in her tracks, a frown appearing out of nowhere.

"Misha?"

He was still struggling to place her when she shook her head. "Lyndsey told me you were working here, that you were going to do Brody's surgery." Her mouth twisted. "But I was hoping I'd never have to lay eyes on you again."

He was taken aback by her sudden hostility, and then who she was dawned on him. There'd only be one person besides Lyndsey who could be that angry with him. "Brittany?"

"So you do recognize me."

He hadn't. Not until this very second, when he remembered Lyndsey mentioning that Brittany had driven her to the hospital two days ago when they were going to the music festival.

That the woman wasn't his biggest fan was obvious. Back in high school, they'd all been friends. Close friends. But he got it. He'd been the one to walk out on Lyndsey and hurt her. He imagined he didn't have many friends left at that school.

"Lyndsey said you brought her to the hospital when her car broke down. Thanks for that."

"Don't thank me. I didn't agree with Brody inviting you to that festival." Her brows went up. "You know, you're reason she wound up with that jackass of a husband."

Anger welled up inside of him. "Marrying Wade was her choice. Not mine."

"Her choice? If you knew what he put her through. God…he almost ki—"

"Brittany! That's enough." Lyndsey's voice cut through her friend's tirade like a knife.

Her mouth shut with a snap and she shook her head. "Oh, honey, I'm sorry."

"It's okay." But Lyndsey's voice was cool. Cooler than he'd heard it since that night when he'd told her he was going back to Belarus.

Brittany looked from her to Misha before moving over to her friend. "I came by to tell you your car should be ready soon. I wanted to make sure you were okay." She seemed to stumble over her words before finally adding, "And… I'm really sorry."

Lyndsey pulled in a deep breath and gave her friend a hug. "It's okay. I know why you did it. But none of that has anything to do with Misha. Those choices were mine and mine alone."

So why was there a sense of guilt that was suddenly pressing on his chest like a pile of boulders? Because whatever she'd been about to say was something that Lyndsey hadn't wanted him to hear.

That Brittany blamed him for whatever happened with Wade was obvious. Had her ex felt like she'd never gotten over him? Had it driven them apart? She did say he'd left.

Maybe. But that explanation didn't feel quite right. It was as if a very important piece was missing. Without it, the puzzle would never be complete.

But did Misha even have a right to know? Hadn't he given up any right to know anything about Lyndsey's life when he'd left her behind?

Unexpectedly, her friend turned to him. "Listen, I'm sorry. I shouldn't have said that. Any of that. Lyndsey's heart is more forgiving than mine is. And if she chooses not to blame you for…anything, then that's her right. And I'll respect her wishes." She sent him a hard smile. "Just don't expect me to roll out the welcome mat if you ever come back to Centerville."

He was pretty sure that was one mat that no one was going to roll out. The weirdest thing was, they evidently had one thing in common when it came to

Wade. It sounded like Brittany wasn't a fan of his either. He'd venture even further to say that she might actually hate the other man even more than she hated him.

Or maybe he was mistaken. All he knew was that Brittany seemed to blame him for everything that had gone wrong in Lyndsey's life after he left.

And the sad thing was, she could very well be right.

Lyndsey couldn't believe that Brittany had almost blurted out the truth about Wade. It was something she'd never even told Brody. Her son did not need that weighing down on him, and she knew him well enough to know he'd find a way to blame himself for it. Or somehow imagine that he might grow up just like his lowlife dad.

Nothing could be further from the truth. Brody was one of the kindest, most compassionate human beings she'd ever met. Maybe she was biased because he was her son, but she wasn't the only one who felt that way. Look at how he'd included Misha in their little circle at the music festival.

She just wished he didn't seem so attached to Misha. But right now, it was what it was. She was pretty sure it was hero worship over what Misha might be able to do for his hearing. And she wasn't about to let anything or anyone jeopardize him getting that surgery. So she needed to smooth whatever damage Brittany had done, if she could.

Once her friend left with a promise to call her later,

she turned to Misha. "I am so sorry about that. She has a big heart."

"I can see that. And it's okay." He paused as if trying to formulate his words with care. He had to have been shocked at how hard Brittany had come at him. "I'm glad you have people like her in your corner. If anyone deserves a friend like that, it's you. And I'm really sorry you had such a hard time in your marriage."

"It's over and done with. And it's something I try my best not to dwell on."

"Brody doesn't know about whatever Brittany was accusing me of?"

She shook her head. "No. And he never will if I have anything to say about it."

Something crystallized in his look that made her want to head him off at the pass. She did not want him asking any more questions about Wade or her marriage. Especially not before Brody's surgery.

"Just know that what Brittany said wasn't really aimed at you."

He smiled. "I'm pretty sure it was. But that's okay. I can take it. And she's probably right in a lot of ways."

"No. She's not. People are responsible for their own choices. And I owned mine a long time ago. That doesn't mean I can't move forward or do the best I know how for Brody. I have done that and I'll continue to do so, as long as these lungs have breath."

And it was because of Brody that she'd given that last huge effort to get Wade off her. And it had worked. Thank God, it had worked.

"I get it."

Maybe that was how he'd felt when he needed to go back to Belarus. That he'd move heaven and earth for his family. Now that she was older, she could see how he might have been torn between staying and going. But he could have told her that. Instead, he'd withdrawn emotionally in a way that she had a hard time doing.

One thing was for sure. He was never going to know the truth about Wade, unless she someday decided she wanted him to know.

But honestly, she didn't see that happening anytime soon. If ever. There was no reason to tell him.

"Anyway, thanks again for understanding. I just wish Brody's surgery was over and done with and that we get the results we're hoping for."

"We only have a week to go, and unless something awful happens, there's no reason why this surgery won't be a success. Brody is young, he's in the beginning stages of otosclerosis, and he's in excellent health. He's the perfect candidate for surgery. Let's just take things one day at a time. And before you know it this will all be over."

A shudder rolled through her. Someone had once said almost that exact same thing as she lay on a hospital gurney praying that her son had somehow survived the attack, that his tiny life was still safe inside of her.

Just go to sleep. And before you know it, this will be all over.

She had. And when she had woken up, she'd instinctively known that Brody was still there. Still alive. And so was she. She was never going to take that for granted again. For anyone. So it was a very good thing that he'd put a stop to that kiss outside of her home. It was a mistake she hoped she'd never make again.

She and Misha had a past, yes. But that didn't mean they had a future. They didn't. And the sooner she realized that, the better.

CHAPTER SIX

MISHA SPOKE TO the woman in tones that he hoped were soothing, but he wasn't the best at doing that. Especially where young children were concerned. And this worried mom was cradling a child around five years old who'd shoved a pencil through his ear. The blood and drainage said he'd perforated his eardrum. The sooner he could look—

Lyndsey pushed through the door, and he gave a sigh of relief. It had been a couple of days since that encounter in the hallway with Brittany, and he could swear Lyndsey had been avoiding him.

And he hadn't minded, especially since that kiss in front of her doorway was still rolling around in his skull toppling over everything in its path. He'd put a stop to it, and it had been the right thing to do. But right now, she was a ray of sunshine in a tense situation. The child did not want Misha looking at his ear and had screamed bloody murder every time he came anywhere near him with his otoscope. And his mom, who he couldn't blame for being protective, wasn't helping matters.

Misha had felt the same way when there'd been a

hint that Wade had hurt Lyndsey in some way. He'd felt an anger that had almost consumed him, had made him want to protect her from whatever had happened. Except it was probably all in his imagination. And whatever it was, it had happened a long time ago.

Lyndsey hadn't offered any explanation other than to apologize for Brittany's words. In other words, it was none of his business.

She glanced at him and then at the mom and son duo seated on the exam table and he could almost see the wheels in her head sizing up the situation.

Ignoring him, she went over to the mom and whispered something in her ear. The woman looked at her for a second or two and then nodded. "Okay. You can try. His name is Lucas."

"Lucas. I know your ear hurts right now, but I have something at my desk I think you might like to look at."

The face that had been buried in his mother's chest peeked out at her, his cheeks and nose red from all the crying he'd done. "W-what is it?"

She lowered her voice to a conspiratorial whisper. "An elf on a shelf is living in a drawer at the nurses' desk."

"No there isn't." There was a sniffle, but there was also interest.

"There is. Really. I don't let many people see him." She glanced at Misha. "Dr. Lukyanov has never seen him. But if you promise you won't tell anyone but your mom about him, I might let you peek inside."

"Really?"

"Yes. But you have to promise that afterwards you'll let the doctor look in your ear to see if everything is okay."

Lucas sniffed louder. "Matthew told me to stick my pencil in there. But it hurt, and my mom came and said I had to come here." His small chin wobbled. "But I want to go home."

"And you will. But Dr. Lukyanov can help fix your ear so that it doesn't hurt anymore."

"Lyndsey…" Misha said.

She shot him a look that made him swallow the rest of that sentence. "He has magic drops that can make it stop hurting. Don't you, Doctor?"

Hell, she was talking about his anesthetic drops. But he hadn't even seen the ear yet, had no idea if there was damage to anything besides the ear drum. If the boy had dislocated any of the small bones within that canal, he might need surgery. But she was right. He couldn't do any of that if he couldn't get a look inside. And he really didn't want to have to restrain him to do it, if he didn't have to.

"Yes, I really do have some drops."

The boy glared at him for a minute as if he might be lying. Why in the world did he believe Lyndsey and not him? Because she had that kind of personality. One that drew you in and made you want to trust anything she said.

He'd certainly believed her fifteen years ago when she said they were through.

She held her hand out to Lucas. "Will you come with me and see our elf? His name is Ornament, but we call him Ornery for short."

He lifted his head before putting his hand to his ear and looking at Misha. "You promise you'll make it stop hurting afterwards?"

"I promise."

Lyndsey carefully lifted the boy down from the table and took his free hand in hers. "We'll be right back. No one else is allowed to see Ornery, though. Only Lucas."

In other words, he and the boy's mom were to stay put.

He nodded and held his hand over his heart. "I promise I won't peek."

The pair went through the door and Misha quickly relayed what needed to happen next to Lucas's mom and stressed that she needed to work with him, even if Lucas cried. The longer it went without being looked at, the more chance there was of infection or permanent hearing loss.

"I will. It's just so hard to see him in pain."

"I know. Believe me." It had been awful to see Lyndsey in such pain fifteen years ago, knowing there was nothing he could do about it. Nothing he could change.

"When they come back, I'd like to let Lyndsey assist me—the nurse who took him to see the elf—since he now trusts her. If you don't mind standing a little ways away, it would make it easier for you. And ultimately for him."

"I will. My oldest daughter had to be strapped to a board to let her lip be stitched back together. I had to leave the room. My husband was here then, but he's deployed for the next six months. He knew just what to do."

"And so will you. Just trust that we're trying to help Lucas, not hurt him."

"I do trust you. I'll try to channel my husband."

Less than three minutes later, Lyndsey opened the door again and led Lucas inside. He had something clutched in his hand this time.

Misha stared at it. "Is that a...candy cane?"

"Not just any candy cane. It came from Ornery and it's magic, right, Lucas?"

The boy nodded, before moaning and cradling his ear. "I can eat it after the doctor looks at my ear. Ornery told Lyndsey that Mommy has to keep it for me until afterwards." His chin wobbled again. "You promise the drops will make it stop hurting?"

"I promise." He glanced at her then back at Lucas. "Why don't you give the candy cane to your mom while Lyndsey gets the drops?"

He did as Misha asked, but when he tried to hold onto her again, she nudged him back toward the doctor. "You have to let him look. You promised Ornery, didn't you?"

He nodded then looked at the instrument in Misha's hand. "Will that hurt? The pencil hurt when I put it in my ear."

"It won't hurt because it doesn't go in very far." He

knelt down to be at the same level as the child, holding the instrument out to him. "Here, you can look at it. If you press this button a light comes on. Like a flashlight. It lets me see what's going on inside your ear."

Lucas took the otoscope and pressed the button, watching as the light came on. He pointed it at various objects in the room. "It's cool."

"It is. I bet if Ornery had an earache, he would let me look in his ear."

"That's what Lyndsey said too."

When Misha glanced over at her, he found her clutching the drops, watching him with a weird expression on her face. A softness he hadn't seen in a long time. Something in his stomach shifted and he had to look away, forcing himself to concentrate on Lucas instead. "You can stand right there, if you want, while I look. It might hurt a very little bit because I have to tug a little bit on your earlobe, like this." He chose the unaffected ear to demonstrate on to show how much pressure he would put on it. "First, I'm going to look in this ear, okay?"

Lucas nodded, seeming relieved that he wasn't going to start with the injured one.

"Turn this way a little bit." He had Lucas turn his good ear toward him. "Good."

He used the otoscope to look in the boy's ear. "Everything looks perfect in there. Did that hurt?"

"No."

"Okay, turn the other way."

Lucas hesitated, glancing back at his mom, who

nodded at him. Lyndsey came over and knelt next to him. "Here. Hold my hand. Squeeze it as hard as you want."

The boy took her fingers.

Misha showed him the otoscope again. "It'll be the same thing on this ear. It'll just take a little longer because I need to get a very good look at it."

"Okay."

Trying to be as careful as he could, Misha pulled down a bit on the boy's earlobe to open the canal and then looked inside with the otoscope. There was blood and sure enough there was a hole in the tympanic membrane, but it was smaller than it could have been. Probably only the point had penetrated, which was a very good sign. It meant that there'd probably been no damage beyond that point. It should heal on its own. He'd prescribe some antibiotic drops just to ward off any infection from the foreign object, but the drum should heal over without needing to place a patch over it.

He removed the otoscope and sat back. "And that was it."

"Do you need to operate?" Lucas's mom stared at him, the words quivering with the threat of tears.

"No. No operation needed." He couldn't keep his glance from flickering to Lyndsey for a second. Was she wishing that Brody's problem was just as simple to fix?

He shifted his attention to Lucas's mom. "It actually should heal all by itself. It's a very small puncture wound, about this big…" He used his thumb and forefinger to give her an idea of size. "I don't think anything more than the lead went through. But it bled just like any other wound might."

"We don't need to do anything?"

"Nope. I'll give you some ear drops to use for a week. Two drops in the ear, twice a day. If it gets worse or he starts having any kind of discharge from the ear, I want to see him again."

"Thank God."

He looked at the boy. "So how about some of those magic drops now? Do you still want them?"

"Yes."

"And you'll let your mom put the other drops in your ear too? They'll help your ear get all better."

"They won't hurt either?"

"No. They might tickle, but they won't hurt. Mom, if you'll get on the exam table, we'll let Lucas put his head in your lap so I can drop one or two of my magic drops in his ear and help it feel better." Lyndsey's plan had worked like a charm. Maybe because she had a son of her own and had maybe walked some of these same paths with him. Whatever the reason, he was grateful she was in his department and that she was very good at her job.

It took very little effort to get Lucas into position. Misha put a single drop of anesthetic in his ear. "Stay still for just a minute so it can work its magic."

He glanced at his watch and ticked down a minute and a half. "Okay, you can sit up."

Lucas sat up and turned his eyes to Lyndsey first and then Misha. "It worked."

"It doesn't hurt?"

"Not even a little."

Misha smiled. "I'm glad. The magic will wear off after a while and it might start hurting again, but your mom can give you Tylenol and that should make it feel better again." He fixed the boy with a stern look. "Are you going to put anything in your ear again?"

"Nooo." The way Lucas drew the word out made Misha's smile widen.

"That's very good to hear. I think Ornery would be very sad if he heard you'd done something like that again. You can eat your candy cane on your way home, okay?"

He printed off a sheet of care instructions for Lucas's mom and called in a prescription before sending the duo on their way with a sigh of relief.

Lyndsey had worked her magic and he was very glad for it. He only hoped that her magic didn't extend past little boys and their childhood ouchies. But he had a feeling she was even more powerful than Ornery the elf. Misha just had to make sure she had no opportunity to send any of that magic his way. If she did, he might just fall under her spell all over again.

Brody was behind the doors of the surgical suite at this very moment being prepped for his first procedure, and she felt like someone had punched her in the gut.

Breaths were hard to come by and her nerves were wound tighter than tight.

Before he'd been whisked away, he'd told her that he'd be fine. But he hadn't said it with his voice. Instead, he'd signed the message to her. Her eyes had been awash with tears as he'd slowly moved his hands to form each word. He'd been learning it just in case worse came to worst and something went terribly wrong with the surgery.

Lyndsey, with fear in her heart, signed back to him for the first time ever. She'd never admitted to him that she'd also been learning sign language—hadn't wanted him to see that she'd ever doubted they'd find help.

She'd hugged him for a long, long time before Misha had gently pulled her away. "I'll let you know as soon as he's done."

And now it was a waiting game. She'd asked if she could view the surgery up in the observation area, but he'd quietly told her no. That it would be a distraction he didn't need, and it would just cause her unnecessary anxiety.

Brittany, who was now seated next to her, gripped her hand. "He'll be okay, honey. He's strong. And from what you've said, Mikhail is an expert in this surgery."

"He is. I'm so lucky he agreed to do it."

Her friend's jaw tightened, but she didn't say anything beyond what she'd already said. It was one of those things on which they'd had to agree to disagree in order to save their friendship. Brittany blamed Misha for everything that had happened to her. But

Lyndsey didn't. Not anymore. She had at one time. Had convinced herself that she hated him. But seeing him again? She realized she'd vilified someone who hadn't deserved it. She could see that now, even if Brittany couldn't.

And right now, the very person she'd once thought was the worst human being on the planet was fighting to save her son's hearing. And for that, he was a hero. Her hero. Brody's hero. And she would be forever grateful to him in ways she couldn't explain. And maybe she didn't have to. Maybe she could just accept it for what it was.

A gift. One she didn't deserve, but one that was hanging over her head anyway. She just prayed Misha could pull it off.

Misha's concentration was complete. He couldn't see or think of anything beyond what he saw through his loupes and on the monitor to the right of him.

The stapes, all but its footplate, had been lifted free from its spot, and he was preparing it for the prosthesis. First, he drilled a precision hole in the footplate just large enough to accept the base of what looked like a tiny piston. This microprosthesis would transfer the vibrations that the stapes no longer could.

This was the moment of truth.

He was vaguely aware of someone swabbing sweat from his brow and temples but kept moving forward, trying his damnedest not to screw something up. His hand shifted for a millisecond, and he immediately stopped the drill, breathing a prayer that the size of the opening was correct.

He picked up the prosthesis with the pincers of his tool and slid it into place. It was snug but not too tight. It had to be able to move freely but without slipping through the hole he'd made.

On the other end of the prosthesis was a tiny C-clamp that he laid over the bone next to where the stapes had been and checked its position before pinching the ends of the clamp and securing it in place. He nudged either side of the piston and it had just enough give without falling from its new position. He stood there for a moment racking his brain for anything else he needed to check. But he'd done it all. And for now, it looked like Brody's new prosthesis might just work.

He held his fingers up to no one in particular and crossed them in a sign of hope.

Because that's all he could do right now. Hope. Hope he'd thought of everything. Hope that Brody's body accepted its tiny new addition. And hope that everything would heal exactly as it should. Just like their trach patient had done.

Lindsey's reaction that day still puzzled him. The way her hand had gone to her throat with a convulsive movement. The jolt of fear he thought he'd spotted in her face before she got control over herself. Her reaction afterward when he'd asked her about it.

Brittany's words came back to him. "He almost ki…"

He almost what?

Not again. He didn't need to start going through this again.

He finished up the final steps to surgery, checking things one last time.

There was no reason to think this wouldn't be a complete success.

He blew out a breath to release the tension that had been building inside of him. "Okay. Let's wake him up."

The nursing staff shifted Brody so that he was face up on the bed once again while they reversed the medications that had kept him unaware and comfortable during surgery. Soon, a groggy patient was repeating his own name when prompted.

Misha moved himself into Brody's line of sight. "It looks like everything went as planned. It'll take a little time for everything to heal, but I think it's been a success." He touched the teen's arm. "But no loud music for the next several weeks, okay?"

Brody didn't answer, but he nodded his head. That was a good sign his hearing was no worse. He only hoped there would be a significant improvement. "I need to go let your mom know."

Brody nodded his head again, lids flickering shut and staying there. He probably would remember very little of this conversation. And that was okay. Most of it wouldn't matter.

What would matter, however, was how much hearing Brody had now, and how much he could expect to have in the future. If this procedure was as successful as he'd hoped, there was no reason they couldn't do the same for the boy's other ear, which was in the very initial stages of ossification.

He stripped off his gloves and tossed them in the nearest receptacle, then headed for the waiting room, not bothering to take off his surgical scrubs. When he reached the room, he saw Lyndsey and her friend Brittany leaning over something, their heads close together. When he moved closer, he saw it was an article on Brittany's phone.

The headline blazed out from the screen: *Wade McKinna, High School Quarterback, Released from Prison.*

A million thoughts swept through his mind, but he took a step back and cleared his throat to announce his presence. He hadn't meant to pry, and he now wished he could unsee the headline.

Suddenly, Lyndsey's words about Brody's dad being out of the picture took on new meaning. He'd been literally out of the picture. Not because he'd gotten involved with someone else or had disappeared to a different part of the country. No. The man had been in jail.

For what?

Possibilities swirled in his head in quick succession until all he saw was one probable conclusion. One so terrible he wished he could erase it from his mind.

But right now, he couldn't worry about any of that. He needed to tell Lyndsey that her son's surgery had been a complete success. That's all that mattered at the moment.

Brittany was the first to look up, and she snapped off her screen so fast that Lyndsey glanced over at her before seeing him. Then she sat straight up, eyes widening.

"Brody?"

"He's fine. He's just waking up. He'll be in recovery for a while, but as soon as he's transferred to a room, you can see him."

Brittany stood. "That's my cue to leave. Unless you want me to follow you home. I totally can."

"No, I'll be okay. I have no idea how long it will take to release Brody. Go home. I'll be fine." When her friend looked dubious, Lyndsey reiterated the words.

"Okay." Leaning down, she gave Lyndsey a kiss on the cheek. "But call me the minute you get home to let me know you made it and are safely inside your house."

Misha's gut tightened. Were they worried about Wade showing up at her house?

"I will. And thank you."

Brittany gave him a look that, while not quite friendly, was definitely less hostile than what he'd experienced the last time their paths had crossed. Then she headed toward the elevator.

"So you think it went well?" The hope in her face sent a spear through his gut. He was beyond glad that he had good news for her, even if it came on the heels of what looked to be bad news.

He forced his mind back to Brody. "Yes. I think it went very well. We'll have to wait a little while to be sure, but I think the surgery was a complete success. It'll take him a little while to adjust to things, and he might have some tinnitus for a bit, but I'm pretty sure he's going to be playing music with more gusto than ever."

"I can't believe it. The last year has been…"

"Hard." He pulled the word out for her.

"Yes. Hard. Harder than I ever thought it could be."

"If this one works, he'll still need the other ear done at some point in time."

She nodded. "I'm trying not to forget that. Right now, though, I think I just need to get through this one."

"I can understand that. I just want you to keep it in the back of your mind that this is not the end of the line as far as surgery goes."

"Okay. How long do you think it'll be before I can see him?"

"A half hour. Maybe less."

She looked up at him. "I know you're busy, but can you sit with me. Just for a few minutes while I absorb the news I so desperately needed?"

The news about Brody. Not about Wade. "Of course."

He dropped into the chair next to hers and pressed his shoulder against hers in a show of solidarity. She pulled in a deep breath and closed her eyes before slowly letting the air escape from her lungs. She repeated it again.

"God, it feels good just to breathe, doesn't it. We take it for granted, but we shouldn't."

Wade McKinna released from jail.

The suspicions that had appeared out of nowhere returned with a vengeance. The possibility was too horrible to imagine. It had to be for some petty crime or something more like tax evasion. There were myriad reasons why Lyndsey's ex-husband had spent time in prison. Except only one of them made sense to him right now.

But he wasn't going to ask her now. Not with her son lying in a hospital bed hoping beyond hope that he'd be able to hear again.

Unable to force his head to concentrate on anything beyond what Wade might or might not have done, Misha asked if she was ready to go see Brody.

"Absolutely. Do you think he's in a room yet?"

"If he's not, he soon will be, so let's head that way, and I'll tell you what to expect after his procedure."

It took ten minutes of explaining in minute detail what to look for over the next several days. But none of it was overly scary. It was pretty standard medical jargon.

By the time he finished, they'd reached the nurses' station. "Has Brody McKinna been put in a room yet?"

The nurse looked at a chart on her computer screen. "He's just being moved in." She smiled at Lyndsey. "He's evidently been asking for you repeatedly. Enough that it made it into the chart."

"Which room?" he asked.

"321. I would say wait until he's settled, but I know what it feels like to need to see your child after surgery. So go on in."

When Misha made a move to stay where he was, Lyndsey sent him a glance. "Would you come with me? Please?"

With his heart in his throat, he nodded. Not because he'd never gone into a room to see a patient before, but because there was such a look of vulnerability in her eyes as she asked. There was no way he could refuse to go into that room with her.

Steeling himself to see her reaction, he went down the hall with her and pushed open the door to room 321.

Lyndsey had never seen a more beautiful sight than Brody lying in bed asleep. His long lashes cast shadows on his cheek, and his right ear had a pad of gauze placed over it.

She moved closer and touched his face, fingers feathering over her child's skin like she'd done when he'd been a little boy.

But he wasn't little anymore. He was on the cusp of being a man. Just a little younger than she and Misha had been when they'd first started dating.

It was enough to make her weep, but she forced herself to hold it together. It was one of the reasons she'd asked Misha to come in with her. The last thing she wanted to do was fall apart and drape herself over

Brody's bed. He would hate that. He was a pretty stoic kid, and stoicism was what he reacted best to. A quiet, measured approach. He was so different from his dad, yet every once in a while she saw an expression that she recognized. It had bothered her at first, but she'd made her peace with it, reassuring herself that just because he might look like his father, it didn't mean Brody *was* his father. He was the polar opposite of him, in fact.

Brody's eyelids flickered and then slowly parted, his glassy eyes coming to rest on her, and then searching the room. She reached for his hand and gave it a squeeze. "You're okay. The surgery is all done." His gaze tracked back to her again before veering off. He said something nonsensical.

"Don't try to talk right now. Just rest for a while," she murmured. She was hyper aware of Misha standing just behind her not saying anything.

Brody shook his head. "I wish…" His eyes rolled back for a second before coming back to rest on her. "I… I…"

The struggle to find the words broke her heart. Just as she was going to tell him again to rest, his free hand came up, fingers dangling, and kind of waved in Misha's direction.

"I…" Brody licked his lips and took a deep breath. "I wish you…you were my dad. Not…not Wade."

The room went silent, and Lyndsey's hand went to her mouth. She turned to look behind her, whispering the word "sorry" when she saw a muscle ticking away in his jaw.

Of all the things for Brody to say. He wasn't totally aware yet, but to think those words had been rolling around in his subconscious killed her. Because she had to admit she'd thought the same thing. Not because she was still in love with him, but because Misha would have made a great father. And because she wouldn't have had to do this all on her own.

She turned back toward the bed, suddenly exhausted. More exhausted than she could imagine.

When she felt something touch her shoulder, she flinched before she felt Misha give it a squeeze.

Brody was still looking at something behind her. At Misha?

When his big, reassuring voice came from behind her, she tensed. "If I were your dad, Brody, I wouldn't have been able to do your surgery."

"Oh, yeah. That would…have been bad. Very bad." Her son's gaze returned to her, and she could see the awareness trickling back in. He shook his head. "I don't know why I said that. I'm sorry, Mom."

She didn't think her heart could be more shattered than it was right now. "It's okay, baby. You're still waking up. People say silly things when they're under the effects of anesthesia."

Only this hadn't been something silly. Something she could easily laugh at and film for a later date. This was something that had come up from the depths of her son's soul. She had no idea he'd missed having a father that badly. And to choose someone he barely knew…

Well, Misha had probably attained hero status in his book. He'd repaired an ear that another doctor had said was beyond his scope of expertise. And he'd shown an interest in Brody's band and life. Maybe it was time to start limiting contact with Misha. No more side trips or invitations to events that were important to her son. The last thing she wanted was for him to be disappointed when Misha made it clear he had no interest in stepping in or filling any gaps that Brody might feel were there.

A snoring sound from the bed told her that he'd fallen back asleep. Thank God. Maybe next time he woke up, his head would be clearer. As it was, the idea of facing or talking to Misha was a horrifying specter that she couldn't banish.

She realized Misha's hand was still on her shoulder. A warm presence that she was reluctant to shake off. "I really am sorry. I can't believe he said that."

"It's perfectly okay. He'll probably be out for a couple of hours. Let's let him rest. I'm going to take a guess that you haven't eaten much this morning, since Brody wasn't allowed to have anything."

"I had some coffee." Which was now sitting in her stomach like an inky pool of acid.

"Let's go downstairs and grab a bite to eat."

"You don't have to babysit me. I am fine. And I'm sure you have other patients to see."

He shook his head. "Actually, not until tomorrow.

Brody's surgery was complicated, and I wanted to make sure everything went okay, so he was the only thing I scheduled for today."

"Thanks so much. For everything." Okay, he was kind of gaining superhero status in her eyes as well, and she needed to be careful not to confuse gratitude with any more personal emotions.

Like wishing he really had been Brody's dad?

But he wasn't, and Brody wouldn't be Brody if he had been.

They reached the cafeteria, and they went through the line. She picked up a couple of light choices, while Misha went for bacon and eggs. Her brows went up. "Did you not eat either?"

"I did, but nothing too heavy." He smiled. "This is how I celebrate a good outcome. And I can't imagine one better than Brody's."

"I can't believe it's finally done."

"Believe it. As long as his body adapts to the prosthesis, things should be fine." He pushed open the door to the courtyard and waited for her to go through first. It seemed like forever since the first time they met out there. But in reality, it was only a few weeks ago. He hadn't been happy to see her that day in his office, and she couldn't blame him.

And now? Was he over that initial shock?

He certainly seemed to be. And he hadn't reacted angrily to Brody's groggy pronouncement.

"I really am sorry for what happened in that room."

"He probably won't even remember saying it. Anesthesia meds suppress the centers that form lasting memories."

"I hope that's the case. He would be so mortified at having said what he did."

"Like I said, he more than likely won't remember anything about waking up. But I do want to ask you something regarding what Brody said."

He turned to look at her, his frown deep and ominous enough to make her shiver. "What did you want to ask?"

"I want to know what the hell that man did to you. And to Brody."

CHAPTER SEVEN

THERE WAS SILENCE for a few seconds, while she stared at him, eyes wide. "What do you mean?"

"I mean, I was coming to tell you about Brody's surgery and caught sight of the screen on Brittany's phone. I couldn't help but see the headline. Does his jail time have anything to do with you?"

She didn't speak for a full minute, and he thought maybe she was going to jump up, tell him to mind his own *proklyatiye* business and walk away. If she did, he wasn't going to stop her. But Brody's words had crunched something in his gut and the flash of anger it had brought with it was dangerous. If Wade had been in that room, he couldn't guarantee what he would have done to the man if what he thought was true really did turn out to be the case.

"Yes. It had to do with me."

"So I'm going to ask again. What did he do? And are you in any danger now?"

"There was a restraining order in place at the time of his arrest, so I'm hoping it's still in effect. I'll check with the courts before Brody and I return to the house."

He shut his eyes and counted to ten in Russian before looking at her again. "So he did hurt you. Your reaction to Joanna's injuries weren't just a fluke."

She shook her head. "No. It wasn't. She was pregnant. Just like I was at the time."

"*Der'mo…*" He couldn't stop the oath from escaping his mouth as he dragged his hand through his hair. Then he swiveled his body on the concrete bench, straddling it so he could face her fully. "Tell me." He said the words, even though he wasn't sure he wanted to hear what had transpired between her and her ex.

Lyndsey moistened her lips and then started talking, the words pouring out of her so quickly that he had to really concentrate to understand.

"When you left, Wade came and offered a shoulder to cry on. He listened. And he seemed like a perfect gentleman. And when he kissed me…." She shook her head. "I was so angry and confused, it was like everything inside of me rose up, and I accepted it. Maybe I was trying to get back at you, although I can see now how stupid that was.

"And when the kissing turned to other things, I never thought about protection. My emotions were just too dark…too raw."

"You got pregnant." A dark pit of anger and despair opened up inside of him, threatening to swallow him whole. But he had to know. Had to understand the ramifications his decision to leave had had on Lyndsey.

"Yes. And he offered marriage immediately."

She'd obviously accepted. And looking at it through

her eyes, he could see how that might have seemed like the best solution for everyone.

She appeared to gather herself together. "What I didn't know at the time was that he was secretly taking steroids to improve his ball playing. There were scouts looking to fill their college rosters, and Wade was determined to get on one of them. But as the months rolled by, the offers dried up. Maybe Wade's attitude had turned them off. I'm not sure. What I do know is that he started getting angry, and I was the only one around."

He suddenly knew he didn't want to hear the rest of it, but he'd asked the question, and Lyndsey obviously needed to talk to someone about it.

"It started off as ridicule. I didn't dress the right way or talk the right way. He became convinced that the colleges saw his marital status as a detriment. According to him, they wanted single quarterbacks that the girls would flock around. And by that time I was six months pregnant and felt huge and ungainly. Wade started drilling into my head that I was the reason he wasn't getting any offers. And I found myself starting to believe him. When we were out in public, I shrank back and tried my best to become invisible."

"Ethot ubludoc." More words slipped out before he could stop them. But they were true. Wade was a bastard. Cowardly and cruel.

"I don't know what that means."

"You don't want to know. I take it Wade's abuse didn't begin and end with words. It escalated?"

"He tried to blame it on 'roid rage, but there were other girls with similar stories. Some of them during the time we were married. When no scholarships appeared, he started drinking, making what was already a bad situation even worse. He hit me for the first time a week later. He was so remorseful afterwards, and looking back, I can't believe I fell for his promises that it would never happen again.

"Worse, Brittany came and told me that he'd hit on her when he saw her at the store." She pulled in a deep breath. "That night he came home drunk. And when I wouldn't go to bed with him and confronted him about what Brittany had said, he grabbed me, put his hands around my throat…"

"God, Lynds."

"I thought I was going to die. And if it hadn't been for the thought of Brody, I might have. I clawed at his hands with all my might and kneed him in the groin, and he let go. And then I ran and ran and ran, until a neighbor took me into her house and called the police." She bit her lip. "He was sentenced to fifteen years in prison for attempted murder. And that's what you saw on Brittany's phone. He just got out."

"No wonder she hates me so much." He said the words more to himself than anything.

Lyndsey looked at him for a long time, before reaching out and touching his hand. "Brittany doesn't hate you. She hates what happened. And it wasn't your fault. None of it. I made those choices. Not you."

"But if I hadn't left…"

She needed to speak the truth, even if the circumstances around it still hurt. "If you hadn't left, I wouldn't have Brody. It's as simple and as complicated as that."

"Even so. What Wade did—"

"That's on Wade. Not anyone else. And I wouldn't trade my son for anything. Like I said, he saved my life. Literally. And my mom worships the ground he walks on. She loves him. Does it excuse anything Wade did? Absolutely not. And I should have left sooner. But it was hard reconciling the charming star quarterback that I thought I knew with the monster he could become.

"Has he tried to contact you?"

"Yes. And he's begged me to bring Brody to see him at the prison." She touched his hand again. "Brody doesn't know exactly what happened between me and his dad. I haven't told him. I just told him that he went to prison for doing some very bad stuff. And Brody has never once asked to see him. And maybe he knows more. The news articles are out there. And I'm sure some of his friends probably heard about it from their parents. But if he has, he's never said anything."

Brody was a smart kid. And curious. Like Lynds said, he probably knew more than she thought, which may be where his anesthesia-induced comments came from.

"I want to take you home tonight, once Brody is

discharged. Stay the night. Make sure everything is okay at your house."

"I'm sure Wade wouldn't—"

"Maybe not. But I could see someone like him wanting to take some swipes at you. Even though he did all of this to himself. I don't trust him. I never have."

She squirmed. "My car is still in the shop, which is why Brittany was here with me. I planned on staying the night at a hotel."

"Please, Lyndsey. I would never forgive myself if something happened to you or Brody."

She looked down at her food, then back up at him. "I'll accept, but only because of Brody. If there's any hint of him trying to come near us, I'll call the police."

"I can sleep on the couch."

"No need. We have a spare bedroom that my parents use from time to time when I've had to go out of town. And no, it's not the house Wade and I shared. That was in his name, and he sold it off to pay for his defense."

"Defense. That's kind of laughable when you think about it. There's no defending what he did."

"No. Like I said, he tried to blame it on the steroids, but they were able to prove that there was already a pattern of behavior that began in high school. It just wasn't common knowledge. The drugs amplified what was already present. My hope is that he'll leave the area and Brody and I will never have to deal with him again. His parents both passed while he was in prison so there's nothing really holding him here."

The anger that had been flickering in the background flared up. "If he's smart, that's exactly what he'll do. But in case he doesn't, I want to be there for a night or two."

"One night." She smiled. "I'm really a pretty self-sufficient person nowadays."

"Of that I have no doubt."

She glanced down at her plate. "Wow, I can't believe I actually ate it all. I must have been hungrier than I thought."

His fingers moved to hers and linked with them for a few seconds before giving them a quick squeeze and then releasing them, despite the fact that he hadn't quite been ready to let her go. "Thank you for telling me. And for letting me take you home."

In a different place and time that last sentence would have had an entirely different connotation. But it wasn't. It was here and now, and he had no right to expect anything to change between them. His mom had called him last night to let him know he had a new baby cousin. She'd been disappointed that he wouldn't come home to welcome the newborn into the family. But Louisiana was his home now. If his mom became ill, he would of course go and take care of her, but he couldn't see himself staying there for the long term. When he settled down—if he settled down—he wanted it to be here. Wanted to raise any children he might have here.

Not that there were any prospects. He had no interest in trying to meet people. So maybe he would someday die here, alone with no family to stand beside him.

Something that was ridiculous to think about right now.

"I appreciate your concern, Misha, although I'm pretty sure Wade isn't stupid enough to try anything. I'll call Brittany and let her know you'll be driving me home and staying the night."

"I'm sure she'll be over the moon when she hears that news."

"She'll be glad that I'm safe. Like I said, her problem isn't with you. Well, not most of it, anyway."

One brow went up. "That's so very reassuring, Lynds."

She laughed. "She's overprotective, and I love her. I'd do the same for her."

"Speaking of overprotective, how about we go and check in on Brody, while I get the ball rolling on his discharge papers."

"I can't believe you're releasing him already."

"He's fine. He's going to be in pain until some of the swelling goes down, but pain meds should help take care of that. Unfortunately, I'd rather not use any of my so-called magic drops in his ear, due to the risk of them getting into the surgical site. And seriously. Is there really an elf in a drawer at the nurses' station?"

"There really is. And his name really is Ornery. He's an expert in dealing with difficult patients that happen to be under the age of ten or so."

"That is crazy. And yet it obviously works."

"It does indeed." She tilted her head as she looked at him. "Speaking of kids. What if Brody remembers what he said earlier? How should we handle that?"

The "we" in that sentence gave him a wobbly feeling that he couldn't quite banish. It would be easy to get used to that. To making joint decisions with someone about a child.

Hadn't he just thought about having a family someday?

But Brody wasn't his, and Lyndsey hadn't meant it the way he'd taken it. She wasn't likely to ask him for parenting advice.

"I think we laugh it off. I'll say something off the wall and funny. I'm good at that."

"Really? The person who can't tell a joke to save his life?"

He cocked a brow. "I did have my moments, if you remember right."

"Yes, you did. Just not in the stand-up comedy department." When she gave him that cheeky smile from the past, he knew what she was thinking of. The times they'd made love until neither of them could see straight. And afterward, more often than not, they'd start the process all over again.

"Careful, Lynds. You might wind up with more than you bargained for."

"Sorry." It was as if she pulled herself together in a rush, suddenly remembering where she was, who she was with. If he wasn't careful, she was going to change her mind about letting him drive her home, and right now, her and Brody's safety trumped everything. He forced himself to look at that goal and nothing more.

"Let's go see him."

With that, they dumped their trash and walked to the elevators that would take them up to the third floor.

This time, Brody was definitely awake and in his right mind. And as Misha had suspected, he didn't mention anything about Wade or wishing that Misha was his dad. He was fingering the dressing over his ear. "How long does this have to stay on? My ear feels full."

His voice was a little raspy from being intubated, but other than that he wasn't complaining of pain. That would come later.

"That's normal. And the dressing has to stay on a couple of days. We don't want any dirt or dust introduced to your ear until your bone has a chance to heal."

"Where you drilled the hole?"

"Yes."

"And my music?"

"That's a harder answer, but it's necessary, Brody. You need to reintroduce certain sounds slowly. Nothing loud or full of bass for a couple of weeks. We want to see how the prosthesis handles everything. And like I said, I want it to have a chance to heal before it does any heavy lifting."

The boy blew out a breath. "I know you mentioned all of this before, but now that I've had the surgery, everything seems very real. Is it really going to work? I feel like I can't hear anything out of that ear right now and it's freaking me out a little bit."

"I know. But like I said, you need to heal. There's some swelling from where I had to drill, I'm sure. That will take a few days to subside. Then we'll bring you in for some hearing tests and see where we stand."

"And if it works, I'll have to go through it all over again with my left ear?"

"Yes." He didn't want to give false hope that things might stabilize. Otosclerosis was progressive and there was evidence that his left ear was already being affected, although not nearly as much as his right ear had been. But it would get there. It was better for Brody to be prepared for that eventuality. "But you'll be surprised at how quickly this will go."

Lyndsey moved to the head of the bed. "Let's just take this one ear at a time, okay? No jumping ahead to a place we can't yet see."

"Okay." And with that, the conversation about the surgery took a back seat as his mom handed Brody his phone and let him check his messages.

He smiled. "Most of my friends have texted me." His eyes widened. "And one of my bandmates said he's writing a song that he wants me to sing. About my hearing. Listen to the chorus.'

As I sit here in my silence, wondering what is next,

The fear is overwhelming. Is there really nothing left?
Then a tiny blip of sound bursts through my brokenness.
Just a hint of treble. Followed by a touch of bass.
Is any of this possible?
Can a miracle break through?
Or is it all a wishful dream that never will come true?

"Oh, Brody. That is beautiful. I…" She shook her head as if unable to finish her thought. Instead, she leaned over and hugged him for a long moment.

She wasn't the only one who'd been touched by those words. Misha's insides were twisted with emotion. This could have been referring to his first weeks in Belarus after leaving Lyndsey behind. As his dad battled his cancer.

When he could finally bring himself to speak, he said, "That is a keeper, Brody."

"It's awesome. He knows I can't play right now, but they still want to get together and figure out the rest of the lyrics and the music. Maybe use this time to write some original stuff."

Who said high school students weren't wise? He was certainly seeing a whole lot of wisdom in this particular group.

"That's wonderful," Lyndsey said. "Blessings we

can't always see at first, but they're in there, waiting on their chance to peek through all the bad stuff."

Was she talking about her marriage to Wade? About Brody's hearing? Maybe a little bit of both.

Brody nodded. "When can I go home? I want to get started on this."

There was an unmistakable excitement in his voice. The same giddy happiness that he'd had when describing the music festival. His passion and thirst for it were unmistakable. Who knew if he would someday make it in the music industry. He certainly seemed to have the drive for it.

"Let me check you over really quickly and then we can see about breaking you out of here."

Misha was smart enough to realize the next surgery was going to be tricky, if he stayed this particular course. He wasn't related to either Lyndsey or Brody, but he was getting attached. He could feel those threads relentlessly tugging at him. At least when it came to Brody. Would he know when he'd crossed that line?

Or had he already crossed it? Maybe it was time to start researching other ENTs who had expertise in this field, although he was pretty sure Lyndsey would fight him on it. But it wasn't just about the attachments. It was about whether he could objectively do his job if a complication arose. Or would he freeze?

He had no idea, because he'd never been faced with this kind of dilemma before. And to admit to Lyndsey that he cared about Brody too much to continue to be his doctor?

He could imagine her face if he shared that kind of news. She'd be angry. Furious, probably. And he'd be railing over his inability to keep his thoughts and feelings to himself.

Going to her house to make sure it was safe? Did a doctor do that for the parents of his patients? Or just the ones he cared for a little too much?

Maybe a part of him wished that he was Brody's dad too.

But they were a ways out from his next stapedotomy. He still had time to slow down what was happening. But not today. Not when he needed to make sure Lyndsey and Brody were safe. If that wrote him out of the picture as far as being able to provide medical care for the boy, then so be it. He would cross that bridge when he came to it.

He did a quick exam, checking the covering on his ear for excess drainage or active bleeding. There was none. And his blood pressure and vitals were all within the normal range.

"All right. Let's get those discharge papers started."

Lyndsey stepped forward. "Misha will be coming home with us, just to make sure everything is okay overnight."

He wasn't sure he agreed with her about keeping the real reason from her son, but she hadn't technically lied.

"Cool! Will he be in Gram's room?"

Why would Brody think he'd be sleeping anywhere else? Had other men come over who hadn't stayed in that third bedroom?

Something he really didn't want to think about. And something that was none of his business. He'd slept with other women after their breakup. So why should it be any different for her. It wasn't. He was just being an ass.

"Yes, he will. And just for tonight."

He was pretty sure that last part carried a message for him, that one night was all he was allowed.

They wheeled Brody out of the hospital in the required wheelchair, pulling up beside Misha's Jeep.

"Can we put the top down today?"

He smiled. "No. Not with your ear the way it is. Maybe another time."

As if there would be one.

Brody was able to get in the back under his own power and buckled himself in. "My ear is starting to throb a little."

"That's to be expected. We'll pick up your prescription on the way home." He glanced at Lyndsey, who rattled off the name of a pharmacy in Centerville. Then she twisted to look back at her son. "By the way, no talking on the phone tonight, young man."

"Mom! I'm not totally stupid. We text most of the time anyway. It's easier."

Misha smiled. He wasn't exactly sure how typing

out messages on a tiny phone screen was faster than just saying the words into the phone, but maybe he was just a little slower when it came to technology. Besides, he received more texts in a day than he cared to count. He was happy when his phone sat somewhere without pinging every few seconds.

When she looked over at him, he could have sworn she was thinking the exact same thing. In fact, she gave a choked sound that could have even been a laugh. He liked seeing her this way. It was like a huge weight had been lifted from her shoulders, which was odd since the reason he was spending the night at her house should have her just the slightest bit worried.

"Maybe I should have had the prescription called in here in Lafayette instead of Centerville."

"How bad is your ear, Brody?" he asked.

"It's okay. It's just hurting a little. I can make it home."

He paused. "Actually, can you move across to the left side of the car? I'd rather you didn't rest the right side of your head against the window." The vibrations might aggravate where the prosthesis is attached to the footplate of the old stapes.

He waited to start the car until Brody was buckled in behind him. If he fell asleep, he'd feel better about his head resting on the opposite side. Unfortunately, he didn't carry a pillow or a blanket in the car, because it was rare that he ever carried passengers in here. Actually, going to the music festival was one of the few times he could remember anyone besides him being in the vehicle, unless it was for a business lunch with colleagues, which didn't happen all that often either.

They pulled out onto the highway and headed in the direction of Centerville.

CHAPTER EIGHT

LYNDSEY WOKE UP with a start, feeling out of sorts as she tried to figure out where she was. Then she realized. Misha's car. It was no longer moving, and they were parked in her driveway. But there was no sign of either her son or Misha. And the vehicle's back door on the side where Brody was sitting was hanging wide open. The seat was empty.

A sense of horror set in. Had Wade been there waiting for them? Had he kidnapped Brody? Hurt or killed Misha?

Leaping out of the car, her legs barely held her upright as she struggled to run up the walk toward the front door, which was also wide open. It was like one of those movies where something held you glued to the ground, while everything around you moved in slow motion.

"Brody!" Her son's name came out as a long scream of pain.

Misha appeared just in time to catch her as she fell through the doorway. He held onto her as she flailed around, trying to break free.

"What the hell?" he said. "What's wrong?"

She stared at him, her mouth opening and closing several times. "Me? Where is Brody? Where *is* he?"

"He's in bed."

"In bed." She tried to wrap her head around what he'd just said. "So Wade didn't…he's not…?"

"*O milyy…* No, no, no." He gathered her tightly in his arms. "I'm so sorry. I carried Brody into the house. You were both fast asleep and I didn't want to disturb either of you. I never dreamed you might wake up and think…"

She clung to him as relief caused her limbs to buckle, her racing heart making her dizzy. "I've only been that scared one time in my whole life."

He dropped a soft kiss onto her temple. "I'm sorry." He crooned something over and over in his native tongue. She wasn't sure what it was, but she could feel her heartbeat slow, his calm, even voice soothing her nerves in a way she'd never known.

Brody was okay. Misha had somehow wrestled him into the house, although her son was almost as tall as she was.

She was suddenly glad Misha was here. The thought of walking into that empty house and wondering if someone was waiting there inside…

A thought occurred. "How did you get in?"

This time he looked a bit chagrined. "Your keys were hanging from the shoulder strap of your purse so I…took them."

She nodded. "Thank you. Thank you so much."

"I'm not sure if you should be thanking me or cursing me. I never meant to scare you."

"I jumped to conclusions and wasn't thinking straight." She glanced up at him. "Okay, I think I can stand up on my own now."

He let her go gingerly, as if he wasn't as sure as she was that she could manage it. "Do you think any of your neighbors called the police on us?"

Oh, God. That was the last thing she needed. "You mean because of my banshee-like shriek?"

"I wasn't going to say it, but it certainly had me skidding my way to the door." He gave her a half grin that made her insides turn to mush.

"I'll text the ones I know and tell them everything's fine." She retrieved her phone from her pocketbook, surprised it was still on her arm with the way she'd leapt out of the car. Pressing a few keys, she reassured the neighbors she knew that all was well.

"I'll go out and close up and lock the car."

She glanced back and saw that not only Brody's car door was still open, but hers was too. "You must think I'm absolutely insane."

"No. I think you're a mother who loves her child."

"Thanks."

"Let me make you a cup of coffee. I see you have one that uses the pods. I think I can figure that kind out. Cream? Sugar?"

"Thank you. Both. I have flavored creamer in the fridge. I'm going to check on Brody."

"You go. He's got his pain meds on board, I hope

you don't mind. He woke up long enough to take it. Right before I heard you scream."

She managed a low laugh. "You are never going to let me live that down, are you?"

"*Net*."

Even she knew what that word meant. "Gee, thanks."

She headed toward Brody's room and when she got there, true to Misha's word, her son was fast asleep. His shoes were tucked under the bed and his covers were tucked around his narrow form. He looked peaceful and vulnerable. She knelt on the floor beside his bed and stared at him. She didn't know what she'd do if something ever happened to him.

But it hadn't. She leaned her cheek on the mattress next to him and breathed out a prayer of thanks. First thing tomorrow she was going to check on that restraining order and whether or not the prison knew where Wade was headed. Surely, he was on parole and had to report things like that. Not that any of it was a guarantee that he wouldn't try to contact her or Brody. Maybe it was time to tell her son the truth and make sure he knew how dangerous it was to have anything to do with his dad.

When she finally got up and walked back to the living room, she spied two coffee cups on the glass-topped coffee table in front of the couch. A wash of gratitude went through her, not just for the coffee, but for taking at least one layer of worry off her. Brittany had already texted her a few times since they left the hospital, and she'd finally been able to reassure her friend that she was fine and would let her know if she could do anything.

"Thank you." She sat on the leather couch, letting the soft cushions envelope her.

He handed her a cup and she wrapped her hands around it, letting the warmth seep into the iciness of her hands. She didn't even want to think about the shape she'd be in if her worst fears had come to life—if they'd pulled up to her driveway and found Wade waiting for her.

When Misha sat next to her and put his arm around her, she leaned into him, breathing deep and taking a sip of her coffee. She allowed herself to fully relax. Oh, how she'd missed this closeness. Missed the sight and scent of him. Missed how perfectly she fit against his side, her cheek nestled against the warmth of his neck.

It had been even better on hot nights when his shirt had come over his head and she'd been able to snuggle against his bare skin. And the times when it wasn't only his shirt that had come off...

Oh, yes. Those had been the best times. But for now, she was happy to just cruise down memory lane and enjoy this tiny taste of the past.

Neither of them said anything as they drank their coffees. The silence was both wonderful and healing. A balm to her soul.

She thought of the first line in Brody's song. *As I sit here in my silence...*

Silence could mean so many things. It could mean physical silence. Anguish. Grief. Or it could mean comfort and peace, which was what it meant for her right now.

"This is nice."

"Yes, it is, *milyy*." His voice rumbled over her. Through her. All around her. The familiar endearment pulling at her insides.

She couldn't stop herself from tilting her head and looking up at him. The blue eyes gazing back at her contained a crystalline warmth that made her want to stroke tiny circles over the pressure points in his temples until his eyelids swept closed in pleasure.

He was so gorgeous. And he'd once been hers. How had that even happened?

Before she could stop herself, she rolled her body until her front faced his and her thighs were on either side of his.

His face tightened. "Lynds…"

"Tell me you don't feel it." She couldn't help herself. After all that had happened today, she just needed to touch him. Needed to be touched by him.

Wrapping one arm around her back to secure her to him, he leaned forward to put his coffee cup on the table in front of them. "Oh, I feel it. But if you're planning to end this before it gets fully started, I suggest you move to a different location."

She moistened her lips, wondering if she dared. Yes. She did.

Her hands went to his shoulders and her hips slid forward until she was pressed tight against him. And yes, she definitely felt something there. "You mean like…this location?"

He groaned. "Lyndsey, I'm not playing around."

She cupped his face, her thumbs sliding over his cheeks, his eyelids, anything she could reach. "Does it feel like I'm playing?"

"No. It feels like you're about to get exactly what you're asking for. If you are asking, that is."

"Oh, I am. I definitely am."

He glanced at the closed door across the room. "What if Brody comes out and sees us?"

True. She hadn't quite thought about that. "This is kind of a compromising position, isn't it? My bedroom is just down that hallway," she whispered. "As far from his as we can get."

Without hesitation he stood, his arms going beneath her butt to carry her along with him. He then strode to the door and pushed it open, turning and pushing it quietly shut again with his foot. Then he locked it. "It looks like I won't be using your spare bedroom after all." He smiled at her before moving to the bed and unceremoniously dropping her onto the mattress. She squeaked at the unexpectedness of it.

"No, it looks like you won't."

There was no fear in her as he undressed her with slow, careful hands before turning to his own clothing. No fear. Only the pleasure of getting to look at him again, when fifteen years ago, she was sure she'd never have that chance again. Never get to feel his touch again.

And yet here he was. The terrain of his body had changed slightly, but it was still familiar in ways that beckoned to her. Her body had changed as well. And yet, he obviously still desired her. Because he was here. In her house. In her bedroom.

But for how long?

The insidious whisper slithered through her, winding around her synapses and halting the steady flow of communication between her brain and her body.

No. She wasn't going to let anything ruin this. She was going to enjoy this night for what it was: the gift of one more time, when she'd thought there was none to be had.

His palms glided up her thighs, making her squirm with need. "You'll tell me if you don't like something, *milyy*?"

Was that a reference to Wade and what she'd told him? Misha would never do anything to purposely hurt her.

"I like it all."

He sighed, the sound sliding over her like a caress. "Do you…like this?" His palms came to a halt just below her hip bones, his thumbs grazing over the v at the tops of her thighs.

Her breath whooshed in at the jolt of sensation. So close. And yet not close enough.

"Yes. I like it."

He lingered only for a second or two before continuing his journey up her body, dancing over her ribcage with soft swipes of his hands. "And this?"

He had to know he was driving her crazy. Her gaze ran over his body, eyes moving down to the obvious need that was very much on display. She wanted that with a desperation that made her whimper. "Yes." She beckoned to him with her hands. "Misha, come here."

"My pleasure." He lowered himself onto the bed, fitting his hips in the juncture of her thighs. "And now, I can do this…"

His mouth moved over her left breast with tiny kisses that pebbled her nipples and made her arch into him. "Yes."

And then he was there, sucking her into his mouth, sending fiery shots of need racing through her. She twined her legs around his, desperately seeking a friction that he hadn't given her yet. Looping her arms around his neck, she pulled him in for her kiss, her tongue sliding deep into his mouth.

His groaned response told her all she needed to know. He used to love this when they were together. And he evidently still loved it. That knowledge was satisfying in a way she didn't quite understand. And maybe she didn't want to. But it made her feel powerful. And in control. It was heady. And awe-inspiring.

His hands went to either side of her face, caressing her cheeks, her lips, his fingertips periodically touching her tongue as it continued to press forward in his mouth in a way that was so very sensuous.

Everything about this man was built for sex. His physique. His hands…his voice. That voice that could send shivers down her spine with a single syllable. It was rough and throaty, the Russian intonations scraping across her senses like callused hands on her most sensitive spots.

He did it for her. He always had. From the moment she'd met him all those years ago.

He still did.

She didn't fear Misha. But she feared that. The craving for him that hadn't lessened after all these years.

It was okay. She was giving herself permission to crave him. But just for tonight. So she had to make it worth both their whiles. She untwined her legs. Loosened her arms from around his neck. Pulled free from his mouth.

When he lifted his head to look at her, a frown darkened his face. She smiled. "Don't worry. This isn't the end. It's just the beginning."

With that, she pushed hard at his chest, rolling him onto his back. Before he could do anything, she had straddled him, just like she'd done on the couch. She pressed her hands onto the mattress on either side of his head, leaning over him, her hair falling around them.

"It's your turn to tell me what you like. Do you like this?" She slid her tongue across his lips, darting inside for a second then sliding back out.

"You know I do."

"I do know." She leaned down and kissed him softly. Slowly. "But pretend that I don't."

She moved her hips forward, sliding over his erection with slow steady pressure that made him jerk against her.

His hands moved to her hips, holding them still as if his life depended on it.

"I liked that a little too much."

"Did you?" She licked her lips. "Then show me."

She took one of his hands and drew it to his flesh, wrapping his fingers around it and holding it there with her own. "Show me, Misha."

His eyes on hers, he slowly pumped his hand, a muscle ticking in his jaw as if trying to keep a tight hold on his control. Seeing him this way pushed her own need to an all-time high. Less than a minute later, he let go and lifted her up and onto him, seating her all the way down in one quick move.

"Ahh…" her breath whistled through suddenly tight vocal cords, the numbing pleasure almost overtaking her. If he had moved another inch, she would have gone over the edge. But he didn't. He held her there. Tight against him.

They stayed completely still, and she saw the strain in his beautiful face as he wrestled to hold back.

Suddenly she didn't want to hold back. Didn't want to wait. Maybe there would be other times, and yet here they were acting as if they were going to fall off the face of the earth if they let themselves go.

She looked at him. Really looked at him.

"Misha. It's okay."

He understood exactly what she was saying, his

body relaxing as he allowed himself to feel. As he allowed *her* to feel.

And it was an ecstasy of a different kind as they relearned their rhythm. The one that had once been so natural, so unique to them as a couple. He knew just how much pressure to put where. Knew that rotating his pubic bone against that tiny nub of flesh could drive her wild with need. And so he did, with each thrust of his hips.

And it was good and familiar and...*them*.

Lyndsey let it flow around her, the snapping electricity that crackled and coaxed and periodically bit.

She let herself rise and fall in tune with his body's moves, the realization that she had never felt so in sync with another human being as she had with Misha.

Pleasure washed over her, the waves rushing in and then flowing out, making her anticipate when they would come again. Her hands wouldn't be still, needing to touch him everywhere. He was the same, and God, she wasn't sure she would ever be whole again by the time they were done.

Misha's thumb touched her, and the shock of the direct contact made her go still, her every nerve ending focusing inward on that pleasure center. He teased and coaxed and demanded. Her hips made a shuddery descent and then rose again before pushing back down with an urgency that swelled inside of her.

"Yes, *milyy,* just like that."

She kept going, her rhythm quickening to match his thumb's movements. The fingers of his free hand intertwined with hers, creating an intimacy that drove her even higher.

She couldn't hold back anymore. Didn't want to hold back. She suddenly pumped with jerky movements, her control slipping from her fingers. And then it was here, the wave that crashed over her...pulsed around her, giving everything up. She moaned, leaning over and taking his mouth, kissing him like there was no tomorrow.

No tomorrow.

She closed her eyes as the world began to slow and her movements with it. She felt, more than saw, Misha carry their joined hands to his mouth and kiss them And something about that gesture...

No tomorrow.

It finally entered her brain, bringing with it the reality that the thought probably held an element of truth.

Hadn't she thought how good it was to have him one more time?

And now she had. It was already in the past. As if defying that reality, her hips rose one last time before settling with a finality against him.

She wanted to cry. But she wasn't going to.

Gentle fingers touched her cheek, and she realized one tear had already escaped somehow.

"Lynds...are you okay?"

She forced a smile and somehow manufactured a satisfied sigh. "Yes. You?"

Twining his fingers in her hair, he drew her down for a kiss. "More than okay. That was...*potryasayushchiy*."

She had no idea what that word meant. She only knew it was good. Very good.

"So are you, Misha."

And now it was time. Time to move back to reality. Before she could chicken out, she lifted her hips, allowing him to slide free. Each second she stayed joined to him was another second that she wanted to ask him to stay. In more ways than one. But she couldn't. At least not yet.

"*Net*." His soft complaint caught at her soul.

"We have to. Brody is just down the hallway."

It had nothing to do with Brody, and everything to do with self-preservation, but it was the only excuse she could think of.

He tugged her onto the bed and moved in close behind her, wrapping his arm around her. "Then let me lie with you for a while. I promise I'll be in the other bedroom by morning."

How could she argue with that, when she wanted so badly to feel him against her, to imagine them as they were all those years ago. Hadn't he said the same thing to her then, as they lay together in her bedroom?

"Let me lie with you for a while. I promise I'll be gone by morning."

And Misha had always kept that promise. Sometime in the middle of the night, as she slept, he would silently slip from her bed. In the morning, she was always alone.

As those words filtered through her, a part of her

mourned. Because in the morning…tomorrow morning. She would be all alone.

Just as she always was.

CHAPTER NINE

MISHA HADN'T GONE to the spare bedroom. In the early hours of dawn, he had lain in Lyndsey's bed and watched her sleep for a long time, already knowing he wasn't going to press her for anything more than what they'd shared last night.

She'd tossed and turned, one time crying out the word "no!" in her sleep. It had ripped through him in a way that had him gritting his teeth in pain. Was her restlessness due to what they'd shared? She'd said she liked it, but maybe something inside said something else. Or maybe it was memories of Wade. Memories that sleeping with Misha had reawakened? Either way, her sleep was not that of someone who was at ease with where they were. With who they were with.

Why couldn't things ever be simple for them?

He had no idea. But they weren't. And for the life of him, he couldn't figure out a way to magically make them so.

The reality was Lyndsey had a teenaged son who might lose his hearing in his left ear if he didn't have surgery. A surgery Misha was no longer sure he could perform.

And if nothing else he'd ever done had hurt her, refusing to operate on Brody would. And he wasn't sure he knew how to tell her.

Unless he could somehow turn this ship around and put them back on solidly professional ground. That meant not seeing her. Not touching her. Not going to anything special that Brody might want him to go to.

But there was one thing he could never unhear, and it was Brody saying, *I wish you were my dad and not Wade.*

He wasn't sure how he would get past that statement enough to be objective. Because in his heart of hearts, last night as he'd lain in that bed and watched a sleeping Lyndsey, he'd wished the very same thing, that it had been him who'd made a family with her and not Wade.

So he'd slipped from her bed in the early morning hours and quietly exited the house, locking the front door and pulling it tight. Then he'd gone out to his car and sat in it and watched to make sure no one tried to creep in while Lyndsey and Brody were asleep. When the sun came up and neighbors started stirring, he knew it was safe to leave. So he drove to his office before anyone got there and sat at his desk. He then laid his head on the flat surface and set his watch alarm before letting himself get a couple of hours rest. Maybe by then, the answer would come to him.

The awkwardness was the worst. She knew he was trying hard to maintain a professional demeanor in front of their colleagues, but it was slowly driving her crazy. She'd woken up three days ago—after making crazy love to him—to an empty house. Oh, Brody was there. And she'd thought Misha was too. So she'd cooked this fabulous breakfast, thinking that maybe she'd overreacted the night before. Surely, they didn't have to go back to being strangers.

But when she'd sent Brody to wake Misha up, his son came back with a frown. "He's not there." He shook his head. "It doesn't look like he even slept in the bed."

She'd gone to see for herself. He was right. There'd been no sign of Misha having been in that room. Had she imagined the whole thing? She moved the wrong way and a twinge in a certain region told her muscles that hadn't been used in years had indeed been put to the test during the night. And what a test it was. It had been everything she could have hoped for.

Then why had he left the way he had?

She hadn't asked him when she saw him the next day because he was acting funny. Kind of withdrawn. Like he didn't want to be seen talking to her. She'd backed off immediately and thought she'd try the next day. But he was the same way yesterday.

It was now a week after Brody's surgery, and today she didn't even try. She'd gone to the courthouse yesterday and found out that in his release agreement, Wade wasn't allowed to come anywhere near her or Brody. Nor was he allowed to contact them. That helped alleviate her fear a little bit. But it was still there humming in the background, and honestly, it might always be that way. A man that had once hurt her was out there somewhere, and the way Misha was acting, there was no way she was going to call him if she was afraid in the middle of the night.

Actually, Brody had a follow-up appointment with him at ten this morning and she didn't want to get into a big discussion about that night and somehow cause a bigger rift than there already was.

It was as if that night had never happened. Or maybe he only wished it had never happened.

God. She hoped he didn't present this strained, unfriendly side to her son too. It would hurt him. Maybe she should go talk to him before the appointment and ask him what was wrong.

But in the end, she chickened out. Besides, he was doing the exact thing that she'd originally planned to do: pull back and protect herself and Brody.

She hadn't needed to withdraw, because he'd done it for her. And actually, she wasn't thrilled with it.

And now it was ten, and Misha was late. Brody on the other hand was brimming with excitement at the idea of getting the packing and gauze removed from his ear. They would also be testing his hearing for the first time since the surgery.

Fifteen minutes later, Misha breezed into the room as if he didn't have a care in the world and sat behind the desk. "Hello, Brody, how are you feeling?"

He said nothing to her, and it stung more than it should have. But if he didn't want to interact with her, then that was his prerogative. Hell, she'd supposedly prepared herself for just this possibility. So why wasn't she handling it better than she was.

Brody looked from her to Misha with a frown. It was kind of hard *not* to notice the tension between them was thick enough to cut with a knife. And her kid was nothing if not intuitive.

But in the end, all that mattered was that Misha talk to Brody about his surgery and the possible outcomes. She was his mother, yes, but she was positive Misha wouldn't move in a direction that she wouldn't approve of. He wasn't that kind of man. Or that kind of doctor.

"I'm looking forward to getting this stuff out of my ear." He smiled at Misha.

There was no return smile. "You know you won't be able to submerge your head for three more weeks. I have some ear plugs you can use, if you go swimming. But it's very important until your eardrum fully heals. Do you understand?"

Brody's head tilted as he looked at the man. "Sure. I get it."

"And no heavy lifting for the same period of time."

Brody nodded, but his frown had grown, and she knew why. Because Misha had gone from acting like a friend to acting like a doctor who was seeing a routine patient.

Brody was hurt by the change. Just like she knew he would be.

And, oh, how she knew that hurt. She'd felt it for the past week. Did he regret their night together so much that he'd had to withdraw into his little box and close the lid so that she and Brody had no access except that which he allowed? Which was pretty much none at all.

And it stunk. It stunk for Brody who'd had no say in what the two adults had done that night. And it stunk for her, who'd not fully weighed the possible ramifications of sleeping with him again.

How easy he made it seem to walk away. Whether it was emotionally, like he was doing right now, or physically like he'd done back in high school. She hadn't seen him after he'd left for Belarus, but she remembered thinking she hoped he was suffering as much as she was. But seeing him now? She doubted he had. There was some wall he was able to erect that kept him from looking at anything except what he chose to look at. And right now, that wall was keeping him from seeing them. Really, seeing them. It was as if he could talk to them without looking at them.

Doing it to her was one thing. But doing it to Brody?

Hell no. As soon as this appointment was over, she was going to have it out with him. He could damn well be late for his next appointment just like he'd been late for theirs, while she had her say.

"Why don't you hop up on that table, and we'll see what we've got." He finally gave her son a smile that didn't quite make it to his eyes.

By the time he'd silently removed layers of gauze and packing and examined Brody's ear with the otoscope, Lyndsey was boiling mad.

She could practically see Brody shrinking into himself as if he sensed Misha's indifference to him as a person. All Misha seemed interested in were the results of the procedure he'd done on him. Stoking his own ego?

No. She didn't think so. Misha had never been egotistical. So what was going on?

They went through a few hearing tests using the tuning fork again, as well as the booth where an audiologist measured his hearing.

Brody came out of the booth and the audiologist handed the results to Misha, who rested a hip on the exam table. Brody came over and sat next to her, no longer even trying to engage with him.

And Misha seemed oblivious to the change in his patient. "So, how do you feel the hearing in your right ear is? Better? Worse? No change?"

"It's better."

The words were said in a monotone that bothered her. He'd been so very excited about this appointment. Excited about seeing Misha, whom Brody hadn't seen since he had taken them home from the hospital.

That excitement was nowhere to be found right now, and she hated that Misha made him feel rejected. He could reject her all he wanted, but to reject Brody?

What was it he'd said at her first appointment? That he would never penalize someone for something they had no control over.

Well, from Lyndsey's perspective, he was doing exactly that. Penalizing Brody for something he'd had no control over.

Sleeping with him had obviously been a mistake. At least for him. And if she'd known the consequences of giving in to her fantasies, she would have never let things head in that direction. She would have shown him to her spare bedroom and wished him a snippy good night.

But she'd had no idea Misha was capable of transforming into this cold stranger who had gotten what he wanted and then walked away without a second glance. It made her feel cheap. Something she hadn't felt since Wade. That had always been the difference between them. Misha had always made her feel special, while Wade made her feel like nothing.

"What are your goals for your other ear, Brody? The left one?"

Her son sat there in silence for a second, then he turned to look at her, and she could see from the expression on his face and the quivering of his lips that he was on the edge of breaking down. And she wasn't going to let that happen. Not in front of Misha.

She stood, pulling Brody up with her, and lifted her chin as she stared icy daggers at Misha. "This appointment is over. We've heard all we need to hear. When you can be bothered to set up a time for his next surgery, please give *me* a call."

With that she hustled Brody out of the office, right past the office assistant—who tried to call them back—and out into the hallway, where Brody immediately fell apart.

She held him in her arms, pulling him close and murmuring to him.

When he finally looked up, scrubbing at his face with his knuckles, he whispered. "Why does he suddenly hate me?"

Oh, God. She closed her eyes to keep from weeping for a boy who looked lost and confused. "He doesn't hate you."

He might hate her, but he didn't hate Brody. Her son was simply collateral damage for whatever was going on between Misha and her.

"Then why is he acting like that."

"Come with me. I want to tell you something." She wasn't going to tell him about what had transpired a week ago in their house. But she could tell him a little about her and Misha's past.

They made it to the cafeteria and Lyndsey got them each a drink and headed for a table in a far corner where people were less likely to hear what she had to say. They sat.

"You remember I told you that Misha and I went to school together?"

He nodded.

Pulling in a deep breath, she forced the next words from her mouth. "Well, it was a little more than that. We were close. Very close."

"You dated him?"

"Yes."

"That's wonderful, I think. Did you break up or something?"

She took a long pull of her drink as memories of their last day together trailed icy fingers over her.

"Something like that. He had to move back to Belarus with his family."

"And you never saw him again?"

"Nope. Not until the first appointment I made with him."

Brody seemed to mull that over. "So he's decided he no longer wants to date you, is that what this is about?"

Leave it to her son to break things down into their most basic components. "I think that's exactly what this is about. He's taking a few steps backward and trying to return to a more professional relationship. It has nothing to do with you personally."

"But not dating you doesn't mean he can't be friends with me, right?"

"You would think that would be the case, but human relationships are more complicated than that."

Brody seemed to relax into his chair with a smile. "Well, in that case, thanks for ruining things for me, Mom."

That made her laugh. He could pin it on her all he wanted. She would welcome it, in fact. That did not mean Misha wasn't still in the hot seat. Oh, not by a long shot. It was just something she was not going to do in front of her son. "You're welcome." She gave him a mock bow from her seat. "Hey, I'm going to ask Brittany to take you home, okay? This is about the time she gets off. I have a few things here at the hospital to take care of." She didn't tell him what or with whom.

He shrugged and then said, "Misha didn't say I

couldn't listen to any music, right? I just can't listen to anything loud for the next few weeks."

"That seems to be what I remember, why?"

"We're going to try to nail down the melody to that new song we've been working on this afternoon. If that's okay with you, that is."

"It's fine. Just don't do anything you know you shouldn't do. That prosthesis has to last a very long time."

"Don't worry. I'll be careful."

She looked at him. "So your hearing is better. How much better."

He smiled, his eyes finally showing some sparkle again. "It's a lot better."

"That is exactly what I was hoping for."

They waited for Brittany out in front of the hospital. When she glanced at her watch, she saw it was almost noon. Misha normally took a two-hour lunch break if she remembered correctly.

Once Brittany arrived, she waved goodbye with a wide smile on her face. Her friend was taking Brody back to her place rather than dropping him off at home. Misha had kind of gotten her spooked about that, despite her calls to both the courthouse and her lawyer. But it was better to err on the side of caution, wasn't that how the saying went? Besides, she wouldn't be away from home for long. She just needed to have a word with a certain clueless ENT.

She went back into the hospital and headed for the elevator. Once on the floor where his office was, she went straight to the reception desk and smiled at the staff member. "Is Dr. Lukyanov finished with his morning patients? I'd like to have a word if so."

"Um…well, he normally goes to lunch now."

"That's okay, it won't take long. If you could just let him know that Lyndsey would like to speak with him for a moment. If he can't right now, I'll catch him on the floor tomorrow."

He couldn't run forever. They were eventually going to stand face-to-face. And she was pretty sure he'd rather do this in private than in front of the nurses on the floor, although she wasn't opposed to doing exactly that.

The woman picked up her phone, turning her back to Lyndsey and speaking in low tones. Lyndsey moved away from the desk so that she didn't appear to be eavesdropping on their conversation.

A minute later, the woman nodded at the door that led to the exam areas. "He'll see you in his office."

She sent her a brilliant smile. "Thanks so much."

Pushing through the double doors as if she had every right to be there, she turned the corner and then strolled down the hallway. She was going to arrive when she was good and ready. No rushing or nervous stuttering. She was going to say what she had to say and then leave.

She got to his office. The door was already open, so she went in. He looked up. "Lyndsey."

One corner of her mouth quirked up, even though

nothing about this situation was funny. "You didn't tell me that sleeping with you carried a lifetime penalty for everyone associated with me."

"Excuse me?"

"You know exactly what I'm trying to say. You hurt my son in there with your little act. We left that room, and he bawled in my arms, thinking that you hate him."

Misha leaned back in his chair and closed his eyes. When they opened again, they were rife with an emotion she didn't understand. "I did what I had to do."

"You had to spit out orders and edicts to a fifteen-year-old boy without even asking him how his day was? What his band was working on?"

"I treated him the same way I would treat any patient."

She shook her head. "I don't believe that for a second."

"Believe what you like." He shot the words at her like bullets, each one hitting their mark.

They stared at each other, and she wasn't exactly sure what else she could say or what she even hoped to accomplish here. Try to reason with his softer side?

Kind of hard when apparently that part of him had been sent into exile. If it had even been there in the first place. Had it all been an act?

He was the first one to break the charged silence. "Look, Lyndsey, if I don't pull back, I can no longer be his doctor. It's as simple as that. I'll have to refer him elsewhere."

"What?" Shock went through her. He was now threatening to not do Brody's next surgery? She'd been spitting mad, yes, but she hadn't said anything inappropriate, so she had no idea where any of this was coming from.

He blew out a breath and got up and shut the door, before coming to sit beside her. "There's a reason doctors can't operate on their relatives or loved ones. Their emotions can cloud their judgment, making it more dangerous for the patient."

He sounded like he was reading something straight from the hospital's personnel manual. "Did someone say something to you about me or Brody?"

"No. But I care about him. Maybe too much. I thought if I reeled myself in and changed my approach, I could go back to where I should be, which is looking at Brody as a patient rather than someone who means a lot to me."

"I trust you to do your job."

"Maybe *you* do. But in the end, that's not what matters. I have to trust myself enough to do my job. And I'm not sure I do right now."

"I see." Her mouth twisted as she tried to think. "So this was your idea of a solution? You don't think you could have talked to Brody and explained that to him. He's actually a pretty smart kid. He probably would have been fine with it. As it is, I'm not sure he'll agree to go through with the second surgery after today's visit."

"*Proklyatiye.* That was never my intention, Lyndsey. But I realized after being with you that I'd crossed a line I never should have crossed. Not while Brody was my patient."

"It wasn't like you seduced me. We were once involved. That has to count for something. Besides, I seem to remember being the one to climb into your lap, not the other way around."

Misha grinned. "Okay, that's an image I'm going to have a hard time erasing from my head." He touched her hand. "So what can I do to make things right with Brody?"

"Talk to him. Tell him you need to stay on professional footing with him until after the second surgery. He'll understand, I promise. And at least I won't have a confused and upset son who thinks he's done something wrong."

"Jesus, I never intended to send him that kind of message."

"Well, you did. I thought the same thing he did. Oh, not that he'd done something wrong, but that you regretted sleeping with me so much that you were going to brush us off every chance you got. And if it was that, I could handle it. But Brody can't. He's a sensitive kid—a musician who feels everything deeply. He doesn't understand adults who can turn their feelings on and off with the flick of a switch."

"And you think I can do that?"

"Apparently."

Misha turned to her and before she could say anything, he leaned over and kissed her mouth. Softly. Gently. "This is what I wanted to do the entire time you and Brody were in the room. Does that sound like someone who can turn their emotions…er…on and off at the flip of a switch?"

"You wanted to kiss me?"

"*Da*. And it's part of my problem. If something goes wrong in that operating room, will it be because my mind is somewhere else or something that would have happened whether or not you and I are involved?"

He thought there was a chance they could be involved? That was news to her. And there'd been no hint of any of that in the exam room.

"Are all Belarusians able to set aside their emotions at the drop of a hat?"

"When there is a need, I think. When it would hurt someone else if they don't."

She finally understood. "And you thought it would hurt Brody in the long run if you hadn't acted the way you had during his appointment."

"I think going to another surgeon would hurt him in the long run."

If his words were taken at face value, someone might think that Misha was conceited as hell. Well, he wasn't. She knew he had more experience with the procedure in this part of Louisiana than anyone else in his field. It was what had made Lyndsey come to him in the first place, telling him she didn't want to uproot Brody unless it was absolutely necessary. "I agree."

"I mean he could go to a surgeon in another state, like Texas, but that would be a lot of driving. And it's better to have whoever put in the first prosthesis fit the second one as well, so that there's as little variation as possible between the left and right ears."

She saw how that would be true.

"Then will you talk to him?" She hesitated. "I already told him that we were once involved with each other in high school."

"We were a little more than involved, don't you think?"

Her lips twisted. "I wasn't going to get into the nitty gritty facts of our relationship with my son. But I did say that it had maybe played a factor in how you acted toward him today."

His fingers dragged through his hair in that way that made her tummy shimmy inside of her. And discovering the reasons for his behavior had helped mitigate her anger quite a bit.

"And I don't have to say anything about that night at your house."

"No. I'd rather you didn't, in fact."

He tilted his head. "Then I'll talk to him. Where do you suggest?"

"Maybe somewhere neutral, off hospital grounds.

Maybe at one of his jam sessions?" She hurried to say, "It doesn't mean you have to start going to all of his practices or start palling around with him. He'll understand, once you explain it to him. I know he will. But it has to come from you, rather than me."

"I understand. And after his second surgery?"

"What do you mean?"

"Is there any chance we can see each other periodically?"

Shock held her silent for a minute or two. "Y-you *want* to start seeing me?"

"It's a possibility. I'd want to take it slowly and see where it leads."

"I'm all for going slow."

He gave a smile that lit up his face. "That's not what I experienced recently."

Relief made her words flow a little more freely than maybe they should have, but she couldn't resist. "Oh, no? Well, I'm all for trying again. *After* Brody's second surgery, that is."

"In that case, we'll see where we are in a couple months' time."

A couple of months had never seemed so far away. But it was a smart plan. And a better alternative to trying to find another doctor. A surgeon she didn't know or trust. She wanted Misha on his case, and just like in the beginning of this journey, she was willing to do anything to make that happen. Even wait on her own happiness.

And did he make her happy?

Yes, she thought he did. And that was as far as she was willing to explore that thought. At least for the time being.

CHAPTER TEN

OVER THE NEXT couple of weeks, Misha found himself letting his guard down more and more while keeping to the boundaries they'd jointly set:

Rule number one: no sex.

That seemed obvious enough.

Rule number two: no sly touches or innuendos.

Rule number three: no kissing.

This one was personally hard for him, because he found himself wanting to do that every time he was in a room with her.

Rule number four: no waggling eyebrows.

When he'd made up that last rule, she challenged it by saying she never did that with her brows. He countered by saying yes, she did, and she knew it. Just like she'd done years ago. And they'd waggled a lot back then. Lyndsey had smacked him in the arm, which he'd claimed violated rule number two.

There'd been some laughter that had made him think it might just be possible to be friends during this interim time before Brody's second surgery, which was scheduled for two months from now. Surely they could hold out until then.

He moved across the nurses' area on his way to a patient's room. Lyndsey came up beside him and passed him a note. Then she turned and headed the other way.

When he looked down at the scrap of paper, the words *waggle-waggle* were scribbled across it. He laughed before crumpling the paper up and stuffing it in his scrubs.

Right then it hit him. He loved her. Had probably never stopped loving her. Maybe that's why there'd never been any real interest in dating other women, either when he was in Belarus or after he'd moved back to the States.

Did she feel the same about him?

He pulled the note out of his pocked and opened it up, smoothing it on one of the desks. *Waggle-waggle.* That would seem to indicate she might. Why else write something like that if she wasn't showing some kind of affection toward him?

Maybe she did. Maybe she wasn't yet sure. But that was a conversation to be had after Brody's next surgery. He was doing his damnedest to do right by the kid, so he wasn't going to ruin it all by skipping over the steps they'd laid out. They had all the time in the world, from what he was seeing. He just had to stay the course until he could come right out and say the words. But that time was not yet, and recently he'd read a journal article about a family who was suing their son's doctor for gross misconduct after their son died on the operating table. They claimed he was no longer able to be an objective party after the doctor fell in love with the boy's mother. Yes, it was different in that there was a love triangle involved, and in the fact that he couldn't see Lyndsey suing him for sleeping with her. But it still seemed wise to be careful. *Waggle-waggle* or no *waggle-waggle*.

The next day, Lyndsey spotted Misha walking across the lobby floor, just as she was coming from a patient's room. She wanted to ask him about another patient, so she rounded the corner to catch up with him.

She realized as she moved closer that he was on the phone with someone, and he was speaking in Russian. His words were crisp and succinct. No nonsense. In their time together as kids, she'd picked up some words here and there, and before she could move away, she heard the word Belarus and that whatever it was, Misha was going to think about it.

Something sharp struck her heart and went deep. Was he thinking of leaving again?

A sick sense of déjà vu came over her. Of course he would go back to visit his family—his mom. Just as she would if she'd been in his shoes. But what if this wasn't that? What if there was a business opportunity or the chance to head up the ENT department at a prestigious hospital over there? Misha would be quite a catch for a hospital in any part of the world.

She swallowed, knowing she was probably overreacting. But her dad had never really reentered her life once he'd left it. He'd withdrawn both emotionally and physically, always making promises he'd never kept.

And she'd seen firsthand how Misha could withdraw emotionally when he wanted—or needed—to.

And hadn't Brody told her just yesterday that he wanted to learn Russian in case Misha needed to move back to Belarus? Had Misha hinted that he might?

She couldn't go through that again. Couldn't watch him fly away and wonder if he was going to end up being like her dad. Misha had been in the States for ten years now. Ten years and he never wondered about what happened to her. Whether she was alive or dead or living with a man who had almost killed her. If she'd known he was back in the States, would she have tried to call him?

Yes. She thought she would have.

But to live with that fear all over again, knowing he might walk away and not look back? That wasn't her. And she was pretty sure she couldn't be with someone who was capable of it. And she had Brody to think about. He'd understood Misha's reasons for being standoffish, but she was hoping after his surgery, they could go back to being friends.

But if Misha went back to Belarus and dropped off the face of the planet, her son would be crushed. And while she knew she'd never do anything stupid the next time around, like jump into bed with the first guy who looked her way, she was not sure how Brody would react. Would he turn moody and depressed like he'd been in the exam room that day when he'd thought Misha hated him? Or maybe something worse?

Maybe it was time to be proactive and ask him outright if he was thinking of moving back to his home country. And if he was? Well, then she was going to have to do one of the hardest things she'd ever done and tell him there could be no future for them if he was.

"Hey, can I talk to you for a minute?"

Misha looked up from the chart he was reading and smiled at her. "Sure, come on in."

She hesitated for a second or two before coming into the space and sitting down. Well…it wasn't actually sitting. It was more like she was perched, ready to take flight at any moment.

He frowned. "What's up?"

"The other day on the floor I was coming around the corner to say something to you and I realized you were on your phone with someone. Before I could turn around and leave you to your conversation, you mentioned Belarus and said you'd think about something."

His brows went up. "You understood all of that? I'm impressed."

"So I was right?"

"About what?"

She moistened her lips in a way that drew his attention, just like it always did. The woman was a distraction like none other had ever been. But that made sense, didn't it? He'd never been in love before. Not really.

"Are you thinking about going back to Belarus?"

He leaned back in his chair. "Is that what this is about? You thought I might be moving back there?"

"So you're not?"

"No, I'm not. There's a conference on otosclerosis that my mom thought I might be interested in presenting at. I told her I would think about it." The reason he hadn't said yes right away was precisely for this reason. He knew that Belarus was a touchy subject with her because of their past.

"I see."

There was something about the tone of her voice that gave him pause. "What do you see?"

"Can you think of a circumstance that might have you actually moving back there?"

What exactly was she trying to say? "Is there a reason why you're asking this?"

Her mouth twisted. "You haven't exactly answered my question."

He thought carefully about what to say. "I would never dare to predict the future. But there are a couple of reasons I might think about going back for an extended stay."

"As in months? Or years?"

"My answer would be, it depends. My dad died while I was in Belarus. If my mother became ill like he did, I would go back and care for her. It would be my duty as her son, in my culture. But it is also because she is my mother. Would you not do the same for Brody if the situation was reversed?"

"But it's not. Brody lives here in the States."

"And my mother prefers to live in Belarus. I will not uproot her from her home."

"I'm not asking you to. What I'm asking is…" She shook her head, her lower lip trembling as if she was trying to contain some terrible emotion. "God, Misha. I… I know you would need to go back. I would never expect you not to. But is there a time limit on any of that? You were gone for five years the last time you left. I'm just not sure I could go through that again."

"And yet I've been here in the States for ten. Longer than I was gone. Military families deal with this kind of absence all the time. Is it really so different?"

"In the life of a child, five years is forever. The milestones that would be missed, the growth that will happen. Could you really pull yourself away for that long?"

"We haven't even talked about children yet." His words were shorter than they should have been. He could chalk it up to impatience, but he wasn't sure that was all of it. This was like the past all over again. He couldn't make the promises she seemed to want him to make.

"Again, you've avoided the question rather than answering it. And I was talking about Brody. Not children of our own." Her voice wasn't as soft as it was a minute ago. Then she closed her eyes for a long minute. "I think I have to walk away, Misha. I know there are people who live apart for extended periods of time. Years even. But I'm not wired that way. I can't do it. And realistically, you've said yourself there are times when you might have to leave for years. So I think it's better to pull the word relationship from our vocabulary and go back to being colleagues. Or friends even."

So she was allowed to move heaven and earth for her family, while he was not afforded the same luxury? He didn't think so.

"If you think we could ever be friends with the conditions you've put on our relationship, you are very much mistaken. If it ends here, it ends here for good. We may have to work together. But one thing we don't have to be is friends."

Her lower lip trembled again for a second before it returned to normal. "And Brody?"

"What about him?"

"Please don't hurt him. We don't have to be friends, but please don't punish him for my inability to deal with the realities of being in a relationship with you."

He saw her point. "In that, you won't have to worry. Brody will always be special to me. And I'll make sure I don't make him feel any less than the great kid he is."

"Thank you."

His brows went up. "How do you say it here in Louisiana? It's been real. See you around."

She didn't say anything else, she simply got up from her chair, turned and walked out of his office and out of his life. And he couldn't think of anything that would change the outcome. He couldn't promise he would never go back for an extended period of time. And she couldn't deal with the possibility that he might. So he didn't try to stop her. Didn't try to feed her lies and make promises that he might not be able to keep down the road. To do that would be no better than what her ex-husband had done when he promised to change his ways. So he did what the old adage said: when you loved someone, you set them free.

Two weeks after her conversation with Misha, Lyndsey did two things. She found out that Wade had moved away from his hometown, which was a huge relief, and she decided that she was making a job move back to Centerville for good. She'd given her notice at Louisiana Southern. The other nurses had tried to talk her out of it but had finally accepted her excuse that after a year of trying, the hour-long commute had simply become too much. They'd given her a small going-away party, one that Misha hadn't attended. Not that she'd expected him to. She'd contacted him only once to make sure that he was still willing to do Brody's surgery that had been moved up to just a few short weeks away. His answer had been curt and to the point. He'd said he would do it, and she'd find he didn't go back on his promises.

She found herself not going to as many of Brody's garage practices after seeing Misha's Jeep pull up once. She'd made a beeline out of there so she wouldn't have to say anything to him. Even seeing him made a fire ignite in the acid that now hung out in her stomach on a regular basis. But one thing she was glad of was that he was maintaining his relationship with her son. There was always a risk of seeing him, but it was a risk she was willing to take.

Not like the risk of having someone she loved leave the country for good.

Wait. Back up a minute. She loved him?

Of course she did. Why else would she write him off the way she had?

Except she'd just now realized it. She loved him. Was terrified of being hurt by him again like she had been in the past. Like her father had hurt her. But Misha, in leaving the last time, had never sealed off wanting to keep in contact. Of wanting to try to have a long-distance relationship. She was the one who'd done that.

He'd been willing to live with the risk of it not working out. Of being gutted if she walked away. And she *had* been the one to walk away. Misha might have left the country, but *she'd* been the one to leave the relationship.

She hadn't been able to go with him back then. She'd still been in her late teens living with her parents. But now she was an adult, with the adult ability to make choices she hadn't been able to make back then.

And weren't there risks to everything in life? There'd been the risk of Brody going deaf. Had she cast him aside because of it? No. She'd learned sign language and prepared for the possibility. Why couldn't she do the same for Misha? Why couldn't she prepare for the possibility and find a way to make it work? Just like she'd done with her son. Because she loved him. Loved them both.

But how? How could she prepare for another five-year absence? Like Misha said, military families did it. Some of them lived overseas with their deployed loved ones, when possible. Some settled for daily video chats. They made it work. Because they loved each other. Lyndsey could see that she'd been totally selfish. It was no wonder he said they could never be friends. Because she hadn't acted like one. At least not like a good one. It had been her way or the highway, and she could see how wrong she'd been, both now and fifteen years ago. They could have found a way to make it work, but she'd chosen not to. And now she realized she'd handled both situations like a child.

So she had a choice. She could go on acting like a child, or she could do some growing up and figure out a way to make things with Misha work. If he was even willing to after everything she'd said to him.

Her lips twisted. Maybe that was part of what being an adult meant—going to someone and trying to make amends. Apologizing and then acting on that apology, making changes that would prove you really were sorry. And then, after all that, if Misha no longer wanted to maintain a relationship or even friendship, then it was something she would have to accept. Because it was the grown-up thing to do.

But she'd already quit her job in Lafayette. Well…an hour wasn't so far away in the scheme of things, was it? But first she had to find out if Misha even wanted to make it work.

And she prayed for both her sake and Brody's that saying she was sorry wasn't too little too late.

"Misha, I have someone out front who would like to have a word with you, if you have a minute."

Great. He was bone tired and had been looking forward to going home and eating some cold cornflakes and milk for dinner. Then he could mope until it was time to go to bed. He had a feeling he'd be doing a lot of that over the coming months.

"Is it a patient, Marie?"

"Not exactly, but she is related to a patient."

His heart jolted for a second before he remembered that a lot of his patients were kids and were brought in by their parents or other relatives. It didn't mean it was Lyndsey. He hadn't heard from her since that terse phone call three weeks ago. He'd actually gone to a couple of Brody's garage practices and only realized afterward that part of the reason he went was the hope that he might catch sight of her. His declaration that they couldn't be friends had been a ridiculous attempt to force her hand. But he hadn't been all wrong. She couldn't expect him to never visit his home country any more than he could expect her to never visit Brody should he move away someday.

"Misha?"

Marie was waiting for an answer. He shoved his hand into his pocket and felt something crinkle as he did. A piece of paper. He pulled it out and saw something familiar scribbled there. He turned it sideways to read it. *Waggle-waggle.*

Hellfire. That seemed like years ago, when in reality it had only been a few short weeks.

There had to be a way to get back to that. Or at least try.

He finally said, "Tell them I'll meet them out in reception."

And then once he was done with that, he was going to make a very difficult phone call. But it had to be done if he expected to have any kind of closure.

He set the note on his desk, smoothing it out. When he got back, it would serve as a reminder of why he was going to do what he hadn't done fifteen years ago and call her, even if she said she didn't want to hear from him. And since she'd quit her job at Louisiana Southern, she'd made it pretty plain that she'd cut ties with him and had no plans to see him again, except for Brody's next surgery. Well, she was going to hear from him one last time, whether she wanted to or not. And then he would know for sure if it was truly over or if it was something that could be revived with enough time and effort, both of which he was willing to put in, if she was willing to do the same. With that decision made, he walked out to reception.

And came face-to-face with the very woman he'd been thinking of.

"What are you doing here?"

"Sorry for coming unannounced. It seems like I make a habit of doing that."

"I'm sorry?" He had no idea what she was talking about. Had she come by when he wasn't here?

"You didn't know who I was at our first meeting, and that was my doing."

"Ah yes. I think I was just as shocked to see you then as I am now."

She paused, glancing at where Marie was still working on some patient files on her monitor. "Is there someplace we can talk?"

"Come back to my office." He was trying very hard to believe this was something about Brody and not about them, because if he let hope creep in where it wasn't wanted, he would be gutted when all she wanted to talk about was a scheduling need.

The last time she'd been back here, she'd broken things off with him. Maybe he should have chosen someplace like the courtyard, where those specters weren't lurking, waiting to say "I told you so" when he was wrong about the possibility of finding a compromise.

He closed the door and motioned her to a chair. But this time, instead of sitting behind his desk, he came around to sit next to her.

Before he could say anything, she started talking. "You know, I thought I had learned all about taking risks when Brody got his diagnosis. I hoped for the best, but planned for the worst. I fought with all I had to get him the help he needed. But on the side, I was busy learning sign language. Just in case. And neither Brody nor I had known the other was studying it until the surgery, when he signed to me. And I signed back."

Misha blinked. "I didn't know that."

"No one did." She smiled. "So yeah, I thought I knew all about risk. Thought I was pretty much an expert on it. Until I overheard a small part of your phone conversation with your mom and almost made the same mistake that I made fifteen years ago. I realized I knew nothing about real risk. The kind that forces you to make sacrifices—big ones—because you love that person."

The tentacles of hope that he'd been trying to keep from gaining a foothold ripped down a whole wall and sauntered in. He made no move to stop it. Because she'd said three very important words. Risk, sacrifice, and love.

Because he realized when he'd been thinking about calling her, those three words had not been very far from his mind, either.

He smiled. "That's funny. You know what I realized just a few minutes ago?"

She shook her head.

"I realized that this…" he reached across the desk and pulled that slip of paper toward him and held it up. "These words scribbled on a piece of paper make the risks seem a little less scary, they make the sacrifices seem a little bit smaller, and they make the love worth fighting for."

"You kept that?"

"Not on purpose. But it seems that it was kept there

for a purpose, maybe by some higher power, so I could find it again at the right moment." He took a deep breath and said the words. "I love you, Lynds. And as long as you waggle your brows at me, everything in my life will have meaning and purpose and fulfillment. No matter the risks. No matter the sacrifices."

She stared at him before reaching over and touching his face as if in wonder. "I realized almost the exact same thing. Not about the waggly brows—I still deny doing that—but that love makes all the rest worthwhile."

He hesitated before asking. "And if I ever have to go to Belarus for an extended stay?" He held his breath as he waited for her answer.

"Well, then you'd better start teaching me some Russian so I don't look like a total goofball to your family and friends."

He laughed. "You could never look like a goofball—whatever that is." His smile faded. "And what about Brody? You think he'd be okay coming with us, if he's still a minor?"

"Here's the funny thing about Brody. He's already been preparing, even before he knew I was coming here. He secretly bought a well-known study program and has been studying Russian. Because, in his words, 'If he ever moves back to Belarus, I'm going to go visit him.' How's that for being a risk-taker?"

"I truly love that kid." A thought just occurred to him. "But—"

"If this is about his surgery, listen. This is a risk

both Brody and I are willing to take. If you choose not to do his surgery and want another surgeon to take over, we'll be okay with that decision. We'll just find the next best surgeon and worm our way into their heart the same way we did yours."

He laughed. God. It felt so good to be able to feel true joy again. "Just don't worm too hard, because the only one who is allowed to love you with the love of a family is me. Well, and your blood relatives, of course." He stopped for a minute before saying. "You'll really be okay if I feel too attached to do the surgery? I'm not even sure the hospital will let me, unless we hide our relationship. Which I'm not willing to do."

"So are you saying we have a relationship?"

"Oh, yes, we have a relationship."

She leaned over and kissed him, and the touch was sweeter than anything they'd done before. Because this touch had a promise none of the others had had. The promise of forever, and that was something he never wanted to take for granted ever again.

"Except this time no rules. I want to be able to waggle my eyebrows whenever I choose to, no matter who is around. I just have to learn how to do it first."

"Agreed." A subject came to mind that he wanted to clear up, because he'd thrown something at her in anger the last time they were together. "About children…"

Her face clouded. "If you don't want any, that's okay. It's a sacrifice I'm willing to make."

"Oh, but I do want them, and given our ages…"

"Excuse me?"

"I'm not calling you old. All I'm saying is we might want to start trying sooner rather than later. I don't think I'll have the energy to have kids when I'm ninety."

"Hmm. I bet you'll be a pretty sexy ninety-year-old."

"Are you calling me pretty? Or pretty sexy?"

"Once your receptionist finishes with those files, I think we should lock this door and find out. Although to be honest, I do find you pretty, in the most masculine sense. And those eyes…they just do it for me."

Misha picked up his cell phone and dialed Marie's extension. She picked up almost immediately. "I just wanted to see how you're coming with those files. I don't want you to have to work too late." He glanced at Lynds. "So you've just finished the last one? Great. Have a wonderful evening, and I'll see you in the morning." With that, he pressed the button to end the call. "She's done."

"So I heard. So all that's left is for you to get up and lock that door."

The last thing he saw as he went to do just that was Lyndsey trying to waggle her brows at him. It didn't look quite as sexy as he'd envisioned. But it was still adorable.

He stifled a laugh. This could prove to be quite interesting. But one thing he knew for sure was that this room was going to be filled with love. And promises that would be kept no matter the risk. No matter the sacrifice. Because love was worth it all.

EPILOGUE

THEY WERE GETTING MARRIED.

In Belarus.

She could hardly believe it was really happening. But it was.

She and Brody had arrived two weeks ago, and Misha had met them at the airport. She'd wanted it that way, wanted him to be able to go and arrange things with his family and friends. His mom had been lovely and understanding and had welcomed her and Brody into the family with open arms.

Biting her lip, she waited at the back of the huge cathedral and looked in wonder at the beauty all around her. A hand squeezed hers, and she turned to look at Brody who was smiling at her. "Imagine the acoustics in this place."

She laughed, then covered her mouth when it echoed through the space. "Do not make me laugh."

"You've been laughing a lot recently. I like the sound of it. Actually, I like the sound of everything. I'll never take my hearing for granted again."

Her son had had the surgery on his other ear. And it had been performed by Misha's mentor, the one who'd overseen his training in the technique. They'd had to go all the way to New York to have it done, but it had been worth it.

The strains of an organ sounded at the front of the space. "I think it's time."

"Are you sure you want me to walk you down the aisle, Mom?"

She hugged him close. "More sure than anything."

"It's kind of like the baby is walking you down the aisle too, isn't it?"

"Shh…"

"Oh, right. Sorry."

She and Misha had found out a month ago that they were expecting a child, which was why he'd made the trip to Belarus to fast-track their wedding. No one knew about the pregnancy yet, except their little family, and she wanted to keep it that way for right now. Just for a little while longer. Once they got back to the States, they would have a second smaller wedding with her mom and their friends in attendance. And the funny thing was, it didn't feel like a sacrifice to either of them.

She and Brody started their trek down the long, carpeted aisle, her eyes locking with Misha's as he stood tall and proud at the front of the cathedral.

It seemed to take forever to reach him, but reach him she did. And when he took her hand to escort her up the steps, a shiver went through her. Just like it did every time he touched her. She suspected it would always be this way. They may have gotten off to a late start, but they both intended to finish this race well. And to finish it together.

A clergyman recited words she barely understood, but Misha had gone over what she needed to say and when. And he nodded at her, whispering a word to her when she stumbled over the pronunciation, but she was proud and happy to stand beside him. To finally be able to declare to the world that they belonged together.

When it was time for him to kiss her, they clung together for a little longer than was customary, judging by the titter of laughter that came from behind them. They broke apart and turned to face the relatives who'd gathered there to celebrate with them. Her eyes sought out Brody, surprised when she saw he had a microphone in his hand.

"What?" she whispered to Misha, only to have him say, "He and I both agreed this was the perfect way to celebrate the start of our new family."

From somewhere behind her came the familiar notes that she'd heard time and time again in a garage in Centerville, Louisiana. Her glance swung to Misha with an unspoken question.

"Yes, they're all here, actually." He nodded to a place she hadn't noticed when she came down the aisle. But Brody's band members were all there, playing a song she knew by heart. And he was right. The acoustics were out of this world. She had no idea how any of them had managed this, but she was beyond grateful.

Then her son's voice came to her, singing words that

were filled with a wistfulness and a question that only the listeners could answer.

As I sit here in my silence, wondering what is next,
The fear is overwhelming.
Is there really nothing left?
Then a tiny blip of sound bursts through my bro-
kenness.
Just a hint of treble. Followed by a touch of bass.
Is any of this possible?
Can a miracle break through?
Or is it all a wishful dream that never will come
true.

As tears poured down her face, she knew it wasn't just a dream. It was reality. Their reality. And it only promised to get better with time.

She squeezed Misha's hand and looked up at him, trying to contain the huge ball of emotion that grew and grew with every breath she took. Looking up at the man she loved as the song drew to a close, she did the only thing she could think of. Sent a message that only the man she loved could fully comprehend: she waggled her brows at him.

* * * * *

ONE SUMMER
IN SYDNEY

ANNIE CLAYDON

MILLS & BOON

To Soraya,
with thanks for wise thoughts and encouragement.

CHAPTER ONE

A TWENTY-FOUR-HOUR JOURNEY. As they'd flown over the baked heart of Australia, it had occurred to Dr Allie Maitland-Hill that if she wasn't far enough away from London yet, there was nowhere else left to run.

The thought made her feel *more* determined, rather than less. When the news had first broken at the hospital, whispers turning into rumours, and then firmed up by a bland official announcement that had given precious few details, Allie had run to Hampshire for the weekend. Two days tramping the countryside with Aunt Sal had always fixed whatever life had thrown at her, but this time it hadn't even come close.

On Monday morning she'd returned to work to find that the hospital had made another announcement, this time with further details. The online group, where members had posted pictures and videos—Allie's blood had run cold with panic at the thought of videos—was no longer a suspicion but a reality. Several of the ringleaders had been identified and immediately suspended. They weren't named, but James wasn't there when she'd happened to pass his work station at the hospital and it had lain empty for the whole week.

The following weekend, she'd tried to run a little further. Surely Yorkshire would do what Hampshire had failed to accomplish? But two nights in a hotel, most of it spent in her room looking out at the glorious view and trying to think of an alternative to the one possibility that was boring its way into her heart, had been fruitless.

James had been affable and charming, almost shy, but he'd left her under no illusions that he was interested in her. Allie had liked the gentle three-month courtship that moved slowly from looks and smiles towards a coffee date and then an evening meal together. She'd ignored the veiled hints she'd heard from a friend that he wasn't all that he seemed, because everyone else who knew him seemed to like him, and he'd never pressed their relationship to go any faster than it should.

When they'd spent the night together he'd seemed so perfect. He'd pulled back the bedcovers, keeping the lights on, because he said that he wanted to see everything that passed between them, and they'd made love for hours.

He'd called her the next day, seeming genuinely upset. They'd had a wonderful time together but he had a lot going on right now, and couldn't take things any further. He'd been vague and uncharacteristically thoughtless, but Allie had swallowed the questions that had come to mind and put it down to experience. James had said that he'd always remember their time together with fondness, and then hung up.

As she'd sat miserably in her hotel room, Allie had wondered whether James had more than just fond recollections to remember her by. Maybe he had an aide-memoire, to recall their time together, that she didn't know about. The thought had eaten away at her, like corrosive acid, and when she'd returned to London she'd called the confidential hotline that the hospital had set up for anyone with concerns that images of them might have been shared without their knowledge.

* * *

That had been eighteen months ago, now. Time spent facing the truth and not running from it. Finally Allie had buckled under the pressure and decided she needed a change. Some anonymity where she didn't feel that everyone knew what had happened and where she was constantly wondering who had seen what on the internet. When she'd gone to her line manager to tell him that she was giving up her job, he'd suggested an alternative. Dr Zac Forbes had been in Sydney for the last two years, as part of an exchange scheme between her own hospital and a sister hospital in Australia. His tenure was due to finish soon, and since there were currently no suitable candidates to replace him Allie's application could be pushed through quickly. She could keep her job in London open, and return without losing any seniority.

And Australia could be a new start. Or—it was impossible to run any further without going into space. Whichever way Allie was minded to think about it, it had seemed to open up options for a future that increasingly seemed to offer very little, apart from just getting through the day, and then surviving the night.

In a daze of weariness, she followed the line of passengers slowly making their way off the plane, and through customs. Someone had directed her to the meeting area and she'd followed a group of people, just off the plane and clearly looking forward to a reunion with family or friends. Allie watched as they fell into the arms of the people waiting for them, smiling a little at the warmth that escaped the tight circle. Maybe if she concentrated on that, it would stop her from shivering.

Zac had said he'd be waiting for her here and she summoned up the two-year-old image of him, from her own hospital. Pale brown hair, and…she didn't know what colour his eyes were, they'd never had much to do with each other back in England. Probably some shade of brown, which went with the muted colours he always wore. Perhaps he'd be carrying a placard with her name on it, which would distinguish him from all of the other anonymous faces that surrounded her.

Allie sat down at the end of a row of seats, clutching the handle of her suitcase tightly and scanning the people in the waiting area. She couldn't see Zac; maybe he'd been detained at the hospital… The impulse to flop to one side, curl up on a couple of seats and take a nap seized her and she opened her eyes with an effort, only to see a card propped up against the cash register of a coffee cart. *Dr Alexandra Maitland-Hill.*

Maybe she was supposed to ask there where she was supposed to go next. Then the man who had just paid for coffee picked up the disposable cup along with the card with her name on it and turned. Zac…?

There was nothing anonymous about him. This was a man who met someone's gaze, a lot broader across the shoulders than she remembered Zac, his hair kissed blond by the sun and his skin golden. He wore a pair of casual trousers, along with a dark blue T-shirt emblazoned with a brightly coloured design on the front. Something about him reminded her of the shy, gentle man that she remembered, whose only two aims in life seemed to be study and merging into the background. But there was a lot that didn't.

Australia had obviously been good to him. Allie automatically raised her hand, waving to catch his attention, and he gave a frank, open smile that made her wonder momentarily whether this really *was* Zac and she wasn't fast asleep on the plane still, dreaming her own version of *Revenge of the Body Snatchers*.

Blue. His eyes were dark blue. And Zac Forbes was absolutely gorgeous.

Zac had thought about this a lot. When the news had broken at the hospital, the police had contacted him to ask whether he knew anything about the abuse that had been taking place and although Zac wished he could tell them something that would be of help, he was also relieved to be able to say that he'd no clue about what had been going on. He'd watched the situation from afar, seen Allie's bravery in coming forward and encouraging others to do the same, and realised the toll that must have taken.

And now he could see it in her face. She was smiling, clearly disoriented at finding herself in a strange place with precious little sleep, and no one could be expected to come off a long international flight looking completely self-possessed. But there was more. A drawn watchfulness that she probably didn't even know that she was exhibiting. He'd hardly recognised the bright, bubbly woman that he remembered from two years ago.

And now her bravery and what Zac assumed must be a wish for a new start had carried her here, and he'd made up his mind that he would make this transition as painless as possible for her. It was up to him to provide as much security and success that he could for her during their five-week handover period.

He sat down next to her, leaving one seat empty between them. 'How was your flight?' Zac decided that sticking with obvious questions was probably best at the moment.

'Fine…good.' She answered too quickly for that to be

anything other than a pleasantry. 'I could do with some fresh air.'

He nodded. 'Would you like a coffee before we get going? We can take it outside.'

She hesitated. Zac wondered whether she'd lost the ability to trust in the simple offer of a drink. Too late, the thought that any drink might be spiked occurred to him, and it tore at his heart that this kind of precaution might be the first and most important thing that occurred to Allie these days.

Then he saw a flash of the bright warmth that he recognised from two years ago. He'd always felt a little envious of her carefree, outgoing spirit, and Allie's sudden smile made his heart lurch in his chest.

'Yes. Thanks, that would be nice. Unless you have to be somewhere?'

'I'll be dropping in to the hospital this afternoon, but there's no rush. We've plenty of time.' He got to his feet, and Allie strung the strap of her handbag across her shoulder. 'Let me take your case.'

One more thing that she had to think about. Allie was clearly apprehensive and feeling vulnerable in an unfamiliar place, but she was making a determined effort to return his overtures of friendship. The impulse to protect her, to tell her that he'd do everything and anything to keep her safe, made his heart ache.

'Thanks.'

There was a trace of reluctance as she pushed the large case towards him, and Zac picked up her cabin bag, propping it on the top and then waiting for Allie to get to her feet before he started to walk over to the coffee cart.

'Um…' She was scanning the list taped to the front of the cart, frowning. Zac searched his memory and coffee with

milk popped out from one of the creases of a past that he'd
thought he had carefully folded away.

'A flat white is somewhere between a cappuccino and
a latte. Frothed milk without the foam.' He grinned at her.

'That sounds good.' She reached into her bag, fiddling
with a zipped pouch inside, and Zac handed her a ten-dollar
note. He'd been in the same place two years ago, picking a
random brew from a list and sorting through the bundle of
unfamiliar notes he'd got from the bank in England.

'Thanks.' She examined the note and then grinned at
him, the dark shadows under her eyes seeming to disappear for a moment.

Such beautiful eyes, wide and brown, shot with gold
when she turned her face towards the light. Allie's dark
curls and her smile had always brightened his day back
in London, even if approaching her to talk about anything
other than work was out of the question.

He had to stop this. Wanting to make Allie smile meant
that he had to get close to her. And he guessed that getting
close would be a whole new challenge after all that she'd
been through. He'd made up his mind to make her welcome,
and do as much as he could to give her a safe place to live,
while she was finding her feet here. He really needed to stop
thinking about the feeling in the pit of his stomach that he
wanted to roll back everything that had happened to Allie
in the last two years, and somehow make it all go away.

After the air-conditioned hum of the plane, the sounds
and smells of the open air began to dispel the fog that had
formed in Allie's mind. She could look around her and drink
in her surroundings, a cup of coffee in her hand, Zac sitting
quietly next to her. She took off her hoodie, turning her face

up to the warmth of the sun. Everything seemed brighter somehow, and clearer.

'I think I'm going to like it here.' Allie decided that since this *was* a fresh start, she should be optimistic.

'I do. There's something about moving to the other side of the world that gets everything into perspective.'

Did he know? It wouldn't be beyond the bounds of possibility, he must have friends back at the hospital, although Zac had always seemed too busy with his books and his work to socialise much. Allie rejected the thought. Fresh start. Time to stop wondering what everyone she met knew and what they'd seen on the internet. What they *might* see if it occurred to them to look.

'Did you?' She sipped her coffee, trying to make the question seem casual.

'I think so. A little less work and a little more play. Although there's still plenty of work and a lot to learn.'

Allie had been banking on that. Something to keep her mind occupied, and to tire her out so that she might sleep. Right now she was more interested in the leisure side of Zac's metamorphosis, because work was something that was always there, both here and at home. And the change in him was even more marked now that they were in the open air. He seemed relaxed and so at one with the world around him.

'What do you do? In your spare time.'

He chuckled, stretching his legs out in front of him. 'Well… I've learned to surf.'

'Surfing! So you're a real Australian now, are you?'

'Nah. Still noticeably English. Ask anyone at the hospital.' He shrugged. 'I hear that Cornwall's good for surfing.'

'So when you get home you'll be driving down there for weekends?'

'Who knows. I may well give it a go.' He spun his coffee cup into a nearby recycling bin, and Allie yawned behind her hand. 'Do you want to get going?'

She nodded. 'I could do with a couple of hours' sleep. Then hopefully I'll make it through the afternoon without dozing off and sleep tonight...'

Zac had put her luggage in the back of a rather battered SUV, which seemed to fit perfectly with his new persona of a man who liked to spend time at the beach. He'd held the door open, frowning awkwardly and brushing a few specks of sand from the seat before she got in, in a nod to the shy, apologetic man who she'd thought would be picking her up at the airport. In a place that seemed so like home in some ways, and so different in others, contradictions might be something she ought to expect.

They drove for half an hour, along free-flowing highways and then through residential districts, with houses set back from the road and shaded by trees. Finally, Zac turned onto a coastal road.

'You live here?'

He smiled. 'Cronulla's handy for the hospital, it's on the same side of Sydney. And it's only half an hour by car, or an hour by train from the centre of town if you want to go out for the evening.'

Going out. Two years ago, Allie would have been up for that. But she couldn't remember the last time she'd been on an evening out, now. Handy for the hospital would be good, though.

'And it's by the sea.'

'Yeah. And not too far from the Royal National Park, if you want to go walking or cycling.'

She hadn't done much walking or cycling recently either.

Or been to a beach, although the deep blue of the sky, merging in the distance with the water, did seem inviting. Allie would settle for the privacy of four walls, and some peace and quiet in which to sleep right now. That vision seemed to disintegrate a little as Zac turned in to a covered parking spot, next to a brightly painted shop front.

'You live above a surf shop?' She couldn't suppress the note of surprised disappointment in her voice as she got out of the car. Zac definitely hadn't mentioned *that* in their brief set of exchanged emails.

'I'm friendly with the owners. They used to live above the shop but they have a growing family now, and they need a bit more space. Don't make any judgements just yet—wait until you see it…' He took her suitcase from the boot, then ushered her along a path that led around the side of the building, to a set of steps that led up to a first-floor doorway. He pulled his keys from his pocket, unlocking the door and standing back to let her step inside.

The curtains were drawn against the morning sun, and the place was fresh and cool. Wooden floors and neutral colours gave the feeling of even more space to an already huge area by English standards, which combined a kitchen and living room. Everything was neat and gleaming, and Allie could see none of the personal items that made a place look lived in.

'I've packed up my stuff and put it all in the spare bedroom.' Zac was hanging back, clearly waiting for Allie's verdict.

'You didn't need to do that…' Suddenly she was glad that he had. Accepting his offer to live here while she found her feet had seemed like a sensible thing to do, but Allie had already decided that finding her own space was her top priority. But staying here for a while didn't seem quite so challenging as she'd thought it might be.

'It's very quiet.'

Zac raised his eyebrows. 'You're expecting to have to fight your way through a throng of beach bums sipping beer to get to the front door? Mark and Naomi sell high-end surfing equipment so the place doesn't attract that crowd. You won't find them holding any midnight beach parties either, they have young children.'

'That's a relief. It seems really nice here.'

He smiled suddenly. 'You haven't seen the best part yet.' Leaving her suitcase by the open doorway, Zac strode across to the full-length curtains and pulled them back.

Allie caught her breath. There were sliding doors leading out onto a large shaded balcony, with chairs and a small table. And beyond that the sea, with views of a curving, wooded peninsular to one side. Suddenly the neutral tones of the room made absolute sense, because who needed colour and decoration inside when there was the animated beauty of the panorama outside?

'It's gorgeous, Zac!'

He nodded, seeming to relax a little. 'The view's actually better from upstairs. And it's never quite the same two days running.' Zac turned as a woman's voice sounded from the doorway.

'Knock, knock!'

'Hey Naomi. Come in.'

The woman standing in the doorway stepped inside. She was about Allie's age, with blonde hair and golden skin, and was carrying a baby in a brightly coloured wrap. A little girl of about four stood next to her, holding a large bunch of flowers.

'Hi.' Naomi grinned at Allie. 'We just popped in to say

hello and to welcome you.' Naomi let go of the little girl's hand, and she ran to Zac.

'Hey, Izzy.' He squatted down on his heels in front of the child, and she pushed the flowers into his hands. Zac chuckled, leaning towards her, speaking in a stage whisper. 'They're beautiful. But I don't think they're for me.'

Naomi chuckled. 'No, they're not, you can go and pick your own flowers, Zac. Izzy, give them to Allie.'

Izzy snatched the bunch of flowers back, and walked over to Allie. Despite the ache in her back, Allie bent down towards the little girl. 'Hey, are you Izzy? I'm Allie.'

'These are for you. Welcome to Australia.' Izzy proffered the bunch of flowers.

'Thank you, Izzy. They're so pretty.'

Izzy nodded. 'That one's waratah…' She pointed to the lavish, dark pink blooms, bound together with dark green foliage. 'I helped pick them.'

'You did? You chose such nice ones.' Allie smiled at Naomi. 'Thank you so much.'

'Waratah's the floral emblem of New South Wales.' Naomi gave her a bright smile back, beckoning to Izzy. 'We won't stay, you must be exhausted, but I just want you to know that if Zac's not around and there's something you need, my husband Mark or I are always downstairs during the day. Our house is at the top of the hill right behind here, so I hope you'll pop in for coffee some time.'

'Mark and Naomi's place is the one with the waratah bushes,' Zac interjected.

'Yep. And before I forget—Zac's lease is up in six weeks, but you're welcome to stay as long as you want after that. If you like the place we can sort out a lease, or if you'd prefer somewhere different feel free to stay on a weekly basis while you're looking round.'

'Thank you. That's really kind of you.' Allie was beginning to feel that her feet were really back on solid ground again. Naomi exchanged a wordless smile with Zac and Allie wondered whether he'd had something to do with the plan.

'It's our pleasure to have you here.' Naomi grabbed Izzy's hand. 'Zac, why don't you go and bother Mark in the workshop? I expect Allie wants some time to herself to settle in and catch some sleep.'

'No can do, I'm afraid. I said I'd pop in to the hospital for a couple of hours. If he's still there when I get back, I'll catch him then.'

'He'll be there, he's got a lot to do.' Naomi gave a smile and left them alone.

Allie was finally feeling that she was grinding to a halt. Zac had put the flowers in water, saying she could arrange them later, and carried her suitcase upstairs. The bedroom overlooking the sea had the same balcony and panoramic views, and it was cool enough to be able to sleep. Zac snapped the front door key from his keyring and handed it to her.

'Why don't you take it? You'll need to get back in again when you return from the hospital, won't you?'

'I won't disturb you. I'll be over in Mark's workshop if you want anything. Just put your head around the door downstairs and Naomi will point you in the right direction. Dinner at six?'

'That's fine. I just need to close my eyes for a few hours.'

Zac nodded. 'I'll leave you to it.'

He turned, walking downstairs, and Allie heard the front door close behind him, suddenly realising that she was breathing a sigh of relief. Alone. In a room that had been stripped of all his belongings, with just empty fitted wardrobes and freshly laundered sheets on the bed. And her fingers closing around the front door key, which meant she could let down her guard.

Did he know? Had he done all of this to give her some space and make her feel safe? Allie wasn't sure how she felt about that, or whether she should feel an echo of that humiliation she'd felt at the hospital in London, where everyone knew. She was too weary to even think about it.

Allie stumbled into the en suite shower room and then changed her mind. Sleep first. She closed the curtains, making sure that there were no chinks that allowed the outside world to intrude, then sat down on the bed, looking around her. There was a thumb turn for a bolt, under the handle of the door.

No. She was making a new start and she didn't need to do that. She should take off her clothes, lie down and sleep, like any other normal person. All the same, she walked over to the door, turning the stiff bolt back and forth a couple of times so that it engaged more easily, and then locked the door.

CHAPTER TWO

ZAC RETURNED TO the apartment at five o'clock to find that Allie was already showered and dressed, the flowers arranged neatly in a vase from under the sink. From the carrier bag that lay on the kitchen counter, she'd clearly ventured out for ten minutes to the newsagent.

'Anything happening?' He gestured towards the newspaper that was spread out on the breakfast bar.

'I can't tell. I'm not sure who all the people in the headlines are yet.' She smiled at him impishly. A few hours' sleep and she was clearly feeling a little more in charge of the situation, and Zac reckoned that might be exactly what she was aiming for.

'There's a place by the hospital where you can order the English papers if you want them.'

She shook her head. 'I'm in Australia now.'

Right. So she was serious about making a new start. *Really* serious—even Zac hadn't gone to those lengths. He supposed that it mattered what a person was trying to leave behind. His own demons had been intensely personal, but Allie's had been bound up with the hospital authorities and the courts, and ultimately the newspapers.

He prepared dinner and after they'd eaten Zac suggested they take a walk. Allie was interested in everything, questioning him about his life here and the things that she saw.

They talked and joked together, but the one thing that wasn't discussed was the thing most on his mind. The one thing that seemed to dictate everything she did.

Allie said that she was ready for an early night, and Zac sat downstairs, watching the moon rise across the sea, unable to stop himself from listening to the quiet sounds of her moving around upstairs. The almost imperceptible sound as the bolt turned on the bedroom door...

He tried not to take that personally, telling himself that Allie had probably bolted the door when she was alone in the apartment. What kind of humiliation led a person to even think of bolting the door to their bedroom, to give them the courage to lie down and sleep?

Zac sighed. He knew something about humiliation. He'd said nothing about his own parents' jibes when he was growing up, resorting to the safety of books in an attempt never to meet anyone's gaze. He'd found his own space, and now it was time to give Allie the space she needed.

After a restless night, Zac decided that getting up at six on a Saturday morning was preferable to staying in bed thinking about things he couldn't change. He'd weighed up all of the pros and cons—his suspicion that Allie wanted a fresh start and wouldn't be happy about anyone here knowing what had happened back in England, against the idea that she'd already been treated dishonestly and the first thing she needed from him was the truth, even if she didn't much like it.

Early Saturday mornings were usually spent putting in a couple of hours' surfing, but Mark had things to do today before he opened the shop. Zac couldn't work up much enthusiasm to go alone, so he made coffee and went out to the balcony, staring out over the deserted beach. When he heard movement in the kitchen and turned, he realised from the clock on the wall that he'd been sitting there for an hour.

'Good morning. How did you sleep?'

'Like a log. It's so quiet here.'

Yes, it was. If you kept the sliding doors that led out onto the balcony closed. Zac preferred to open them and fall asleep to the sound of the sea, but he supposed that was a small pleasure that Allie couldn't allow herself.

'Would you like some breakfast? There's bacon and eggs in the fridge, or toast…' Allie's slim figure was accentuated by the T-shirt and Bermuda shorts she wore this morning, and he could see that she'd lost weight.

'Bacon and eggs *and* toast? And coffee?'

He grinned. 'Coming right up.'

Setting to work, Zac filled two plates with eggs and bacon, and a third with toast, while Allie made the coffee. They sat at the breakfast bar and he realised that his appetite wasn't quite equal to the task in front of him, although Allie was tucking in hungrily.

'Will you be sorry to leave?' Allie pushed her plate away and picked up her coffee mug. 'You seem really settled here.'

Zac had thought about it. 'It's time I got back to London. I'm not looking forward to the winter, though.'

She nodded. 'You have things to do back home?'

He nodded. Zac had his reservations about going home but at the same time he needed to make that journey. When he'd left England he'd been looking for something that he now felt he'd found. Going back was the final step in re-claiming the man he'd become.

'Not quite. It's more…things to rediscover.'

She was clearly considering what that might mean. He should say what he had to say now, before worrying about it tore a hole in him. Try to reassure her that even if he couldn't completely understand what she'd been through, he'd fought his own battles, and he knew how tough it could be to leave the past behind.

'Allie, there's something I wanted to mention.' Now he *couldn't* go back…

She turned to him, a flash of alarm showing in her eyes. Suddenly she seemed very small and frail, and Zac wanted to reach out and protect her.

'It's just… These last two years have been good to me in a lot of ways. I had to get away and do some major re-assessment.' Just saying it was harder than he'd thought it would be.

'You seem different. More at home with yourself.'

It was nice that she'd noticed. And since he was about to tell Allie that he knew all about what had happened to her it was only fair to stop using generalisations about what had happened to him. He'd made up his mind that he was going to be honest, and so his next step should be obvious.

'I spent most of my childhood being bullied by my mother. My father as well, although he wasn't around much. My reaction to that ended up being my escape. I buried myself in my books and got to university.' Zac was staring at the grain of the wooden breakfast bar now, and with an effort he turned to meet Allie's gaze.

Her reaction hit him like a blow to the chest. Allie's eyes were dark and wide with shock, her cheeks flushed. And there was a look of not just concern, but real pain on her face.

'I'm so sorry, Zac. I wish…' She shrugged. 'I wish I'd known that you were going through something like that.'

He shook his head. 'I was determined that no one should ever know, or be able to reach me, and I'd had plenty of practice in keeping it a secret. Allie, I'm only telling you this because I've had a chance to make my peace with what happened while I've been here. I know what happened to you and...'

The expression on her face, and the way she seemed to shrink away from him without really moving, silenced Zac. Allie's cheeks were bright red now.

'I wondered if you'd heard. I suppose you're still in touch with friends at the hospital.' She seemed utterly miserable, suddenly.

'I guess I might have been if I'd been that close to anyone there. I was actually contacted by the police, and I had to go down to the station in Cronulla and answer questions from the investigating officers in London by video link.'

Her hand flew to her mouth. 'They thought you had something to do with it? That's crazy.'

'They had to speak to everyone who'd worked at the hospital. I'd only been gone for six months and presumably the whole thing had been going on for longer than that.'

'I meant...' She pressed her lips together. 'I would never have thought you'd be involved in something like that. Even if I have proved my judgement's not particularly sound at times.'

Two contrasting emotions almost knocked him from his seat. The rush of warm gratitude that Allie thought him incapable of the kind of crime that had hurt her so was followed by the chilling realisation that she thought that some failing on her part had contributed to what had happened to her.

'We're all capable of being deceived. And we're all capable of feeling ourselves to blame for things that aren't our fault.' He could attest to the latter.

She nodded, clearly not really believing him. 'Thanks.'

'Allie, all I want to say is that I know what it's like to

want to make a new start. It happened for me, and I believe it can happen for you. And... I just want to be honest with you and to make sure that you get whatever space you need right now.'

'Does anyone else know?' A tear rolled down her cheek, and she brushed it away impatiently.

'I haven't spoken of it to anyone. I didn't think it was my place to then, and it certainly isn't now. And no one's mentioned it to me in our discussions about the handover period.' Zac wondered if people here *did* know and they were just keeping quiet about it.

'I was going to hand my notice in, and my boss persuaded me to come here instead. He said that what had happened wouldn't be discussed with anyone here and even though I'd waived my anonymity to make a plea for people who might be affected to come forward...' She seemed to choke on the words, but Allie fanned her face with her hand, pressing on. 'It was some time ago. I doubt anyone will put two and two together.'

Clearly Allie was *hoping* they wouldn't. His own uncertainty, the worried examination of every conversation that he'd had with anyone for the last two weeks, was something that Allie had been living with for a long time now. It felt as if he was peeling off the layers, finding a different possibility for hurt in every one.

'I'm sure you're right. The exchange programme is intended to share medical expertise, and in my experience there's no interaction concerning anything else. It's for you to decide who knows what.'

That was clearly something of a relief to Allie and she reached across and took his hand. 'Zac, I really appreciate... everything. I don't quite know what to say...'

'Nothing's always an option. You could always leave it at that until you do have something to say.'

Happiness was beginning to eat away at all of Zac's uncertainty, all of his fears about going too far, or maybe not far enough. All he needed right now was to feel her hand in his.

Allie gave a teary smile, squeezing his fingers. 'That's a really good thought, Zac. Shall we take our coffee out onto the balcony and decide what to do today?'

There was always something not to like, even in the most perfect housemate. Allie had had her share of navigating those waters when she'd first gone to London to study, and when she'd finally been able to put a deposit down on her own place it had been heaven. Going home, shutting the door and being able to just exist in her own environment.

She was still looking for the thing not to like in Zac. He was easygoing, he'd given her a room to call her own and he was a great cook. And he'd set out the terms of their relationship right from the start. He'd told her that he knew about what had happened to her back in England, and even thrown in a little of his own experience, so that she didn't feel too much like a project in vulnerability. Back in the day, when she had a full social schedule she'd appreciated the solitary refuge of her own home at times, but Zac seemed like that one in a million that you'd actually want to come home to.

And he was horribly easy on the eye as well. When she'd come downstairs this morning and seen him sitting on the balcony, an exercise in relaxed harmony with the world around him, she'd caught her breath.

There had been a time she'd know just what to do about that. Get to know Zac again, find out all the ways in which he'd changed and see where that led them. Allie knew just what to do now too. Stay away, because absolute trust was far too great a gift to risk giving anyone.

But it was the weekend, she was in a new place and she could go as far as enjoying his company. A supermarket for the weekly shop wasn't the most enticing of venues but Zac had said that his stocks of fresh food were running low.

Their first stop was at a small market that dealt in tropical fruits. Allie chose dragon fruit, because she'd never tried it before, and they came away with several paper bags filled with the kinds of things you'd never see in the shops at home. The supermarket had a more familiar range of foodstuffs, but Zac seemed to be in no particular hurry, dawdling after her with the trolley as Allie inspected everything carefully.

'Why did you get that one?' He'd thrown a packet of breakfast cereal into the trolley.

Zac shrugged. 'It's the one I always get. I used to eat it back in England.'

Allie inspected an unfamiliar brand. 'This one's got raisins and less sugar. I might try it.'

He grinned, removing his own purchase from the trolley. 'I'll join you then. It would be a shame to leave without having tried the full gamut of Australian breakfast cereals.'

He was joking, and Allie smiled with him. If different brands and unfamiliar fruit were about as far as she was prepared to go in terms of trying new things right now, then at least they might get her into the habit.

'What made you come to live here?' The place seemed to suit him so well, but she couldn't quite imagine the old Zac fitting in so seamlessly.

'I was living in hospital accommodation for starters—I dare say they offered you a room?'

Allie nodded. She'd weighed it up against Zac's offer and

reckoned that the risk of living with one person she knew was probably less than that of sharing accommodation with a group of strangers.

'The hospital units are nice, but I can't really recommend it long-term. I was desperate to get a place of my own, so I made up a checklist and started touring around the different neighbourhoods in Sydney. There are a lot of great places that are closer to the centre of the city, and ex-pats tend to gravitate there because there's plenty to do and a thriving nightlife. Places like The Rocks or the North Shore.'

'I'm not really looking for nightlife at the moment.' Two years ago Allie would have been spending her free time making new friends and seeing new places. Now, she just wanted somewhere to escape the incessant chatter, and the constant worry that some of it might be about her.

'Yeah, they didn't tick all of my boxes. Cronulla's quieter, a bit more relaxed and more residential. It's considered quite a long commute into the centre of Sydney so a lot of people who live here work locally. When I came here I made a detour through the Royal National Park, and then drove down to the beach and took a walk. That was enough to fall in love with the place, and I went to the real estate agent and got a list, then came down the next weekend to take a look around. I saw the rental sign up at the surf shop downstairs and popped in to ask about it, just for comparison's sake really.'

'And you ended up taking it?'

Zac smiled, reaching for some gravy browning, and then put the packet back onto the shelf, waiting for Allie to choose.

'Naomi showed me the apartment, and I really liked it. There's such a great connection with the outside...' He glanced at her, and Allie nodded. She knew what he meant;

the barrier between outside and inside didn't seem to exist. That had made her very grateful for the comfort factor of closely woven curtains in her bedroom.

'I asked what they wanted for the place, so Naomi left Mark to deal with the customers and collected up Izzy and we went down onto the beach to talk terms.' Zac grinned. 'Apparently I passed the Izzy test.'

It made sense that one of Naomi's first priorities would be to find someone who'd be child-friendly, and Zac's quiet, gentle nature would have been in his favour.

'What was the Izzy test?'

'I make good sandcastles. The moat cinched the deal; Izzy loved it. And Naomi made me an offer I couldn't refuse.'

'Which was…?' From the look on Zac's face, Allie reckoned she wasn't going to manage to guess it.

'She threw in a paddleboard. She said that I couldn't live so close to the sea without having some kind of beach equipment and guessed—quite rightly—that I hadn't brought anything of the sort with me from London. The morning after I moved in, she appeared at the front door and told me that we were going down onto the beach to try it out.'

Allie laughed. 'That's nice.'

'Yeah. It wasn't so nice when I fell off it for the fourth time, but I got the hang of it. That was what prompted me to try surfing. At this time on a Saturday morning, the beach is usually beginning to fill up and Mark and I are sitting outside the shop drinking coffee, after a couple of hours out catching waves.'

'I thought you said that the shop didn't attract any rowdy elements?' Allie smiled up at him and Zac chuckled.

'I'll be back in London soon, so it's not an ongoing problem…'

They called in at the shop after they'd put the shopping

away, and Allie was introduced to Mark, who shook her hand and asked her if she could swim. Zac waved him away laughingly.

'Give Allie a chance to get her feet back on the ground before you try to get her onto the water, eh?'

'I can swim.' Allie exchanged a smile with Naomi.

'I can swim too!' Izzy declared, tugging at the hem of Zac's T-shirt, clearly wanting to be included in the conversation. Zac lifted her up and she wrapped her arms around his neck, clearly happy to be on the same level as the adults.

'Yeah, you're a mermaid, aren't you? Your mum says that you swam before you could walk.'

Naomi chuckled. 'Yes, she could. And before Mark notices that you've admitted to being able to swim, Allie, I'm going to make a cup of tea. It's time for a break, we've been busy this morning.'

'I showed a man a surfboard.' Izzy piped up.

Mark smiled. 'Yeah, that's the ticket, Iz. He wanted a tin of wax, but I expect he'll keep your choice of boards in mind for the future.'

'I'll leave you here to help Dad, then.' Naomi jerked her thumb towards the baby bouncer. 'Zac, you take Finn outside and find a place in the shade, and I'll make the tea.'

CHAPTER THREE

JUST AS ZAC was beginning to think that Allie was beginning to relax and settle into watching the world go by from the small shaded area in front of the shop, the call came. Bad timing. But then the timing was infinitely worse for the people who'd been involved in the accident...

'I'm sorry...' He drained the last dregs from his cup and then got to his feet. 'Got to go to the hospital. There's an emergency.'

'One of your patients?' Allie gave him a questioning look.

'No, there's been a bus accident. There are a lot of people coming in to the ED—that's A&E—and they need some help to deal with everyone.'

'I'll come.' Before Zac could shake his head in reply, Allie stood up.

'Are you...officially on the staff?' He wondered what the position was with that, and guessed that Allie might find herself sitting waiting for someone to sort the necessary paperwork out before she was allowed to see any patients.

'As of last week. I signed everything, and video-conferenced with HR before I came.'

'Really?' Zac's eyebrows shot up.

'Allie's just told you, Zac.' Naomi frowned at him. 'Will you go already?'

Fair enough. Naomi was less protective of Allie than he

was, and maybe he should stop treating her as if she was about to break into small pieces. She might be vulnerable, but she'd showed a lot of strength too.

'You're a lot more efficient than I was.' He murmured the words as he backed the car out of its parking spot, and Allie gave a grim chuckle.

'Not really. I did it so that I wouldn't chicken out of getting on the plane at the last minute...'

Allie hardly looked around her as they hurried into the hospital and through to the Emergency Department. She'd clearly retained the same focus when it came to her work, and Zac privately admonished himself for wondering if that would be the case. There was no way that the hospital in London would have allowed her to come here if her work had suffered.

He steered her over to where Beth Kramer, the head of the ED, was directing everyone to the right place, keeping the atmosphere busy but calm. She smiled when she saw Zac, beckoning him over.

'Thanks for coming, Zac.'

'No worries. This is Dr Allie Maitland-Hill, she's my replacement from London.'

'Are you officially employed here yet, Allie?' Beth dispensed with the introductions and got straight to the point.

'I signed everything and spoke with HR—Joe Simmons,' Allie replied.

'Okay, I'll have to give him a quick call at home, just to make sure everything's in order. You understand...?'

'Of course. I just want to help if I can.'

'Great. Over your jet lag?'

'I'm fine.' Allie's firm answers seemed to reassure Beth, and she nodded.

'And your specialty?'

'Paediatrics, the same as Zac.'

'Good. Zac will sort you out with some scrubs and anything else you need.' Beth glanced at him and Zac nodded compliantly. 'By the time you're ready I'll have spoken to Joe, just to make sure there's nothing outstanding, but I'd like you to work with Zac this afternoon if you would. I have no doubts about your abilities—'

'Thanks.' Allie waved away Beth's explanations. 'Since I'm new, I'll need someone to tell me how everything works here.'

By the time they returned, Allie wearing a set of scrubs that one of the admin staff had found for her, Beth had everything sorted. She beckoned to an ambulance crew who had just arrived, pointing to one of the cubicles and murmuring to Zac to, 'Get on with it, then.'

As he led Allie to the door of the cubicle she grinned at him, almost stopping him in his tracks. There she was. The old Allie, who met every challenge head-on and did her absolute best for every one of her patients. He'd watched her from afar, back in London, admiring her confidence and her ability to connect with people. She was no different now, and he shouldn't assume that she was vulnerable in every area of her life.

'Don't take it personally that Beth wanted you to work with me...' He stopped by the door of the cubicle as the ambos wheeled their patient towards them.

'Why should I? She's just being sensible. Medicine's medicine, but I was told to expect a few differences in admin and procedures here.'

Zac nodded. He'd reckoned that her first day might cover those, but since Allie was being thrown in at the deep end here, there wasn't much opportunity for that.

'I'll stick to the admin and procedures then. Let you get on with the medicine?'

The amused look in her eyes made his stomach lurch. Something that resembled the normal interplay between a gorgeously attractive woman and a rather starstruck man. 'You can help with the medicine if you like.'

He chuckled. 'Okay, thanks.'

The ambos wheeled the trolley bed into the cubicle, and quickly gave Zac a status report on their patient. He'd been travelling with his mother, who had also been injured, and had been brought here. It looked as if she'd broken her jaw, so they couldn't get any information about the child from her, but he'd told them his name was Billy and that he was five years old. They suspected concussion and a broken ankle. Billy had become increasingly drowsy in the ambulance, but had initially been complaining that his head hurt, and he seemed bothered by the light.

'Where do you want me?' Allie would understand this was a vote of confidence. Zac didn't make gestures that might compromise the welfare of a patient.

'You take his leg. I'll see if I can rouse him and check on his reactions.'

Zac nodded. Good choice. If the boy was going to respond to anyone's smile it would be Allie's. He set about carefully removing the temporary support that the ambulance paramedic had placed around the boy's leg.

'What do you see, Zac?'

'I think the ankle's fractured, but the skin's not broken and it doesn't feel displaced. Should be reasonably straightforward. You?'

Allie puffed out a breath. 'I don't know. Something's wrong…'

Zac glanced at her. 'You think he may have sustained

a TBI?' Traumatic Brain Injury was always something to watch for after an accident, and in a bus the passengers might well have been thrown around.

'Maybe… I don't know. I don't see any signs of injury to his head, and his pupils aren't dilated, even though he seems drowsy and unresponsive.' She puffed out a breath and then seemed to come to a decision. 'Zac, is his leg all right for the moment? I think we should order a CT scan, but I'd really like to just see if it is possible to get any more information from the mother.'

'Sure. I'll put the scan into motion. There's a board by the nurses' station that shows who's in which cubicle, or you can ask Beth. She always knows exactly what's happening.'

'Great, thanks.' Allie hurried from the room and Zac pulled his phone from his pocket, to check on how soon Billy could be sent for a CT scan.

She was gone for a while, and Zac was about to call a nurse to see if they could find her when Allie reappeared in the doorway.

'Where have you been?'

'In the next-door cubicle. The mother's jaw is definitely broken, and I had to ask yes and no questions. But it seems that Billy was sick before the crash. The nurse with her said that the bus that crashed goes straight past the hospital. She was bringing him here to see a doctor.'

'So…' Zac thought quickly. 'He's pale, difficult to wake, the ambos said he was complaining of a headache and seemed photosensitive.'

'A rash…?' Allie beat him to the next question and Zac nodded.

Carefully they sat Billy up, taking off his T-shirt and examining his skin. 'Here… Look.' Allie lifted Billy's arm, and Zac saw a group of red pinpricks on the boy's side.

'You were right. This looks like meningitis.'

'So we'll do a blood test and get ready to start him on fluids and broad-spectrum antibiotics?'

'Yes—I won't cancel the scan, there's still a chance he may have bumped his head in the crash, and it would be good to check that the infection hasn't caused any swelling around the brain.' Allie was nodding in agreement and Zac smiled. It was always good to find a doctor who seemed in tune with his own thoughts, and when that doctor was Allie it felt even better.

'Shall I go and see if I can get more details from the mother? I think if I give her a pen she may be able to write her answers down.'

'Sounds good. Could you ask Beth to find a nurse and send her in, please?'

'Will do...'

It had been a busy afternoon. Billy's mother had refused any treatment other than analgesics until she'd told the doctors all she knew about Billy's condition before they'd arrived at the hospital, and Allie had spent a while at her bedside, gathering information from her. Zac had stayed with Billy, monitoring him carefully and expediting his treatment, until he was transferred to the children's ward.

He joined Allie at Billy's mum's bedside, and was able to reassure her that Billy was having treatment and seemed to be responding well. Only then had she allowed her own doctors to come anywhere near her, and Zac had practically had to drag Allie from the room as a nurse sat down beside her bed, taking her hand.

Then there were cuts and bruises, sprains and a broken wrist, as the doctors worked their way through the patients with less serious injuries.

Beth appeared in the doorway of the cubicle. 'Time to go home, people. I can't thank you enough, but we've got this now. Get lost, both of you.' She turned to Allie. 'Good to meet you, Allie. I hope I have an opportunity to work with you again.'

As Beth abruptly turned away, already focused on the next thing she had to do, Zac nudged Allie. 'That's about the highest praise you'll ever get from Beth, you know.'

Allie smiled up at him. 'I got that. I'm feeling it.'

She'd shown no sign of fatigue all afternoon, but as they walked out of the hospital together Allie seemed to tire suddenly. She sat in the passenger seat of the car, her eyes closed, and when they reached the apartment she fell asleep on the sofa.

When Zac prepared something to eat, and gently touched her shoulder to wake her, she sat up with a start. He pretended not to notice, and fetched the plates of sandwiches and fruit from the kitchen, setting them down on the coffee table.

Allie leaned over, inspecting the fruit. 'This is the dragon fruit?'

Zac nodded. 'Try it.'

She reached out, picking up one of the chunks of fruit and inspecting it carefully and then taking the tiniest of bites. This was a world away from the confident doctor who was able to think outside of the box and make a diagnosis that went against everything that the situation seemed to suggest.

'What do you think?'

'I'm…not sure. Perhaps it's an acquired taste.'

'Yeah, I guess so. Would you like some tea?'

'Some of the herbal tea we got this morning would be nice, thanks.' She seemed suddenly listless, staring at the sandwiches as if she was wondering what to do with them. Zac knew she must be hungry, they hadn't eaten since breakfast.

But when he returned with the tea she seemed to have rallied and had picked up a plate and was tucking into the food.

He sat down, taking a sandwich from the pile. 'Bit much to ask, really. You've only been in the country for thirty-six hours.' He floated the idea.

'It was good. I don't do time off all that well these days. I like to keep busy.'

Keeping busy until she dropped, in the hope that she wouldn't have nightmares? Zac decided not to suggest the idea. 'If you want to keep busy, I'm going to call Mark and see if he's going to catch some waves first thing tomorrow. I could always bring the paddleboard along, in case you decide to try it out.'

She seemed to be turning the idea over in her head. 'What time?'

'Just get up whenever you wake, and look out of the window. If we're there and you feel like it then come down and join us.'

'You make it sound so simple.'

Sometimes things *were* simple. He'd been agonising over his motives—whether his protectiveness towards Allie was strictly down to his horror at what had happened to her, or whether he was beginning to care for her on a completely different level. The two could co-exist—quite separately—as long as he concentrated on acting on the first, and ignoring the second. Allie needed a friend, and wanting to become a lover felt as if it was a betrayal.

'You're very quiet.' He felt her elbow nudge at his ribs. This easy friendship that was developing between them suddenly seemed far too precious to put at risk by wanting more.

'Yeah. I guess I'm tired too. Early night, I reckon.'
Allie stifled a yawn. 'Sounds like a plan.'

Maybe it was sheer fatigue and jet lag. Maybe that she just
felt safe here. But Allie had only woken with a start once
during the night, and even then she'd managed to relax and
go back to sleep. When the first strands of light began to
filter through the curtains she got out of bed, showering
and dressing before she let the morning in by drawing the
thick drapes back.

She could see two figures on the beach, one dark-haired
and dark-skinned, the other sun-blond and golden. Mark and
Zac both wore board shorts with short-sleeved rash vests,
which she'd seen on sale in the shop and were designed to
protect them from sun and water. And she couldn't take
her eyes off Zac.

Watching while he didn't know it. More precisely, *ogling*
while he didn't know it. Her first instinct was to turn away,
but something about the way he moved, the way that he
seemed so confident and at home in his own skin made her
open the sliding doors and step out onto the balcony. Zac
was on the beach and he didn't care who saw him. Maybe
he didn't much care that the thoughts running through her
head at the moment centred largely on how it might feel to
touch his golden skin.

All the same she waved, calling to him to announce her
presence. Her voice must have been drowned in the crash
of the ocean, but something made him turn and he lifted his
arm, waving back. This she was allowed to enjoy. An innocent wave and a smile, with hundreds of metres of clear
space between them. Even if it did feel wholly intimate.

He was walking up the beach now, leaving Mark behind

with the surfboards. Moments of sheer pleasure, when she had every reason to watch every move he made.

You could give a girl a break, Zac. Walk a little slower.

'Are you coming down?' He'd reached the empty road that separated the surf shop from the beach.

'I can see from here.' All she really *wanted* to see, anyway. Surfing she could take or leave.

'Fair enough.' He began to turn away and Allie's heart sank. Maybe being out on the beach, where it was natural to want to feel the sun on your skin and for people to watch each other, wasn't so confronting at this time in the morning. Maybe being with Zac would mean that the feeling of freedom, which seemed to leak out of him, would rub off on her.

Then he turned back. Walking across the road, he came to stand under the balcony, the sun shining in his hair. 'You don't want to go paddleboarding?'

She did, but there was one problem. 'What do I wear?'

'As long as you're comfortable and you don't mind getting a bit splashed, you can wear your best dress. What you have on will be fine.' He gestured towards her shorts and T-shirt. 'Sunglasses probably, and plenty of sunscreen...'

'I thought you said you fell in four times on your first go.'

'Yeah, I did. But I'm not Naomi, I don't think it's funny to rock the board and tip the newbie into the water. And I've borrowed her lifejacket, just in case.'

'In case of what?' Allie was already going paddleboarding, but having Zac persuade her to join him was just too delicious for words.

'Uh... We get a few giant squid around these beaches at this time of year. They'll swallow you in one but they don't like the taste of neoprene, so they might throw you back in if you're wearing a life jacket.' Somehow Zac managed to keep a straight face, and Allie nodded sagely.

'Okay, that sounds like a good precaution.'

'It's a lot safer here than jumping into the Thames...' This time he did betray a smile. He must remember the day when the group of newly qualified doctors had jumped into the Thames in fancy dress to raise money for charity. The scheme hadn't been as reckless as it sounded, they'd chosen their spot and taken precautions against infection, and Allie had thrown herself into the water with joyous gusto.

'I didn't see you there...'

'No, that's because I wasn't. I'm not quite as adventurous as you.'

Zac was clearly beginning to get what so few others did. That *being* hurt and anxious didn't make her a hurt and anxious person. He didn't have the air of someone who was stepping on eggshells around her, and Allie was grateful for that.

'Okay, you're on. Give me ten minutes to get my sunscreen and stilettos on.'

He laughed. 'No stilettos. I'll go and inflate the board.'

Allie would have liked to have watched him walk back down onto the beach again. Compare the back view with the front. But she was too eager for the beach herself, and she hurried inside to grab her sunscreen from the en suite bathroom.

CHAPTER FOUR

THE AIR WAS fresh and warm, the ever-present breeze from the sea ruffling her hair. A perfect morning for the beach, but then Allie imagined that there were a lot of perfect mornings for the beach here. Mark was looking thoughtfully out to sea and Zac had taken the paddleboard further up the beach, to where the water seemed a bit calmer.

'Hey, Allie. Ready for your first dip?'

'Zac said I wouldn't be getting my hair wet.' Allie grinned back at him.

'Right then. I'm sure you won't.'

Allie wrinkled her nose. 'Don't try to put me off, it's not going to work. Can't we do it here?'

Mark shrugged. 'You could, but it's a bit choppy for a first outing. The first really good beach break of the summer has formed just here, you see it?' He indicated the line of higher waves, which crashed onto the shore.

'They move?'

'Yeah, the sandbanks shift, and they may last a few days, or maybe a week.'

'So the same beach can be different?'

Mark nodded. 'That's why I like it. Zac's shifted up a bit to get out of my road.'

Allie was beginning to feel guilty about that. 'Am I keeping him from this...uh...?'

'Good beach break?' Mark supplied the correct terminology. 'No, you're not. Well, you are, but it appears that Zac would rather be paddleboarding this morning.'

That sounded as if Zac found her company preferable to the waves that Mark found so absorbing. But since Mark's attention was back out to sea, she probably wasn't going to get a solid answer out of him. Allie contented herself with letting the idea form and roll around in her head for a moment.

'I'd better go and see what he's up to then.'

'Uh huh…' Mark was still engrossed in the waves. 'Oh, don't forget the life jacket, it's in my bag. The pink one.'

'Okay. Thanks.' Allie left him to his deliberations, finding a fuchsia-pink lifejacket in Mark's bag and then walking along the beach towards Zac.

'It's bigger than I thought it would be.' Allie surveyed the board.

'This is a two-person board, it's Mark and Naomi's. They take Izzy out on it. Ready to go?'

'Definitely. How do I get on?'

'Just follow me…' Zac picked up the board, walking down to the shore with it, while Allie followed, trying not to think about strong shoulders. She liked strong shoulders on a man, and she liked Zac as well. Coupled with a sunny morning and a crystal ocean, this was getting to be a perfect storm of enjoyment.

Walking out into the water, he stopped when they were knee-deep and set the board down, showing her how to get on to the front of the board and then sit down. That was easy enough, and Allie felt the board dip a little under his weight as he got on behind her. The board started to move forward as Zac paddled away from the shore. Further along the beach, Allie could see Mark, carrying his surfboard into the water.

'You want to stop and see how he does?'

'With the beach break?' Allie decided to show off her latest piece of jargon. 'Yes please.'

Zac chuckled, sitting down on one side of the board, his legs dangling in the water. Allie shifted carefully around to sit next to him.

'See, he's paddled out, and he's ready to catch the next wave. If he gets it right...' Allie saw Mark gain his footing on the board, travelling fast across its peak, and then suddenly he and the board parted company and Zac let out a groan.

'Where is he? I can't see him...'

'He's okay. There, look.' Zac pointed to where Mark was swimming strongly for the beach, the board towed behind him.

'He's going to try again?'

'What do you think? He'll try until he gets it right.'

'So this is what you do out here in the mornings. Falling off your boards until you get it right?'

'More or less. I'm not as good as Mark is, so I've been known to give up on the tricky ones. Mark just keeps going.'

'The waves aren't quite as big as I thought they'd be.'

Zac raised his eyebrows, laughing. 'It's not always a matter of size. What Mark's doing isn't easy.'

Mark was paddling back out again, and they both watched intently. This time he stayed on his board, riding the wave for its full length. Zac let out a *'Yes'* under his breath.

'Don't you want to go and try it? Mark said that this sandbank was new.'

He turned suddenly, looking at her, so much warmth in his eyes that it made Allie shiver. 'No, I'd rather be here.'

'But…' The words died, strangled by the lump in her throat. His eyes were as blue as the sea and far more inviting. In that moment, everything that a man and a woman could possibly do together seemed just a word away.

A word that she was too afraid to say. What if all the things that had been taken from her couldn't be claimed back again? Those private moments that had been shared with the world felt irretrievably spoiled. If she tried to experience them again with Zac, would she just relive the humiliation? Would that humiliation be all that he saw if she let him make love to her?

Zac was looking at her speculatively now. 'You want to give paddling a go?'

'It is a paddleboard. It wouldn't be right to come all the way out here without at least trying it out.' Allie breathed a sigh that hovered somewhere between disappointment and relief. This would be a lot easier to handle than staring into his eyes and all of the promise they held.

'Right then. First thing to remember is, whatever you do don't drop the paddle.'

'Okay. That's straightforward. Do I have to stand up?' The gentle rock of the board was soothing when she was sitting down, but if she was on her feet it might be a little more tricky.

'No, that's somewhere around lesson four. You can start off by just kneeling, like this…' He carefully moved to demonstrate, showing her how to move the paddle.

'Okay. I can do that. Let me try…'

Allie *had* dropped the paddle, when she'd become a little too enthusiastic and lost her balance, almost falling off the board. Zac's arm had coiled around her waist, steadying her, but before she'd had a chance to shiver at the deliciousness of feeling him so close he'd drawn back again and slipped into the water, swimming to recover the paddle before it was borne away by the waves.

'Try again.' He climbed back onto the board. Zac wasn't afraid to push her, to encourage her to try something one more time and get it right.

'Like this?' Allie tried again and this time something clicked into place and the movement felt right.

'Yes, exactly like that. That's great. Do you want to take us back to the beach, or are you getting tired?'

Allie's fingers curled tightly around the paddle. 'I'm not tired. Show me how to get us back.' She'd achieved something this morning, and it was the first time in a long time that her battles hadn't been all about simply getting through the day. She wasn't going to give up now.

'Okay, it's easy. Let the movement of the waves do all the hard work, and concentrate on steering...'

It had turned into a good day. No—a great day. Zac was beginning to get a feel for where he should back off and when he should push Allie, and something had clicked between them. A kind of closeness which felt right. Just as long as he didn't think too much about where it might lead.

But there hadn't been too much opportunity for thinking. Naomi had joined them on the beach with Izzy and Finn, and Mark had gone back to the shop to open up. Weekends were their busiest time, and when Naomi had seen three cars draw up in the forecourt she'd left Izzy with them on the beach and taken Finn back up with her to help Mark.

'How do you feel about a trip up to the Royal National Park this afternoon?' Izzy had finally managed to expend enough energy to tire her out, and Naomi had taken her and

Finn home for lunch and a quiet time. 'There's a nice little pizza place on the way.'

'Sounds good. Is it cool?' As the beach had filled up, the sun had been climbing in the sky and this afternoon promised to be hot.

'You get air-con with your pizza and…' He shrugged. 'Forests are pretty shady places.'

Allie grinned at him. 'What are we waiting for?'

They'd eaten and then driven to the edge of a thickly wooded area of the park. Zac had stopped the car, letting Allie choose one of the paths that wound into the thickly forested valley floor. She set off, clearly keen to explore.

They wound their way past tall trees and the giant leaves of lush plants, all of which had been unfamiliar to Zac when he'd arrived here. He'd wanted to bring her here because the giant proportions of this place never failed to instil a sense of peace.

'These plants…' Allie was looking around her, drinking everything in. 'They're so big. It's how I imagine a prehistoric forest might be.'

'It's pretty impressive, isn't it.'

'Wonderful. It makes me feel very small. The ocean and this forest.'

'There's more than just forest here. There are lakes, coastal areas and mangroves, along with rocky plateaus on higher ground. I'm not sure you ever could see it all.'

This was a start, though. They walked for a while under the high canopy of the trees, slowly falling under the spell of a world that was far removed from their everyday lives.

'Do you mind…if I ask you something? I'm not expecting an answer.' Allie had seemed deep in thought and suddenly she looked up at him.

Zac thought he knew what the question was, and fully expected to answer. 'Sure. Go ahead.'

'You seem… You *have* changed from the person I knew in London.' She smiled up at him. 'How did you make that journey?'

He could see why the answer would be important to Allie. It was important to him as well. There had been hints and scraps of information dropped along the way to one person or another, but Zac wasn't sure he'd ever said it all in one go.

'Bit of a long story.'

'This seems like a place for a long story. If you want to tell it.'

Yeah. Suddenly he wanted to tell it very badly.

'My parents were…different. My father was a pilot and he was away from home a lot. I suspect he didn't make much effort to change that state of affairs. My mother stayed home and…she kept the place immaculate. No mess, nothing out of place. Now I know that she was exhibiting signs of an obsessive disorder, but when I was a child all I knew was that the house was cold and pretty scary.'

'Scary?'

'I got very good at staying under the radar. If I made a mess or damaged anything then I was punished for it. She locked me in my room for two consecutive weekends once, because I'd been ambushed by a gang of kids from my school, who smeared some mud onto my uniform.'

'Zac, I wish I'd realised. I'm so sorry.' He felt her fingers graze his arm as Allie reached out to him.

'I know that you spoke out about what happened to you, and I admire your courage. I never did that, even as a child. I knew that my way out was to study and get to university and when I left home I thought that I was finally free. Of course things don't quite work out that way. As you know.'

'Yeah.' Allie shot him a wry smile. 'You can't walk away from yourself.'

'Sometimes a bit of space gives you perspective, though. I went for therapy—probably not enough, but it helped me make a start. I still didn't know how to reach out to the people around me, but I'd at least come to the conclusion that I wanted to live my life differently.'

'Are you in touch with your parents now?'

'There was a fire in the house, when I was in my second year of university. They must have gone to bed and, although the fire never spread upstairs, they both died in their sleep from smoke inhalation.'

'That must have been so hard for you, to lose them like that.'

'It was…confusing.' The complex set of emotions around his parents' death rolled over him, almost as if he was feeling it for the first time. When he looked down at Allie, he saw tears in her eyes. Before Zac could stop himself, with a reminder that this was risky, he'd taken her hand in his.

'Sorry…sorry.' Allie wiped her face with her other hand. 'It should be you that's upset, not me.'

'Don't be, I appreciate the sentiment. At the funeral…' He shook his head, trying to make sense of a day when he should have cried but all he could feel was numb anger and despair.

'You were on your own?'

He shook his head. 'My parents did have family, but they never spoke about them. I only found out about my uncles and aunts by looking them up on a genealogy website. But I reckoned they had a right to know what had happened, and I managed to track them down. Two of my aunts came, the others didn't want to. And one of my tutors from university turned up as well, with his wife. It was a nice gesture.

Everyone said all of the right words, how sorry they were, but no one cried.'

Suddenly, Allie reached out and hugged him. She stepped back again immediately, before he could even return the hug, but Zac knew how careful she was of her own space and how much it had cost her. When he'd reached out to stop her from falling off the paddleboard, he'd felt her instinctively flinch.

'I've left most of that behind now.'

Allie looked up at him. 'Not all of it, though?'

There was one thing he'd never spoken to anyone about. But those few brief moments when he'd felt Allie's arms around him had torn down the defences that shielded the most hurtful secret, and now he couldn't hold it back.

'I've never quite been able to come to terms with the broken promises. My mother's idea of punishment was to take things I wanted away from me. If I did something wrong at the dinner table she'd grab my plate and empty my food into the bin. Or I'd be promised something for Christmas and never get it because of something I'd done.' Zac felt a shiver run through him, as if he was physically trying to drive the memories away.

'That's…not something I'd be able to come to terms with either. Every kid has to believe that they have something that's theirs, which no one can take away.'

Every adult too. Zac had made a rational decision that the abuse that Allie had suffered meant he shouldn't act on the attraction he felt for her. But in a world where anything could be withdrawn, becoming too close to her would also mean he had to face the possibility of losing her.

Not at this moment, though. She'd slipped her hand into the crook of his arm, anchoring him down in a present that could escape the past, and allow the future to look after itself.

'Things are different now...better. I've made a lot of changes in my life.'

She nodded. 'I see them. And you're ready to go home?'

'Yeah. It's important to me to join the pieces of my life back together again—the person who left England and the one who goes back there. Revisit things and places back home and... Does regaining it all on my own terms make sense?'

'I can identify with that.' Allie chuckled. 'Are you still in contact with your aunts?'

'Yeah. We've been exchanging emails and a few video calls. I'm actually really looking forward to seeing them. I'm not quite sure what to expect, but it would be nice to build some kind of relationship.'

She'd understood all that he'd said to her. Being able to explain it all was getting it straight in Zac's head too.

'I really hope you can. It's nice to feel that going back might be a positive step that's in my future somewhere.'

'I'm sorry. I'm talking about my baggage, and that's all in the past now.' Zac had done so in an attempt to be honest and to let Allie know that it was okay for her to talk, but it had turned into something more. Something precious that he felt he could keep.

'You prefer mine?' She smiled sweetly up at him. 'I thought that was one of the things I liked about you, Zac. That you see me first as a person, and only second as someone who's been abused.'

He shrugged. 'That's the way I'd like to be seen.'

The answer obviously pleased her. 'So let's address a more immediate concern, shall we? Do you have any idea about how to get back to the car, or are we going to have to stay here all night and forage for roots to eat for breakfast?'

Zac grinned, pulling out his keyring and flipping the

cover on the tiny compass that hung from it. They'd strayed away from the path while they'd been talking and he'd lost his bearings as well.

'That way.'

She followed the line of his pointing finger, along a narrow, overgrown pathway. Zac had to admit that it didn't look the most promising way to go.

'Okay, we'll give it a try. What's the worst that can happen?'

CHAPTER FIVE

ZAC HAD TO admit to feeling nervous about Allie's first day at work. Not that he doubted she could handle it, but caring about someone brought with it the ability to be nervous on their behalf. Allie seemed to have picked up on his reaction and was exuding confidence.

She'd dressed for success. A plain cream-coloured blouse and skirt, the blouse embellished with rows of buttons at each cuff and a double buttoned fastening at the front, which gave it a unique look. Heels that were just low enough to be comfortable, a little make-up and shining dark curls. The judgement of anyone who failed to be impressed by her might rightly be questioned, and Zac privately added his own, more subjective opinion. She might be laughing on the beach or ready for a business meeting, but Allie was always the most beautiful woman he'd ever seen.

He parked in the hospital car park, and they went their separate ways. Zac wondered whether he should have wished her good luck, but doubted very much that Allie would need luck. All the same, he contrived to think about her and wonder what she was doing for most of the day.

They met back at his car after work, Allie looking as fresh and excited as when they'd parted that morning. The only difference was that when she got into the passenger seat she bent down and removed her shoes.

'Been on your feet all day?'

'Not all day. But these shoes are new, I'll have to wear something a bit more comfortable tomorrow. I got the full tour of the hospital though.'

'And…?'

'It's amazing what you can do with a little more space than we have available in London. And good people, of course. Along with good facilities and a little thought.' She grinned suddenly. 'Great patients.'

That was Allie all over. She never forgot that the patient was at the centre of everything she did, and when he'd come in contact with her in London Zac had been impressed with the way that she seemed to approach each patient with a greater than usual knowledge of who they were and the things they cared about, in addition to knowing what was wrong with them.

'So you're ready to start work in earnest tomorrow?' Zac was already looking forward to seeing a little more of her than he had today.

'Not quite. The exchange scheme co-ordinator's suggested that I spend this week working with Beth. It gives me a good overview of the continuity between admissions through A&E and onto the wards and Beth wants to carve out some time on Friday to discuss any differences in approach between London and here.' Allie grinned. 'Maybe by that time I'll be remembering to call it the ED and not A&E.'

Good idea. That would help prepare future candidates for the exchange programme and also outline a few of the areas where each hospital might learn from the other. Zac swallowed his own disappointment.

'So you'll be back with the adolescent and young adult team next week, then?'

'You bet, I can't wait. I'm really looking forward to getting to grips with a slightly different balance with my work.'

The team that Zac had been working with for the last two years, and where Allie was due to take over from him, was a little different from the paediatric team at home. It catered for young people from the ages of ten to twenty-four, and there was an emphasis on meeting the specific issues that teenagers and young adults faced when they were in hospital.

'It's challenging.'

She gave him a smile. 'That's what you like about it?'

'Yeah. One of the things. You?'

She nodded, and Zac started the car.

When they arrived back at the apartment Allie insisted on making dinner, although she must have been tired. They took a walk on the beach and he tumbled into bed for an early night, exhausted by a day spent worrying needlessly about her.

Managing his own expectations had been a survival measure when Zac was growing up, proofing him against the promises that had failed to materialise. But it had its good side. When Allie walked into the unit on Friday morning, all he could feel was unexpected and complete pleasure.

'Just visiting?' Spending these few unscheduled moments with her was more than enough to brighten his day.

'Beth's busy today, so we've arranged a sit-down with the exchange scheme co-ordinator on Monday afternoon. Which puts me at a loose end today, so I wondered if you'd mind my joining you for your morning rounds?'

Allie *really* didn't need to ask. 'Yeah, no problem.' Zac decided he could risk being a little more effusive. 'That would be great.'

Bright sunshine wasn't that much of a novelty here, but when Allie's own brand of sunshine was walking next to him it made the day seem warmer. The morning rounds took a little longer than usual because he had to get Allie up to speed with the history of each patient, and afterwards she joined him in a secluded corner of the large food hall for lunch.

'So we've seen everyone now. Apart from Carly. How is she today?'

Zac started guiltily. Carly had arrived on the ward yesterday, and he'd wondered briefly whether Allie had seen her in the ED when she was first brought in to the hospital.

'She was being assessed by Psychiatric Services this morning, and I'm anticipating that their recommendation will be a course of counselling, to start now and continue after she's discharged. There's some concern about permanent disability in her left hand, but I think with minor surgery and physiotherapy we can avoid that.' Carly was eighteen years old and had attempted suicide by cutting her wrists.

'Good. I was worried about that too.' Allie regarded him thoughtfully. 'I was expecting to see her again this morning.'

She always cut to the chase, asking the questions that were the most difficult to answer. Zac had sat alone last night watching the sea, after Allie had gone up to bed, wondering how he might deal with this and coming to no definite conclusion. Zac took a sip of his coffee, trying to clear the lump that had suddenly formed in his throat.

'I had a long conversation with her mother yesterday. Carly's at art school, majoring in photography. She was friends with a guy in the same class as her and they'd go out together on photographic shoots. One thing led to another, they got close and they took photographs of a more private nature. When they split up, he shared all of her photographs on the college's social network.'

'What?' Allie's eyes filled suddenly with tears. 'Why did you wait until now to tell me this?'

'Because I think, given the circumstances, it may be best if you take a step back, and let me continue with her general treatment alone.'

That familiar motion of wiping tears away. Now, more than ever, he realised the fine line that Allie walked between living her life and being dragged down by what had happened to her.

'Don't you think I'm uniquely equipped to help her?'

Zac had anticipated that this would be Allie's first instinct, but he wasn't convinced it was the way to go.

'I know this sounds heartless, but you know as well as I do that we have to retain some distance from time to time, so that we can continue to do our jobs. Compromising yourself isn't going to help anyone.'

'But—'

'I think you should at least think about it over the weekend before you decide.'

He saw a flash of anger in her eyes. 'There's nothing to think about, Zac. The internet group who shared my most private moments, without my knowledge or permission, they took everything from me. They took my trust and my confidence. They locked me up in my flat for eighteen months, afraid to go out and meet people. They took my friends and my home...'

Her cheeks were flushed now, and she was stabbing the table with her finger. Wound so tightly that he thought she might break. Maybe he should have waited until this evening to tell her, but there was no going back now.

'Allie...'

'They will *not* take my voice away. And they won't take away the oath I made, to do the best I can for my patients.'

'First, do no harm, Allie. We have to tread carefully with Carly, and maybe…' There was no tactful way to say this. 'Maybe you're not ready for this. Maybe Carly's not ready for your anger yet.'

She was still staring at him, her gaze refusing to let him go. But Allie seemed to simmer down a little, leaning back in her seat.

'I'm angry with *you* at the moment, Zac.'

Another challenge. One that Zac wasn't going to back away from.

'Fair enough, I'll take your anger. As much as you want, whenever you want, I thought I'd made that clear.' He hadn't quite anticipated how hard it might be, how much it wounded him to hear Allie say what her life had been like in the last eighteen months, but he'd learned one thing from Australia. You committed yourself and then you rode the wave, wherever it took you.

'*Can* you take it?'

'Try me. One of the reasons I told you about my own childhood was because I wanted you to know that I wasn't going to shrink from what's happened to you. I became an expert in denying what's going on when I was a kid, and I'm not going to pretend that it works.'

She broke the connection between them, looking down at her tightly clasped hands. There was something that could hurt him more than hearing what had happened to her, and this was it.

'Allie…?'

She waved her hand, still refusing to meet his gaze. 'It doesn't matter.'

'Clearly it does.' He lowered his voice, trying to resist the temptation to vent his feelings openly.

Suddenly she got to her feet. Allie left her lunch behind on the table, walking towards the entrance doors to the canteen. Maybe he should let her go.

Maybe he shouldn't. She might regain her cool, but that would just be a first step towards freezing him out. Zac caught up with her outside the canteen, where she'd stopped for a moment, looking around, clearly deciding which way she needed to go. He grabbed her hand, hoping that she wasn't going to protest loudly enough for someone to have to intervene. Kidnapping a fellow doctor was just as much frowned on here as it was at home.

But Allie didn't say a word. She followed him through the busy reception area and out into the sunshine. Zac led her to a secluded spot in the hospital grounds, sitting down on a bench. Allie joined him, keeping her distance, which was just as well because Zac imagined that a few explosive gestures might be part of the arsenal that she was about to launch at him.

But instead she looked at him blankly. Hiding behind those carefully constructed defences of hers.

'Talk to me Allie. Please.'

'I think you're wrong.'

'Yeah, that's pretty obvious. Can you tell me something I don't know, and change my mind?'

Allie took a deep breath, clearly considering the idea. 'Okay, I take your point. Whatever my reaction to this is, it has to put Carly front and centre. She's the one who's been abused and that makes her the most important person in the room.'

'Along with you.'

'Yes, okay, then. Along with me, because I have to work here.'

At least she'd acknowledged that, and it was the only thing that Zac had wanted to stress. That Allie was here for a reason, and she shouldn't ignore her own well-being. He nodded, deciding that it was about time he stopped making assumptions and listened to her.

'It's all about taking things back, Zac. And the important thing I want to say right now is that you're not one of the people who's made me feel disempowered.'

That really mattered to him. He hadn't always got things right, but he'd tried his best.

'Thank you.'

'I want to help Carly, and I think I can. I think that I can approach her in a way that prioritises how she feels, not what anyone else thinks, and that I can make it clear to her that this is something that's been done to her, and has nothing to do with who she is.'

'I'm not in any disagreement with that.' He ventured an opinion and Allie nodded. 'What about you?'

Allie's brow creased. 'You're right, that's something I have to consider and it's more difficult. I'll have to liaise with Carly's counsellor before I do anything, and that means telling them why I think I'm able to understand how Carly feels. Probably a few other people as well. One of the reasons I came here was because I didn't want to be in an environment where everyone knew what had happened.'

'And...?'

'I'll be telling them my own story, from my own perspective. I didn't realise until now how different that feels and how much it matters to me. It'll be hard and I might need a friend...'

She was asking? But the fact that Allie *had* asked him

made Zac feel slightly dizzy. It was the kind of compliment that didn't just slip off the tongue, it came from the heart.

'I'll be there. Probably upsetting you from time to time with opinions you don't want to hear.'

She smiled suddenly. 'That's the deal, Zac. I might upset you from time to time as well.'

But that was okay, because suddenly their relationship seemed stronger than that. He and Allie were both stronger than that, and they could weather a little honest disagreement.

'Yeah. That's the deal.'

They went back to the canteen, expecting that their sandwiches would have disappeared and they'd have to get more. But they were beckoned over by one of the servers, who smilingly produced their plates from under the counter for them, and poured two fresh cups of coffee.

'Thought you hadn't finished yet. Called away?'

Allie smiled at her gratefully. 'Only a minor emergency. Thanks.'

Philippa, Carly's counsellor, had already spent some time with her and decided to allow Carly to get settled into the safe environment of the hospital for a few days, before starting work with her next week. Zac was keeping a close eye on her physical condition and when Allie followed him into her room Carly recognised her from the ED and smiled.

When she admitted that he was right, and it *was* probably best to think everything through over the weekend, he simply nodded as if that had been Allie's idea all along.

She was up early the following morning, and when Zac got back from his Saturday morning surfing with Mark and started to make bacon sandwiches and brew coffee, Allie already had a list of bullet points.

'What do you think?' She slid the paper across the breakfast bar towards him, and Zac leaned over to read it.

'Yeah. Looks good. There's more on the back?' He was holding his greasy fingers away from the sheet, and Allie turned it over for him.

'I like the part about this being something that both you and Carly can learn and benefit from, and that you're not comfortable with doing it without Philippa's advice and support.' His gaze moved from the paper. 'Do you really mean it, or are you just courting her agreement?'

'No! I thought about it, and when my righteous indignation wore off I decided that I was going to need some support. Some clinical support in addition to the friendly support, that is.'

He chuckled. 'Yeah, gotcha. I'll just stay in my friend box, shall I?'

'It's not such a bad box for us to be in, is it?'

Zac was very far from stupid, and he couldn't have missed the way that their relationship had slipped from colleagues to friends to… Something more, that lived in the times when they touched, and when his gaze met hers. When that happened, Zac backed off as suddenly and as often as she did.

'Turn it over again…'

Allie turned the paper back to her initial points and he read them through again, nodding. 'I like your point about not calling it *revenge porn*. I feel pretty uncomfortable when people call it that. It's like asking what a woman was wearing when she was attacked, as if she's done something to warrant a crime being committed against her.'

'Yes, I prefer Image Based Sexual Abuse.'

'Hmm. That sounds more like it. Although, considering the medical penchant for acronyms…' He grinned at her.

'I'll risk it. Do you think I have everything in the right order?'

'No. I think you should put your last points, about being able to reach Carly and your willingness to accept support for yourself, first. That's what you've decided you want to do, and the rest is important but they're supporting points. At the moment it sounds as if you're trying to justify what you want, and I think you need to go in a little stronger than that, and let Philippa bring up anything she disagrees with.' He moved back to the cooker, turning the bacon in the pan. 'Not that I think she's going to disagree, by the way. In my experience, Philippa's always open to a joined-up approach and a bit of good sense.'

He managed to make that sound like a compliment instead of an I-told-you-so.

'I appreciate your input. I was thinking of writing a separate sheet, just noting down what happened to me. What do you think?'

Zac nodded, buttering the toast before he turned to face her. 'I think it's relevant. Do you prefer to write it down or is it easier to talk about it face to face?'

Allie thought for a moment. 'I could do either. But somehow writing it down…'

'Gives you a sense of ownership?'

'Yes. That.'

'Well, that's a point you could make as well. Are you happy to discuss and answer questions?'

'Yes, very much so.'

'Then perhaps that's one of your bullet points. I think it's a good one, how you take control of the way you tell your own story.' He grinned. 'Maybe that's one of your introductory paragraphs as well?'

'Yes, that's a good idea.' Allie wrote it down at the end of the list, starring it to go at the top. This felt right. As if she *was* in control of her own story.

'Put that away now.' Zac put her sandwich and a mug of coffee in front of her. 'We'll come back to it when we've eaten.'

CHAPTER SIX

SHE'D RETURNED TO her list, between shopping and cooking, and by the evening Allie was pleased with what she'd done and had typed it all up, along with her account of what had happened to her. Zac had suggested they go out for some fresh air and they'd walked along the beach for a while, sitting down on the sand when the sky began to darken.

'I want you to hear it first, Zac. Before anyone else.'

'I don't need to…'

'But you'll listen, if that's what I want?'

He nodded. 'Of course. I feel honoured that you're trusting me with this.'

Allie took a breath. This was the hardest thing, because Zac's reaction meant more to her than that of anyone else here. And the easiest, because she trusted him better than anyone else.

'James seemed like a really nice person. He was fun, and he seemed very respectful as well. Sent me little notes and flowers. He didn't push for sex. In fact, I think that was my idea.'

Zac nodded, opening his mouth to speak, and then stopped himself, seeming to think better of whatever he was about to say.

'In the context of what happened next you could call that grooming, but I didn't have any idea at the time.' Allie voiced the obvious, wondering if that was what Zac had been about to say.

'Yeah. Flowers can be just...nice. I guess that's the problem, isn't it. Nice gestures become weaponised.'

Allie let that go. She'd stared at the bunch of waratah that stood on the table next to the sofa, wondering if she might have enjoyed it a little more if it didn't remind her of James. Zac didn't need to know that Naomi's gesture wasn't appreciated quite as much as it should have been.

'What I didn't know was that he'd rigged his bedroom with cameras and that he had everything, the whole night and the next morning. There must have been at least two because there were two distinct angles that were cut together in the video. The IT guy said it was pretty professional.'

'Oh, nice! Nothing like making you feel better about it, is there?' Zac frowned.

'Yes, that was a bit tactless. Generally speaking, I was interviewed by officers who were trained in dealing with this kind of crime and they were really good. James admitted his guilt soon after he was arrested, and so I was spared a court case.'

He nodded. 'But the video had already been shared.'

'Yes. The way that the group worked was that someone who wanted to join had to submit their own video, as a kind of entrance tariff. That meant that the group had a steady stream of new videos, and also that anyone who did join was immediately implicated so they couldn't betray any of the group's secrets.'

Zac shook his head, a look of utter disgust on his face. 'That's... I'd say it was clever if it wasn't so despicable.'

'It was effective, for quite some time. Not all of the members of the group worked at the hospital, and they still don't know exactly how many there were because when the first enquiries were made it shut down pretty quickly. Apparently most of the members were using burner phones, which didn't make things any easier.'

'And you didn't suspect anything?'

Allie shook her head. 'I just thought that we'd spent a nice night together, and that things hadn't worked out between us. I was hurt, but I got over it. But six months later, when someone blew the whistle on them, the hospital made all of the staff aware of what had happened and asked anyone who had concerns to come forward. And James suddenly wasn't at his desk. I put two and two together and...'

Suddenly it felt as if there wasn't enough air on the beach. Zac's hand hesitantly reached out for hers and she took it and gripped it tight, feeling the panic begin to subside.

'It's okay. I'm all right. Not too much more to go...'

'Take it at your own pace. I'll wait.'

He *would* wait. Even if this took all night. Allie took a breath, feeling stronger now.

'Some of the videos, mine included, had been posted on other closed groups and found their way out onto the internet. The police did what they could, and I did some research on how to find them. I got quite good at it, but as soon as I reported one and the task force got it taken down, another one would pop up.'

'You're still looking?'

Allie shook her head. 'No. It was driving me crazy, for a while it was all that I could think about and I'd be up all night searching. I had to let it go for the sake of my own sanity. Maybe we got everything and maybe we didn't. I've had to come to terms with that.'

Zac was shaking his head. 'How? How do you come to terms with something like this?'

'A lot of people helped me and...there wasn't much

choice. These were things that I couldn't change and I had to learn to live with them.'

His fingers were gripping hers tightly now. 'Saying that I'm sorry this happened to you doesn't really cover it, Allie.'

'It's the best anyone can do. And I appreciate it.' She squeezed his hand, and felt his fingers relax against hers. 'Zac, I didn't tell you this to make you angry. I told you because I've decided I have to share this, and I want you to know first. If I can say it, then I feel a bit more in control of it.'

'Then thank you. For saying it.'

They sat for a while, hand in hand, watching the dark movement of the sea. Just existing, in an interval of time where it didn't seem necessary to do anything else.

'Australia does make a difference, doesn't it,' Allie murmured.

'It did to me. Maybe it's just the distance. If we were Australians we might be taking in a few galleries in London, or exploring the Roman ruins in St Albans. Finding our places there.'

'Maybe. It's a lot less cold here, though.'

'Yeah. Although winter in Sydney can go down to eight or nine degrees.'

'Oh. Freezing, then.'

Zac chuckled. 'It seems a bit colder, somehow. Australian houses are built for the heat so double glazing and central heating aren't so common here.'

'Or heavy curtains?' Allie nudged him. 'The price tag fell out of the curtains in my room this morning.'

'Did it?' Zac attempted an innocent look, shrugging when Allie raised her eyebrows. 'Okay. You've got me there. I didn't have any curtains in the bedroom, because it's not overlooked and I like the sea breeze at night. I thought you might appreciate a bit more privacy.'

'I did, very much. Along with the latch on the door and the new paint job.'

'Give me a break, eh? I'm not admitting to any of that, it could have happened for any reason and at any time. Just give me a few minutes and I'll come up with an alibi.'

Allie laughed. 'Better be a good one…'

He was laughing too, making a show of pretending to think. Out here together on the beach, it seemed so natural that they should be together, and so impossible that something this sweet could ever be happening to her. His fingers were twined around hers, and Allie knew that he felt it too. Zac would never act on it, and she'd never respond, but maybe the man who'd had to work so hard for that frank, open smile of his needed to hear it.

'I like you, Zac.'

The way he let go of her hand, the uncertainty on his face, showed that he knew exactly what she meant. But when he replied there was no trace that he understood the admission she'd just made. That she *wanted* him.

'I like you too, Allie.'

Maybe she should just leave it at that. Then she saw the pulse beating at one side of his brow.

'I meant… I *like* you. I know it's not going to come to anything, and that you'll be leaving soon. I just wanted you to know that it's the first time I've thought of anyone in that way for a long time.'

He smiled slowly, laying his hand on hers again. 'Is this all right, though?'

Holding hands? 'Yes, it's really nice.' Suddenly it felt as intimate as a kiss.

'And this?' He raised her hand, stopping when it was just a few inches from his lips.

Allie caught her breath. 'Yes.'

His lips brushed her fingers, his gaze holding hers in the most delicious of embraces. They both knew that this wasn't going anywhere, but somehow that made it all so much sweeter. There were no uncertainties, no doubts about what might happen next. Just the tender acknowledgement of what might have been, if their lives had been different.

'Look up.' He murmured the words, and Allie couldn't help but trust him and tilt her head towards the sky.

'Oh! Stars!'

'One thing you don't get in London. Too much light pollution. They're brighter still if you go a little further out of town.'

Zac brushed her fingers with his lips one more time, sending shivers up her spine. 'These are the stars I've been sleeping under for the last two years, though. So they're special to me.'

'Can we see the Southern Cross from here?' That was the only constellation from this hemisphere that Allie had heard of.

'Right there. You see, four stars in the shape of a cross.' He pointed towards the sky, just above the horizon, and Allie moved closer, leaning against his shoulder to see exactly where he was indicating. When his arm curled around her, she snuggled against him.

'It's smaller than I thought it would be. It's just those four?'

'There are more, but you need a good pair of binoculars or a telescope to see them.'

'Do you know any more?'

It was nice. Feeling the warmth of another human being.

Someone who seemed to want to be here as much as she did. Feeling *Zac's* warmth.

'Do I know more? How long have you got…?'

Allie was alone now, with the curtains closed and her bedroom door latched. Which was crazy because the only other person in the apartment was Zac. But then the thoughts that had intruded now were crazy too. How James had seemed kind when she'd first met him. How she'd been so wrong once and it was difficult to trust her own judgement again.

But Zac was different. He'd been more than just honest with her, more than considerate. More than a friend in an unfamiliar place. He'd been someone who she could trust. Someone she might so easily have loved, if Allie hadn't found him too late for her to love anyone.

She lay down on the bed, switching out the light and then reaching to pull the covers up over her. In the velvet darkness, all she could think about was Zac's touch and the precious moments they'd spent together. Suddenly there was something very important that she had to do.

Stumbling to the door in the darkness, she quietly disengaged the latch. She might still need heavy curtains and closed windows, but tonight she could sleep without locking her bedroom door.

Last night had been the most exquisite experience…

Zac hadn't dated when he was a teenager. Taking a girl home was out of the question and anyway he was too busy with his studies, too desperate to get away from his mother's volatile moods and constant disapproval. When he'd got to university he'd diffidently embarked on relationships, usually with young women who were as shy as he was. In Australia, his growing confidence and his newfound love of the beach had widened his horizons a little, and he'd found himself with no shortage of offers, but even then his relationships had always been low-key. Always easy to make and easy to let go of. That childhood habit of never wanting anything that might be taken away had clearly controlled him more than he'd thought it did.

Allie was different, though. He'd felt a sizzling excitement from just a simple touch. He couldn't stop thinking about her, and when he managed to stop thinking and go to sleep he couldn't stop dreaming about her. Always wanting more, but knowing that whatever Allie could give him was somehow enough.

Thirty-two, and he was acting like a teenager. And Zac didn't care. Every moment he spent with Allie was confronting, exciting and more fulfilling than he'd ever thought possible. Applying a little logic to the situation, telling himself that it would never work and that he should back off, wasn't an option any more.

He'd woken early out of habit, and automatically pulled on his board shorts. Mark was out on the beach, testing out the waves as they crashed across the ever-shifting sand.

'What's up with you, mate? That's an easy one.' Mark hadn't failed to notice Zac's unforced errors.

'Work stuff.' Zac brushed off his lack of concentration in two words and Mark nodded, walking back out into the water and paddling out to the break.

Zac couldn't resist turning to look up at Allie's window. It was recessed slightly into the building, and screened by the plants and furniture on the deep balcony, but he could see the top of the sliding doors, and he couldn't help catching his breath. The curtains had been drawn back and the doors were slightly open.

Had she done the unthinkable, and allowed herself to

sleep with the stars and the sea for company last night? Zac rejected the thought as too much to ask. But as he stared up at the balcony, unable to avert his gaze, he saw movement. Allie was up and dressed, and sitting outside. She waved to him and the effect was electric, as if she were touching him.

One more thing to learn, in a world that already seemed tipped on its head. Just the sight of her, the knowledge that she might have been watching him, was enough to set his heart racing. She walked to the edge of the balcony, leaning on the balustrade. Allie definitely *was* watching him now.

He gave another wave, feeling a sudden, exquisite self-consciousness. That was new too. Zac had always regarded his body as a means to an end, something that allowed him to indulge in the activities that made him feel good. But now all he could think about was whether Allie liked what she saw.

All he wanted to do today was forget all of the harms that the past had dealt them both. Take the sunshine and the un-predictable swell of the ocean, and see where that led. He jabbed his finger towards the paddleboard that lay in its bag on the empty beach, and gestured an invitation to Allie to join them. She nodded, disappearing off the balcony, leaving Zac to wait for her on the beach.

On Monday morning Zac did his ward rounds alone. He'd wished Allie good luck before she'd gone to speak with Philippa, adding the caveat that she didn't really need it, and she'd grinned nervously back at him.

'Thanks. I'll take the luck if you don't mind, all the same.'

Maybe he should have wished himself luck, he was nervous enough for both of them. Zac dismissed the thought and got on with his morning's work.

'What is it today, Jack?' When he'd entered the roomy

four-person ward Zac had been under no illusions about what he'd find his next patient doing. And, true to form, he was playing computer games.

Jack ignored him, concentrating on the screen. He grinned suddenly, typing something and then looking up at Zac.

'Sorry, Dr Forbes.' Jack was nothing if not scrupulously polite. 'Just had to win this one.'

'In the interests of galactic peace and security?' Zac smiled.

'No, that's a different game. This one's Ancient Britain.'

'Right. Well, don't mess with the timeline, will you. I wouldn't want to disappear in a puff of smoke if you happen to vanquish one of my ancestors.'

Jack laughed. 'No chance of that, Dr Forbes. Unless you're descended from cosmic giants.'

'Ah. Should have known outer space would be in there somewhere.' Zac laid the tablet he was carrying down on the bed, well out of Jack's reach. He'd already learned that it took Jack no time at all to call up his own notes and read them.

'Let's take a look at your leg, then.' Zac cleared the trailing cables and closed the laptop, putting it to one side on the cabinet next to the bed. 'Any chance of you going down to the rec room to play there?'

'I get interrupted.' Zac nodded, wordlessly noting that this was the whole point of going to the rec room. 'And this is more private, I'm playing with my girlfriend.'

'Right. Has she been in to see you?' Jack had plenty of visitors, but Zac didn't recall being introduced to a girlfriend.

'That's a bit difficult, she lives in Brisbane. I haven't met her yet IRL, but we're in a relationship.' Jack paused for a moment, frowning. 'IRL is In Real Life.'

'Gotcha.' Zac was already learning that a relationship didn't necessarily depend on the things he'd thought it did, and so he wasn't going to argue. He turned his attention to examining Jack's leg, which had been broken in several places in a car accident.

'The muscles are still wasted, Jack. How are the exercise sessions with your physio going?'

Jack shrugged. 'Okay.'

Zac knew exactly how they were going. Jack did all that was asked of him but no more. And when the session was over he returned to the empty ward and spent his time staring at the screen of his laptop instead of trying to walk as much as he could, as his physiotherapist had advised.

'Okay isn't good enough,' Zac reprimanded him gently. 'Before you leave here, we want to see you starting to do most of the things you usually can.'

'That's what I usually do…' Jack frowned, gesturing towards the laptop.

Zac pulled up a chair and sat down. One of the things he liked about working with teenagers and young adults was the challenge. And one of the things he'd learned was that directness and honesty was usually the best policy.

'Got tickets for the computer games conference in Melbourne next month?' Jack's mother had mentioned that to him, and Zac had stored the information away for future reference.

'Yes, I applied for them as soon as they went on sale…' Jack knew he'd fallen for the ruse, and frowned. 'I expect you're going to say that I'll be wanting to walk around there.'

'What do you think? I would have thought that having to rely on your parents pushing you around in a wheelchair would cramp your style a bit. Is your girlfriend going to be there?'

'Yes, I got her a ticket.'

'Take it from me. You're going to want to be on your feet when you meet her.'

Jack sighed, giving him a look that clearly indicated he thought Zac was around a hundred years old. 'Things are different from when you were young, Dr Forbes.'

'I like to think I'm still young enough to learn a thing or two. Enlighten me.'

'We don't care how someone looks. Everyone's the same inside.'

Excellent point. Jack had a lot going for him, he was intelligent, articulate and valued the people around him. But he was also fourteen, and Zac knew a bit more about life than he did.

'You fight with your girlfriend, do you?'

The question appeared to put Zac nearer to a hundred and fifty in Jack's eyes. 'I don't fight *with* her. We fight together, to vanquish oppression and injustice. We're comrades.'

Comrades was a good word. One that he might remember when talking with Allie. 'And, as comrades, you both have to be the best you can be, in order to face…whatever it is you're facing.'

'S'pose so… Yes, we have to keep our wits about us.'

'So here's the thing. If you truly couldn't make it back onto your feet, then you'd be right to expect that your girlfriend wouldn't see you any differently, and I'm glad that's something you both value and feel confident about in your relationship. But if you don't try, that's another thing entirely.'

Jack pursed his lips, thinking for a moment. 'You mean

what's the point in being the best we can for each other on-line, if we can't do it IRL.'

'Couldn't have said it better myself.' Zac grinned at him. 'I know it's not easy to get back up and start moving around, but I wouldn't be pushing you if I didn't think you could do it.'

Jack frowned, clearly turning the idea over in his head. 'Yeah, okay. Chloe's a really good person and I'd like her to be proud of me. I'm really proud of the things she does.'

Jack gestured towards his laptop and Zac leaned back in his seat, not moving. The boy grinned at him and pulled himself across the bed, swinging his legs around. Zac helped him to stand, so that he could reach the laptop.

'Look, here...' Jack sank back onto the bed and tapped an address into the browser. 'This is Chloe's site.'

Zac stared at the screen. The website looked really profes-sional, its message immediately clear, warning of the dan-gers of pollution and the erosion of the Australian coastline.

'How old is Chloe, Jack?'

The boy rolled his eyes. 'Don't worry. She's fourteen, same as me, we both know how to be careful online. We video-conference all the time, and my parents have met hers.'

'Right. Sorry. It's just that this looks amazing. Did she do it by herself?'

'No, I helped her. It's an important issue, and we both believe in preserving our natural resources. We don't just play games, you know.'

'Okay, I'm learning something.' Zac reached forward, tapping on a few of the menu links. The other pages were just as striking as the first. 'Is this kind of thing easy to do?'

'Where have you been, Dr Forbes?' Jack's voice held a

note of resigned frustration. 'Don't you have to get stuff off the internet to be a doctor?'

'Yes, all the time. I don't have much to do with it apart from that.'

'Well, we're in the twenty-first century now. It's really easy to do something like this.'

Zac ignored the implied insult. 'Okay. Can I do you a deal? I'll share some of my knowledge with you, and we'll make a concerted effort to get you back on your feet. You share some of your knowledge with me, and show me how to make a website like that.'

'Cool. You're on.' Jack started to enter another web address into the browser and Zac stopped him.

'Not right now. First I'm going to take you through some of the exercises that your physiotherapist has given you to do in your own time, and we'll see how you do with them. Maybe we can meet up in the rec room, when I'm not on duty and you don't have any visitors, and you can impart some knowledge as regards web development.'

'The rec room.' Jack hadn't failed to notice that, and turned the corners of his mouth down in disapproval. 'Okay, whatever.'

Zac's head was buzzing with possibilities. Maybe Allie wasn't ready yet, but this was one way to take back something that had been taken from her. He'd have to test the water, but he couldn't even suggest it to her if he had no idea of how to accomplish it. He reached for Jack's walker, and put it by the side of the bed.

'This stays here, so you can reach it. Let's see you take a few steps. I want to see how much you can do...'

CHAPTER SEVEN

ALLIE HADN'T BEEN able to stop thinking about Zac lately. Surely he couldn't be unaware of the bonds that increasingly seemed to be pulling them together.

He'd been there for her this weekend and during her meeting with Philippa, as well. Not physically there, but she'd been able to explain what she wanted to do, despite the constant tug of anxiety that always accompanied talking about what had happened to her. Going through everything first with Zac hadn't just helped her arrange her thoughts effectively, it had given her the strength to speak out.

When she walked back onto the ward he was deep in conversation with the senior nurse, but he looked up and saw her as the doors closed behind her, flashing her a smile. He was clearly busy and when they found themselves alone for a moment she murmured that they'd talk later.

Later turned out to be lunchtime, when they fetched sandwiches and a drink from the canteen and Zac guided her to a quiet place in the hospital grounds, where they could eat outside.

'How did it go?'

'Good. Great.' Allie was still slightly breathless from the feel of his light touch on her arm.

He nodded, clearly waiting for something a bit more tangible than that.

'Philippa suggested that we sit down together and talk about my experiences first. I agreed with her that it'll help us both move forward with a joint approach that might help Carly.'

He nodded. 'That sounds really sensible. How do you feel about it?'

'I'm really happy with it. It's practical and I feel supported in what I want to do. *More* supported, that is. I couldn't have done this without you, Zac.'

He pressed his lips together, looking a little disappointed. 'I'm glad I could help.'

Zac had his own set of insecurities about their relationship, and perhaps he thought that Allie needed him more than she wanted him. 'It's Philippa's job to help. You're my friend, and that's a bit different.'

He nodded. 'Philippa's very good. I'm sure she'll give you all of the professional support you need.'

'I've no doubt of it. I like her a lot.'

Something stirred in his eyes. Sweet shadows of a dark sea and glimmering stars. And there was an uncertainty in his face that matched her own. Allie supposed that was natural, when they were making their own rules and everything meant so much more than either of them were prepared to admit.

'You do? That's good.'

Allie leaned towards him. 'I *like* you a lot.'

Zac grinned suddenly. Job done. 'I *like* you a lot too. And I'm really glad that it went well for you this morning.'

Pure pleasure washed through her. It seemed they'd both needed a bit of reassurance.

There was still something on his mind, though. Zac was studying the ground in front of the bench where they were sitting as if it might be about to open up and swallow him.

'I was wondering. Since that's the case, how would you feel about coming on a date with me?'

A date? They were living in the same apartment, and Zac had already been eager to show Allie the best features of his adopted home.

She cleared her throat nervously. 'What kind of date, Zac?'

His face took on a pained expression and he seemed to be concentrating on fiddling with the wrapping of his sandwich. 'I was afraid you were going to ask that. You're quite right, we need to set a few boundaries...'

Silence. Zac was clearly struggling with this as much as she was. A sudden glimpse of the shy man who found it difficult to meet anyone's gaze reminded Allie that of course he found this difficult.

'Zac, I...' She searched for a way to phrase what she really wanted to say to him.

And then he said it for her. Suddenly his gaze met hers. 'I guess that the least I can do while asking someone out is to look at them.'

'Yes, it inspires confidence. Lets me know where you're coming from.'

He acknowledged the heavy hint with a smile. 'Well... I was talking with Jack this morning, about putting his laptop down and concentrating a bit more on his rehab.'

Allie couldn't see the connection, but she went with the flow, nodding him on.

'He was telling me that his generation makes their own rules, as if I was about a hundred years old. He's got a point, though, it is up to us to make the rules. I'd like to be a special friend to you, and I think that means finding out the things that we each want to give and accept.'

Allie stared at him, dumbstruck, for a moment. Zac's

expression became pained and she had to give him a reply before he decided he'd said the wrong thing and he should forget all about the idea.

'Zac, I think that's one of the nicest things anyone's ever said to me.'

'Really?' He grinned suddenly. 'I'm not great at this, am I...?'

'Has anyone ever told you that a guy who doesn't rely on his looks when he asks a woman on a date, but thinks about what she might want from him, is a sure winner?'

'Uh...? No, I don't think so. Maybe they did and I was a bit too nervous to notice.'

'Then listen up, Zac. I'd really like to go on a date with you, and you don't need to say any of the right things to me, just tell me what you want. And, in case you're in any doubt, I'm not saying yes because I've been hurt, it's because I won't settle for anything less.'

That intoxicating warmth filtered into his gaze and Allie wondered for a moment what she *would* actually settle for. Right now it seemed a possibility that she might forget the hurt...

She could forget James. She could even trust Zac. But the shame and humiliation that had been heaped on her had changed Allie's relationship with her own body, making her conscious of it and uncomfortable with it. Zac had been willing to talk about anything in his life, and if being with him felt like having sex with a stranger, it wasn't because *he* was the stranger. Her own body was the stranger.

'Hey. You want to change your mind?' His voice was tender.

'No, I'm just getting used to the idea.' Holding hands with him was nice. That was one thing she could take back right now, and she curled her fingers around his.

'Okay. How does Saturday evening sound?'

Allie smiled up at him. 'I think I'm free on Saturday evening. Did you have something in mind?'

'I thought I'd just weigh up the options for a while. Agonise a bit over them...' He gave her a cheery smile. 'Do you have any preferences?'

'I'd like...' in for a penny, in for a pound '...somewhere I can wear a dress.'

He nodded, smiling. 'A dress it is. I'm looking forward to it.'

In one way, Allie's obvious caution about their date made things a lot easier. Zac wasn't in the habit of steering his relationships the way he wanted them to go, and even if he'd aspired to do that he reckoned he didn't have the panache to get away with it. Allie was clearly unsure about how far she wanted to take this, and it was nice to be able to start a relationship without any preconceptions. Nothing assumed, nothing taken for granted.

Zac's usual choice of venue for a summer date involved the open air—a barbecue maybe, or the beach. Somewhere that Allie could wear a dress was a little more of a challenge for him to rise to. But he'd come up with an idea and some last-minute tickets. The weekend had finally arrived—anticipation making the journey a little slower than usual—and an hour before they needed to leave the apartment, he'd changed into a pale-coloured lightweight suit with an open-necked shirt. Then he waited for Allie to come back downstairs.

He wasn't aware of jumping to his feet when he saw her, just that he was suddenly standing. Allie was wearing a plain dark blue sleeveless dress with high heels. Her hair was artfully arranged so that her curls seemed softer and wilder, and she wore make-up. The wrap that covered her shoulders might be there for protection rather than warmth, but she'd clearly made an effort.

'You look beautiful.' He wasn't sure where they stood with regards to compliments yet, but he allowed himself this one on the basis that it was more understatement than compliment. She shone, like moonlight over the sea.

And then she smiled, adding a whole new dimension to his pleasure. 'Thank you. Not so bad yourself...'

She walked towards him and Zac's heart nearly stopped when she reached out, deftly pulling the collar of his shirt straight. Trying to catch his breath without seeming to, he held his arm out and she took it, letting him walk with her down to the car and open the passenger seat door for her.

Her eyes widened a little when he parked the car for their first stop. A food truck on the beach wasn't the obvious start to a date with a dress, but they had to eat.

'I couldn't get a dinner reservation for the restaurant at our final destination.' Zac felt a little flutter of excitement when Allie glared at him in frustration over the secret. 'So I reckoned that the best burger in town and the finest dining area imaginable would have to do.'

She looked at the wooden trestle tables set out on the beach. There were a few families, clearly relaxing after a hard day at the beach, and another couple who seemed on their way out for the evening.

'This is perfect, Zac. I love the décor.' She reached down, taking off her shoes and leaving them in the footwell.

Zac guided her to an empty seat and Allie sat with her back straight and her feet tucked under her seat, looking like a queen. He fetched hamburgers and a fresh green salad to share, along with plenty of napkins, and Allie ate with the kind of appreciation that would generally be reserved for a five-star restaurant. Then he hurried her back to the car, and started to drive again.

He took a slightly longer route into Sydney, taking in some of the best sightseeing locations of the city centre. By the time he parked at Darling Harbour, Allie was looking around her, drinking it all in.

'A ferry?' She was holding his arm, practically dragging him towards the pedestrian walkway that led onto the craft.

'Best way to see the harbour...' Actually the second best way. Their route home again, surrounded by the lights of the city, would be the best way, but Zac wasn't going to give up even that small detail of his plans for the evening.

Allie insisted on sitting on the open deck, despite his warnings that they might encounter some spray as the ferry began to move. It was a twenty-minute ride to Circular Quay and she hung onto his arm the whole way, craning her neck to get the best views of the Harbour Bridge and the Opera House. When Zac rose, guiding her off the ferry, she seemed almost disappointed, but then Allie turned her attention to the next thing on their agenda.

'We're going to see the Opera House?'

He nodded, loath to give away any more details. Zac led the way up the long series of steps, letting her stop every now and then to take everything in, and then into the building.

'A recital?' Allie was looking around her as they followed the path of the foyer, winding around the concert hall. 'You're a fan of the opera?'

Zac grinned. 'I've never been. It's about time I did, though, and even if it's not our thing then at least we can both say we've been to the Sydney Opera House.'

'Good thinking. How on earth did you get tickets at such short notice?'

'Beth helped, she's a real music buff and has a member-
ship of the Opera House. She called the priority booking
line for me and asked if there were any ticket returns.'

'That was nice of her.' Allie grinned up at him. 'Did you
tell her who you were taking?'

Zac hadn't told anyone, not even Mark and Naomi. It had
seemed somehow wrong to say even one word about this,
when everyone back in London knew far too much about
Allie's last relationship.

'I said I had a date with someone I wanted to impress.
Beth interrogated me a bit, and when I wouldn't give her
a name she said that she was glad to see I was finally taking a more serious attitude to dating. So if you happen to
mention it to her, I'd be grateful if you didn't say that we
ate on the beach.'

Allie's sudden shiver and the warmth in her face reminded him again just how wounded she was. When she
moved a little closer to him, as if she'd just gained more
confidence in his protection, Zac thanked his lucky stars
that he'd been careful.

'Not a word about the beach, I promise. Although it did
seem quite in keeping with the occasion, since we didn't
get our feet wet.'

Zac laughed, and she squeezed his arm. This was already
shaping up to be the best date he'd ever been on. A redefi-
nition of the word *date* in fact…

They had great seats, and the music… Zac knew nothing about music, and wasn't accustomed to sitting quietly
in an auditorium, but the music had a texture all of its own.
Swelling and then receding, like the ocean. Washing over
them in the darkness, an almost physical pleasure that made
him shiver at times. Allie seemed to feel it too, forgetting
to adjust the wrap when it slipped from her shoulders. If he

chose to see it that way, Zac could imagine her beginning to let down her guard and letting the music in to sit beside her. He could almost feel jealous of it, but he knew that this was precious. If the music could reach Allie, then so could he.

'What did you think?' As they walked back down the steps of the Opera House, Zac asked the question.

'I loved it. Thank you.' Allie pulled her wrap back around her shoulders, but since most of the other women he could see were donning jackets, Zac decided not to take it personally. Although maybe he could take the shining look on Allie's face a little personally.

They turned to see the projections that now caressed the sails of the Opera House. And then he hurried her back down to the terminus to catch the next ferry.

'It's wonderful! Sydney's such a beautiful city.' Allie had again decided that only the deck of the ferry would do, and she was shivering slightly in the cool breeze. Zac took off his jacket, deciding that it was possible to worry too much about how everything he did might seem, and offered it to her.

'Thanks. Aren't you chilly now?'

He chuckled. 'Yeah. Don't give it back, whatever you do.'

She laughed, pulling his jacket around her gratefully. 'I've really enjoyed this evening, Zac. It feels…like a taste of the life I used to have.'

'That's good?' Zac wondered whether Allie had really thought that through.

'I just…' Allie leaned against the handrail, looking down at the water. 'I just want to go back to the way things were. The way *I* used to be.'

She seemed to be asking him something. Zac could hardly bear the answer that he knew he had to give, because anything else was wishful thinking at best. At worst, a bare-faced lie.

'You can't go back, Allie. I wish that were possible, but none of us can, we can only go forward. And you never know, forward might be better than back.'

She looked up at him, seeming to be blinking away tears. 'Thank you. I've been telling myself that over and over again and… It's nice when someone else is honest enough to say it.'

Allie pressed her lips together, looking round. The ferry was nearing the dock and the impetus to go forward seemed to seize her once more. 'It's time to go.'

'Not yet. Allie, listen…' She must have heard the urgency in his voice because she turned, looking back at him.

'I don't know how I'd cope with the kind of abuse that you've been subjected to. I have no idea how you're going to cope with it either. But I believe that you will. Things won't be the same, but you'll find your own peace and make a life that you can care about.'

'You *believe?*' She threw the question at him, as if it were a challenge.

'If you don't, what are you doing here with me? It's far less trouble to sit at home…'

The hurt must have sounded in his voice, because Allie's face suddenly softened. She reached out, slipping her hand around his elbow, and Zac automatically crooked his arm.

'I'm here because I want to be. With you.'

That was suddenly enough. More than just enough. It was everything. Zac laid his hand on hers, feeling her fingers squeeze his arm.

He made another detour on the way home, to take in the lights of Sydney, glinting across the water of the bay. Allie held his hand as they climbed the steps back up to the apartment, stopping outside the door.

'The Opera House was wonderful. Thank you, Zac.'

'Thank *you*. I have a great memory to take back to London with me.'

Allie laughed. 'I can't believe you've been here all this time and you hadn't been there.'

She didn't seem about to move, and Zac felt in his pocket for his key to the apartment. Suddenly Allie reached up, smoothing the lapel of his jacket. A brief, intoxicating trace of her scent made him stop in his tracks, and when he looked down at her Allie's gaze met his.

First date. Doorstep. He was getting the message. Zac just didn't quite know how to respond to it. Then it occurred to him that he should just ask, because Allie was perfectly capable of saying no.

'Could we do this again?'

'I'd love to. Only next time I'd like it to be my surprise. Are you free next weekend?'

Zac thought the matter over. He might know the area better than she did, but where they went really wasn't the point. He just wanted to go there with Allie.

'Nothing planned. Any time next weekend sounds perfect.'

He probably should open the door now. Maybe make some hot chocolate to round the evening off, in the hope that would put him in the mood for sleep because right now it felt as if every one of his senses was on high alert. He could feel the movement of the breeze, hear the crash of the sea behind them. And all he could see was Allie…

'May I…' He lost his nerve and then she stepped a little closer. 'May I kiss you?'

'I'd like that, very much.'

He caught her hand, raising her fingers to his lips. Each sensation seemed magnified, dizzying. Then Zac brushed his lips against her cheek. Allie moved a little closer still, resting her hand on his shoulder, and he bent to kiss her mouth.

As kisses went, it wasn't the longest or the most passionate. But it was intoxicating, in a way that he'd never experienced before. This slow, make-your-own-rules way of doing everything made everything more uncertain, but a hundred times more pleasurable. Each time they touched he knew for sure that it was because Allie wanted to touch him, enough to cross the line that she'd drawn around herself.

'That was gorgeous. Perhaps we should go in now.' He felt her breath against his neck, and shivered at its caress.

'I could…see you inside and then go back to the car. You could watch me from the window.' He teased her and Allie laughed.

'Where are you going to go? You live here!'

'I'd just drive for a while and then sneak in. I'll be quiet, in case you're asleep.'

'You think I could sleep, when I'd be wondering if I'll hear you creeping up the stairs at any moment? And if I didn't hear you, then I'd have to go out and look for you in case you'd had an accident. That's not a good ending to the evening, is it, Zac?'

'Probably not.' Zac decided to revert to the original plan. 'Hot chocolate then?'

'That would be nice.' She took the key from his hand, and opened the door.

Allie perched herself on one of the breakfast bar stools, slipping her shoes off and watching him as he prepared the hot chocolate. Zac could almost feel her gaze, and concentrated on steadying his hands so he didn't burn himself.

When he slid a full mug across to her she picked it up and took a taste.

'Mmm. That's really nice, thank you. I'm going to take it upstairs if that's okay?'

'Of course. Sleep well.'

'You too. And thank you again for a lovely evening…'

Zac watched as she bent to pick up her shoes. She blew a kiss which seemed to hit his temple with a dizzying blow, then made for the stairs. He listened for the sound of her footsteps and when he heard her bedroom door open and then close, he slid back the doors that opened onto the balcony.

If he had a *thinking place* then this was probably it. Somehow, the regular crash of the sea and the light from the stars always put everything into its proper focus. But that process wasn't going to work this time, because the correct perspective was that everything Allie said and did mattered a lot more than it should to him.

He was leaving. Allie was… Zac thought for a moment and discounted the word *fragile,* along with *vulnerable.* Allie was neither, but she'd been hurt so badly that it took considerable strength for her just to function, let alone come to a new country and start again. He'd thought that a low-key relationship, more friends than anything else, might be the right way to deal with the instant chemistry between them. It would allow them to acknowledge what was indisputably there, without either of them getting too involved. And that might well have worked if their relationship *was* low-key.

But when they talked there was an honesty that made Zac feel exposed, naked almost. When they touched it set off a chain reaction of pleasure that shot through him with such force that it left him breathless.

He couldn't go back, not now, even if there was the ever-present fear of losing something he cared about. As long as Allie wanted to be with him, he'd be there for her. If it broke his heart to leave, then so be it.

Allie had carefully measured her own footsteps as she climbed the stairs. Made sure she didn't run to her room and bang the door closed behind her. She closed the curtains, flipped on the light and then sat down on the bed.

She'd wanted all of this. Wanted to feel something again, and more than anything she'd wanted to feel it with Zac. And she'd loved everything about the evening and the way he'd planned it so carefully.

He was going back to London and she would be staying here in Sydney. But that didn't make any difference. She felt what she felt, and the shy side of Zac's nature gave her the courage to show it. This was the slow reawakening that she'd longed for, and which was so sweet it almost hurt. Like pale winter skin that was exposed to the sun for the first long hot day of summer and felt tender afterwards.

Allie put the hot chocolate down beside the bed and changed into her nightdress, adding her dressing gown on top of it, even if it was a little too warm for comfort. She was bound to feel a little uncertain about this. All that Allie really knew was that she finally felt she had a choice about what she was going to do next, and that she chose not to give Zac up until the time came for him to leave.

CHAPTER EIGHT

WORK HAD BEEN Allie's way of surviving over the last eighteen months. She'd piled everything into it, as a way of shutting out the thoughts that tormented her, but now she was beginning to realise that she'd forgotten something. Having a life outside the hospital made her sharper and better during the hours she spent working.

She and Zac stared at the empty bed, the pillows still showing the indentation of a head. The leads from the intravenous drips were draped along the floor, along with a few spots of blood where their patient had pulled the catheter from the back of her hand. Corinne had been brought into the ward this morning from the ED, suffering from a kidney infection and sepsis, and she'd been started on broad spectrum antibiotics and fluids immediately. By the time she'd reached the ward all of the necessary tests to check that her other organs hadn't been compromised had been completed, and Allie and Zac had reviewed her condition and medication, then left her to rest. And now, two hours later, she was gone.

'I've only been away five minutes...' The nurse who was attending her had re-entered the room behind them.

'You were monitoring her condition regularly,' Zac murmured, reassuring the nurse. 'We need to put the search procedure in place though. Will you go and speak with the ward manager, please.'

The nurse hurried away, and Zac shot Allie a worried look. Corinne's condition had been caught early and, although sepsis was always a cause for concern, she was stable and hadn't displayed any of the confusion that was one of the possible symptoms.

'What's the procedure, Zac?'

'The doctor on shift for a missing patient checks their room, and reports back to the ward manager. You'll look through her personal items?'

Allie nodded, opening the closet. There was precious little in it, just a crumpled T-shirt, a bra and a folded newspaper. 'Nothing here, she's probably wearing her clothes on top of her hospital gown. I remember the nurse putting them in here for her, there was a red hoodie. And I got her to let go of her handbag and put it in here, it was one of those leather courier bags.'

Zac nodded, taking the pillows from the bed and pulling the covers back to check beneath them. 'Nothing here to give us a clue. There are some spots of blood on the floor, and a smudge on the towel dispenser so her hand's probably bleeding from where she pulled the IV out. It doesn't look as if she's touched anything else.'

They made their way to the ward manager's office, reporting back to her.

'Thanks. Let's hope she's wearing the hoodie, eh, she'll stand out a bit in that. Can you go and do Sector Six now?' She handed Zac a sheet of paper from the file that was already open on her desk, and Allie saw a plan of the ward with different sectors outlined in red, and a checklist.

'Right you are. Thanks.'

Allie followed him to the rec room, and then on to the

kitchen next door. They methodically checked everything for any signs that Corinne had been this way, ticking items from the checklist as they went. When they returned to the ward manager's office she was already on the phone.

'I've got the last sector check complete now.' She took the sheet of paper back from Zac. 'We're sure she's not still on the ward… Yes, okay… Thanks.'

'No sign of her?' Zac pressed his lips together in disappointment.

'No. There's quite a large smudge of blood on the wall next to the door release button, which can't have been there for long, so we think she's left the ward. We checked outside in the corridor and there's nothing there to show which way she went. All of the other wards in this block are doing a missing patient check, and we already have security on all of the possible exits and the walkway through to the main building.'

'So the common area search will be starting now?' Zac asked.

The ward manager nodded. 'Yes. It might take a while, but they'll find her.'

Allie puffed out a breath as they walked out of the office. 'I dare say there are as many places to hide in this hospital as there are at the one back home in London.'

Zac nodded. 'More, possibly. The footprint's bigger so there's a bit more space. She may not be hiding.'

'She's in a strange place and we know she isn't thinking straight, because if she was she wouldn't have pulled out her IVs. I reckon we'd better hope she's hiding, because otherwise she's managed to slip past security.'

'That doesn't bear thinking about. She could be anywhere.'

'I reckon she would have gone home.' The idea started

to take hold in Allie's head and she suddenly couldn't let it go. 'It's unlikely but...'

Zac nodded. '*Highly* unlikely. We missed her pretty quickly and she would have had to move quickly to slip past security before we raised the alarm.'

'Coming to the wrong conclusions doesn't make some-one any less determined. Confusion and thinking that you're going to die are both symptoms of sepsis, and patients have been known to try to walk out of hospitals before. Where else do you go when you're feeling awful?'

'There's not much more we can do here, other than search places we've already searched.' Zac marched back to Corinne's room, picking up the tablet that contained all of their patients' notes for the morning and tapping it. 'We have her address and it's not far.'

He was suddenly on the move again, hurrying back to the small bank of lockers in the staff kitchen and retrieving his car keys. Her instinct and his capacity for action car-ried them into the ward manager's office and then through security and into the car park.

'This is the street.' They'd driven for ten minutes. 'Can you look out for the numbers?'

Small one-storey properties, set back from the road. Allie scanned them, trying to see house numbers, and then she didn't need to. Up ahead, a taxi had drawn up and she saw a flash of red as a slight figure got out of the back seat.

'There, Zac!'

He put his foot down, accelerating up the road. As they went past the taxi the driver wound down his window, lean-ing out.

'Hey! Miss...!'

Corinne had clearly been so focused on getting to her front door that she'd forgotten to pay, and she didn't look round. Zac stopped beside the taxi, pulling his wallet from his pocket.

'What's the damage, mate?'

Allie kept going, running to head Corinne off. She caught up with her halfway up the path, seeing Zac pull out his phone as the taxi drew away and speaking quickly into it, clearly calling to let the ward manager know that she could call off the search now. He waited at the end of the path, keeping his distance so that he didn't spook Corinne.

'Hey, Corinne. How are you doing?' Allie slowed down, smiling at her. Corinne had a paper towel wrapped around her hand, and her hospital gown was tucked into her jeans, showing only at the neck of her hoodie.

'Okay...' She clearly wasn't okay but she kept walking, probably more out of muscle memory than anything else.

'Corinne, stop.' Allie blocked her path, and Corinne stared blankly at her. 'You know who I am—Allie, the doctor from the hospital.'

Recognition showed in Corinne's eyes. 'I'm... I need to go inside now. I'll be okay.'

Allie addressed the balance between telling Corinne that she definitely wouldn't be okay if she didn't come back to the hospital, and frightening her with that information.

'If you come back to the hospital with us, you'll be okay. If you stay here, you won't.'

'If I'm going to die, I'd rather do it at home. Thanks for all the trouble you've taken, but you don't need to worry any more.' Corinne's face was impassive, which was what worried Allie the most. The feeling of dying was a symptom of sepsis, and Corinne seemed to have accepted that this was what was going to happen.

'Listen to me, Corinne. I'm a doctor...' Allie knew she had to give Corinne a clear way forward right now. 'It's not unusual for people to feel the way you do right now, but you need to come back to the hospital with me. If you do, I promise you that I can get you better and you won't die.'

Rash promises, based on probabilities rather than all the things that could possibly happen in real life. But Allie recognised the annoyed look that Corinne shot in her direction. There was a measure of peace in accepting that things couldn't get better, and when others—most notably Zac—had changed her own view of life, it had hit Allie hard.

'I've been so much trouble...' A tear rolled down Corinne's face.

'That's what I get paid for, taking trouble. Without any patients I'd be out of a job.' Allie took her arm, firmly starting to walk her back along the front path.

'I don't know. I feel bad. Maybe I should just stay here and lie down for a while...' Corinne started to protest and Allie ignored her, keeping her walking.

'Let me decide what's best. I've got you, Corinne, and you'll be safe with me, I promise.'

Corinne didn't reply but she didn't stop walking. Allie decided to take that as an agreement for treatment, but as Corinne's blind focus on getting home seemed to dissipate, her legs began to buckle. Allie tried to hold her up, but Zac was there, lifting Corinne up in his arms and carrying her towards the car.

Allie fished his car keys from his pocket, trying not to think about the intimacy involved in the necessary gesture. She opened the back door, pushing a bag full of surfing equipment to one side, and Zac deposited Corinne gently on the seat, pulling the seat belt across her. Allie put his car keys into his hand and got in next to Corinne, putting her arm around her to reassure her. Zac got into the driver's seat, performing a U-turn in the road, and Allie allowed herself to breathe a sigh of relief.

A nurse was waiting at the edge of the car park with a wheelchair, and Zac drew up next to her. They walked briskly past the security officer at the main door and took Corinne back up to the ward. She was gently undressed and put back to bed, and Allie turned her attention to re-inserting the catheter and starting up the lifesaving drips again.

'Doesn't look too bad.' Zac had clipped a blood pressure and heart rate sensor to Corinne's finger and was looking at the screen by the side of the bed. 'Will you stay and check her over more thoroughly?'

'Yes, and I'll take a look at where she pulled the catheter out.' Blood was soaking through the paper towel that was wrapped around Corinne's hand. 'I'd like to sit with her for a while as well.'

Zac nodded. 'Good idea. I can get on and finish the rounds.'

Corinne was curled up in the bed, her eyes closed, and Allie suspected that she was zoning out rather than sleeping. That was fine, but it would be good to be able to talk with her a little and reassure her. When the antibiotics started to take effect she should start to feel much better and would be more receptive.

Zac made his way to the door, and she felt a sudden sense of loss. Allie swallowed it down, turning to Corinne.

'Good call, by the way.' Zac had turned and was smiling at her, and suddenly Allie's world turned from shadow into sunshine.

'You too.' She smiled back at him. Zac's approbation shouldn't be important, they'd taken a chance that might have been wrong but had turned out to be right. But he'd trusted her judgement, weighed the matter up and decided it was worth a try. That meant more than it should.

Allie had stayed with Corinne for two hours, and then popped back during the afternoon to check on her, while Zac busied himself with all of the other things on their schedule. That was the advantage of having two doctors doing one person's job for a few weeks, but Zac was pleased it had worked out that way. Her own battle to find peace seemed to have deepened and broadened the already good relationship Allie created with her patients.

'We'll pop in to see Corinne before we go?' As they wrapped up their shift Zac knew that Allie would ask, and reckoned he might as well save her the trouble.

They found her sitting up in bed with a half-eaten plate of food in front of her. Zac motioned to the nurse who was taking her blood pressure that it would be okay to leave them here with Corinne for a while.

'Hey! You've managed to eat something.' Allie's smile showed that she wasn't going to bother about the half of the plate that was full and was concentrating on the half that was empty.

'Yeah, I was hungry, I hadn't eaten in a while. I wasn't well for a few days before I called for help.' Corinne gave her an embarrassed smile. 'I'm really sorry. About earlier...'

Allie plumped herself down on the chair next to Corinne's bed. 'I'm just happy to see you looking so much better. And there's something I want to say to you.'

Corinne turned the corners of her mouth down, obviously expecting a telling-off. Zac begged to differ. Whatever it was that Allie had to say, she wouldn't be reproving Corinne. He decided that she didn't need him to help her and sat down on a chair in the corner.

'One of the symptoms of sepsis is that people tend to do things they wouldn't normally do. That's really well understood. So I don't want you to apologise or beat yourself up over it. It's like saying sorry for not being able to walk when you've broken your leg.'

Corinne nodded, still looking unconvinced.

'What is it, Corinne?' Allie sat back and waited.

'Did I...? I did, didn't I? I said that if I was going to die, then I wanted to do it at home. That was really stupid.'

'No, it's not. Feeling as if you're dying is a recognised symptom of sepsis and in these situations instinct takes over and your first priority is to be somewhere that's familiar. Not many people get as far as you did, but I guess that just means you're a bit more resourceful than most.'

Corinne stared at her, wide-eyed. 'You're just saying that, aren't you?'

Allie turned to Zac, indicating that it was time for him to back her up on this. 'No, Allie's not just saying it. Ask any ambulance crew, they've all had to persuade people with very serious injuries that they won't be okay to go home if they're allowed to just rest for a minute.'

Corinne nodded. 'Thanks. I appreciate that.'

'Glad you're taking his word for it over mine...' Allie grinned, raising an eyebrow.

Corinne's hand flew to her mouth and then suddenly she started to laugh. Allie's teasing had done its job and taken the tension out of the situation. 'There's no right answer to that, is there?'

Zac chuckled. 'None that won't get you into trouble. I'd keep quiet if I were you.'

'Sounds like good advice.' Allie shot Zac a grin. 'Do you have someone who can bring you in some things?'

'Yes, thanks. My parents are in Melbourne, but my

brother and sister-in-law will be coming this evening. With some clothes and probably a set of shackles in case the nursing staff need them.' Corinne was able to venture a joke about it now.

'They won't. You're looking much better now, and all of your charts tell me that you're on the mend.' Allie pursed her lips. 'Would you like me to speak to your brother, and tell him what I've told you?'

Corinne nodded. 'He won't be here for another hour or so but… I don't suppose you could phone him, could you? If it's not too much trouble.'

'Of course, that's no trouble at all. Give me his number…'

Allie spent some time with Corinne's brother on the phone, but she smilingly reported back that everything was fine, and that her brother understood. Corinne seemed a great deal happier now, and Allie bade her a cheerful farewell.

'What are the arrangements here with regards to Post Sepsis Syndrome?' Allie asked as they walked down to the car together.

'There's an information pack, and we usually have a session with patients or caregivers, to go through it with them and chat about any specific concerns they have. They have a number they can call for help after they're discharged.' The emotional and physical after-effects of sepsis were well recognised now.

'That's good, thanks. Can I have a copy of the pack to look through it?'

'I'll get you one tomorrow. I think you've made a good start in allaying Corinne's fears though. I didn't hear her say that she'd gone home because she was sure she was going to die.'

Allie nodded. 'She was so unemotional about it, as if

she'd accepted that was going to happen and was acting accordingly. When she stumbled, I knew I'd got through to her...'

'That you'd persuaded her there was an alternative?'

'Yes. When she realised that, she lost her focus and almost fell.' Allie pressed her lips together, clearly deep in thought. 'It must have been hard for her. Suddenly realising that she had something to lose.'

Zac nodded. It must have been hard, but he got the impression that Allie wasn't talking only about Corinne. 'Better than not allowing yourself anything, in case you lose it.'

'Really?'

He nodded. 'Yes. Really.'

She smiled up at him suddenly. 'Are you still up for letting me drive us home this evening?'

'Absolutely.' He took his car keys from his pocket and dropped them into her hand. 'Or you could just tell me where we're going at the weekend, so that I can drive. I may be able to suggest a better route.'

Allie chuckled. 'Nice try, Zac. You're not convincing me. I can read a map.'

Zac shrugged. They were both beginning to focus on the delicious possibilities of the present instead of the past, and there was always a possibility that either he or Allie might stumble. But, for now, they were both keeping their footing.

He got into the car and Allie started the engine, driving confidently out of the car park.

CHAPTER NINE

ALLIE HAD DRIVEN to and from the hospital a few times now, with Zac sitting next to her in the passenger seat. Driving a car as large as Zac's was unfamiliar, and she kept forgetting that it had an automatic transmission and reaching for the gear stick. But after a bit of practice, and a careful read-through of the Australian Road Rules, she was confident she could make the longer drive in the dark that she had in mind for their date on Friday evening.

He'd complied without question when she'd told him to bring a sweater with him, although Allie could see that he had his doubts about whether that was absolutely necessary. And she'd been through the large closet in the apartment's entrance lobby, moving the mountain of surfing gear out of the way to find a warm jacket with gloves in the pockets at the back. Allie had surreptitiously added that to her own jacket in the boot of the car. They were ready to go, and Allie switched on the satnav, calling up the route she'd programmed in.

After they'd been driving for a while, heading away from the centre of Sydney, Zac began to get a little restive.

'We're not lost, are we?' He was staring out at the high bushes that bordered the highway.

'No.' She grinned at him. 'I'm not, anyway.'

'Okay. I'll just go with the flow, shall I? Unless you have any navigational questions you want to ask...'

'Like, how do I get to where we're going?'

He chuckled. 'Yeah. That would be ideal.'

'I've held out this long and I'm not going to give it away now. I have an innate sense of direction and a satnav.' And Allie was increasingly nervous. What if Zac didn't enjoy the evening she'd planned? What if it gave too much away about her feelings for him and he was embarrassed by them?

It wasn't long before they entered the Royal National Park, which gave their destination away, but Zac still seemed mystified, obviously wondering what they'd be doing here when it would be getting dark in less than an hour. But as they climbed towards higher ground he started to grin, and when Allie turned off the road and he caught sight of the observatory platform he chuckled.

'Stargazing?'

'Yes, I hope you'll like it.'

'It's a great idea, Allie. Thank you.' He got out of the car, looking around to get his bearings. 'I haven't heard of an observation point in this area.'

'It's new, they've just opened up this year apparently. When I compared the various websites it seemed to be good, and it has the advantage of being close to Sydney. This is why we had to come on a Friday, all of the tickets for Saturday were already gone.'

He nodded, looking around. The advertised telescope looked reassuringly large and complicated, and there was a man standing next to it chatting to a few of the other people who were here for the evening. The breeze was already cooler at this height, and Zac shrugged off a shiver.

'I've brought our coats.' She opened the boot of the car, handing him his, and he grinned, pulling it on.

'Thanks. When you said dress warmly, I didn't think I'd need any more than a sweater.'

She led him over to the small kiosk that was serving thick soup and submarine rolls and they ate hungrily. The light was fading fast and the first few stars were beginning to appear in the sky, and they joined the other stargazers in a group around the telescope as the astronomer began to explain which star was which and what they'd be doing this evening. High-powered binoculars were available for everyone, and they would all have their turn with the telescope.

But just her own eyes and the scattering of bright stars that were appearing in the sky were enough to make Allie catch her breath. She nudged Zac, whose attention seemed taken up by the telescope. 'I saw pictures of this on the web. I thought they were enhanced in some way.' She grinned up at him.

'No, this is what it's really like. You can capture it with a photograph, but it doesn't really do it justice, does it?'

Photographs lied. Even when they weren't enhanced or changed in any way, the lens could only capture one moment that didn't take any notice of the human heart... Allie rejected the thought, and her own shiver of humiliation.

'It's amazing.' Something that was an unchangeable force of nature. 'Have you been stargazing before?'

'I've seen the stars from the park before, but never with a telescope or anyone to explain it all.' His gaze settled back eagerly onto the telescope. 'I can't wait for our turn...'

The time was spent chatting with the others in the small group, swapping stories and impressions. Allie found that the binoculars allowed her to see the craters of the moon, and the long sweep of the Milky Way. The clarity of the universe around her made her catch her breath.

'It makes you feel as if you're a part of it all, doesn't it?'

Zac chuckled. 'Yes, I'm feeling like an extremely small part of it all at the moment. It puts everything into perspective.'

Passing unnoticed, under the great panorama of the sky. It was a great feeling. Allie snuggled against Zac and he put his arm around her shoulders. *That* was a great feeling too.

The first hour was taken up with images from the telescope, displayed on a screen so that everyone could see them. There was something about stars that made everyone move just a little closer together.

Then came their chance to direct the telescope wherever they wanted in the night sky. Zac was so transfixed by it all, so excited, but he didn't forget to give Allie her turn and she saw a bright nebula, swirling slowly but unstoppably in a blaze of colour. Far distant stars, the images of which were hundreds of years old after having travelled at the speed of light through the universe. The moon, their closest neighbour, was revealed in intricate detail which made Allie almost feel that she could reach out and touch it.

It all lasted for longer than had been advertised, and the young woman who was dispensing more soup from the kiosk told Allie laughingly that it always did.

'We give a time, but we never expect to stick to it. People always want to stay a bit longer. Between you and me, *I* always want to stay a bit longer, the sky's different every night.'

'So you never get bored with your job?'

'How could I? Would you like me to take a photograph of you?'

Allie hesitated. She'd seen several people standing in front of the camera that was mounted on a tripod to one side of the kiosk, and decided not to join in with that part of the evening.

'I'm not really…very photogenic.'

The woman raised one eyebrow, but clearly decided not to make a point of it. That was good. Most people allowed Allie to melt away quietly when photographs were being taken, but there was always someone who insisted she move a little closer to be included in the shot.

'The camera's adjusted to capture the stars. Anything on the ground comes out as just a silhouette.'

Allie thought about the idea, beginning to like it. 'Okay. If you don't mind.'

There was no one else waiting for soup, and the woman climbed down from behind the counter in the kiosk. Allie chose the section of the night sky that she wanted the photograph to capture, and suddenly Zac was there, standing beside her, wanting to know what was going on.

'We're taking a photo…' Allie couldn't help feeling slightly apologetic as she looked up at him, as if this was some kind of guilty secret.

'Ah. With an anonymous shadow beneath it?' Zac got the point almost immediately.

'Yes. Don't you feel a bit like an anonymous shadow at the moment?'

He chuckled. 'A lot like one. This is all too big for us to be anything else, isn't it?'

'Both of you?' The woman had finished fiddling with the camera and was looking up at them now.

'Yes. Both of us.' Being a shadow didn't seem quite so melancholy if Zac was going to join her. 'Where do we stand?'

It was late when everyone said their goodbyes, and they got back into the car. Allie followed the line of headlights moving slowly along the road that led off the mountain, trying to concentrate in the darkness. Zac was in the passenger seat, flipping through the photographs that had been downloaded from the telescope onto his phone.

'You want me to drive?' He looked up suddenly as Allie slowed, confused by the shadows that formed around the edge of the beam of the headlights.

'Uh… Maybe.' She brought the vehicle to a stop, still hanging onto the steering wheel. 'I'm not used to this.'

'I should have remembered. Finding yourself in complete darkness comes as a bit of a shock after London.' He grinned, reaching to open the passenger door, and Allie remembered just in time to disengage the locks.

Stupid. Whenever she drove alone these days, she locked the car doors. But there was nothing out here… Nothing but shadows that suddenly seemed menacing. And creatures that she'd heard about but hadn't yet seen.

As Zac walked around to her side of the car she saw something move in the furthest reaches of the headlights. What seemed like a pair of eyes, reflecting the light, and then disappearing back into the shadows of the trees around them. And she panicked…

Allie knew exactly what was happening to her. These attacks had become frighteningly familiar when she'd first learned about what James had done, but she'd thought she had them under control. But in this unfamiliar darkness, surrounded by goodness only knew what…

She tried to breathe. Tried to let go of the steering wheel, but she couldn't, because that was the one thing that seemed to afford her a measure of control. She was aware of Zac opening the driver's door beside her, and couldn't help letting out a whimper of panic.

What must he think? That only made things worse, and she felt tears roll silently down her cheeks.

'Allie?' She heard Zac's voice beside her. Beckoning her back into the real world, where she could cope with the everyday things that surrounded her, but it wasn't enough. He closed the car door, walking back round to get into the passenger seat.

'You're okay. Breathe.'

That was what she was trying to do. Allie closed her eyes, trying to dispel the image of the scene around her. Darkness. Unknown things that seemed to be moving around in that darkness. It suddenly felt even more terrifying and she opened her eyes again, blinking into the pool of light around them. Searching...

Zac leaned forward slowly, engaging the locks on the car doors. She tried to focus on him, but shame wouldn't allow her to meet his gaze.

'Allie, listen. You're okay, you're safe. Just breathe with me.' His voice held no trace of reproach, just gentle reassurance. This time she *could* follow his lead, and as he counted slowly she managed to regulate the panicky gasps of air. Her head began to stop swimming.

'That's great. Now let go of the steering wheel before you break it in half.' His quiet humour cut into the panic, and Allie focused on her hands, willing her fingers to unclench.

'Good. Give it another try, you're nearly there.'

It was an effort, but she managed to let go, in favour of clasping her hands tightly together in her lap. 'Zac... I'm so sorry...'

'Don't be. You're on new territory and you're allowed to be uncertain. I should have thought about it sooner.'

Allie shook her head. 'I've spoiled everything...'

'No, you haven't. Get your phone out.'

Allie felt miserably in her pocket, pulling her phone out with trembling fingers.

'Let's take a look at that picture, eh?'

It was easy enough to find, it was the only image on her phone. Allie tapped on the screen and the picture of the stars, with two unrecognisable silhouettes beneath them, opened up.

'It's...' She cleared the lump that had formed in her throat. 'It's a great picture.'

'It was a wonderful moment. Thank you for sharing it with me.'

'You want me to send it to you?' The thought made her feel a little breathless, even if there was nothing to worry about.

He shook his head. 'No, I don't think so. I prefer having it up here.' Zac gave a diffident shrug, tapping his temple with one finger.

'I really *am* sorry, Zac. I was making a fuss over nothing.' She reached over, taking his hand. Zac hadn't touched her once, and his instincts had been good. If he had, it would only have made her panic even more.

'It's not nothing, Allie. It's something you've had to go through and I wish that you hadn't. But it doesn't change anything, about you or me.' He frowned suddenly. 'Am I explaining this properly?'

'You mean it's something that happens to me, not who I am?' Allie hoped that was what he was thinking, anyway.

'Yes, exactly.' He squeezed her hand. 'This is who *I* want to be.'

'Me too.'

Zac grinned. 'Since we have that sorted, I'll remind you that I consider getting you back home safe and sound is my responsibility, irrespective of what number date this is.'

Allie managed a smile. 'Okay. As long as you'll agree that it's also my responsibility to get *you* back home safe and sound. Which in this instance probably involves handing over the car keys.'

'Agreed. Mutual accountability.' He let go of her hand and the car rocked slightly as he squeezed through into the back seat. 'Shift over.'

Allie undid her seat belt, sliding over into the passenger seat. Zac moved forward again, settling himself behind the wheel. 'Ready to go?'

He drove slowly towards the highway, coming to a stop when a couple of kangaroos decided that it would be a good idea to race them, and then gave up when Zac refused to take up the challenge.

'You can't outdrive a kangaroo.' He flashed her a smile. 'Just give them the road and let them get out of the way...'

'Maybe I shouldn't have been quite so ambitious. No streetlights makes the headlights on their own really spooky.'

'Yeah, I don't know anywhere in London that gets completely dark at night, there's always a bit of light coming from somewhere. But you chose a great place for a date and we'll be back on the highway in a minute.' He was relaxed and easygoing, and seemed to have forgotten all about Allie's sudden panic. When they arrived back at the apartment he didn't delay on the doorstep though and had his keys out ready to let them inside. Allie supposed that since this was the second date...

He closed the door behind them and she caught his hand. This time she felt a lot more confident about what should happen next.

'Thank you. I had a wonderful evening.' She reached up, clasping her hands behind his neck, wondering if Zac would take the initiative this time and kiss her.

'So did I.' She felt his hands, gentle on the back of her waist. Not moving, not pulling her close. That was what she liked about Zac. He generally gave her plenty of space but when he did touch her he owned the gesture. Ready to change it if it wasn't what Allie wanted, and never pretending that it was anything other than what it was.

She stared up into his eyes, and he returned her smile. Then he gently brushed his lips against her cheek, murmuring quiet words against her skin. 'I'd really like to kiss you.'

'I'd like that too.'

This time he was more confident. His kiss was right on the edge of searching and dominant, turning her knees to jelly. But Zac's gentle responsiveness still allowed Allie to feel that everything which happened between them was her choice. She moved closer, holding him tight, feeling his strong body taut against hers.

He drew back, his gaze telling her everything that she didn't dare say. Then he kissed her again, this time a light rhapsody of pleasure on her lips. His gentle goodnight sent her upstairs to her room still buzzing with feelings that only a wide sky and the universe could contain.

CHAPTER TEN

AFTER A LATE NIGHT Zac woke late. He'd needed the sleep, but he also needed exercise, balance and the cooling rush of water against his skin, to rid him of the sensual drowsiness that owed more to last night than it did this morning. Mark had already gone inside to open up the shop, and Zac decided to take a swim.

He arrived back in the apartment an hour later, the muscles in his shoulders now looser and aching a little from the amount of exercise he'd put them through. Allie was sitting at the breakfast bar with her laptop open in front of her and a cup of coffee to keep her company.

'Hey there. What are you up to?' He went to the fridge, taking out some fruit to chop and mix with a bowl of granola.

'I'm just looking for some websites to recommend to Carly. I mentioned that there were a few that had helped me, but she won't go onto the web and find them herself.'

'I can see her point. How have things been going with her?' Zac flipped on the coffee machine.

'Good. Now that she's ready physically to be discharged, Philippa and I are working on some of the things she'll be facing when she goes home. It's been really helpful for the three of us to discuss that. I think we've all learned something.'

'And you think she's ready to start going back on the internet now?'

Allie turned the corners of her mouth down. 'I'm not sure that *ready* is quite the word. But it's a fact of life, the same as going back to college when Carly knows that everyone will have seen those pictures. If we can help her feel safe and protected while she reclaims her space, that's really the best we can hope for at the moment.'

Maybe now was the time for Zac to say something. Maybe not...

'So... Tell me more.' He sat down opposite her at the breakfast bar and took a sip of his coffee. 'I'm interested.'

Allie shrugged. 'There's not much more to tell, really. The one thing that the internet's really good at is sharing—information, images and so on. I learned that to my cost, and I've always felt that I wanted to take a part of it back.'

'That's a tall order.'

'Yes, but knowing that there may be images out there which I never wanted to share is a pretty tall order as well. I can try to get things taken down, but it doesn't always work. I reckon that maybe the thing that does work would be to make my own voice heard, but I'm not sure how to do that.'

Zac stirred his granola thoughtfully. She'd said something of the sort before. And if he didn't say what was on his mind now then he was going to have to forget all about the idea.

'You mean your own website?'

Allie puffed out a breath. 'That seems a bit grand. It's well beyond my technical capabilities as well.'

'I know how to make a website. It's actually really easy.'

She stared at him, shaking her head. Then she frowned. This was a *no*, then.

'When you say easy...?'

'How many times have you seen me messing about with computers?'

Allie shrugged. 'Never. But I've only been here for three weeks.'

Three weeks that felt like a lifetime.

'That's pretty representative. When I was a teenager I didn't do social media because I didn't have anyone to socialise with. I used the internet for my studies a lot but that was it. The same when I went to medical school. And when I came here... I just wanted to experience life—the kind you can reach out and touch. I've got my own website, though.' Zac couldn't help feeling a touch of pride at the achievement.

'You have? How come...?' Understanding dawned on Allie's face. 'Does this have anything to do with those mysterious lunchtime and after-work meetings with Jack in the rec room. That I never get invited to?'

Zac nodded. 'I had to get him out of his room and communicating with the real world. So we did a deal. I've been telling him how rehab works and giving him some things to read, and he's taught me how to make my own website. Doing it in the rec room has been really good for him, people get interested and he's started to make friends. He's been exercising a lot more as well.'

'Yes, I noticed that. The muscles in his leg are starting to get stronger...' Allie fixed him with a questioning look. 'Did you do this so that you'd know how to make me a website?'

He hadn't really expected her not to ask. Allie was perceptive enough to understand most things about any given situation and Zac had only justified not telling her about this by promising himself that he'd be honest if it ever came to the crunch.

'It was a good way to get Jack moving around again. And since you'd been talking about taking the things that had been stolen from you back again, it seemed to me to be a good skill to have. If you ever needed it.'

'Two birds with one stone, then.'

Zac shrugged. 'I wouldn't quite put it like that. But yes, I suppose so.'

'And if I'd never mentioned it?' Allie clearly wasn't about to let him off the hook as easily as she might have done.

'Then I wouldn't have said anything about it. I'd have reckoned I'd learned something, and that it had done Jack good as well.'

She stared at him. And then she started to laugh. Zac didn't quite know how to respond to that.

'Zac…!' Her shoulders were shaking, and she clapped her hand over her mouth.

Okay. He hadn't thought that this was particularly funny. Zac picked up his empty cup, emptying the dregs of coffee into the sink and switching the machine back on. Maybe they both needed a few moments.

'Zac… Come here.'

He turned and walked back over to the breakfast bar.

Allie stretched out her hands, taking his. 'Zac, that's the nicest, sweetest thing anyone's ever done for me.'

'And the funniest?' That hurt a little, and Zac wasn't sure why.

Allie must have seen his discomfiture, and her face straightened suddenly. 'I wasn't laughing at you, Zac, I was laughing at me. I came all this way, thinking that Australia had to be far enough to go to get away from everything that had happened, because I couldn't run any further. And then I met you and I'm beginning to feel that I can do what I wanted to all along, stop running and fight back.'

From somewhere, deep in his past, his mother's laughter echoed in his head. The way he'd tried so hard to please her, and been met with nothing but derision. So different from Allie, who had every reason to be bitter, but had somehow retained the ability to love.

'I misjudged you.' Zac turned the corners of his mouth down, wondering how he was going to make this up to Allie.

'If you mean that you judged me by the way you've been treated in the past, then that's not your fault. I'd should have been more thoughtful. I will be in future, because I want to earn your trust.' Her gaze searched his face.

He let go of her hands, leaning over the breakfast bar to kiss her cheek. It felt so soft against his, so warm, that he couldn't draw back. 'You have that already.'

She turned her head slightly, whispering in his ear, 'So what were you saying about a website?'

In other words, Allie trusted him too. Zac smiled, whispering back, 'Think about it. Let me know what you decide.'

They spent more than twice the amount of time in the supermarket than Zac usually allocated for his weekly shop, because Allie was still intent on examining everything that was new and different. It was twice as much fun too, as was dropping into the shop to drink tea with Mark and Naomi afterwards.

'A paddleboard's an investment,' Mark told her sternly as she examined the display. Zac would have characterised it more as something to have fun with, and Naomi's elbow in his ribs indicated her agreement.

'That's the best one!' Izzy piped up, and Allie looked down at her.

'Why's that, Izzy?'

'Because it's yellow.'

Allie squatted down on her heels next to the little girl. 'Do I have to wear yellow as well?'

Izzy thought for a moment. 'You can wear a yellow T-shirt with a wiggly blue stripe on it.' She described her current favourite from her own collection of T-shirts.

'Sounds good. It's nice to have something that matches.' Allie looked up at the paddleboard.

'The valve on this one is rather more robust. Saves time when you're inflating it…' Mark tried to restore a more serious tone to the process. 'And it's well priced.'

'Dad!' Izzy pushed at her father's leg, trying to move him out of the way. 'It's not yellow!'

Mark scratched his head thoughtfully. 'Yeah. There is that to it.'

'You don't have to buy one now,' Naomi called over to Allie. 'Borrow mine, I'm not using it. Too busy with the next generation of surfers.' She grinned at the baby bouncer, where Finn was waving his arms ferociously.

Mark nodded. 'That's the thing to do. Then you'll know if you want to keep going with it.'

Zac kept his own disagreement with the idea to himself. If Allie had a board of her own she'd use it and going out onto the water seemed to him to be one more step towards a place where she could feel and appreciate the world around her. But he'd be gone soon, and she had to find her own way.

Not everything was about healing, though. Some things you just had to do because you wanted to do them, which in Zac's experience was part of the healing process too. A couple of other customers, clearly serious surfers, had caught Mark's attention and Izzy followed him over to give her own opinion of their choice.

'She's getting to be a handful, isn't she?' Zac grinned at Naomi.

'You don't know the half of it.' Naomi smiled back. 'They

talk about the *terrible twos* but just wait until you have a four-year-old.'

Zac had never envisaged that. He loved Izzy, but had never really imagined he'd want to be part of a family again. But somehow, that solid determination that had grown in his heart, the feeling that he'd do anything to make Allie happy even if it meant walking away and leaving her here... That was family, wasn't it? Wanting the best for someone, however much it cost?

Izzy ran over to him, looking up expectantly. Now that Mark was involved in a conversation about the wicking properties of various materials, which didn't appear to take account of their colour, she was getting bored.

'Want to go down onto the beach, Izzy?'

The little girl started in an expression of delight, looking pleadingly up at her mother, and Naomi grinned.

'Haven't you got something to do, Zac?'

'Yeah.' He lifted Izzy up in his arms and she hung on tight to his T-shirt in an indication that whatever it was he had to do, she'd be coming along to help. 'I'm thinking of going down onto the beach...'

'Sandcastles?' Allie had been lingering by the paddle-boards, still sorting through them, but she looked round suddenly.

'*Plee-ee-ase*, Mum.'

'Okay, Izzy.' Naomi shot him a grateful smile. 'Drop in for lunch on the way back, eh?'

Allie and Izzy had embarked on an ambitious sandcastle project, which had temporarily sapped Izzy's excess of energy. Zac carried the little girl up the hill to Mark and Naomi's house, Allie stopping to admire the carefully tended waratah bushes.

'Are we staying for lunch?' Seeing himself and Allie as a unit which made its decisions together was becoming more and more natural.

'If you want. I'd like to see your website, though...' Allie looked up at him questioningly.

Somewhere between paddleboards and sandcastles, she'd made her decision. Zac grinned down at her.

'Right then. Prepare yourself to be impressed. Jack's done a really good job with it.'

He gave their apologies to Naomi, promising to drop in again soon, and tried not to rush Allie back to the apartment before she changed her mind. But she seemed enthusiastic enough for the both of them, waving away his offer of something to eat first as she sat down at the breakfast bar and opened her laptop. Zac typed the address into her browser, hitting the enter key.

'Zac! That's amazing!' The entry page consisted of a picture that Zac particularly liked. Mark had caught him right at the head of a large wave, a plume of spray following his trajectory.

'Only time I ever managed to do that without falling off. You have to scroll down.'

Allie nodded, clearly having already seen the down arrow at the bottom of the picture. Jack had told him that people would expect that and know how to navigate without being told. Allie studied the picture a little more closely and then started to scroll.

She didn't take her eyes from the screen, finding the menu without any trouble at all and tapping first on the *About Me* icon and reading through the text that Jack had made him write. Then she moved onto the surfing section, which largely consisted of images from his phone. Zac decided to leave her to it and that sandwiches were a good idea, since Allie was clearly reckoning on taking her time with this.

'Who's *InternetWarrior2*?' She'd clearly worked her way down to the comments section of the page.

'That's Jack. See, *InternetWarrior1* has liked the comment. That's his girlfriend.'

'That's sweet. And I suppose *SurfinDoc* is you, is it?'

'How did you guess?'

Allie grinned. 'The heavy-handed hint that he needs to do his exercises before he'll be ready to surf gives you away. You could be a bit more easy-going, you know.'

Zac shrugged. '*InternetWarrior1* gave me a like. So did *WarriorMum*.'

'I suppose his mother knows best.' Allie made the leap from real life, where Jack's mother was a neat, friendly women who wouldn't say boo to a goose, to her internet persona without any apparent difficulty.

By the time he'd slid the plate of ham and cheese sandwiches and a mug of coffee over the breakfast bar, Allie had been through the page where Zac talked about his work as a doctor, and was clicking on the link which gave hints and tips on water safety.

'There's nothing there!'

'That's the most important part of it, so I'm thinking about what I want to say. What do you reckon?'

Allie reached for a sandwich. 'I think it's great. It looks really professional and I certainly wanted to keep reading. But be honest, Zac. How much of this is your work and how much did Jack do?'

'Jack showed me how to do it, but all the words and pictures are mine, and I chose the template and set up the pages. I had to go back with some questions, of course, but I know the answers to them now.'

'And the comments section?' Allie had seemed particularly interested in that.

'That comes with the template. You just have to select what elements you want on the page.'

'And how long did this all take you?'

'Jack and I got the general shape of it really quickly, in our first session in the rec room. I spent a bit more time getting everything right in the evenings, after you went to bed.'

'Well, I'm impressed. I know lots of people have websites, but I'd never thought much about how they did it...' Allie turned the corners of her mouth down.

'Too busy in the real world.' An image of the Allie who worked hard and played hard, seemingly without a care in the world, hit him. Two years ago, Zac had felt an obscure longing to be a little more like her, not so much because he wanted to change, but for the opportunity it might give to enter the circle of light that always seemed to surround her.

They'd both changed. His own life had moved on when he'd realised that he needed to change for himself and not anyone else. Allie's... He wouldn't wish that change on anyone, even if it had started her on the long road that led here.

'I didn't need a website then. I need one now.'

Zac thought about the proposition. 'But do you *want* one? It's a big commitment.'

She shrugged. 'I don't know if anyone's even going to read it. I'm not sure if that even matters.'

'You just want to say it?' Allie gave him a silent nod. 'That's okay, but what if people *do* read it? Can you be there for someone like Carly, who might find the site and need help? And what if someone comes on your site and doesn't agree with you?' Jack had told him all about trolling and Zac didn't want to think about that right now. That would add an even greater dimension to Allie's pain.

'It'll be my site. Presumably I can delete comments?'

'Yes, but you've got to look at them first. Don't get me wrong, Allie, I'll help the best I can with whatever you want to do. That's why I did this in the first place. But I'm not going to pretend that it'll be easy. Getting up the courage to say what you want to say is just the beginning. And you know better than I do that what goes onto the internet is difficult to erase, so once you start it's not necessarily that easy to go back again.'

'Don't make it sound too much like a walk in the park, will you?' Allie's rather feeble joke fell flat and a tear rolled down her cheek. All of her enthusiasm, all of that precious glow, was gone now. He'd burst that bubble as efficiently as his mother had stamped on all of his own enthusiasms.

'Allie, if you really want to do this, then I'm with you all the way.' He reached forward, wiping the tear away. 'I truly believe you can do it, but I won't lie to you and tell you it's going to be easy.'

He saw her hand fist in her lap. Allie was going to fight back. It occurred to Zac that all his parents had ever wanted was to subdue his wants and needs with theirs, and the fierce excitement that he felt at Allie's defiance freed him from the nagging worry that his actions owed anything to theirs.

'Don't run away with the idea that this is all your idea, Zac. I've been thinking about something like this for a long time. Now's the time for me to do it, and if I have you to thank for that then…' she shrugged, throwing up her hands in an expression of frustration '…thank you. And if you don't help me set it up, then you're in *real* trouble.'

Zac couldn't help grinning at the thought that somehow he'd played a part in bringing her to this *right time*. 'What kind of trouble?'

'Trouble you won't like.' Allie smiled suddenly, leaning forward to plant a kiss on his cheek.

'I'll warn you now that I can stand any amount of that kind of trouble...'

Allie knew her power over him, and she no longer seemed afraid of it. Zac wasn't afraid of it either. He knew that she'd tell him what she wanted and that she wouldn't break if he pushed her a little. He kissed her, his lips lingering on hers to explore the exquisite sensuality of her response.

'I could pack my bags and go to live in the hospital accommodation...' Allie's threat was accompanied by the sweetest of smiles imaginable.

'You'd be miserable there.' Zac caressed her cheek with his fingertips.

'Yes, I'm sure I would. But I've made up my mind and I'm going to stop at nothing, Zac...'

If only they had more time. Zac would be here for another two weeks, and then he was off to Queensland for a week, before flying home to England. But Allie knew that trying to force the pace between them wouldn't work. She'd be fearful and ashamed of her own body, and he was bound to know it, however hard she tried to hide her feelings from him. She'd become practised in smiling and keeping going, even though she was dying inside, but this relationship with Zac didn't allow anything but complete honesty.

But there were plenty of things they *could* share. Things that seemed to demand the same trust and the same kind of caring and sharing as making love. And, strangely, she and Zac were now strengthening their relationship in the one place that Allie had thought she might never be at peace with. The internet.

He'd shown her the site that Jack had used to construct his

website, and Allie had liked a lot of the templates, and the idea that she could incorporate a blog onto her site. By the time the sun started to sink in the sky, Allie had a website.

'What do you reckon, so far?' They'd decided to celebrate with cocktails on the balcony, and the ice clinked in her glass as Allie stirred her drink thoughtfully.

'It's good. I like the idea of having one page for who you are, and another for your personal statement about what happened to you. It makes the distinction between the two clear. And using blogs to cover different aspects of image-based abuse, and your own journey, gives you a forum to update it regularly.' He paused, looking at her thoughtfully. 'It could do with a few photos.'

That was confronting. But it was important to her as well. 'I want to present the image of myself that I've chosen.'

Zac nodded. 'But you're understandably not that keen on a camera lens. What about the one we took last night, with the stars?'

'I can use it? You're in it as well…'

He laughed. 'It's nice of you to ask. Yes, of course you can.'

Allie thought the idea through. 'I'd like to do a blog about the stargazing. What it meant to me to be able to go and do something new, just because I wanted to. But if I can't show my face to the people I'm trying to reach, what kind of message does that give?'

'That you're cautious. The people you really want to speak to will understand that, won't they?'

'Yes, but… Why should I, Zac? Why should I feel I have to hide from a camera?'

'Because it was a tool that someone used to abuse you. If someone's been stabbed, then no one questions it if they're a little wary of kitchen knives. You don't have to do any more than you're comfortable with, Allie, that's important.'

He'd been cautious and given her some good advice. But this didn't feel right.

'Can we take some pictures tomorrow, Zac? Just to try things out, and I'll see how I feel about them.'

'Sure. Any time.'

Allie could feel a frown coming on, and looked down at her drink, stirring it disconsolately. The jangle of the ice cubes didn't seem quite so perfect, suddenly.

'We'll have to do it soon. In another two weeks…' He'd be gone. Allie would be alone here, albeit with a good place to live and new friends close by, which was more than she could have ever expected to achieve in the course of three weeks.

'I was going to ask you about that.' Zac's voice interrupted her reverie. 'I was thinking of giving Queensland a miss and staying here for the extra week before I fly back to London. Would that be okay?'

A jangle of competing emotions left her numb. 'It's your apartment, Zac. Of course you should stay, for as long as you want.'

His gaze caught hers. 'That's not what I meant. I was wondering if I could stay here with *you*.'

It was hard not to just say *yes*—forget about why he'd offered, and just take this extra time with him. Maybe it was pride and maybe caution that wouldn't allow her to.

'It's really good of you to offer, Zac. But I'll be okay here on my own.'

'I know you will.' He puffed out a breath. 'I made a complete hash of asking you out the first time and so I'm going to try and do better this time around. I've really enjoyed spending these last three weeks. I have two more weeks at work and then another week before I go back to London, and I'd like to spend all of that time with you. If you'd like to spend it with me, that is.'

He couldn't make it any plainer, and that was absolutely fine with Allie.

'Yes. I'd like that too, very much.'

Zac grinned. 'Then it's settled. What do you say we finish our drinks, go for a stroll on the beach and then get an early night? Scout out some places for photographs in the morning, eh?'

CHAPTER ELEVEN

ZAC HAD BEEN up early, finding his camera and download-ing his own photographs onto his laptop. He left it on the breakfast bar, with a note for Allie, saying that the now empty memory card was for her to use and then keep, then went outside to join Mark on the beach. The waves were small and uneven this morning, and they spent quite a bit of time sitting on their boards and exchanging ideas about where the sandbank might move to next.

He saw Allie walking towards them, chatting to Naomi, who was bringing the children down to play while the beach was still empty. As he waved to them, he heard Mark's voice behind him.

'You're not going into work today, are you, mate?'

The question wasn't entirely unwarranted. Allie was wearing a pair of neat trousers and a long-sleeved blouse, with a pair of low-heeled sandals. She looked as if she was about to go to a business meeting.

'No. Not as far as I know, anyway.' He waited for Allie to pick her way down the beach towards them. He'd leave it to her to explain if she wanted to.

'I hear you're taking photographs,' Naomi greeted him. 'For a blog.'

Zac nodded. Allie clearly hadn't gone into details, but it

seemed that she'd decided to start as she meant to go on, and not make a secret of it either.

'I thought some pictures on the beach for starters, maybe.' Allie was pushing her curls behind her ears, in an effort to stop the breeze from catching them.

Zac decided to put his reservations aside. This was hard for Allie, and she didn't need his criticism to make it harder. 'Great. Where do you want to stand?'

'Um…maybe a little further up, so we can get some sand and the sea in?' Allie started to make her way back up the beach, looking for a good spot, and Zac decided to let her go.

'Are we sure about this?' Mark murmured in Naomi's direction and Zac shot him a warning glance. 'What? She just looks a bit uncomfortable.'

Uncomfortable wasn't the word for it. Allie looked as if she expected a giant octopus to rise up out of the sea and grab her at any moment.

Naomi rolled her eyes. 'This isn't as easy as it looks, Mark. I know *you* don't label people, but there are plenty who do.'

'What's that supposed to mean?'

'People see you with a child, and you're a mum. If you're in a bikini on the beach then they reckon you don't have a brain, just a body. Wear something a bit more businesslike and they take you more seriously, but heaven forbid you're able to do all three.'

Naomi had a point. And this was all about not allowing herself to be defined by the camera for Allie.

'You do all three.' Mark glanced over in his direction for some support and Zac decided that he was going to have to fend for himself in this discussion. Naomi had given him a place to start and he needed to talk to Allie.

He walked over to where she was standing. 'More difficult than you thought it would be?'

She turned the corners of her mouth down. 'Yes. I don't
know where to stand or… I couldn't decide what to wear
either.'

'And you wanted to look like someone that people would
take seriously?'

Allie shrugged. 'I just want people to hear what I have
to say.'

'Fair enough. I'm wearing shorts and a rash vest so I
suppose you can completely discount anything I've got to
offer…'

'It's different for you, Zac.'

'Granted. But I thought that the whole point of this was
to be unashamed of who you are, and to show others that
they should be too. What was it you told me that Carly had
said? About someone who has their photograph taken being
called a *subject* when really they're the centre of it all and
in charge of everything that's happening.'

Allie dumped the camera into his hands suddenly, turning to walk back up the beach. 'I'm going to change.' She
flung the words over her shoulder at him and Zac grinned.

When he turned, he saw that Mark had taken charge of
the children and was wandering along the beach chatting
to Izzy, and Naomi was making a beeline for him.

'Everything okay?'

'Yep. I was listening to what you said, there.'

Naomi shot him a sceptical look. 'You were?'

'Allie's gone to change. Something a bit more formal. We
were thinking that a tiara might give her a bit more gravitas.'

'You'd better be joking, Zac…'

Naomi's mood improved markedly when, ten minutes
later, Allie appeared. She was wearing the light cargo shorts

that she usually wore for the beach, with a cap-sleeved blouse. Allie always looked stunning, but now she also looked ready for a day at the beach.

'What do you think?' She smiled at Naomi.

'Fantastic.' Naomi handed Allie her sunglasses. 'Want to try these?'

Allie took the sunglasses, and Naomi nodded in approval. Zac wished he'd thought to suggest them, because they offered the sensation of privacy and at the same time suggested free time and a sunny day.

She stood a little stiffly at first, but soon enough Allie started to relax. Zac took plenty of pictures, reckoning that Allie *had* to find one that she liked amongst them, and then a few with Allie and Naomi together, their arms around each other.

'You just need one?' Naomi asked as the three of them sat together, watching Mark dangle his son's feet over the waves that broke gently onto the beach, while Izzy did her best to drench her father and brother.

'I think I'll have another one of me at work. Not actually *at* work, because that's private, but looking like a doctor.'

'Hmm. How do you look like a doctor?' Naomi asked.

'Large hypodermic and an evil grin?' Zac flopped onto his back in the sand, feeling the sun warm him. 'Or a stethoscope?'

Allie chuckled. 'I think I'll go for the stethoscope.'

'You could borrow Finn and pretend to be examining him if you wanted.' Naomi floated the idea and Allie shook her head quickly.

'Thanks, but it's got to be just me. The blog's about some pretty serious issues. I'm writing an opinion piece and I shouldn't implicate your family in that, especially a child.'

Zac saw a flash of curiosity in Naomi's face. She was obviously wondering what this was all about.

'That's thoughtful. I wish you well with it.' Naomi decided not to ask, and Zac felt the tightness at the back of his neck relax a little.

Maybe Allie was thinking the same as he was. He was faced with the reality of it now, a chance conversation on the beach becoming something that was challenging and painful. Allie was putting herself in the position of having nowhere left to hide from what had happened to her, but he supposed that he was just experiencing the smallest taste of what she'd been living with for the last eighteen months.

'It's about…' Allie whispered the words so quietly that Naomi didn't hear them, her attention caught by Izzy, who had fallen flat on her face in the sand. Naomi got to her feet, walking over to pick her up, brush her down and give her a hug and a kiss, and the little girl scampered back to Mark.

'Can I tell her?'

'You don't have to.' Zac pulled himself up, leaning on his elbow. The moment was gone now, and Allie didn't need to explain herself.

Allie's gaze met his. 'I want to.'

'That's okay too. Naomi and Mark are good people.' He'd known them both for a while now, and he trusted them.

'Sorry…' Naomi was back now, and she plumped herself down on the sand. 'What were we saying?'

'About the blog. It's *my* blog. Zac's been helping me with it.'

'Ah. Nice.' Naomi shot him a bright, approving smile. 'Making good use of your time then, Zac.'

'It's about…'

Suddenly, Allie lost her nerve. Zac opened his mouth,

about to direct the conversation away to a less difficult subject, and then he caught sight of Allie's pleading look.

'Back in London...' he started slowly, and Allie gave a small sigh of relief, nodding him on. 'In London, Allie was a target of image based sexual abuse. The perpetrator went to prison, and Allie wants to speak out about what happened to her, in the hope of helping others.'

Naomi's eyes widened in horror. 'Allie...?'

'It was eighteen months ago, now. It's okay...'

'No, it is *not* okay.' Naomi reached out, laying her hand on Allie's arm. 'It really isn't. I'm so sorry this happened to you.'

Tears of relief started to spill down Allie's cheeks.

Naomi spread her arms, enveloping her in a hug. 'I can understand that you don't want to talk about this. But I'll read your blog.'

'Thanks. That's what I want people to do.' Allie took the tissue that Naomi had produced from her pocket and wiped her eyes, smiling now.

'I could email my friends. Tell them to pass the word on?'

'Thanks, Naomi. Read the blog first, and if you agree with what I say and feel you can share it with other people, that would be a big help.'

Zac hadn't thought of that. He'd been so concerned about Allie, so determined that she should be able to have her own voice heard if that was what she wanted, that he hadn't considered who was going to hear it.

'That's a really good offer, eh, Allie.'

Naomi shrugged it off. 'It's the least I can do. Lots of people are worried about this. I hear that being pressured to swap photos is becoming increasingly common amongst teenagers these days. It's one of the gazillion things I worry for Izzy about and if there's anything I can do to help then just shout.'

'Allie didn't swap photographs.' It seemed somehow important to Zac that he should make the point, although he wasn't entirely sure why. 'It was a video taken without her knowledge...'

'I know you're saying that it wasn't my fault, Zac, but you don't need to defend me. If I had known about the video and made it in the expectation of it being private, then my ex still wouldn't have had any right to share it, and the consequences of it would have been equally devastating,' Allie corrected him gently.

'Yeah. You're right, I didn't think. Sorry.'

Naomi had blanched at the mention of the word *video*, and it looked as if she was still coming to terms with that piece of information. But she shot Zac a sudden smile.

'I always thought you had hidden depths, Zac. Good on you.' Naomi gave him an approving nod. 'Mark'll be opening up the shop in a minute and he can manage on his own for a bit. Why don't you both come back to mine, and we can find a blank piece of wall for that doctor photograph. I have chocolate fudge brownies.'

The chocolate fudge brownies seemed to seal the deal, and if he was honest Zac needed a few calories. Naomi went to fetch Finn and Izzy, while Zac tucked his surfboard under his arm and started to stroll back up to the apartment with Allie.

'You okay with all of this?'

Allie puffed out a breath. 'I feel as if I've just run a marathon, and my knees are still shaking. But yes, I'm better than okay.'

'And you're ready for the doctor photos?'

'Yes. What shall I wear, do you think?'

It was the first time that Allie had asked him that, and it felt like another small step for man and an enormous leap for womankind.

'What you had on earlier is great. Pin your hair back and hang a stethoscope around your neck and you'll look just as you do at work.'

She nodded, laying her hand on his back, even though Naomi and Mark were probably watching. When Zac put his arm around her shoulders she walked a little closer, falling into step with him.

'You smell nice. Like the sea.'

Despite everything, Zac felt suddenly happy. In moments like these if felt as if they could do anything together and Zac's urgent wish to protect Allie gave way to a more potent ambition. He wanted to fight next to her, in the knowledge that they would protect each other.

It was the closest to someone staging an intervention that Allie had ever experienced. Zac had mentioned that Mark had asked them to pop in on Monday evening, after work. Naomi made tea and the two men sat silently, nodding their agreement while Naomi spoke for all three of them.

They all admired her for standing up for what she believed in and wanting to help others. Both Mark and Naomi had read every word of what she'd written on the site, after she'd given Naomi the address and the password to view it, and they both believed in what she was doing. But she didn't need to stand alone. They were her friends, and if Allie would agree to add a picture of all four of them on the beach together they'd be honoured.

Allie cried, and Naomi produced a box of tissues out of nowhere, pushing it towards her. 'Think of it like this.

You're showing that you have friends who support you. People need to know that too.'

'You're sure?' Allie looked around the group for reassurance and Zac rolled his eyes.

'We're sure. If you need written confirmation, we're happy to provide it. In large letters in the sand.' He gave her that irresistible grin of his, and Allie laughed through her tears.

By Wednesday the site was finished. Allie had asked Naomi for honest comments, and she'd made a couple of suggestions that Allie really liked. All four of them had drawn up a list of friends that they could email, to try and spread the word about the site. But the most touching thing, the thing that always made her smile, was the photograph at the bottom of the *About Me* page. Allie and Naomi, standing on the beach together, with Zac and Mark on either side of them, Zac's arm around her shoulders and Naomi's around her waist.

Allie and Zac walked up to the house at the top of the hill, Zac carrying his laptop and Allie a bottle of iced champagne. Zac ceremoniously removed the password from the site, making it officially live, and they all sent their emails. Then Zac popped the champagne cork while Mark fetched some glasses, so they could drink a toast together to the success of Allie's new venture.

'Now we wait.' Zac put his arm around her shoulders as they walked back down to the apartment.

'I'm not expecting miracles. Maybe a few people will see it as a result of our emails, but I don't mind if I'm talking to an empty room. I've done it, and that's the main thing.'

Zac nodded. 'We'll see. We've worked pretty hard over the last few days—you fancy catching a movie tomorrow evening?'

'Yes, that would be great. Something to look forward to.'

* * *

If one man's hope could do anything to drive a website's stats up, then Zac reckoned that Allie's site would have garnered about a thousand hits by now. They hadn't had time to look at the site on Thursday morning before work, but Allie had switched her phone on during their coffee break and it had started to chime furiously.

'What's that?'

'I set the first blog post up so that I'd get an email when someone commented.' Allie was scrolling furiously. 'I've got over fifty unread emails here, look.'

Zac leaned over to see her phone, his heart suddenly thumping in his chest. He knew he'd wanted this for Allie, but he didn't realise how much. She'd got to the bottom of the list and was smiling.

'Ah! My first comment is from *SurfinDoc*. He's a pretty nice guy. And then there's *Naomi1357* and *Mark2468*.'

'Hardly imaginative.' Zac tried to curb his glee. They had to go back to work in a minute.

'Oh, shush, Zac. It's really sweet of them.' Allie started to scroll back up again. 'I don't recognise any of these names—who *are* they all?'

'Um—stop, that's a guy I know who used to work here and moved to Melbourne—Geoff Andrews.'

She opened up the email, scanning the text quickly. 'That's a really good comment. He makes some great points about how health professionals can support people who've been abused.'

'Yeah, Geoff's a nice guy. His wife teaches at a high school, so I wouldn't be surprised if she's commented as well… Allie, I'm sorry, but we've got to get back to work. We can read them all at lunchtime…'

By the time they managed to get away for a late lunch,

there were more comments. Allie worked her way down all of them, liking each one, and added her own comment thanking everyone for their interest, and saying she was overwhelmed by the response.

'That'll do it. People like an acknowledgement.' She took a bite from her sandwich, jumping as yet another email pinged into her inbox. 'This is getting crazy.'

Zac nodded, smiling at her. He'd wanted this so much, but now that there were more comments than he'd ever dared hope for, he was afraid that they would overwhelm Allie.

Careful what you wish for...

Zac had been wishing for a great deal lately. He knew that his relationship with Allie had to end, but he was recklessly moving ahead, as if he'd never heard the word *loss* before. And now the website was threatening to overwhelm Allie. But he couldn't bring himself to regret any of it, because he'd never felt quite so alive. He was on a rollercoaster and the only choice available to him now was to hang on.

'What do you say we give the pictures a miss tonight, to give you a bit of time to respond to this?'

She thought for a moment. 'I have to keep this sustainable. I've got to work as well and I could spend for ever getting into discussions with everyone. I'll like things and drop in with a few general comments, but I can't reply to everyone individually, there are only so many ways of saying thank you. I'll post again at the weekend as I'd intended, and if you still want to go to the pictures tonight...?'

'That's a great plan, Allie. You need to keep some time for yourself. And I'd love it if you'd come to the pictures with me tonight.'

CHAPTER TWELVE

WHAT WAS IT they said? Careful what you wish for? The number of comments coming in had subsided after the first day, and Allie spent the day on Saturday taking a tour of central Sydney to see some of the sights with Zac. They had a great time, and when they got back home their kisses were sweeter than ever. Everything was going well and the only cloud on the horizon was that Zac would be going back to London soon.

The second post on her blog had already been prepared and scheduled to post on Saturday evening. Allie had switched off the email alerts that flooded her inbox, in favour of carving out an hour every day to go through them all and write a comment at the bottom thanking everyone for their thoughts.

Then, on Sunday morning, the first challenge came. Luckily, Allie spotted it while Zac was out surfing, and he never saw her reaction. It was just one line, but a cold hand seemed to close around her heart, squeezing hard.

Letting someone take videos of you is just asking for trouble.

For a moment, she was right back where she'd started. Humiliated and afraid, wanting to run to her room, lock the door and cower there. Allie slammed the lid of her laptop closed, shaking.

She could delete that comment. Make it go away. She opened her laptop again, scrolling down a little further, and began to realise that she didn't need to do anything. Five replies did it all for her, explaining why the comment was so hurtful and wrong, and defending her.

'Thank you. *Thank you!*' She sent the thought out into the ether, and then typed her own comment, thanking those who had spoken up for her and closing down that thread. All the same, she still felt sick to her stomach. She decided she'd done enough for today, and opened her email to see if there was anything there for her.

Then she saw the email, and Allie's blood ran cold. It was from one of the nurses at the hospital in London, who started off by saying she'd got Allie's email address from an old round robin invitation for birthday drinks. Anya Patel congratulated her on her new website, and thanked her for standing up to be counted. On behalf of herself and three friends, who had never had the courage to come forward and say that they too had been victims of the group who'd shared Allie's video...

'Hey there.' Allie jumped, slamming her laptop closed, as she heard Zac's voice. 'We caught a few good ones this morning...'

'You did?' Allie forced a smile.

'Are you okay?'

He looked so carefree, tanned and handsome, his clothes dried by the sun. Zac was golden at any time but right now he seemed almost gleaming. She couldn't spoil that.

'Yes, fine. I'm just a bit tired, we walked an awfully long way yesterday.'

Zac grinned at the memory of it. Allie had carefully

stowed the day away in her cache of treasured memories, but it felt as if this morning had warped even that.

'You looked as if you'd just seen a ghost when I walked in.' She couldn't escape his gaze now. Perceptive and yet forgiving. As blue as the sea, and about a hundred times more inviting. And she didn't have an answer for him.

'Okay. I could go upstairs and grab a shower. Make some breakfast and maybe go down and get a paper and read it. Any time you'd like to share I'll stop what I'm doing...'

'It's really nothing, Zac.' And it wasn't fair to share this with him. Zac deserved only sunny days, blue skies with no hint of cloud.

'Now I *know* it's something.' He frowned. Try as she might, it seemed that Zac wasn't going to allow her to save him from this.

'Could I have a hug?'

He nodded, walking over to where Allie was sitting at the breakfast bar. Surrounded by the intoxicating mix of his own scent and that of the sea and feeling his arms around her strengthened Allie's resolve. Zac didn't deserve the fall-out from this when he'd done so much to give her back her voice. More than that—she loved him and couldn't bear to hurt him.

'I never really said this. But I have a lot to thank you for, Allie.'

'Me?' Allie didn't know how to reply to that. 'Why would you want to thank me?'

He looked down at her, holding her tight in his gaze. 'You really don't know, do you? For your kindness and your respect. Your bravery. I used to think that functioning well in the world was as much as I could expect, but you've taught me to want more. I won't forget that.'

'I don't think I taught you anything that you didn't already know, Zac.'

'That's where you're wrong. I care about you and that makes me bold. And it's why it hurts when you shut me out.'

Allie shook her head. 'You don't need to keep supporting and protecting me.'

'No, I don't. I want to, though. I want to share whatever's bothering you as well.'

He'd turned the tables on her, in the most loving way possible, and now Allie had no choice.

'There was quite a negative comment on the blog this morning. I felt really bad about it and then I saw that people had defended me, telling the person who posted it exactly why they were wrong in saying what they did.'

'That's...really upsetting. And really nice, all at the same time.'

'Yeah. I'm going to concentrate on the really nice part of it.'

'And...?' Zac knew this wasn't all of it.

Allie heaved a sigh. 'I got an email, from someone I used to know at work. I can't tell you who, because it must have been really hard for her to write to me, and I have to respect the confidence.'

'Understood. Can you tell me what it said? I'd keep that to myself, of course.'

'I think you must, Zac. However angry it makes you.'

He nodded. 'Fair enough. We can be angry together, eh?'

Allie took a moment to gather her thoughts. 'The person who wrote to me said that she'd been a victim of the group that shared my video. There are three others as well, who didn't come forward.'

She felt Zac catch his breath. 'There are more?'

'At least four. And they've been bearing this weight all

of this time, without any support from the hospital. I had that, at least.'

'And you've replied to the email?'

'Not yet. I want to get back to her as soon as possible because I know it must have taken a lot to write to me, but I'm not sure what to say.'

Suddenly it was Zac who was clinging to her, needing her support. Allie hung onto him tightly, and he let out a sigh.

'How about asking if she'd like to talk about things? It seems she does or she wouldn't have written to you, and perhaps you could video-conference. You know this person already.'

'Yes, and I think she might be comfortable with a conversation. It's a good idea. I could tell her that if she or her friends do want to talk a little more then I'd like to be there for them, whenever they're ready.'

'Just as long as you're ready.' The balance tipped again and now Zac was supporting her.

'I can do this. I've learned a lot from working with Philippa and sharing my own story with Carly and listening to hers. A lot of the things that Carly says strike a chord with me, and I think we've both realised that we're not alone.'

'Why don't you write back now then and I'll make some breakfast?'

'Sounds good. Then we'll spend a lazy day on the beach, being good to ourselves. And each other, of course.'

Zac smiled that warm golden smile of his. 'That sounds really good to me.'

One of the nice things about working with young adults was that they were challenging and demanding, a whole complex bag of medical and emotional issues to solve. Another nice thing about them was that some days they did your job for you.

Jack had made a lot of progress and had been discharged to a rehab facility, but he still messaged the friends he'd made here at the hospital, and Zac had made time to pop in and see how he was doing. Corinne was recovering well, but still found any exertion difficult and was being kept in the hospital because there were concerns that her heart might have been affected by the massive trauma that her body had been through. But she'd struck up a friendship with Carly, who came back to visit her regularly. The two young women were spending time together, providing much-needed companionship for each other.

Zac seemed to navigate the complex web of new friendships and new challenges, ever-changing personalities and needs with ease. That was deceptive, and Allie knew that giving each of his patients the impression that he had all of the time in the world for them was the result of a great deal of hard work, and sometimes a juggling act. But this afternoon everything seemed to have fallen into place. The ward was quiet and running like clockwork, which was just as well because Allie was exhausted from four late nights in a row.

Carly was in Corinne's room, the two of them watching afternoon soap operas on TV. Allie had sat down for just one minute to go through Corinne's notes…

Then she felt Zac shaking her. She opened her eyes with a start, suddenly fully awake. Zac was only moments ahead of the head of the unit, Dr Jamieson, who'd stopped outside Corinne's room to talk with the ward manager.

'Ah, I've been wondering where you were, Dr Maitland-Hill.' Dr Jamieson ran the unit like a precision machine, which made everyone's lives easier, but sleeping on the job wasn't included in his policy that his staff should have time to spend with their patients.

'We've been going through our ongoing recovery plans.' Corinne had hastily switched off the TV and answered for Allie. 'Carly and I are keeping in touch after I leave here, so that we can give each other a bit of encouragement.'

Quick thinking. Allie shot Corinne a grateful look, hoping that her hair wasn't as wild as it usually was when she woke up in the morning, and wondering whether she might become invisible in the now slightly crowded room.

'Excellent.' Dr Jamieson seemed pleased. 'It's nice to see you again, Carly. Do either of you have any concerns that you'd like to raise with me?'

That was Dr Jamieson's purpose in being here. He was an advocate of the principle of management by walking around, and made sure that staff and patients all saw his face at least once a day, and knew that they could speak directly to him if they wanted to.

'No. Everything's fine.' Carly was beginning to speak up for herself a bit more now, and Dr Jamieson's nod of approval showed that he was aware of the work that had gone into that.

'Right then. Nothing for me to do here.' Dr Jamieson beamed at them both. 'I'll be seeing you tomorrow, Corinne.'

No doubt he would. Allie made a pledge to herself that she'd contrive to be awake. Dr Jamieson swept out of the room, and Carly and Corinne exchanged amused looks.

'What? We *are* keeping in contact, aren't we?' Corinne grinned up at Zac, who didn't seem to share her amusement. A quick motion of his hand indicated that he wanted to speak to Allie alone.

'I'd better go. I really appreciate the…um…chat.' Allie grinned at Corinne and Carly.

'No trouble.'

Carly reached for the TV remote, and Allie caught Zac rolling his eyes as he left the room. She shot a grimace in Corinne's direction and picked up the tablet that contained her patient notes, tucking it under her arm.

As she followed Zac, she heard Corinne murmur to Carly, 'I'd be aiming for some late nights if I were working with Dr Gorgeous all day...'

'Hmph...' Carly rejected the idea, turning the sound on the television up.

They didn't know the half of it. That was probably just as well, and Allie followed Zac, who was heading along the corridor as if he were on an urgent mission of some kind. He opened the door to the main stockroom, looking around and then motioning her inside. Overreacting much?

'What's going on, Allie?' He folded his arms, his face grim.

'I'm sorry. And thanks for covering for me. It won't happen again.' Allie decided that attack might be the best form of defence. 'But can you honestly say that you've never had an opportunity to sit down for a moment and then fallen asleep at work?'

'When I first qualified and was on call, yes. I can't say I've done it recently. That's not my point, Allie.'

'What *is* your point, then?' Guilt, knowing she'd done the wrong thing, lent a note of irritation to her voice.

'How late were you up last night?'

'Not that late.' Allie had gone to her bedroom to video-conference with Anya, and then written a follow-up email that had taken a while. But she'd been in bed at a reasonable time. 'I just didn't sleep all that well.'

'Yeah, I got that. I heard you getting up at three in the

morning and going downstairs, and was awake for half an hour wondering if you'd come back up again...'

She hadn't. Allie's head had been spinning and she'd been pacing around downstairs, trying to work off her agitation.

'What, I'm under surveillance now, am I?'

The look on his face made her regret the words as soon as they left her mouth. 'I'm sorry, Zac. I didn't mean that. It was a horrible thing to suggest, to you of all people.'

'But that's the kind of thing that happens when you're bone-weary?' His expression had softened a little in the face of her apology.

'I suppose so. But... I can't just leave them on their own with this, Zac. I don't have it in me.'

'I know. But you've been video-conferencing and email-ing every evening for the last three days now. You have a demanding job here, and you're burning the candle at both ends. It's not going to work, Allie. You're going to have to find a way to make your website a sustainable effort. And find it quickly.'

She knew that. Zac would be leaving in another ten days' time, and he wouldn't be here to cook dinners and support her in all the other little ways he'd been contriving to help.

'Please don't be so angry with me, Zac...' She couldn't take it right now.

'I'm not angry, I'm worried. We need to talk about this, and find some way through it.'

Actually, Zac didn't need to do anything at all. He could turn his back and walk away, leaving her to try and cope with what seemed to be two jobs in one day. But Zac didn't walk away, not from his patients or from her.

'We'll talk, I promise. I'm really grateful that you're con-cerned for me, and to tell you the truth I'm concerned for myself. I'll make dinner this evening, and then we'll take a walk on the beach and then get an early night. Tomorrow's Friday and we can talk then.'

'I may confiscate your laptop. And your phone.'

'That's okay. I'd be grateful if you did, actually. There are only so many hours that I can give to the people who've come onto my blog. I almost wish I hadn't done it, or at least left it a while until I was more settled.'

He reached out, his fingers brushing her cheek. All of the warmth, all the feeling that she never wanted to let him go, flooded through her veins.

'No you don't.'

Allie sighed. 'You're right, I don't. It's a lot of work, but I feel that I've finally begun to own myself and what's happened to me. I couldn't have done that without you, Zac. It's your achievement just as much as it is mine.'

He nodded, smiling. 'Heard and appreciated.'

'Are you going to forgive me now?'

Zac chuckled. 'No, I don't think I will until we talk tomorrow and find a way through this.'

A good night's sleep had done wonders. Allie flew through her day's work, and Zac suggested that they catch the food truck on the beach for their evening meal before going back to the apartment for coffee, and to get out of their work clothes. Sitting on the balcony, overlooking the beach, the sound of the sea added a calm to the mood.

'I've got a proposal for you. We'll both have to agree to make it work.' Zac had thought for a while before opening the conversation.

They'd always made their own rules. And maybe Zac was about to come up with another rule that would work better than Allie had ever imagined it might. 'I'm listening.'

He nodded. 'It's clear that you can't go on the way you

have been. You could decide to limit the amount of time that you spend on your website, but in practice that's going to be hard because you feel so strongly about the issues it raises and you want to help people. I've assumed that I'll go back to the London hospital when I go home, but I haven't committed myself to that yet.'

Sudden joyous hope made Allie's heart beat faster. Zac was going to tell her he'd stay...

'But...going home's important to you, Zac. You've always said it was the final step in reclaiming your life.' Allie smothered her own selfish wish to say *yes* to the plan before Zac had even had a chance to suggest it. He'd always considered her needs, and she had to consider his.

'Yeah. I could do that now, or I could do it next year. As long as I do it, and I know I will, it's not going to be an issue.'

He was going to ask. They'd live together, here in the sunshine, and in time they'd learn how to make a life together.

'You're sure?' Before she got carried away, Allie had to ask.

'I'm sure.'

A future seemed to be forming, right there in front of her.

Allie swallowed hard. 'Are you saying that you've been considering staying here?' *With me.* Allie didn't dare say the words but it was all she could think about.

'I've been considering a lot of things. What I most want is to be able to stay with you and find out where our relationship might lead but...' He shook his head, as if saying a regretful goodbye to the dream. 'The only thing that I can see working for both of us is that I stay so that you can go home.'

'What? Zac...?' She'd been mistaken, and the world felt

suddenly as if it was crashing down, burying her under the rubble of her shattered hopes.

'I've thought about this a lot, and I know two things for sure. You can't abandon the people back in London who need your help, even if it means you have to tear yourself in half. And this is your chance to make a difference, and to take back everything that's been stolen from you. Your website has shown you can do it. It's just the beginning.'

'But...' Allie brushed a tear away. She couldn't let him see her cry, and Zac mustn't know what had prompted her tears. Hadn't she promised herself that she would never allow a man to humiliate her again?

'I'm moving on here, Zac. There's no way back for me.'

'We can make that way back. I can meet your commitments here, and you'll have the opportunity to go and do something that could put your whole life back in focus. It's a lot to ask of you, but it's not impossible.'

Allie couldn't meet his gaze now, for fear that he'd see what was going on in her head. She was grabbing at straws, trying to find something that would allow them to be together. But, deep down, she knew that Zac was right.

'Can I think about this?'

He smiled suddenly. 'And try to find a way to talk me out of it?'

'Yes, actually. How do you always know what I'm thinking, Zac?'

'Because you know what I'm thinking. Which is why you can't bring yourself to argue with this idea...'

Neither she nor Zac had anything more left to say. They both knew what they had to do, but Allie wasn't ready to agree to it yet. And even though it was Zac's plan, he seemed positively relieved when she brought the conversation to a close by saying she was going out for a walk.

A month ago, she would have gone upstairs and locked herself in her room. But now the need to think brought with it an urge to go outside, and let the open air blow away some of the cobwebs. Maybe some of the bitter disappointment too.

She'd tried to tell herself that she hated Zac, and that he'd turned out to be just the same as James, hurting her and letting her down. But Allie knew that wasn't true. He'd never promised her anything that he couldn't deliver on. And he was right about this. They both needed different things. She needed to go back to London, and he needed to stay here and cover for her at the hospital.

If it meant they had to part, then maybe that was what they both needed to do too. They were both afraid of commitment, and both of them had their reasons to fear promises that couldn't be kept. They didn't have the luxury of time, to allow their relationship to evolve and heal those wounds. They had to act now, before they were ready.

Allie walked for a long time, trying to think of another solution, or at least dispel some of the disappointment that haunted her. When dusk began to fall and she returned to the apartment, she found Zac stretched out on the sofa, fast asleep. He seemed so peaceful, but Allie didn't want him to wake after she'd gone to bed and find she'd left him here.

'Allie…?' He sat up with a start, almost as soon as she touched his shoulder.

'You didn't sleep last night?' Zac had always seemed inexhaustible but tonight he *had* appeared tired. As if his usual spark had gone out.

'No, not much.' He pressed his lips together in a look of regret. 'You're angry with me?'

'Not with you. I'm angry that life doesn't seem to want to give us a break.' And that neither she nor Zac could make the promises that were needed to fight that.

'I've got to believe that it will.' Zac's shrug told Allie that currently he wasn't too sure.

'Me too.' She leaned forward, kissing his cheek. 'I'm going to get an early night, and you should too.'

CHAPTER THIRTEEN

THE WEEKEND HAD been hard. They'd done all of the same things but they'd lost their lustre because there would be no going back on this parting. Zac knew that he'd have to stay in Australia for the next year or put the whole exchange programme into jeopardy. And if Allie went home to London she'd have to stay there to meet the commitments she'd made to the people who she felt she'd left behind by coming here.

But there were no arguments because they both knew this was right. They'd talked again on Sunday afternoon and finally made their decision together. Zac had suggested a clean break, knowing that it would at least spare them the pain of losing a little more each day, and Allie had agreed.

He'd called Dr Jamieson and asked for a meeting with him and the exchange scheme co-ordinator. The four of them sat down together at ten in the morning, Allie looking pale and nervous. Zac explained what he and Allie wanted to do, making it clear that he would stay in his post for the full year, in order to fulfil the contractual commitments that Allie had made. True to form, Dr Jamieson didn't look pleased. He'd never been a man who liked surprises.

'So you've decided this between you.' He frowned. 'Do we have any say in the matter?'

'Of course. Allie needs to go back to London for urgent personal reasons. If you'd like me to stay here to maintain continuity and fulfil the commitments that London's made to the exchange programme, then I'm at your disposal.' The idea that Dr Jamieson might give them both the sack on the spot occurred to Zac and he dismissed it as being far too optimistic.

'Quite honestly, I'm not happy with this, Dr Forbes. We can't have our exchange doctors changing their plans on a mere whim, and since neither of you have given any reasons for Dr Maitland-Hill's return to London then I'm not able to assess them.'

'But in practice it's a good solution, Dr Jamieson.' The exchange scheme co-ordinator was one of the people who knew what had happened to Allie before she'd come here, and had listened with a sympathetic air. 'Zac's record here is exemplary, and we'd be lucky to keep him on here for another year.'

'That's not the point.' Dr Jamieson frowned. 'Reliability is a key requirement and I'm minded to write to London and register my disapproval in the strongest terms—'

'No.' Three heads turned to Allie as she interrupted. 'Dr Jamieson, *I'm* the one who's being unreliable, and Zac's simply offering to regularise the situation.'

'But you've dreamed this plan up together, obviously.' Dr Jamieson seemed only slightly mollified by Allie's defence of him. Zac shook his head in a signal that she didn't need say any more and Allie ignored him.

'I'm sure you're aware of the issue at the London hospital, regarding image-based sexual abuse—about eighteen months ago now.'

'I am.' Dr Jamieson's face softened suddenly.

'I was one of the people who was touched by that...'

Allie told her whole story clearly and concisely, which did nothing to lessen its impact. She'd come so far, and Zac was so proud of her, even if he hadn't wanted her to have to do this.

'This is something I have to do, Dr Jamieson, for my own sake and for the sake of the others who have been involved with this and haven't yet stepped forward. And for the sake of patients like Carly, who've been traumatised by this kind of abuse and who need a practical, joined up response from their healthcare providers. I feel very strongly about this, and I also feel strongly that you're being unfair to Zac. He's done nothing but support me and this hospital.'

Allie stopped, apparently having run out of breath, because she gulped in a lungful of air. Dr Jamieson looked at the exchange scheme co-ordinator, who gave a slight shrug.

'Go ahead, Dr Jamieson. I'll let you give your views first.'

'Thank you, Sheena.' Dr Jamieson faced Allie. 'Thank you for sharing this with us, and I hope you'll accept my personal apology for putting you into a position where you felt you had to do so.'

Zac wasn't surprised at Dr Jamieson's response. He was outspoken and firm, but he could never be accused of lacking compassion.

Allie smiled suddenly. 'It's all right. I'm learning that this kind of abuse thrives on secrets, and being here has helped me find my own voice. We shouldn't have asked you to accept our proposal without explaining a little more fully.'

Dr Jamieson glanced at Zac and he shrugged. Allie seemed to have this all in hand.

'That's as may be, Allie. Zac, if you're willing to stay on then we'd be delighted to have the opportunity of keeping you for another year. And Allie, I wish you well. If I can help you in any way, I hope you'll see your way clear to letting me know immediately.'

* * *

'You didn't need to do that.' Zac murmured the words to Allie as they left the meeting room together.

'Yes, I really did. I appreciate the gesture, but you were about to take whatever Dr Jamieson said without defending yourself. I want to speak up for people affected by image-based abuse, and I won't have you compromised by its secrets, Zac.'

He nodded. 'Thank you. I had a horrible feeling that he was about to throw the book at me there.'

He felt her fingers brush against his. 'I'm not going to stand aside and let anyone put you down, Zac.'

Warmth penetrated the heavy sadness that Zac had been feeling at this final confirmation of their plan. Allie meant so much to him and what she'd done meant a lot too—she might well have saved him from a serious blot on his copybook, but that didn't matter so much as the fact that she clearly cared enough about him to want to defend him.

'So what would you like to do for the rest of the day? Since we unexpectedly have it to ourselves.' Sheena had suggested that they take the afternoon off, and Dr Jamieson had agreed.

'I suppose that I'd better get my ticket home sorted. That shouldn't take too long though, so perhaps we could take the paddleboards out for a while this afternoon? One more thing I can take back to London with me—a crash course in paddleboarding.'

Zac chuckled. 'I'm glad you have your priorities straight. That definitely sounds like a plan.'

The whole week had been an exercise in priorities and squeezing everything they could from Allie's last few days in Australia. Their last few days together. She'd driven him in to work every morning and met him each evening so that they could spend time together, visiting all of the places that Zac loved and wanted to share with her.

On Thursday evening Allie pulled out her phone as soon as he got into the car. 'I have to ask you this now, because I need to get back to the guy by six-thirty...' She looked at her watch. 'I was thinking of something we might do at the weekend, rather than moping around the apartment and feeling sad.'

Zac had been wondering about that too. 'What have you come up with?'

'There's a log cabin in the Blue Mountains. We can drive up there on Friday evening and come back on Monday morning, before my flight on Monday afternoon. I managed to find a last-minute cancellation but, as I said, I have to let the guy know soon. And there's a catch.' She squeezed her face into an expression of both apology and...something else. Zac didn't know what.

'What's the catch?'

'It looks beautiful in the pictures, and the area's gorgeous. But there's only one bedroom.'

That didn't sound like much of a problem to Zac, but he had to remember Allie's feelings. And the fact that they'd be on two different continents next week. 'That's not a problem. I'll throw a camp bed into the car and use that.'

Allie pursed her lips. 'Or we could just both use the bedroom.'

Zac shook his head. 'I don't think that's a good idea. A man can only take so much temptation.' He could admit to that now.

'So can a woman. That would be okay.' She was gripping her phone in one hand and the steering wheel in the other, and Zac wondered which of them might shatter under the pressure of her fingers first.

'You're saying…a last weekend? Together?' Against all of his better judgement that sounded wonderful. And perhaps there was a freedom in having no more left to lose.

'I'm saying a last weekend where we can make any memories we want to take with us. Where nothing's planned and we just go with the flow. Talk a bit, and do whatever feels right at the time.'

Zac leaned over, kissing her. 'That sounds perfect, Allie. Make the call.'

Zac had spent one restless night alone, before Allie drove him to work on Friday morning. She'd anticipated his own feeling that memories which centred around the apartment might be too much to bear, and made it clear that the weekend was something separate and very special. Zac had to admit that he was looking forward to the *very special* part.

She picked him up from work, his bag packed and in the back of the car. They headed west out of Sydney and before dark fell they'd found their way to the log cabin, set on top of a ridge, amongst a stunning panorama of wooded peaks.

'We can see for miles!' Allie exclaimed as she got out of the car, stretching her limbs. 'It's so beautiful, Zac.'

He hugged her. 'And we'll have the stars tonight for company.'

'Hmm. They might have to wait their turn. I have *you* for company as well.'

They took their bags inside, finding that the log cabin was small but well equipped and decorated just as beautifully as the pictures on the website that Allie had shown him. She set about making dinner in the tiny kitchen, and they sat down for a leisurely meal outside. Allie was slowing the pace, letting the quiet majesty of their surroundings slowly work its magic, and Zac was on board with that. This weekend wasn't about rushing to do all of the things that they wanted to do before they had to part. It was about getting away from the realities of the world, and taking their time to enjoy whatever the weekend might hold.

They talked for hours, moving inside when the cool of the mountain air started to make them shiver, to sit together by the stove in the cosy wood-panelled living room.

'It's almost nice to be cold, isn't it.' Allie snuggled against him and he laughed.

'Yeah. Particularly when I have you to keep me warm.'

Their talk evolved into a long, slow piece of foreplay, as Allie questioned him about what made him feel good. He told her how the feel of salt water rushing against his body and the roar of the waves had seemed to free him. He described the pleasure he got from feeling her fingertips brush his skin, and when Allie asked he gave her the ultimate power over him and told her what turned him on during lovemaking.

'I never told anyone that before. I'm feeling a little exposed...'

Allie chuckled. 'You're a doctor. You imagine I have no understanding of the physiology of sex?'

Zac resisted the temptation to clamp his hand over his private parts and tell her that they were out of bounds. 'I suppose I'll just have to rely on you to use the information wisely.'

She kissed his cheek, mischief glinting in her eyes. 'Yes, I suppose you will.'

'So I reckon it's your turn now. Since I'm now at your mercy.'

Allie shot him a shy smile, whispering in his ear. Zac

chuckled. 'Yeah, I checked too. I think we can both be confident that no one's put cameras anywhere here.'

'That's so sweet of you, Zac.' Allie kissed him. 'It's silly of me...'

'No, it isn't. It makes you feel more comfortable and that's all that matters.'

'Now that we're so close, I'm a little afraid.'

'That's okay too.' Zac knew that Allie was telling him her greatest secrets, and the pleasure that gave him far outweighed anything that she might say. 'Of me?'

'Never of you.'

He smiled. 'That's good to know.'

'I just don't want to spoil things. I've spent eighteen months willing people not to even see me. What happens if you look at me and I panic?'

Zac didn't need to even think about that. 'If it happens, we'll deal with it. All I ask of you is that you tell me if you're feeling uncertain about anything. Otherwise *I* might start to panic.'

'I promise, Zac. You can rely on me to keep that promise.'

Warmth began to spread through his body. Allie knew how much an unbreakable promise meant to him. Maybe this was what they'd really come here for. To give each other these precious gifts.

She slid onto his lap, her legs astride him, her gaze full of tender fire. Like a conquering queen who had cleared every obstacle from their path and who was now claiming what was hers. He *had* been hers, from the first moment he'd seen her.

She kissed him, still holding him tight in her gaze. It was the most intoxicating thing he'd ever experienced, and he slid his hands upwards from her waist, stopping just before his touch met her breasts. Allie shivered, as if she could already feel what he wanted to do now.

'Are we going to do this?' It was okay if her answer was no, but he really hoped it would be yes.

Allie put one hand on his chest, over his heart, and he felt himself give every beat of it to her. Her other hand moved his, and the way she suddenly caught her breath as his fingers closed over the exquisite swell of her breast told Zac that she wanted him as much as he did her.

'Yes, Zac. We're going to do this.'

Every touch. Every move. Zac's gaze never left hers, and she could see her own desire reflected in his. She was already more naked than she'd ever been, and no one could ever take this from her. It was hers and Zac's alone.

When he kissed her, she could feel fire in her veins. And when his hand cupped her breast the delicious ache for him became even more insistent. Then Zac moved, leading her the few short yards to the bedroom.

He switched the lamp on, and the honey shades of the wood turned to gold. Allie sat down on the edge of the bed, but when she reached for him Zac shook his head.

'Don't move.'

He pulled his sweater and shirt off in one smooth movement, dropping them onto the floor. Then his boots and jeans, and finally his underpants. All of those hours on the beach had left him unashamed of his body, and there were no unnecessary flourishes to hide any embarrassment at being watched. And she *was* watching him.

She nervously tugged at the top button of her cardigan, and he shook his head. 'Don't you want to find out a bit more about me first?'

Allie got to her feet. 'Come here.'

He was within reach now, and she could caress his skin and feel the ripple of muscle as his body reacted to her touch. There was a hungry insistence to his kiss, and when she slid her hands downwards she felt his erection swell at the brush of her fingers.

And he was holding back. Letting her do whatever she wanted with him, and trying to subsume his own desires. That made Allie want him even more.

'Buttons, Zac.' She stood on her toes, whispering in his ear. 'Help me with my buttons.'

His hands were trembling, but he did as he was told. When she stood naked before him, Allie felt no shame, just an overwhelming need to take their lovemaking further. She backed towards the bed, and he bent to pull the covers to one side. She caught his hand.

'I'd like to see you, Zac. Is that okay?'

His grin told her that it was better than okay, and that he didn't want to hide beneath the covers any more than she did. Zac got onto the bed, propping himself up against the pillows, stretching his long legs out in front of him.

'Is that all right?'

'Beautiful. You're beautiful, Zac.' Allie laid her finger across his mouth. She didn't need him to say it back. She knew that he was looking, and the response that he couldn't control told her that he liked what he saw.

She'd left the condoms tucked behind the head of the bed, and when Allie leaned forward to get them she felt his hand slide gently along her thigh.

'We're not quite ready for that yet, are we?'

She was ready. He was definitely ready. Allie clutched at the condoms as he pulled her down onto his lap. He moved her astride him again, and set about redefining the word *ready*.

'Zac! *Please*...'

If she'd known that was the word he'd been waiting for Allie would have said it a little sooner. But then she wouldn't have known exactly what one man could accomplish with just his fingers and his mouth. She felt him prise the packet of condoms from her hand and let go of them gratefully.

Zac kissed her as she carefully guided him inside. His arm coiled around her waist and he began to move, gently at first and then faster and harder, encouraged by her garbled words of encouragement.

Then she felt it. The first tremulous signs of an orgasm. Allie had wondered if she'd ever have the courage to experience this again with any man, and she whimpered with longing, not just for Zac but for what they'd made together. She squeezed her eyes shut, trying to concentrate on the feeling and nurture it, afraid that her body might betray her. And then she felt Zac still suddenly.

'No, Zac. Don't stop. I don't want you to stop...' She felt her hand fist against his shoulder.

Then he moved again, holding her tight in his arms as he flexed his hips. He'd learned her body now and knew just what to do, and the feeling was back again, stronger and more insistent. Allie almost wept with relief, clinging onto him as waves of sensation crashed through her. She collapsed against him, her heart pounding.

'Are you okay?'

No, actually. He'd given her everything and taken so little for himself. But a *no* was likely to give Zac the wrong impression.

'Okay doesn't cover it, Zac. I loved every moment.'

'So did I. Do you want to rest now?'

She lifted her weight from his body, pushing at his shoulder until he slid himself down on the bed. 'You've just given me something that I didn't think I'd ever want from a man again. We're not done yet, Zac.'

That pleased him, and he smiled up at her as she positioned one of the pillows under his head. Then his grin broadened as she reached down, her fingers caressing him.

'I don't need...' His body arched suddenly as she dialled the pressure up a little. 'Yeah. On second thoughts, I do.'

Taking him inside her again was pure pleasure. Moving the way he wanted her to move. Making sure that he felt all of the things that she'd felt so keenly. Zac took it all, pushing hard against her until she came again, just from the pure pleasure of seeing and feeling his arousal.

Then suddenly he flipped her over onto her back. Allie yelped with delight, seeing desire burn bright in his eyes. He tilted her hips, sinking deeper inside, and she felt a deep satisfaction roll over her as he cried out, his limbs shaking.

It was nice that he couldn't speak straight away. She wound her arms around him, feeling the warmth of his skin and the frantic beat of his heart. This was her time to remember him by and it had seared itself into her, becoming a part of her now.

'Allie. This time I'm not asking. I have to rest now.'

CHAPTER FOURTEEN

ZAC HAD WATCHED as Allie took a thin cotton nightshirt from beneath the scattered pillows, pulling it over her head before she lay down with him. In the warmth of the bed, she'd curled her body around his, and he didn't even care that he couldn't feel her skin. Allie had dared so much tonight, and this was nothing.

He had the pleasure of stripping the nightshirt off her again in the morning. They'd found their balance now, trusting each other enough to be able to combine his pleasure with hers. With trust came confidence, and Zac was in no doubt that Allie loved it as much as he did when their lovemaking became bolder and more assertive.

Isolated here, in the spectacular beauty of the mountains, made it easier to feel that time was standing still. There were no more secrets to keep, no promises to break, and that allowed them to take all they could from the forty-eight hours that they did have. But when they loaded their bags into the car, and Allie bade him a tearful farewell from the cabin that had sheltered them from the world, there was no escaping what would come next.

When they arrived home Allie's bags were still waiting for her. There was time enough for lunch, and for Allie to hug Naomi and Mark, and then came the silent journey to the airport. Zac hung onto her hand as they made their way towards the security checkpoint.

'I don't want to go, Zac. I can't…' Now that he could go no further, the realities of their decision seemed to hit home.

'We talked about this, Allie.'

'I know, but can't we talk about it again? Isn't there something we can do?'

'We've made promises. We can't go back on them and…' Zac shrugged '… I don't want you to go back on this, because it's what you need to do.'

She reached up, winding her arms around his neck. 'I really wish that you weren't right.'

'Yeah. Me too.' He kissed her. One last taste of her lips, to hold and to keep with his other memories. 'Allie, it's time now. Let's make a promise to each other, that we'll say goodbye and then walk away. No looking back. We'll just take what we have now.'

Allie heaved a sigh. 'Yes. Yes, that's the best thing. We'll do that. I'll always love you, Zac. Always…'

He felt his resolve begin to falter. Zac had to do this now, or he'd break every promise he'd made, fall on his knees and beg her to stay. If he did that, he knew that Allie would break her promises, and he would never be able to forgive himself.

'Goodbye, Allie.' Zac turned, forcing himself to walk away. Trying not to think about the look of shock he'd seen in her eyes as she realised that the moment they'd both been dreading had finally come.

Somehow he made it back to his car. The sun seemed harsher now, and the air in the vehicle was stale and uncomfortably hot.

I'll always love you…

Why hadn't he been able to tell Allie that he'd always love her too? Zac pulled out his phone, wondering if his call would get through to her. Just to say those words, as he should have done when he had the chance.

But it was too late. It was the wrong promise to make, one that could only be broken. The road back to Cronulla was the only one left open to him now.

It had been a month, and every single day of it had been hard. Allie had stepped off the plane, fresh tears still in her eyes, and London had seemed very cold and grey. Her flat hadn't been heated for a month, and she'd shivered under her duvet until the central heating finally began to warm the place up. She'd cursed herself for falling in love with the most honourable man she knew, and woken in the night crying.

And then she'd got up and gone to work.

The money she'd saved, by never going out or buying herself anything nice, was standing her in good stead now because Allie had more than six months before she needed to find a job. She'd got in touch with Anya, who had introduced Allie to the three other women from the hospital whose images had been stolen and shared on the internet. She'd knocked on every door, talked to everyone who would talk to her and spent hours on the internet, trying to track down videos and photographs so that they could be reported and taken down. She'd made a nuisance of herself with the HR department of the hospital, who considered that the matter of image-based abuse had been dealt with and was closed, and advised her to let this go and move on.

Then she received a phone call.

'Dr Maitland-Hill.' The woman didn't wait for confirmation. 'I'm Sir Anthony Greve's secretary and he would like to arrange a meeting with you. He is, of course, extremely busy, but I have a free slot in his diary at ten past two this afternoon.'

Sir Anthony Greve, the Chief Executive Officer of the hospital. Allie was either in very deep trouble or this was a breakthrough, and from the tone of his secretary's voice and the specific time slot it sounded like the latter.

'Hold on one moment.' Allie laid her phone down on the kitchen counter, counting silently to ten. That seemed about the right amount of time to consult a diary. 'Yes, I'm free at ten past two.'

'In that case, please come to my office at two...'

There was a pause and Allie raised her eyebrows. Maybe the secretary was consulting her own diary to see if she was free.

'No, I have a note from Sir Anthony saying that he'll meet you for coffee at Sloanes in Mayfair. You know it?'

Yes. Sloanes was a very exclusive restaurant, the booking of which was said to be practically impossible unless you were at least a knight of the realm, or known personally to the management. One of those places that no one ever talked about, and Allie only knew about because several people from the upper echelons of the hospital had been there at Sir Anthony's invitation and the news had filtered down.

'I know it.'

'I'll send you a confirmation and directions, anyway.'

Sir Anthony's secretary rattled off Allie's personal email address for confirmation, and abruptly ended the call.

Was this a joke? Or something more sinister? All the old fears suddenly slapped her in the face. She was being watched. There was a shadowy group of people who wanted to stop her from speaking out, for fear of their own part in the image-based abuse becoming known. If only Zac were here, he'd know what to do.

She finished making coffee and opened her laptop. Several emails pinged into her inbox, one of which was from Sir Anthony's secretary. Clearly what the woman lacked in personal warmth she made up for with efficiency. Allie examined the email carefully, displaying the metadata. The hospital address was genuine, and it all looked legitimate.

This could still be some kind of trap, and it was still impossible to work out where her own paranoia ended and sensible caution began at times. Or she could be in for a polite but firm offer that she couldn't refuse, to shut her website down. That wasn't going to happen. Allie had given up too much for this. An image of Zac, tanned and golden, walking out of the sea, assailed her and she almost wished that Sir Anthony *would* shut her down and pack her off back to Australia in disgrace…

But she had to go. Zac would have grasped the nettle and gone, and the thought gave her courage.

Sloanes was entered via an inconsequential-looking door, in a very select part of Mayfair. It had no need to advertise—anyone who would be allowed to enter would know where it was. Allie was wearing her best suit and coat, which doubtless wouldn't impress anyone, and she arrived early, waiting across the street.

At five past two she saw Sir Anthony walking along the opposite pavement. He stopped at the door, which opened almost immediately, and he gained admittance just as quickly. So at least he was here, which ruled out some of Allie's fears. She shouldn't keep him waiting, and she dodged across the street, thick with taxis and high-end cars.

As soon as she gave her name she was welcomed inside. There was an air of quiet quality about the place, obviously designed to confront anyone who shouldn't be here, and

Allie ignored it. One advantage of having been to the most terrifying places that the internet could offer was that an establishment that hung the real thing on its walls instead of just prints didn't frighten her. Zac wouldn't have been afraid either.

The coffee lounge boasted widely spaced groups of tables. Very quiet, very discreet, and the waiters seemed to glide soundlessly across the thick carpet. Allie was shown to a door, which opened onto a beautifully furnished room, where Sir Anthony got quickly to his feet from a leather armchair.

'Dr Maitland-Hill. Thank you so much for taking the trouble to meet me.' Sir Anthony's soft Yorkshire accent, ready smile and rather crumpled appearance belied the real influence he wielded.

'I'm a little puzzled, Sir Anthony. What's this all about?'

'Straight to the point. Good.' Sir Anthony gave her a jovial smile and the waiter took her coat and her order for coffee. Sir Anthony instructed him to leave the door open, and waved her to one of the other armchairs around a highly polished coffee table.

'Little bit musty in here. I think some fresh air is in order.'

He was being tactful. Allie had written that, amongst many other things, closed doors in unfamiliar places made her fearful. She should start as she meant to go on, however challenging that felt.

'I appreciate the gesture, Sir Anthony. It doesn't seem musty in here to me.'

Sir Anthony laughed suddenly. 'No, it isn't, is it? A rather clumsy attempt on my part to put you at your ease. Perhaps you'll forgive me for asking you here as well. It's one of the Minister's favourite haunts, which gives me an entrée, and

I wanted to talk to you in a more discreet atmosphere than the hospital provides.'

There were few secrets at a hospital. Allie had learned that to her cost. 'That's appreciated too. It's very nice here.'

'Yes, they pride themselves on *nice*. I'd like to talk to you about your website and the initiative that's already been set up at the hospital to do what we can to help those who've been affected by image-based sexual abuse. I'd be grateful for any observations you might have…'

Allie was walking so quickly along the street that people were actually moving out of her way. She needed the speed because her head was spinning.

Sir Anthony had been as down-to-earth as everyone said he was, and he seemed to know everything that went on at the hospital. Clearly the rumours of him turning up in the waiting room in A&E at midnight, or in the elderly care ward at visiting times, and sitting quietly, watching and talking to people weren't an exaggeration.

He'd also obviously read pretty much everything on her website, including the comments and the post she'd made last night, and he'd clearly put two and two together from the pictures on the site, throwing in a few very nice remarks about Zac's professionalism and the success of his tenure in Australia. His avuncular manner disguised a mind that was as sharp as a surgical blade.

Allie was aware of the initiative that had been set up at the hospital. She'd seen the posters and read the guidelines that had been provided for the care of both staff and patients. They'd all seemed a little too official for something that was so agonisingly personal, and she'd gravitated towards seeking help from survivor accounts. And that was what Sir Anthony had wanted to talk to her about.

He'd shared his own experience of horrified helplessness when he'd discovered that his own niece had been sharing personal images at school. He'd also offered Allie her own office and job title at the hospital and she'd turned him down, telling him that the contacts she'd made required a discreet and impartial listening ear from someone who'd been through the same as they had. Sir Anthony had understood, wondering if his own personal advocacy and support, along with his extensive list of contacts in the media, the health service and the judiciary might be of any assistance to her. It had taken a measure of self-control to stop herself from jumping to her feet and punching the air.

She was on her way. There was still a very long road ahead of her, but she had a powerful ally in Sir Anthony, and all of her instincts told her that he'd listen to what she and the other survivors wanted and come through on his promises.

All she wanted to do now was to call Zac. The one man who'd already come through on all of his promises, the man she'd walked away from because he'd been so adamant that it was the right thing to do. The man whose loss had hurt her more than anything else.

He'd know. Allie had to trust that, despite Zac's insistence on a clean break, he wouldn't let go of her so easily, and that he'd be keeping a close eye on her campaign. One of the good things about the internet… She'd already passed two Underground stations and it was time to stop walking and go home.

Walking down the steps into the busy, floodlit station concourse, all Allie could think about was the open air and the warm feel of Zac's touch on her skin. And how much she missed him.

* * *

Zac was cradling Finn in his arms, under the shade of the large awning that stretched across one end of the patio. Mark was managing to combine keeping Izzy away from the heat of the barbecue with not burning the steaks, and Naomi was fetching the drinks.

'Any news from Allie?' he asked as Naomi put an ice-cold beer in a Surf City stubby holder in front of him.

'I asked you here to eat, Zac, not interrogate me. Remember eating? That thing you do to keep body and soul together.'

Zac ate. He surfed as well. Just not with the same enthusiasm he'd once shown.

'Interrogate is a bit of a harsh word.' He smiled at Naomi. He didn't do that with the same enthusiasm he'd once felt either.

'The cap fits, Zac.'

Fair enough. Zac knew that Naomi kept in touch with Allie, and his hunger for news of her wasn't slaked by reading through the website every evening. He supposed that asking Naomi if she'd had an email every time he saw her was overdoing it a bit.

'Why don't you just email her? You know email? The thing that normal people do when they want to find out what's happening with someone?'

'She has to do this on her own. I can't interfere.'

'Granted. And she's doing it—she landed an interview on local radio the other day.'

Zac felt his ears prick. He hadn't heard about that. 'What station?'

'Some London station. I don't know.' Naomi rolled her eyes and then took pity on him. 'You want me to send you the link to the stream?'

'Yes please. Thank you.' Now would be good.

'I'll send it tonight. *After* we've eaten.' Naomi's attention was drawn to Izzy, who was pouring water over the chalk line on the patio, drawn at a safe distance from the barbecue.'

'Izzy! Rubbing out the line doesn't mean that Dad and I will forget it's there. You still can't cross it.'

Izzy stuck out her lower lip and took her half-full bucket back into the house, followed by Mark's watchful gaze.

Zac chuckled. 'Off to think of another way to cross the line?'

'Yeah, of course. She hasn't quite learned that however sneaky she can be, I can be sneakier.' Naomi turned her attention back to Zac. 'So what's the problem with just emailing Allie then? It's perfectly possible to let her get on with what she has to do and still make a civil enquiry about how she is, isn't it?'

'There were no hard feelings between us when she left.' Zac answered Naomi's implied question. 'The opposite, in fact.'

'Yeah, I noticed the part about the opposite. Zac, Allie's the best thing that ever happened to you.'

Grief squeezed at his heart, and Zac looked down at the child in his arms, wondering if Finn would wake up any time soon and give him the opportunity of a little mindless play. Thinking about things really didn't help.

'I know. We made a clean break. Going back to London was the right thing for Allie to do—the thing she needed to do. I just facilitated the one thing that would help her move forward.'

'I get that, and I know it was a difficult gesture for you to make. But honestly, Zac, it doesn't look like a very clean break to me. You've been miserable this last six weeks.'

Miserable was Zac's more positive face, the one he showed to the world. Naomi should see him when he was on his own.

'I made a promise.'

Naomi rolled her eyes. 'Yes, and you keep your promises, even when it's hard. That's a very commendable thing. But you see that child?' She nodded towards Finn. 'I'd break every rule, every promise I ever made for him and Izzy. And for Mark too, although if you ever tell him that you're toast.'

'I don't need to, do I?' Something ignited in Zac's chest. Hard, glittering, painful hope.

'I suppose not… Uh—hang on…' Naomi got to her feet, walking over to Izzy, who had just appeared from the kitchen, a plastic tumbler in her hand. Zac watched as Naomi bent down, putting her arm around Izzy's shoulders and whispering in her ear. The little girl nodded, and made her way over to Zac.

'Mum says that Dad doesn't need a drink, but you do, Uncle Zac.'

No doubt because he was on the right side of the chalk line. Zac leaned forward, taking the tumbler from her hand and gulping down the water.

'Just what I needed, Izzy, thank you.' The little girl nodded, clearly appeased, and Zac made room for her to climb up onto his lap, hugging her with his free arm.

'There you go.' Naomi walked back over to him, bending to plant a kiss on each of her children's heads. 'All my promises in one place.'

'Am I a promise, Uncle Zac?' Izzy snuggled against him.

'Course you are. Ask your mum about the story of the Golden Promise.' Naomi seemed to have an endless ability to make up stories for her kids at the drop of a hat.

'Ah, yes! The Golden Promise.' Naomi shot him a look

that plainly indicated he'd pay for this later, and embarked on the story.

Izzy was listening intently to her mother now, which left Zac a little space to think. He really did need to consider which promises needed to be broken.

Friday evening. On Monday it would be six weeks to the day since he'd seen Allie off at the airport. Zac tried not to indulge in sums like that, but when he was tired it was difficult to resist.

He walked up the steps to his apartment, glad to get home. Throwing his keys onto the breakfast bar and his bag onto the floor, he walked over to the sliding doors that overlooked the sea and then changed his mind. He didn't want to engage with the world at the moment, or at least not this side of it. Zac slumped down onto the long sofa, closing his eyes.

After a great deal of thought, he *had* emailed Allie, just two days ago. He'd told her that he read her blog still, and that he'd heard the several radio interviews she'd given, and that he was impressed with how much success she'd had in so short a time. And then one short paragraph, saying the things he regretted bitterly he hadn't said at the airport. He treasured the time they'd spent together, and wished her only love and happiness.

He hadn't expected a reply, and had said as much in his email. But he'd got one, written while he'd slept and which he'd read the following morning. It hurt more than Zac had words to describe. Allie had told him that she loved him.

It made everything so much harder. She'd said that at the airport, even though they both knew that she had to go. He'd almost hoped that she didn't really mean it, or that *love* could be taken in the context of the way that he loved Naomi and

Izzy, Mark and Finn. Wanting only the best for them and being happy when they were, without needing them to be there on a daily basis.

He heard a knock at the door. Probably Naomi with another food parcel. He was going to have to make her coffee, sit her down and tell her that tough love demanded she stop and make him fend for himself. He'd go to the supermarket tomorrow, and have them all round for lunch on Sunday.

Naomi didn't burst straight in as she usually did.

'It's open. You can come in, I'm decent...' He hadn't yet got to the Friday evening, living-on-his-own ritual of throwing off his work clothes, taking a shower and then padding around the apartment naked to cool off.

'That's a disappointment...'

Zac opened his eyes with a start.

Allie was standing in the open doorway. For a moment he thought that she must be a mirage, because she looked refreshed and awake. Zac tried to do the calculation regarding time differences, flight times and the amount of time it would take to look as fragrant and bright-eyed as Allie did, and failed miserably.

'Allie...? I thought you were in London.' That was unnecessary. She *had* been in London last week, when she'd given that radio interview. Hadn't she? In a world where suddenly everything was tipped upside down, anything was possible.

'I got your email on the morning before I left to come here.'

That was one mystery solved. Allie pressed her lips together in a half-frown, and he realised that she was waiting for him to invite her in.

'Come in. I'll make coffee...' She probably didn't need coffee after such a long flight. 'Or some juice. Where are you staying?'

'Naomi picked me up at the airport. I've been asleep in her spare room for most of the day.'

Second mystery solved. Zac couldn't bring himself to ask about the third, agonisingly important one.

He walked to the kitchen, flipping on the coffee machine. If Allie didn't need coffee then he did. And he needed some way of keeping his eyes off her. She looked amazing, in a yellow sleeveless dress, her pale skin an enticing novelty in the heat of a Sydney summer.

'So…how's it all going?' He asked the question over his shoulder, pretending to fiddle with the coffee filter, and Allie came to sit down at the breakfast bar.

'It's good. I suppose you've heard from Naomi that I had an approach from Sir Anthony Greve, and he's been a big help in introducing me to people who can push for change and making sure that anyone who does want to come forward is treated with respect and cared for.'

'I…um…' Zac turned, wondering how he should put this.

'It's okay, Zac. Naomi told me you'd been asking, and I said that it was quite all right for her to answer any questions you had. I didn't want to put her on the spot.'

Zac studied the floor. 'I wasn't quite so considerate.'

'No, well, you didn't need to be. They're your friends, Zac, and they love you.'

That word again. In *that* context. Zac bit back his disappointment.

'Has anyone else come forward?'

'Yes. It turned out that the nurse at the hospital, who I was talking with when I was here, actually had a copy of the video that was made of her. I went with her to the police and as they had proof they were able to arrest the perpetrator very quickly. And that was a breakthrough, because he hadn't disposed of the phone he used for the group, and they were able to retrieve all of the numbers of the other members. We've managed to find other victims as well and to reach out to them…' Allie frowned and Zac saw her hand shake as she passed her fingers wearily over her eyes. 'Zac, this isn't important right now…'

'Yes. It's important. I want to know.' He gritted the words out. This was what he'd given Allie up for, and he needed to know.

'I meant…' Allie's breath seemed to catch in her throat and she looked down at her fingers, wound tightly together in her lap. Zac thought he saw tears in her eyes.

'What did you mean, Allie?' He spoke more gently this time.

'It's important but it's not why I'm here. You were right to say that I needed to leave, and that I could never forgive myself if I abandoned the people who'd contacted me. But we were both wrong too. I couldn't trust that I'd ever be able to heal enough to properly commit myself to you, and you couldn't believe that some promises can never be broken.'

'But I broke my promise to you, when I wrote that email.' Zac wasn't sure whether to apologise or tell her that he never should have committed himself in the first place.

'Yes, and I knew you were serious, because you don't break promises. That wasn't why I came back. I was already packed and was ready to leave. It did make the journey much easier, though.'

Maybe he should wait. Let Allie tell him exactly what she was here for and what she wanted of him. But Zac couldn't. He knew already, and it didn't need words. He strode around the breakfast bar, taking her hands in his.

'Allie, I love you. Maybe we needed this time apart to know that our relationship is stronger than anything that's happened in the past. But I know now that it is, and I want to be with you. You're the most important thing in my life, and we can work something out. I don't know how, but...'

A tear rolled down her cheek. A happy one, because Allie was smiling. 'We don't need to work anything out. When I first went back to London, Sir Anthony offered me a job and I turned it down. But I've done everything I can working alone, and now he's talking about setting up a joint venture with the hospital here in Australia, to help patients like Carly and their families and to reach out into local communities and on the web. I've agreed to head it up, as long as I get the choice of working either here or in London. If I come here, he'll arrange my work permit—'

She could stop talking now. Zac kissed her and she flung her arms around his neck.

'I love you.' He whispered the words, planting a kiss on her neck.

'I love you too, Zac.'

'Will you marry me?'

Allie squealed with delight, kissing him again. 'Yes, Zac. I'll marry you.'

No more words needed. No plans because they'd just made the one and only plan that they needed to. Everything else would fall into place around that.

EPILOGUE

Five months later...

ZAC AND ALLIE'S summer together in Sydney had contained so many days that were perfect. But this had been the best of all. They'd been married at a joyous informal ceremony at one of the lookout points above Sydney Harbour, surrounded by friends and colleagues. Allie's mum and dad had made the journey to be here, and even Sir Anthony had altered the timing of a planned visit to the hospital in Sydney so that he could attend. When she'd looked into Zac's eyes to say her vows she knew that he heard her promises and that he knew they'd never be broken.

The reception was held in the shade of massive trees, an afternoon full of love and plans for the future. Carly was there, having agreed to act as the official wedding photographer, and although she still preferred to stay behind the camera rather than in front of it her photography had taken on a new dimension. She and Allie had talked a lot about the relationship that formed across a camera lens, and that had informed her work. She was making her way back to being a young artist full of promise, whose photographs truly portrayed the people framed within them.

As the sun began to fall in the sky there were kisses and farewells. One last toast, and then it was time for Allie and

Zac to leave. They would spend one night by the beach—their beach—in Cronulla and then drive to the cabin in the Blue Mountains the following morning for their honeymoon.

'You're sure about this?' Zac asked as they stood on the balcony of their apartment, surrounded by the sounds of the sea. 'It's such a beautiful dress, and you could always wear it again...'

Allie had decided on a light dress, trimmed with cotton lace, to suit the informality of the day. Zac's cream linen suit, worn with an open-necked shirt, matched the tone perfectly too.

'I suppose so. But this dress was always just for today, Zac.'

He smiled down at her. 'Because our memories of today will always be fresh. Never yellowed with age, or stained, or torn.'

'Don't you like the idea?'

He took her in his arms, kissing her. It seemed that neither of them could get enough of each other's kisses today. 'I love it. I just wanted to make sure that you hadn't changed your mind.'

'I'll never change my mind about anything we've done today.'

Zac chuckled. 'Me neither. I'll meet you on the beach?' He kissed her again, as if parting for only five minutes was far too much to bear, and then shooshed her up the stairs.

The first red streaks were beginning to appear in the sky, and they had the beach to themselves now. Mark was clearly taking his best man duties seriously, and was lounging in a fold-up chair at the top of the beach, flipping through a surfing magazine, while Zac waited at the water's edge.

'You're still keeping an eye on Zac?' Allie grinned at Mark.

'Someone's got to. As well as unobtrusive lifeguard and clearing up duties so we don't contribute to the marine litter situation. And since Naomi's busy putting the kids to bed I'm deputising as matron of honour. Your hair and your dress look absolutely fine.'

Allie chuckled. 'Great job, Mark. Covering all the bases.'

'So you're going to do it, then? Trash the dress?'

'No! This is my way of keeping it, just as it is. My special dress for one day only.'

'Not really as catchy,' Mark observed dryly. 'You'd better get on with it then, before it gets dark. Your husband's right there...'

And Allie couldn't get to him fast enough. The man she'd always love, waiting for her on the beach, his trouser legs rolled up and the evening breeze tugging at his shirt. She savoured the moment though, resisting the temptation to run into Zac's arms in favour of walking towards him.

'That's a picture I'll keep.' He smiled at her. 'My wife, barefoot on the beach, in a white dress.'

Allie laughed. 'And my husband, waiting for me in the sunset...'

The two-person paddleboard was already inflated, and Zac picked it up, wading with it into the water. Allie gathered her dress up around her knees and got onto the board, sitting down so that Zac could paddle them out. Alone at last amongst the quiet swell of the waves, Zac took her hand, steadying her as she got to her feet.

'Ready?' He grinned at her.

'I'm ready.' Before he could ask her again whether she really wanted to do this, Allie jumped into the water, taking Zac with her.

The feeling of leaping into the unknown with him, knowing that he'd be there always, was exhilarating. But as Allie hit the water the dress became tangled around her legs and it was only Zac's arm around her waist that kept her afloat.

'Oh! This is more complicated than I'd anticipated.'

'You're doing fine.' Zac kissed her and she felt herself melt against him.

'Hang onto me while I get the buttons…' Allie grimaced. The row of small buttons down the back of the dress were going to be fiddly.

'No need. Put your arms around my neck…' Zac reached up onto the paddleboard, flipping open the box that was secured to the back of it and withdrawing a button hook. 'I came prepared.'

He supported her in the water, one arm holding onto the side of the paddleboard, the other behind her back. He'd clearly been practising how to do this and the hook made short work of the buttons. Then Allie floated in his arms while she undid the buttons at her cuffs.

'I've just got to get it over my head now.' Now that the dress was waterlogged that seemed a little more difficult than she'd thought it might be.

'That's okay. Hold onto the board.'

Allie grabbed the board, feeling his hand slide up her leg. 'Zac! Stop messing around.'

'I'm your husband. Isn't that part of the job?'

Allie kissed him. 'It's definitely part of the job. Later…'

'I'll look forward to it.' He disappeared under the water, swimming around her legs, and the dress blossomed around her as he folded it upwards. When he surfaced, taking hold of her cuff, Allie found that she could get her free arm out of the dress easily.

'One more thing and you're out.' He held her against him,

and Allie wrapped her legs around his waist. She could lift the dress over her head now, leaving just the white swimming costume she wore underneath it.

'Am I going to get to undress you now?'

He grinned. 'Later. You could undo my shirt if you wanted...'

Allie didn't need to be asked twice and she tugged at the buttons on his shirt. There was an unfamiliar chain around his neck and Zac was grinning.

'What's this?' She followed the chain with her finger. 'A key! Does this mean we have a front door to go with it?'

'A back door as well. And windows.'

'Zac!' Allie flung her arms around his neck. 'Our beautiful new house has doors and windows!'

'Yes, and that's your key. I had your initials engraved on it. AF.'

'That's so sweet!' Allie inspected the engraving on the key, her new initials surrounded by a heart. Zac pulled the chain over his head, putting it around her neck.

'While we're on our honeymoon the plasterers will be going in and then they'll start laying the floors and fitting the kitchen. Mark said he'd keep an eye on it all while we're away, and with any luck we'll be able to move in, in a couple of months.'

A wedding. A house built overlooking the sea in Cronulla. And maybe, after spending two weeks in a log cabin in the Blue Mountains...

'I'm working on keeping all of my promises, Allie.' He seemed to know what she was thinking. Zac had promised they'd have a family and she knew it was what he wanted. His childhood might have given him no idea of what it was like to have two supportive and loving parents, but he was writing his own script now. Zac was going to be a great dad.

'And I'm working on mine.' Allie had promised Zac that she would never give up on regaining her own space. She'd made a lot of progress with her counsellor, and worked hard to make the new joint initiative, sponsored by the Sydney and London hospitals, a success. Helping others who'd been hurt the way she had was hard, but it gave her a sense of deep satisfaction.

She watched as Zac launched himself backwards in the water, easing out of his shirt and trousers, to reveal a pair of board shorts. Then he hoisted himself onto the paddle-board and stretched out his hand to help Allie climb up with him.

'No regrets?' Zac nodded towards their wet clothes, piled beside her in a tangle of fabric and seaweed.

'Not one.'

'Me neither' He grinned, reaching into the box again and drawing out a bottle of champagne, two plastic beakers and a foil-wrapped package. 'Can I interest you in a few left-overs? Champagne and wedding cake?'

'Oh! Yes please. I was far too happy to eat or drink much this afternoon…'

'I noticed. So did your mum and she wrapped a couple of pieces and slipped them to me as we were leaving.'

Zac handed her the cake and Allie unwrapped it, while he popped the cork of the champagne bottle and poured a splash into each of their beakers.

They watched the sun go down on their wedding day, and then, as the warm breeze began to cool a little, Zac wrapped a fleece jacket around her shoulders and paddled them back to the shore.

They walked back to their apartment, hand in hand.

'The first day of our marriage. Thank you so much for making it perfect, Zac.'

He leaned over, kissing her. 'I have a feeling it's only going to get better. I can't wait to find out everything we'll do together.'

* * * * *

COMING SOON!

We really hope you enjoyed reading this book. If you're looking for more romance be sure to head to the shops when new books are available on

Thursday 31st August

To see which titles are coming soon, please visit

millsandboon.co.uk/nextmonth

MILLS & BOON

MILLS & BOON®

Coming next month

THE VET'S CONVENIENT BRIDE
Luana DaRosa

Rafael released her hand and stepped forward when the judge turned the paper around for him to sign. He placed the pen on the paper with no hesitation, signing his name on the indicated line. Then he stepped back, holding his hand out to her.

Maria took the pen and focused on the paper in front of her. A small tremble shook her hand as she put the tip down on the line and she hesitated, the weight of what she was about to do coming down on her shoulders. This was the price she had to pay to keep her sanctuary from financial ruin.

She swallowed the lump in her throat and signed her name with a flutter in her stomach. The pen came down on the table with a clang of finality. Done.

Maria was now married to Rafael.

They turned to look at each other, an unbidden current springing to life in her chest and arcing through the air between them. She shivered, biting her lower lip to stop her heart from racing and keeping her mind in the present. Nothing they were doing was real. It was all a ruse. The heat in her veins, the quiver in her stomach—they were results of the circumstances they were in and not true feelings.

Loud clapping spooked her out of the moment passing between them, and her head whipped around. The other party in the room cheered at them, clapping and hooting for the union they thought was as real as their own.

Maria's spine stiffened when a person from the group called out, "Aren't you going to kiss your bride?"

Cheers erupted again, and Rafael glanced at her with a slight frown. The question in his eyes was easy to read. He wanted to know if he could kiss her.

Maria swallowed and gave the faintest of nods. His features softened at her consent and everything around her slowed down as his hands wrapped around hers, pulling her closer to him. His scent enveloped her, the smell of lavender and something primal which eluded words. A tremble clawed through her when she watched his hazel eyes narrow and his face come closer.

For a moment, Maria couldn't breathe as the anticipation thickened the air. Then, his lips brushed against hers, and the connection this touch created stoked the tiny flame she'd been carrying for Rafael into a roaring fire that pumped through her veins with every beat of her racing heart.

Continue reading
THE VET'S CONVENIENT BRIDE
Luana DaRosa

Available next month
www.millsandboon.co.uk

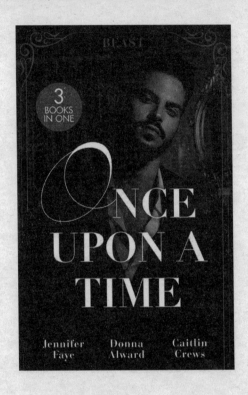

LET'S TALK
Romance

For exclusive extracts, competitions
and special offers, find us online:

f MillsandBoon

𝕏 @MillsandBoon

◉ @MillsandBoonUK

♪ @MillsandBoonUK

Get in touch on 01413 063 232

MILLS & BOON

THE HEART OF ROMANCE

A ROMANCE FOR EVERY READER

MODERN
Prepare to be swept off your feet by sophisticated, sexy and seductive heroes, in some of the world's most glamourous and romantic locations, where power and passion collide.

HISTORICAL
Escape with historical heroes from time gone by. Whether your passion is for wicked Regency Rakes, muscled Vikings or rugged Highlanders, awaken the romance of the past.

MEDICAL
Set your pulse racing with dedicated, delectable doctors in the high-pressure world of medicine, where emotions run high and passion, comfort and love are the best medicine.

True Love
Celebrate true love with tender stories of heartfelt romance, from the rush of falling in love to the joy a new baby can bring, and a focus on the emotional heart of a relationship.

Desire
Indulge in secrets and scandal, intense drama and sizzling hot action with heroes who have it all: wealth, status, good looks…everything but the right woman.

HEROES
The excitement of a gripping thriller, with intense romance at its heart. Resourceful, true-to-life women and strong, fearless men face danger and desire - a killer combination!

To see which titles are coming soon, please visit

millsandboon.co.uk/nextmonth